A Primitive In Paradise

by Josh Langston

1st Edition

DEDICATION

To Annie, my first love, without whom I would be lost. My only regret is that writing, my second love, keeps me from spending all my time with you.

And also to my writer's group, the Verb Mongers. You keep me smiling, entertained, challenged, and motivated. It is an honor to be associated with people of such high character and low humor. Thanks, gang.

--Josh

Chapter 1

Hormones don't care how big you are.

As Klaus Becker strolled through a park on the outskirts of Friedrichshafen, near the Swiss border in southern Germany, someone struck his temple with an industrial-size *rohrzange*, which English speakers would call a pipe wrench. It is unlikely that Becker felt any pain as the blow was both profound and fatal. Once securely wrapped in plastic, Becker's remains were weighted down with rocks and sunk in the depths of nearby Lake Constance, never to be seen again.

As the last remaining member of his family, Becker left no one to mourn his passing, nor-- more importantly--to alert authorities that he'd gone missing the day before he was to report to Zeppelin Luftschifftechnik, GmbH for training as a flight officer on the NT50, a radically new, semi-rigid, double-bodied airship. The huge dirigible, while considerably shorter than the *Hindenburg*, its ill-fated ancestor which had been crashed and burned some 70+ years earlier, could still accommodate an astonishing payload. The number 50 in its official designation stood for the 50,000 cubic meters of envelope volume which could house enough helium to lift a payload of nearly 10 tons.

Josh Langston

No red flags went up the next day at the Zeppelin offices in Friedrichshafen because a man bearing all of Klaus Becker's identification, licenses and documentation arrived on time and eager to learn his duties as an airship pilot. Not only was he expected, he paid for his education-- in full, and in advance. The staff at Zeppelin Luftschifftechnik, GmbH assured him he would learn everything he needed to know well before the magnificent, new, almost-lighter-than-air NT50 departed for its exotic destination.

The man calling himself Klaus Becker seemed very pleased.

~*~

Mato heard the giants long before he saw them though they made no effort to conceal themselves. They were giants, after all, and therefore incapable of stealth. As usual for their race, the giants talked in loud voices, and rattled and clanked about in their camp like the war machines Mato had seen in Tori's house on the box that held moving pictures.

But these were men, not machines. And they had come too close to The People's encampment. Shadow, the great black dog Tori shared with Mato, sniffed the air and growled. He'd smelled the two even before Mato heard them.

Knowing he'd be unable to prevent Shadow from investigating the intruders, Mato waited for his companion to advance. Once the dog's route became clear, Mato chose an alternate course and

2

raced the animal to their quarry.

The men would see the dog; that couldn't be helped. But they'd never see the little Indian. Mato would stay hidden, prepared to defend Shadow if the giants proved unfriendly, or worse, if they attempted to capture the dog.

The giant's camp consisted of a clearing near a ravine carved by winter run-off. The men squatted in the ravine examining the exposed rock. Shadow approached with caution, his movements those of a hunter.

One of the men held a pipe between clenched teeth which Mato could smell even though it wasn't lit. Many other smells competed with that of the pipe. The men had left food in their campsite and smoldering ash in their fire. Partially burned garbage gave off still more odors. Mato knew it wouldn't be long before a bear came to see who had provided such an offering. Of course, he and Shadow would be long gone by then, but the giants seemed intent on studying rocks.

Shadow broke the silence with a throaty bark. Both men looked up, startled by the harsh sound. Then, they laughed. One of them tossed a rock at the dog and yelled for him to go away. Mato resisted the impulse to throw a rock back at the giant. He had better things to do. Besides, the bear would be here soon, and Mato had no intention of interfering. Let the giants deal with it.

Mato chuckled to himself. If not for Shadow,

he'd be tempted to stick around to watch the fun. But the dog might get into trouble. Bears could move with astonishing speed, and while Shadow was every bit as agile as Mato, he'd be no match for a bear.

Mato had to deal with a second temptation as well. The giants were but a short walk away from the caves where The People had camped for the winter. Giants rarely came anywhere near the area, so The People likely had no idea they had visitors. Mato considered doubling back to warn them, but taking his leave of the camp had been an ordeal, one he had no wish to repeat.

Surely The People would discover them before being discovered themselves. Mato decided to let them fend for themselves. He had a more pressing need.

As he turned to continue his journey, content that Shadow had lost interest in the intruders and would soon join him, Mato heard the great black dog bark again. Accustomed to variations in Shadow's pitch and intensity, Mato recognized the danger signal. His breathing slowed, and his muscles tightened as he watched the giant with the pipe draw a gun and aim it at the dog.

At that range, Shadow had no chance.

~*~

Every chair at the long boardroom table held a suited participant in the on-going negotiations for the biggest non-government development ever contemplated for the state of Hawaii. Daniel

Kwan searched the eyes of every man and woman in the room. He never claimed he could see into anyone's heart; he much preferred to gaze into their wallets. But more often than not, his blank-eyed stare revealed which of his opponents–anyone he didn't *own* was an opponent–might dare to fight him. Not that they'd have much luck. He'd proven that often enough, but for the sake of his reputation, he needed to continue proving it. Once every couple years would be enough. Sadly, no one had tried to take him on in the last four or five. He couldn't afford for those who counted to forget about him.

Kwan did not believe in luck. Good fortune played no part in either his wealth or his status. A powerful man, politically and financially if not physically, Kwan disdained anyone who did believe in luck, for they were weak and simple-minded, unworthy of his esteem.

A columnist for a well-regarded newspaper in Honolulu famously claimed that Kwan would have preferred, and perhaps even envied, the pre-ghost version of Ebenezer Scrooge, except that Kwan didn't believe in ghosts and would never have wasted the time required to suffer through an entire Dickens novel, let alone a condensed theatrical version.

Kwan sued for defamation, won, and bankrupted the paper. No one dared comment on his connection to several of the jurors who heard the case.

His wealth and ambition, to say nothing of his disregard for the footprints he left on the backs of those he trampled to achieve his ends, gave him access to all the big deals which occurred in the islands. More specifically, it gave him a seat at the table for the development discussion about his home island of Kauai.

An outsider--or *haole* in native Hawaiian-- had no chance of building a lemonade stand without his blessing. And his blessings came dear. Anything larger required his involvement. If the discussion about to start went the way he intended it to, Daniel Kwan stood to become an even richer man.

So it came as a complete shock when a man who looked, talked, and Kwan thought, *smelled* like a tourist from Mississippi or some other mainland swamp, stood up to speak.

~*~

Tori Lanier sat in front of her computer screen wondering what in hell had happened. How was it that a desirable young--okay, *relatively* young--woman could find herself alone in a crummy, one-bedroom cabin in the middle of a Godforsaken Wyoming dessert?

The social/psychological/incidental calculus didn't work. She ticked the relevant items off on her fingers.

Good: Her insanely jealous ex-husband had killed himself.

Extra good: Her lover, Nate Sheffield, was hot

6

enough to start a stampede in a bridal salon.

Not good: Nate was absent and had been for too long.

Probably good: Tori had discovered an entire race of tiny little people no one knew existed.

Really bad: She couldn't tell anyone about them.

Good: She'd written two bestselling books based on her great-great uncle.

Bad: She'd run out of interesting relatives to write about.

Add all of it up, and she should have had some positive karma left over. So, why the hell was she sitting, *alone*, in a cabin in the middle of nowhere?

It made no sense. It wasn't fair. It called for wine. Lots and lots of wine. Which she'd run out of the day before.

She hadn't talked to her editor in a month. Maybe two. Shadow, her beloved mongrel dog, had wandered off with Mato, the pompous micro-savage, and God alone knew if the poor thing was even alive. Her only "normal" friends lived a half hour away--by car--and she was drinking bourbon *straight from the goddam bottle!*

When the phone rang she grabbed it like a lifeline.

"Hullo?"

"It's me!"

Nate's voice warmed her almost as much as the bourbon. "Where are you?"

"Somewhere in Manhattan."

"Oh." She made no effort to hide the disappointment in her voice.

"But I should be home sometime tomorrow. Depends on the flights."

"Thank God. I feared you might never come back."

"And risk losing you to somebody else?"

He followed that with a low chuckle, a decidedly yummy low chuckle which smacked of self-assurance. As if he knew she'd wait for him no matter what, which was almost certainly true, but she had no intention of letting him know that.

She responded with silence. Mean, maybe, but damn it, he'd earned it. He'd been gone too long. And the knowledge that his ex-fiancée lived in the Big Apple, and had actually gotten him the assignment that kept him there, occupied an ever-growing portion of her emotional real estate.

"Tori? Did I do something wrong? Is there something you haven't told me?"

"Maybe."

Nate instantly dropped his jovial, in-control tone. "You aren't-- I mean, you're not seeing anyone--"

"Just Jack," she said, staring at the square-sided bottle of Tennessee whiskey in her lap. Technically, it wasn't bourbon. Bourbon only came from Kentucky, but it sure as shit *tasted* like bourbon.

"*Jack?* Jack who?"
"N'mind. Doesn't matter."
"It does to me!" he said.
"When will you be home?"
"Around supper time, I suppose. Gotta change planes in Denver, then drive down from Sheridan. Might be gettin' dark by the time I reach Ten . Sleep."
"Then I guess you'll be too tired to drive all the way out here," she said, allowing disappointment to reoccupy her voice.
"Not after sittin' on my ass all day. Of course I'll drive out to your place. Want me to bring something to eat?"
"Sure," she said. "Or I can scrounge something up. Just get yourself out here, okay?"
"Deal. I'll see you tomorrow night."
Tori needed no mirror to be conscious of the grin stretching her face. She lowered her voice. "Please hurry, Nate. I'm tired of being alone."
"Me, too," he said. "Besides, I've got something important to tell you."
"What is it?" she asked, her emotions recoiling.
"Hold on. Damn phone's doing something weird."
"C'mon, Nate! Don't leave me hangin'." She waited for his response, but the phone remained silent.
"Sorry," he said, moments later. "Business."
"It can wait a couple minutes, can't it? You

said you had something important to tell me."

"Oh, right. That. Actually, now isn't a good time. It'll keep 'til tomorrow."

"*What?*"

"I've gotta hustle if I expect to get outta here on time. Unless--"

"Unless what?"

"Unless you're gonna be tied up with Jake, or Jack," his voice trailed off.

"I can set aside a few minutes for you," she said.

"Good."

"Now, about that thing--"

"Seriously, sweetheart, I can't get into it now. I have to run. I'll make it up to you tomorrow. I promise. You'll love it."

"Nate?"

"Gotta go, sweetheart. Sleep tight."

"Okay. G'nite." She clicked off and forced herself to ignore whatever it was he had to tell her. The thoughts which followed had a simple theme, and all of them ended in her bed. His bed was bigger, but he was coming here, and she was determined to make the homecoming special. No. *Extra*-special. She stood up, only a little bit wobbly, and headed for her closet. There had to be something in there besides jeans and long-sleeved work shirts.

And then she remembered a tiny black box wrapped in velvet ribbon which she'd tucked away in a bottom drawer of her dresser. It contained an anniversary present from her crazy ex, Shawn, before he went to prison. Back then, he'd been just a horny redneck whose fantasies evolved from topless bars and dirty movies.

She knew what lay nestled within the box, though she'd never worn it. Never even tried it on, despite Shawn's threats to force her if she didn't. Somehow, she'd avoided punishment without giving in.

Nate, however, was a whole 'nuther pile of puzzles. Clearly, he needed a little reward, something to keep him focused--on *her*--and not on anything or anyone in New frickin' York.

She opened the box and removed the combination of elastic and feathers, bits of which floated gently toward the floor. It required no imagination to determine where the fluffy bits went since the elastic wasn't wide enough to cover anything.

"My goodness, Nate," she whispered to herself. "I believe I've got your reward right here."

~*~

Mato reacted as quickly as he could, his instincts directing his actions as surely as if he'd planned them from the start. Dropping his bow, he drew back his arm and sent his spear on a nearly flat trajectory toward the man aiming a gun at Shadow.

It never occurred to him that the spear might travel wide of the mark, or that his target might shift away from danger. Neither possibility occurred, and the spear landed with quiet precision, piercing deeply into the giant's upper arm.

The man's gun hand lurched upward, and he fired a round toward the horizon.

Mato dropped to the ground as the spear hit the giant, and the tiny warrior propelled himself toward the cover of newly sprouted vegetation in the woods. Cursing his failure to plan ahead, Mato hoped there might be some potency left in the sleeping paste with which he coated the spearhead on his last hunt for The People. It had completely dried but might still yield some results.

Unfortunately, it had little effect. The giant had no trouble grabbing the spear, and when he tried to dislodge it, his screams shattered the silence.

Such a spear cast would have killed one of Mato's clansmen, but the giant, easily three times as tall and many times heavier than Mato, merely stood upright, groaning as he worked to dislodge the missile.

Enraged, and obviously in pain, the giant broke off the spear shaft and threw it to the ground, then began to rock and moan. His companion hurried closer and tried to examine the wound, but the injured giant, his pipe now long gone, wouldn't let him touch it.

Mato ignored their ensuing argument and

crept away through the tall grass. He found Shadow waiting for him. His goal lay southward, beyond the place the giants called Ten Sleep. Only recently had he learned that Ten Sleep was but a tiny example of gathered giants. They congregated in numbers too great to comprehend, but fortunately, they did so elsewhere.

It would be hours before he and Shadow slept, and Mato was only too happy to leave the giants behind. The dog, however, had other ideas. Far from being done with the giants, he wanted to return and investigate them further. Mato held onto his ear in a partially successful effort to hold him back.

Once the giants vacated the ravine, Mato released the animal. Shadow raced from cover and searched the rocky shallow until he found the remains of Mato's spear. This he returned with a great show of canine pride.

~*~

"I'm Joseph Bannock," said the man. "But most folks call me Joe Bob."

Daniel Kwan turned his eyes toward the ceiling. Why couldn't he just have the redneck shot? It would've saved so much time and aggravation. He signaled one of his cronies to keep an eye on the man.

"I represent McCutcheon Engineering, which has partnered with Puck Productions on developments all over the world. We've built a

13

number of rides for their theme parks, but we're best known for developing infrastructure--the stuff the public never sees. So--"

A deep bass voice from the head of the table rumbled through the room and blotted out Bannock's tenor. "We covered all that before we broke ground three years ago, Bannock, and we've been behind schedule since day one. Tell me why I shouldn't have McCutcheon thrown off the premises?"

"Because we had no control over those things which led to the delays. I assure you, Mr. Archer, that given--"

"I can guarantee there will be no such delays if my company takes over," Kwan said, drawing every eye in the room. His voice held an edge as sharp as a shank, and only a fool would try to talk over him.

Bannock proved himself just such a man. "I should've said *no one* could control such--"

"I can," Kwan said.

When Bannock glared at him, Kwan again gestured to his associate. The man produced a cell phone and punched in a number as he left the room.

Archer continued as if uninterrupted. "My plans for Puck's Paradise are revolutionary. Nothing like it's ever been contemplated. Anywhere. But that doesn't mean I'm willing to suffer any more delays. I want to see this property open and producing revenue before the

14

end of our fiscal year. Anything short of that means disaster. Not for us, but for whoever's controlling the project. My lawyers will see to that."

"I quite agree, Mr. Archer," Bannock said. "And that's why you need to retain McCutcheon Engineering so--"

"Shut up, Bannock."

Kwan watched the redneck take the insult without registering any emotion. That, at least, was something Kwan could admire, though not enough to halt the "consultation" he had just arranged. Once Bannock realized just how hazardous it was to compete with Kwan, he'd bail out on the project and leave the islands.

Kwan turned his attention to Timothy Archer, the reigning CEO of Puck Productions. How could such a small, insignificant man command such a powerful voice? No doubt, technology played a role. Archer was known for his stagecraft. He'd worked his way up the corporate ladder from broom-pusher in Puck's first permanent amusement park to his current position as the reigning mogul of the multimedia entertainment conglomerate.

Puck Productions owned amusement parks, film studios, hotels, and even a small fleet of cruise ships. Puck boutiques dotted shopping malls on every continent, and no summer was complete without a record-setting box office hit from the animation experts at Puck's Fantasy

15

Factory. The company's namesake, an imp who starred in their earliest cartoons, occupied center stage in the corporate logo, and "Puck luck," another term for shrewd marketing and cut-throat business dealing, had turned a tiny, second-rate, traveling circus into a corporate behemoth.

But all that took place elsewhere. And very soon Archer would find himself in Kwan's world. A place where the entertainment czar would have no control, and where his stable of beloved cartoon characters would be unable to shield him from Daniel Kwan, the King of Kauai.

~*~

Nate Sheffield smiled to himself as he thought about what he'd just done to Tori. Some might call him cruel for dangling a nugget like "something important" in front of her, and then dancing away before she could weasel any details out of him. She'd probably dwell on little else until he reached her cabin. But, considering how often he'd complained about being so far away for so long, his decision wouldn't surprise her. Or so he hoped.

He glanced at his watch. Tori would greet him about suppertime tomorrow. He made a mental note to stop in Buffalo and grab steaks, spuds and red wine. He wasn't keen on the sweet stuff Tori liked, but he knew she kept an ample supply of bourbon on hand. He wouldn't go thirsty.

Then he turned his attention to the text

message he'd received from a client. That, too, brought a smile. He only had one client. Nate's presence was required at a mid-morning consultation with his new liaison, someone named Randy Rhoades. Had he not grown up in Wyoming and lived with cowboys all his life, he might have laughed.

Randy Rhoades. Slim Shaw. Buck Barstow. It seemed like every other guy on the rodeo circuit had a name like that. Nate once considered giving that life a try, but he'd seen the kind of damage some of those boys absorbed during their careers. It wasn't pretty. After a few years of bronc busting and bull riding, most of those guys couldn't walk a straight line, sober.

Nate preferred his bones whole and his spine uncompressed. Besides, living out of an Airstream trailer or a pickup truck didn't hold much appeal. Of course, one always had to consider the buckle bunnies. They most definitely appealed to him, but they were only interested in the top performers--the stars. If you didn't have a half pound trophy buckle holdin' up your Wrangler jeans, you didn't stand a chance with one of them.

Besides, he had Tori Lanier, and she was worth more than all the buckle bunnies rolled into one. And, thanks to his one and only client, Nate would be able to show her just how much she meant to him.

He had only one more day to go in New York City, and only one more meeting. He'd be home soon.

His phone chirped to alert him to a second text message.

~*~

Mato examined the remains of his spear. Despite the great strength even the smallest of giants claimed, breaking a spear shaft *before* extracting it from a wound seemed impossible. He looked more closely at the wood near the break and found traces of dirt. That made him feel better. The giant possessed no supernatural muscle, no wondrous power. The spear was already damaged. The bigger surprise was that the spearhead hadn't fallen off before reaching the target.

Of course, the spearhead represented the greater loss. Mato had spent hours napping the flint, carefully shaping it and keeping the edges as sharp as any metal blades the giants made. Losing it stung his pride. Only a poor huntsman cast a broken spear, and Mato considered his hunting skills exceptional. He also had the wisdom to realize he could always make another.

Calling for Shadow, he once again turned his steps toward Ten Sleep. If he hurried, he could reach the outskirts of the settlement by nightfall. After that, he'd need only a day or so to reach Tori's cabin.

As they walked he heard a loud, mechanical growl. The giants they'd left behind were also on the move, but they weren't traveling on foot. He ducked into leafy cover and tugged on Shadow's ear until the dog whined and followed him.

"Silence!" Mato whispered, but the vehicle on which the two giants rode went by so fast, it was clear they weren't looking for Mato or the dog.

Mato wondered briefly if he'd seriously wounded the pipe-smoking giant. That hadn't been his intent, but such things couldn't be guaranteed. He decided the man couldn't be too badly hurt if he could hang onto his partner who operated their vehicle. The little Indian quickly put such considerations aside.

"We need something to eat," he said to Shadow who stood looking down at him, panting. "What shall we have?"

The dog didn't answer. Instead, he continued looking closely at Mato, as if his partner might make a pretty good meal all by himself. Mato rubbed the big dog behind the ears, and Shadow lowered himself to the ground so Mato could reach him more easily.

"There should be birds in the meadow," Mato said. "Let's go get one."

With that, Shadow bounded away toward the distant clearing, virtually assuring that any birds in the area would be long gone before the little hunter caught up with his dog.

~*~

Chapter 2

Subtlety is wasted on dogs, toddlers, and hit men.

After a lengthy "discussion" with Caleb Jones, her long-time beau, park ranger Maggie Scott had finally given in to his demands. She had agreed, if reluctantly, to present herself at the Western Lady Spa in Buffalo, Wyoming, for a full day of pampering. Not that she needed it. Maggie could have been a poster girl for the benefits of outdoor employment. Though she and Caleb were nearly the same age, she could--in fact, *had*--passed for his daughter more than once. Caleb's insistence that she subject herself to spa treatments had to be because he'd already paid for them, and the folks who ran the enterprise likely had a no-refund policy.

Maggie's arguments against going were admittedly thin, and if pressed, she'd confess that she looked forward to it. Still, it felt natural to put up a fight, if only a symbolic one. She had to maintain her "tough gal" persona, even with an old cowboy like Caleb. One didn't stake out a career in the park service, especially when working in a huge wilderness area like the Cloud Peak, without showing a little orneriness once in a while. It was part of Maggie's mystique, and Caleb loved her for it. Besides, if they did a good job on her nails, she'd have an excuse to buy new work gloves.

She didn't know all the specifics, though she'd poured over the brochure Cal had thoughtfully included with the gilt-edged gift certificate he'd given her. The options included several different kinds of massage, a variety of skin treatments and facials, and a couple things which sounded vaguely terrifying--was she really a candidate for a "detoxifying body wrap?" The package also included wine and a gourmet lunch.

How could she lose on a deal like that? Besides, Cal promised to take her to dinner as long as they were in the big city anyway. She'd smiled at his description but didn't correct him. Buffalo's population had been creeping up on 5,000 and would likely reach that lofty number in the next census or two. And, compared to Charm, where Cal and nearly a dozen others chose to reside, Buffalo *was* the big city.

Maggie had an hour to kill before her 10AM appointment, and she had every intention of fully toxifying herself with bacon, eggs and coffee before she reported for pampering. She'd stopped at the IGA and picked up a copy of the *Buffalo Bulletin* on her way to the cafe and while stirring a dollop of honey into her coffee, she glanced at the headline:

Prospector Dies After Park Attack

Ignoring her breakfast, Maggie dove into the

story, absorbing details as fast as possible, trying to determine how something like this could have happened on her watch but without her knowledge. It quickly became clear.

Two prospectors had been working in the Cloud Peak Wilderness area when someone attacked them. One of the two was struck by an arrow. His partner got him out of the park and took him to the Johnson County Healthcare Center in Buffalo. When his condition grew worse, he was transported by helicopter to a hospital in Billings where he died.

According to preliminary reports, the wounded man suffered a fatal allergic reaction to something authorities believe may have been on the arrowhead. The toxic substance was not identified, but the arrowhead was described as being "made of chipped stone, like those the Indians used in the 1800's."

Maggie's brows tightened as she read the closing paragraph stating that what remained of the weapon, which had apparently been damaged in the attack, had been turned over to investigators.

Maggie's coffee cooled as she grabbed her cell phone and dialed Tori Lanier.

~*~

"Joe Bob" Bannock entered his hotel room and helped himself to a couple single serving bottles of scotch from the mini-bar. He poured them over ice, then loosened his tie and kicked off his shoes. The progress assessment meeting where he'd pleaded his case for McCutcheon Engineering had left him drained. The task ahead, to keep his company in charge of the colossal project, would be even harder than he anticipated. For once, the sheer scale of a Puck park didn't scare anyone away--even on an island where the sort of heavy machinery such a project required was scarce at best. Shipping it in had been a nightmare. Hopefully, one he'd never have to repeat.

Having so much economic and political muscle in one room would have intimidated him earlier in his career. Now, after twenty years of dealing with crooks, both the duly elected sort and the more traditional variety, he'd grown comfortable with the game. It changed, of course, from one venue to the next, but the issues generally remained the same: progress required that all the right players got to participate, and that they all prospered. If nothing else, Bannock was an equal opportunity wheel-greaser. He didn't care who got paid off as long as McCutcheon Engineering got the biggest slice of the pie. Though only a pair of company bookkeepers and possibly one forensic accountant knew it, Bannock owned all of McCutcheon Engineering. Their mutual history with Puck Productions went back a long way--a very long, *profitable* way.

He took a sip of his drink and frowned. He'd

recognized the label, but he'd forgotten how shitty that brand of scotch tasted. "Probably aged a full week or two," he muttered. Sadly, it was the only thing he had, so he continued drinking it. Besides, Tim Archer had left an even shittier taste in his mouth.

Bannock had put up with Archer's condescension for so long he thought it no longer bothered him. He was wrong. Though Archer treated everyone like a medieval serf, Joe never stopped taking it personally, though he'd gotten much better at pretending otherwise. That allowed him to focus on a matter of greater concern: the stereotypically inscrutable Asian, Daniel Kwan.

One big swallow finished off the liquor without shifting the focus of Bannock's ire. "What an asshole. He probably thinks he can get his hands on the equipment I brought in." Bannock shook his head as he refilled his glass. "Good luck with that, schmuck."

A knock on his hotel room door curtailed his thoughts. "Who's there?"

"Maintenance," said a male voice.

"One second." He glanced quickly around the room. Nothing seemed out of place, or more importantly, out of order. Moving quietly, he walked to the closet, opened his suitcase, and removed a golf club, or what was left of it after he had shortened the shaft and replaced the grip. Though he'd often contemplated sharpening the

24

edge on the lob wedge club head, he'd never gotten around to it.

"Come in," he said taking up a position within easy striking distance.

"Do you mind opening the door, sir?" said the voice in the hallway. "My hands are full."

Oh, right. Sure. "Okay. No problem."

~*~

Tori hadn't had so much to drink the night before that she suffered any serious side effects. The headache was enough. Maggie Scott's ringtone didn't help, and when Tori heard it she briefly considered walking outside rather than taking the call from her forest ranger friend. But that only meant extending her lonely exile. *Screw that!*

She picked up the phone. "Hey, Mags. What's up?"

"Have you read the paper?"

Tori gave her a snort of laughter. "The last paperboy to venture out this far worked for the Pony Express."

"Sorry. Brain fart. I've been hanging around Caleb too much. Anyway, the reason I called is 'cause of an article I just read. Somebody shot a guy prospectin' up in the Cloud Peak with a bow and arrow."

Tori rubbed her temple with her free hand. She hadn't been up too long. "Say again? Somebody was *prospecting* with a bow and arrow? How the--"

25

"He was *shot* with an arrow."

"Ouch. He okay?"

"No. He's dead, but that's not the worst of it."

"Can't get much worse than dead."

Maggie exhaled her impatience. "Ask me about the tip of the arrow."

"Uh, okay. What about the tip of the arrow?" Maggie could get a little weird sometimes. Tori suspected weed. Folks grew it in national forests all the time, and who could blame a ranger for harvesting a smidgeon now and then?

"It was a flint arrowhead, Tori. Just like the Indians made way back when."

"And?"

"Do you know anyone who still makes and uses stone arrowheads?"

"I, uh. Oh. Shit. You don't think Mato--"

"That's exactly what I think," Maggie said. "Mato."

"And he *killed* the guy? Must've been a head shot."

"Arm, I think. They say it had something to do with what was smeared on the pointy end. Some kinda poison. You know anyone else who uses stuff like that? I mean, outside of a couple tribes in Brazil."

"Geez," Tori said. "What're we gonna do?"

"Hell if I know. Is he there with you?"

"Nope. Haven't seen him since last year. He and Shadow took Reyna home to have her baby."

"And they live somewhere in the Cloud

26

Peak?"

"Could be. I don't know. He never said, and he wouldn't tell me if I asked. We discussed all this, remember?"

"Of course I remember. But that was before he killed somebody."

"C'mon, Mags! We don't *know* he did it. And even if he did, which I'm not sayin' is the case, I doubt he did it on purpose. Unless--"

"Unless what?"

"Unless he was provoked. What if this alleged 'prospector' discovered where Mato's tribe lives? There's no tellin' what an idiot like that might do--alert the media, blab to the law, anything. So, if Mato *did* kill him, there's a good chance he did it in self defense. Or in defense of his tribe."

"I'm no lawyer," Maggie said. "But that sounds a little thin."

"It's early. I'm just gettin' warmed up."

For a moment, neither woman spoke. Then Maggie said, "I've got an appointment in a little while, but I'll make a couple phone calls and see what I can find out. I'll get Cal on it, too. Can you talk to Nate? He knows the law."

"I'm hoping to see him tonight."

"Good. Lemme know what he says."

"Right."

"And keep an eye out for Mato."

As if she had to tell me, Tori thought.

~*~

Mato hated the hard, wide trails the giants

27

Josh Langston

called "roads." Not only did they play host to the insanely fast vehicles the giants traveled in, they offered no place to hide. Crossing one meant being exposed, and for animals without the ability to reason, like dogs and deer, there was a high probability of death.

Holding Shadow's ear seemed to be the only way to make the dog sit still. He didn't like it, but Mato never let up. In a test of wills, Shadow had no chance. So, Mato held him motionless until he felt it safe to cross, then both of them ran as if pursued by demons. Low shrubbery on the far side offered some cover, and they headed directly toward it.

The sun had fallen close to the horizon, and Mato knew he would never make it to Tori's cabin before dark. Therefore, he began to look for a place to spend the night. As long as he had Shadow for a companion, his options improved dramatically. The dog would either alert him or protect him from almost any danger.

The trick was to get the animal to stay by his side throughout the night. Many times beyond counting Mato wished he could talk to the dog and tell him what he should do. Shadow, however, had a mind of his own, and it was primarily focused on chasing anything that moved, be it butterfly or buffalo.

Fortunately, they hadn't wasted too much time searching for game birds in the mountains. Mato kept an arrow nocked in his bow in case

Shadow flushed a prairie chicken or a rabbit. Either would provide a feast.

Sadly, they encountered no game and had to settle for grubs and a spotted lizard Shadow almost stepped on. The chase had been entertaining, and Mato thanked the Spirits for sending the lizard to them. It wasn't much, but he remained grateful. He knew what an empty belly felt like. He'd grown up with one.

As the sun dropped below the horizon, Mato settled on a spot of raised ground. It appeared clear of snakes and offered a good line of sight in all directions. Nothing belonging to the giants stood close enough to be of concern, so Mato settled down for the night. Shadow curled up next to him, his breathing noisy but still somehow comforting.

Mato fell asleep wondering how Reyna and their tiny child fared.

~*~

Nate arrived early at the Crown Plaza hotel on Broadway in Times Square. Though he'd spent the better part of the past six months in the city, he never got used to it. The lights, the sounds, the constant crowds, all reminded him that he was far from his element. Worse, he was too far away from Tori.

Obviously, fate was a cruel bitch. Just when he and Tori realized they needed to be together, most everything else in his steady, measured life came apart. Since the previous year's fiasco near the Hudson River, Nate had been pulled ever deeper into a new career as a security consultant. He'd become part cop and part private eye. But more than anything, he'd become a source for common sense solutions to prevent crime. Only, not in Wyoming.

Elizabeth Torrence, the woman who'd broken their engagement three years earlier, was at the heart of it. Her high level position on a New York state task force aimed at organized crime gave her a host of powerful contacts. They'd spoken often, and she made it clear their mutual interests had to remain platonic. She didn't care who he romanced, or where, so long as it didn't interfere with his work. She knew his abilities when it came to dealing with criminal types, and she trusted him to always do the right thing, which didn't always turn out to be the *legal* thing.

In the process of working with her task force, he'd developed a reputation for honesty and reliability. He was also damned good in a fight. His self-effacing manner and aw shucks attitude garnered friends at every agency with which he worked.

Unfortunately, those agencies were almost all located in New York, mostly in the metro area, and he had grown weary of it. Beth had promised that this latest contact would be far from the east coast, but she declined to be more specific.

Nate checked his watch. Time to take the elevator to the umpteenth floor and meet Randy

Rhoades. The text he'd received the night before changed the venue from the hotel's coffee shop to a suite near the top floor of the hotel.

After double checking that he had the right room number, Nate knocked on the door. It opened almost instantly, and a redheaded goddess waved him into the room. Nate tried to move casually, but the need to keep her in sight made that tricky. She closed the door and glided across the room, drawing his gaze as she went. Tall, with the looks and build of a supermodel, she welcomed him in and directed him to a seat on the sofa.

"I'm Randy Rhoades, Mr. Sheffield," she said. "Can I get you some coffee?"

"Yes, please," he said, removing his cowboy hat and quickly smoothing his hair in place. "With cream if you've got it." Several thoughts raced through his brain, but one in particular poked doggedly at his cortex--*don't let Tori see this gal!* She'd never let him come back to New York.

"I hope you don't mind meeting me up here," she said, handing him a thick-handled, white mug. "The cafe downstairs is just too noisy, and I didn't want to take a chance on anyone overhearing our conversation."

"That's understandable."

"I don't know what Ms. Torrence told you about our situation."

Nate smiled. "Nothing, actually, other than that you needed my services."

31

"Do you even know who I represent?"

"Haven't the foggiest," Nate said.

She handed him a business card with her name embossed on it. In the upper left-hand corner an impish cartoon character peered out from a circle of letters that spelled Puck Productions, Inc. "I presume you're familiar with our company."

"I recall being strapped into one of your roller coasters once," he said. "Scared me silly. I think I was six or seven."

"I'm glad to hear that," she said and backed it up with a dazzling smile. "I hate the damned things."

"Me, too. So, how can I help you?" he asked.

"That depends."

She took a seat beside him on the sofa, and he became aware of the fragrance she wore, very subtle yet inviting. *As if she needed anything else.* He tried not to appear as if he'd just been poleaxed and kept his hat in his lap. "Depends on what, exactly?"

"How much do you know about Hawaii?"

~*~

Much to Joe Bannock's surprise, the man standing in the hallway outside his room carried a toolbox and wore the sort of uniform one would expect to see on a hotel maintenance worker.

"We're changing out all the old thermostats," the man said. "I hope this is an okay time."

Bannock nodded assent. "No problem." He

kept his makeshift weapon behind his back and made way for the visitor who went straight to the wall-mounted appliance, set down his tools, and went to work.

Maybe Kwan hadn't sent one of his goons after all, Bannock thought. He watched while the custodian removed the thermostat's plastic cover to access the screws holding the device in place. He seemed intent on the task, humming to himself and moving with the sort of precision that came from repetition.

A reflection in the mirror gave Bannock a moment's notice, and he turned to face a real threat. Two men stood in the doorway, and neither of them looked like hotel employees. Bannock had never seen either of them before.

"Can I help you?" he asked.

The taller of the two men said, "We need to talk."

"About what?"

"You need to come with us."

"Sorry, no can do. See, I'm having my thermostat replaced."

"We're serious," said the nondescript visitor.

"I can see that, but why should I care?" Bannock asked. His hands had grown sweaty, a condition he'd dealt with all his life. It had been the driving force behind his choice of an enhanced grip on the customized golf club still behind his back.

He looked at the maintenance worker who

now stood silent and unmoving. "Call the police," Bannock told him.

"That's not necessary," the man at the door said. "We're hotel security." He gestured at the custodian. "You can go now."

Bannock waited until the worker reached a spot between himself and the vocal member of the duo, then swung his shortened golf club. He didn't have room for a full swing, but he got enough of his target's throat to disable him. He then took a backhanded swipe at the spokesman.

The bogus hotel security man retreated into the hall. Bannock pressed him, stepping over the man gurgling on the floor. He delivered an overhead strike to the remaining intruder just as he leveled a gun at Bannock.

And fired.

The sound, the muzzle flash, and the pain hit Bannock simultaneously. He watched in a peculiarly detached way as the gunman slumped to a sitting position on the floor with the blade of the lob wedge stuck in the crown of his head. A stream of thick, red blood streamed from the wound, obscuring his face. It dripped from his chin onto his chest into an expanding wine-colored smear.

Bannock then reacted to his own pain. He reached for his side, just below his left armpit. It felt like someone had set him on fire. Still enraged, he grew even angrier at the thought that he would soon die from a stupid gunshot. Looking down, he saw the remaining intruder, still struggling to breathe, his eyes wide as hubcaps at the sight of his partner's crude lobotomy.

There was no sign of the custodian other than his abandoned tools and a partially dismantled thermostat dangling from a wire in the wall.

The man on the floor had enough presence of mind to finally reach for his own gun, so Bannock kicked him, his toe connecting sharply with the man's temple. It turned the thug off as neatly as a light switch. It also jammed Bannock's toe, forcing it into an awkward angle that hurt like hell.

But at least it took his mind off the wound in his side which, he surmised, might not be fatal after all, since he remained very much alive and wasn't bleeding anywhere near as much as the two hoods on the floor.

With both threats addressed, possibly in a permanent fashion, Bannock picked up his room phone and asked the operator to connect him with the police.

"You can dial 911 from your room, sir. Just dial 9 first."

"So, 9-911?"

"Yes sir."

Bannock's hand shook so badly it took him two tries to get it right.

~*~

Maggie Scott had very few contacts in law enforcement, and when Nate Sheffield resigned as deputy sheriff, she had even fewer. Nate, at least, could have suggested where she might inquire about the weapon used in the attack on the prospector. Unfortunately, Nate no longer spent much time in Wyoming as he'd found his calling in New York. Just the thought of so many people and so much concrete gave Maggie the creepin' willies, an expression she'd picked up from Caleb Jones. He used it when referring to certain oversized rodeo bulls he'd encountered during his career on the circuit.

Cal, though a dear heart and a budding romantic, had a no-nonsense attitude when it came to the world of rodeos. That was serious business. And while everyone agreed the primary goal was entertainment, a major component of rodeo life was injury. Bull-riders were especially prone to being stomped, gored, or butted, and Cal swore the breeders had come up with a handful of the beasts which were just downright evil. Those were the ones that inspired the kind of willies that snuck up on a fella in the night and sucked his well of confidence completely dry.

Maggie considered calling Nate and rousting him from his luxurious little New York nest, but he was probably already at work. Then she recalled a contact she'd made with a reporter for a newspaper in Cheyenne, a gal who wrote feature articles and needed to interview a park ranger. Maggie's boss had assigned her to be the park spokesperson. Maggie had been flattered, and the two of them got along well.

That had been a couple years back, and Maggie hadn't thought about it much since then, even though she'd kept a clipping she'd cut from the paper to show Cal. He wanted to have it framed so she could hang it on her wall, but the black and white photo that went with it wasn't very flattering, and the text came out in one long, skinny column. Framing it would have been tricky, if not expensive. Cal dropped the discussion when the word "expensive" cropped up.

But, she still had the clipping, folded neatly and packed away in a side pouch of her handbag. She fished it out and read the byline: Daphne Cutter, Feature Editor. The woman had a pleasant demeanor, and while certainly not an "outdoorsy" type, she seemed to appreciate the challenges faced by someone in a ranger uniform, especially a woman. She had been highly complimentary of the park, its programs, and its staff.

Feeling both stealthy and resourceful, Maggie looked up the number of the newspaper and put in a call. It only took two bounces before she reached her target.

"This is Daphne," a familiar voice said.

"Hi, Daphne," Maggie said. "You may not remember me, but a couple years--"

"It's Margaret, isn't it? You're with the forest service."

"It says 'Margaret' on my drivers license, but I go by Maggie."

37

Josh Langston

"Of course! And how could I ever forget my personal tour guide through the high country wilderness? I've got a photo from that story right here on my desk. So, what can I do for you?"

At the first mention Maggie made of the dead prospector, Daphne picked up the thread.

"Yeah, that's a weird one, isn't it?"

"I thought so," Maggie said. "It happened while I was off duty, but I still felt-- I dunno, a little responsible, I guess."

"Why?" Daphne chuckled. "You didn't shoot the guy with an arrow, did ya?"

"Nah, but you know how it is. It happened on my turf, and I didn't know anything about it 'til I saw something in the paper."

"Are you here, in Cheyenne?"

"Nope, Buffalo." She checked her watch wondering how she'd explain to Cal that she'd missed her appointment. Maybe she could reschedule. "Anyway, the article I read said something about the murder weapon being turned over to investigators. Do you have any idea who that might be?"

"Probably the university up in Billings. They teach forensic science up there, and the instructors moonlight on occasion."

"Do you know anyone up there?"

"I've got a contact or two," Daphne said. "What is it you wanted to know?"

"I'm not sure, exactly," Maggie said, wishing she'd rehearsed this part of the conversation before she called. "The paper said the arrow had a flint tip. I know a couple folks who dabble in that sort of thing as a hobby. Weird, isn't it?"

"Very."

"So, I was just looking for a little more information."

"Lemme make a call or two," Daphne said.

"I hate to ask you to do that."

"It's no problem, really. I got promoted to the news desk, and it's been kinda slow lately, 'cept for the park incident. I'd probably have to look into it sooner or later anyway. Give me your number, and I'll call you back. You can look up some of those stone tool makers you know. I might want to talk to one of 'em."

"Deal," Maggie said, then recited her cell phone number.

Daphne said, "Talk to you soon," and hung up.

Maggie glanced at her watch and smiled. "Guess I'll make it to the spa on time after all." She paid her tab, left a nice tip, and whistled as she left the coffee shop.

~*~

Chapter 3

What doesn't kill you makes you stronger.
Except Bears. Bears will kill you.

Daniel Kwan sat stone-faced as he got the news that the two men sent to discourage the redneck *haole*, Joe Bannock, from further involvement in the Puck project were in the hospital. And they weren't merely hospitalized. They were both in intensive care.

Paku Tanaka, the man who explained the situation, showed a similar lack of emotion. He finished his report with, "How do you want this handled?"

"I have no room in my organization for incompetents," Kwan said. He paused to reflect on his options. The temptation to have both men killed appealed to him, but since neither had regained consciousness, they'd have to be dispatched in their sleep. Hardly a fitting way to respond to their failures.

"Keep an eye on them. If they survive, I'll think about what I'll do to them. Meanwhile, find out what Bannock is up to. How did a pencil pusher like him take out two armed men--with a damned golf club, for God's sake?" That just wasn't right.

Kwan had already experienced an overload of annoyance when Bannock got around the obstacles designed to sidetrack the development. Shipping orders had been lost, canceled or amended. Machinery that should have been delivered in the summer months sat in storage on the mainland until the fall. Special materials not available in the islands had been imported from factories on both sides of the Pacific, and while Kwan got many of them delayed, Bannock had gone ahead with construction.

Other than fracturing the project's calendar and timeline, Kwan hadn't accomplished anything, and the place was almost ready to open. His sole achievement was to anger Puck's CEO, Tim Archer.

That wasn't nearly enough.

~*~

Mato spotted some buildings in the distance. The giants invested much time and energy in constructing their living quarters. It always surprised him. He understood their size made it difficult for them to get by on small structures, but that didn't explain their penchant for putting up *multiple* buildings. They even built houses for their machines! Why? Did they believe the machines would be angry otherwise? Mato would not feel bad if he left a bow or a spear out in the elements while he slept, although he would certainly feel shame. Only the very young or the very stupid would risk sleeping without a weapon handy.

Before he met Tori and found out about the

41

giant's *technology*--a word for which his people had no equivalent--Mato thought that some of the things they called "machines" were alive, which explained the need to keep them sheltered in bad weather.

Eventually, however, he came to realize the giants were simply driven by a need to build *things*. Very often, the things they built were so clever they appeared magical. Tori had often assured him that no magic was involved. She credited something called "science." Mato was too proud to admit he didn't understand the difference, although he felt reasonably sure that magic involved either pleasing or angering the Spirits. Science didn't.

That distinction was enough for him.

Shadow, too, seemed interested in the giant's buildings. Normally, Mato would avoid such dwellings for the huge creatures who lived in them often acted unpredictably. They would race outside for no apparent reason and engage in all sorts of activity. Sometimes, though rarely, such activity made sense to him.

But, since they had been traveling for two days with little to eat or drink, he felt it worth the risk to venture near the giant's enclave in hopes of finding food and water. Mato could get by for a while longer, perhaps even long enough to reach Tori's cabin, but Shadow had lost his spark. So they veered slightly from their course and approached the buildings.

The smell of horses and cattle hit them from a great distance, and though there were quite distinct differences in their scents, the combination proved almost overpowering. How the giants could live amidst such powerful odors amazed him. Being around Shadow was bad enough, and more than once he'd had to protect the dog from others in his tribe who objected to the animal's presence, but Shadow smelled a great deal better than *any* cow.

As they drew closer to their target, Shadow seemed to perk up. It might have been the presence of a new smell: the birds which some giants raised. He'd asked Tori about them and wondered why she didn't maintain a supply since she never did any hunting. It seemed like a good idea as the birds provided eggs, too. Tori claimed she could never kill and eat a pet.

Mato was still trying to figure out the finer distinctions between "pets" and all the rest of the animals in the world. Tori's attempts to explain it only muddied the issue.

For now, Mato wasn't worried about pets. His focus had narrowed significantly. He wanted food.

Listening closely for sounds of the giants, Mato and Shadow crept ever closer to the collection of buildings known as a "ranch." That had been another vastly confusing concept for Mato. Ranches could be big or small. They could come with or without herds of animals, though

43

sometimes the latter configurations were known as "farms." But they, too, could house many, many animals, including chickens. Mato would have been quite satisfied to grab one. A scrawny one would do nicely. He and Shadow could sneak away unseen and have a wonderful feast.

Alas, though the smell of chickens lay heavy on the air, the wire enclosure where they would normally be kept was empty except for feathers and bird droppings. That was the other thing that characterized farms and ranches: the smell of shit. The stuff was everywhere, and for Mato it was often knee-deep. Cows, pigs, and horses generated a prodigious volume of it, and the smell carried for miles. He could not imagine choosing to live near it.

When they heard voices, the pair hid behind a piece of ancient machinery. Mato had no idea what the rusting hulk might be used for. Nor did he care. He watched as a pair of giants, one male and one female exited the building.

"We'll be back soon, Mama. You've got a cell phone. Call if you think of something we need to get in town."

Though they were dressed much the way Tori and Nate, Mato's other friend, dressed, they were both older. Mato held Shadow's ear and whispered calming words. The dog seemed to enjoy calling attention to himself at the worst possible moments, but he obliged by slumping to the ground with his nose parked between his huge front paws. Mato stroked his head.

The couple climbed into a truck like Nate's. Though it was about the same size, the layer of dirt on it appeared much thicker. Mato was happy not to have been born a truck.

They waited for the vehicle to rumble off, then sneaked closer to the house. There, Mato picked up a new scent, a most welcome one. He couldn't understand why Shadow didn't react to it as well. Tori called it "bacon," which Mato translated to mean "gift of the Spirits."

The giants had many, many wondrous things and a variety of foodstuffs that defied imagination. Two such items often occupied Mato's hungry dreams: bacon and peanut butter. He would gladly risk his life to obtain either, though he hoped he wouldn't have to.

Mato climbed atop a rain barrel hoping to peek through a window of the building the giant couple had just vacated. Someone, presumably "Mama," remained inside. He could hear movement and had no intention of being seen.

Shadow, however, entertained no such notions of stealth. His focus had been drawn to the presence of yet another farm/ranch animal--a feline. This one looked eerily familiar. It had the same markings and the same attitude as the cat that attacked him beneath Tori's cabin.

That had been long ago, and while it led to an amazing friendship, it had also produced some scars on Mato's torso which never completely went away. He often dreamed about the experience. This time, however, the cat had become the quarry. And, once again, Shadow's timing could not have been worse.

With a bark and a howl of outrage, Shadow leaped from cover and took off after the offending cat. It responded with an equally defiant screech and raced across the open space between Mato and the house.

It veered sharply at the last moment and in a succession of graceful bounds, climbed to the roof of another farm vehicle. Mato couldn't recall the name of it; the giants had names for everything, though few of them made much sense.

Shadow stayed on the ground with his front paws resting against the machine. There he stood, barking as if his life depended on it. Mato, meanwhile, looked for someplace to hide.

Moments later, a giant came to the door to investigate. Older than the two who had so recently departed, this one appeared no less capable of ruining their morning. With a grunt and a curse, the old woman turned around and went into the house. She quickly came back with the same kind of weapon Tori kept in her cabin. Tori called it a "shotgun."

~*~

"What do I know about *Hawaii*?" Nate asked. It wasn't a question he'd anticipated. At all. Especially from a statuesque redhead who had his mind working overtime to keep his libido in check. Why not, "How good are you in bed?" or "Guess my bra size?"--questions he might have entertained at some point, possibly in junior high. But Hawaii? "I'm uh-- not exactly an expert. Why do you ask?"

"Puck Productions has invested heavily in a new development on the island of Kauai. But we're concerned because the level of unexplained problems there has gone beyond anything we've experienced with other projects."

"I see," he said, blindly. "Maybe you should shift the whole shebang over to Wyoming. I could be a lot of help out there."

Randy Rhoades flashed him another smile, which likely did a number on the northeast power grid. "I wish we could. But the boss is determined to create the ultimate Puck-style vacation get-away. If he could have bought himself an entire Hawaiian island, he would've done it. But he had to settle for a significant chunk of Kauai. I presume you've been there?"

"Nope. But I've been to the rodeo in Sheridan too many times to count." He shook his head, the contents of which had often been rattled at rodeos in Sheridan. "I really don't see how I'd be of any use to you. Sounds to me like you need someone who's part cop and part surfer. I fit about half that bill."

"What we need, Mr. Sheffield, is someone who isn't part of any interest group but ours. We can't tell who's working with us or against us."

"You think the local cops are corrupt?"

"Certainly not all of them. But one or two, in the right positions, can facilitate all kinds of mischief."

"And you're hoping I can figure out who's screwing who?" He coughed a millisecond after realizing what he'd just said. "Sorry. Technical terms."

"I'd have chosen an even earthier way of saying it."

"Ah."

She laughed. "You can't offend me. I work for Tim Archer."

"Oh," he said, wondering where the conversation was headed. "I'll try to do better."

"Don't sweat it. We're not looking for a one-man band. We've got internal security, and we have no qualms about hiring additional guard types locally. What we want is someone smart enough to operate solo, under the radar so to speak. Someone who'll poke around and report back to me, or Mr. Archer. Nobody else."

"You just want me to snoop around?"

"Pretty much. And follow up on anything suspicious you might find. We've gotten some great reports about you. We have no doubt you know how to follow your instincts."

"Who's 'we'?"

"Me, mostly. But I keep Mr. Archer up-to-date. He likes to think he's in charge of everything, which is ridiculous. The company is far too big for anyone to know everything."

"You seem to know a lot," Nate said.

"I do. But I don't pretend to know it all." She winked at him. "There's a lot of stuff I know a little bit about, and that's plenty."

He wasn't sure how to interpret that but figured he'd learn soon enough. If he took the job.

She handed him an envelope. "The details of our offer are in there. I think you'll find them quite generous."

He hefted the envelope without examining it. Obviously it contained no cash. "I don't suppose any of my work would be stateside."

"All of it is," she said.

"Oh. Right. I meant--"

"I know what you meant. You need to get used to the idea that Hawaii *is* a state. Hawaiians get a little prickly when you treat them as foreigners."

"What I was driving at," Nate said, "was that I'd like to spend a little time at home before I jump into the next project."

"You don't like New York?"

"Love it like the plague." He checked his watch. "I promised someone I'd be back in Wyoming tonight."

"Girlfriend?" she asked, staring at his ring-free left hand.

"More than that, I hope."

"Well, you haven't agreed to anything yet, and until you do--"

49

Josh Langston

"How long a flight is it to Hawaii?"

"From where?"

"Ten Sleep, Wyoming."

"I have no idea. I didn't know there was a Ten Sleep, Wyoming. What's it near?"

"Not much of anything, really," he said. "But it's where I live."

"I'm sure it's both rugged and handsome. But you know what? It's not important. We'll send a plane for you, so as long as you can get to an airport somewhere, Puck will pick you up. Our corporate jets are pretty nice. You won't mind the long ride. I promise."

His mind was awash with thoughts, most of them centered on Tori Lanier. "If I take you up on your offer, is there any chance I could take someone with me? You know, like a friend?"

"Your 'more-than-a-girlfriend' friend?"

He grinned. "Yeah. We haven't been able to spend much time together lately. A trip to Hawaii would do wonders for her. I'd cover her expenses, of course."

"Of course *not*," she said. "There are very few limits on the expense account you'll have."

"This is sounding better and better."

"Good!"

"How much time do I have to decide?"

She rubbed her jaw. "Hard to say. When's your flight home?"

"It leaves in a few hours."

"Tell you what," she said, blinding him with

50

another smile, "say yes to our offer, and I'll drop you off on my way home."

"At the airport?"

"No, in Twelve Sleep."

"Ten Sleep."

"Wherever. We're a first class operation, Mr. Sheffield. We don't cut corners, especially for associates who have our best interests at heart. Just say yes, and I'll have you back in your sweetheart's arms--to say nothing of her good graces--in no time."

Just saying yes appealed to him, but he hadn't even glanced at the actual offer. However, if the compensation was anything like the perks, he'd be a jackass to say anything *but* yes.

"What if I say yes but change my mind later."

"Then you'll be happy to know Puck Productions retains the sharpest contract law experts on the planet. They'll screw your ass to the wall so tight, you'll think you just shit a condo."

"That certainly gives a guy something to think about."

"C'mon, Nate. Say yes. We only bite when we're pissed off. Here's your chance to make us happy. Hell, it's your chance to make *everyone* happy. What d'ya say?"

~*~

When the cops arrived, one of them handcuffed Bannock and made him sit in a straight-backed chair while the crime scene technicians scoured the room for evidence.

"I'm the one who called you," Bannock said. "Why am I in cuffs? Geez. They assaulted me. Ask the custodian. He saw it all."

A bored-looking detective told him to be quiet. He didn't use harsh language, but his demeanor carried a threat: failure to shut up would not end well.

Bannock shut up.

Eventually, the two thugs were wheeled away; the photos had all been taken; the room had been cordoned off with yellow, plastic ribbon, and the powers that be finally remembered Joe Bannock still sitting where he'd been for over an hour. His arms hurt from the unnatural position, and he had run through a dozen conversations with his attorney--all of them in his head.

Finally the bored-looking detective returned and sat down next to him. "Okay, then, let's get your side of the story."

"Take these damned cuffs off, and I'll tell you."

The cop stared at him for a long moment, then unlocked the cuffs from behind his back but re-cuffed Bannock to the chair he sat on. If he had to, Joe might have been able to use the chair as a weapon, but it would have been awkward and probably futile. Besides, he had nothing to hide, as they so often said on TV.

Should I stay mum 'til my attorney arrives? That could be a while. A day or two, maybe.

"Talk," said the cop.

Bannock went over what had happened. He felt reasonably sure he hadn't left anything out except for his suspicions about who sent the two men.

"Any idea what they wanted?" the cop asked. "They said they only wanted to talk."

"Then why did they pull their guns on me?"

The cop shook his head. "The custodian said they *didn't* pull their guns."

"Then how'd I get shot?"

"Self defense."

"Whose? Mine or the guy that shot me?"

"The guy that shot you. Hell, you went after him with a damned golf club. I'd have shot you, too." He consulted his notes. "What the hell kinda club was that?"

"Lob wedge."

"No shit?" He finally broke a smile. "I didn't think anyone could hit a lob wedge."

Bannock didn't laugh. "I'd really like to get out of these cuffs."

"Yeah, I suspect so."

The cop's cell phone beeped, and he palmed Bannock to silence while he read a text message the beep signaled. "Looks like your visitors both had records."

"See? I told you they were bad guys."

"Having a record doesn't make you a 'bad guy.'" He said. "As of today, you'll have one, too. You a bad guy?"

Josh Langston

"I'm an engineer! I'm in charge of the Puck Resort construction. And I'm getting damned tired of wearing these restraints."

"I get that," the cop said. "And thank you for confirming your identity. But here's the thing. You damn near killed two men who, according to the only eye witness, didn't actually attack you."

"They intended to drag me out of my room when I refused to go with them."

The cop checked his notes again, then shook his head. "That's not what the custodian said."

"Listen, I had no desire to fight with those two. In fact, I asked the custodian to call you."

"You said *you* placed the call to 911." He flipped through his notes until he found the appropriate one and tapped it with his index finger. "Yep. Got it right here. You made the call."

Bannock wanted to scream his frustration. "I only called because he wouldn't! Besides, it was all over by then. I fought them off and reported it."

"The custodian says you attacked them, not the other way around."

"Then he's lying," Bannock said.

The cop shrugged. "We get that a lot." He helped Bannock to his feet. "We'll look into this further at the station."

"You're *arresting* me?"

"Yep. Better not saying anything we can use against you in court."

"You've got to be kidding me!"

54

"We don't do that very much." And then he led Bannock from the room.

~*~

Maggie had never felt so relaxed in her life. The massage, the skin treatments, the soak in the mud bath, and the wine--she couldn't forget the wine--had all worked their magic on her. She couldn't wait to tell Cal how grateful she was. Better yet, she decided, she'd *show* him. Provided she could stay awake.

Daphne called back as Maggie poured herself into her car. She wasn't drunk, but she was *loose*. Deliciously so. "'Sup?" she said. Somehow they'd even managed to relax her lips.

"You okay?" Daphne asked. "You sound kinda-- I dunno. Funky."

Maggie laughed. "That's me all right. *Fun-kee!*" She tried to say it the way the soul singers did back when she was in college a few thousand years earlier.

"Damn, girl. You're gonna have to tell me where you've been."

"A spa. Heaven on Earth, actually. It was a gift from my boyfriend. He's a sweetie."

"Evidently! Listen, I can't talk long, but I got a little more information, and now I want more than ever to talk to anyone you know who can knap flint to make arrowheads."

Maggie patted her cheeks. *Get with it, girl!* "Uh, sure. No problem. What'd you find out?"

"A couple things. First, the folks at the

university said the size of the arrowhead is a puzzle. It's too big to be an arrowhead, but not really big enough to be a spearhead."

"Hm," Maggie said.

"But they did say it was a terrific example of a type they called-- Hang on."

Maggie heard paper rustling and assumed Daphne was consulting her notes.

"Yeah. It's a Clovis point."

"And that's helpful?"

"Well, not really, 'cause nobody's made 'em for about ten thousand years."

"So, the killer is a caveman?"

Daphne chuckled. "Nope. But he acted like one. There was no way to date the flint. No way to tell how long ago it was shaped. But what was left of the arrow, or spear, or whatever it was attached to, is contemporary. Grown right here in Wyoming. And get this: they found a fingerprint in the gook used to hold the point and the shaft together."

Maggie swallowed hard. "No kidding? Well, that should make it easier to find the guy."

"We don't know it was a guy."

"Of course. But-- Whatever. You know what I meant."

"Sure. Funny thing is, the fingerprint is really, really small. 'Bout the size of an infant's."

"That's odd."

"That ain't all. The print revealed tiny scars, too. It's an *adult* print, even though it's so little.

The lab guys are sure of it."

Daphne had confirmed Maggie's worst fears. "So, what're they saying? The killer is a midget?"

"I think the proper term is 'little person.' But even that designation doesn't fit the facts. One of the guys joked that the cops need to start looking for a leprechaun."

"That's rich," Maggie said. "We see them runnin' around here all the time."

"I know, right? Crazy. I can't wait to start working on my article."

"I can only imagine. I really appreciate your calling me back."

"No problem. Now, about those names?"

"Oh, right. The flint knappers. I'll have to look 'em up when I get home. I don't have my address book handy."

"I'll call you back if I don't hear from you."

"No problem," Maggie said. "Really."

"Good. Talk to you soon!"

Click.

Maggie looked at the phone in her hand. It was time to call Tori again. Between them, maybe they could figure out a way to get their little Indian friend out of town. Or at the very least, back to his own people. Where he went didn't matter so long as the cops couldn't find him.

~*~

Mato had seen what a shotgun could do and knew Shadow was in grave danger. The cat, however, hadn't reached the same conclusion. It chose that moment to vacate its perch and run for another of the buildings on the property.

Shadow followed close behind.

The woman in the doorway pointed the gun in the air and fired.

Fortunately, Mato had heard the sound of such a weapon before and managed to keep quiet. The woman in the doorway ducked back inside once again. As before, she reappeared only moments later, this time wearing heavy, unlaced boots. She marched after the cat and the dog letting the screen door crack against the wooden frame behind her.

Leaving Shadow to care for himself, Mato raced to the house and slipped inside the screen door before it hit a second time. He followed his nose though the building until he reached the kitchen. There, on a table, sat several strips of bacon, still oozing hot grease and permeating the air with a heavenly aroma.

Mato climbed up on a chair and reached for a slice, then quickly withdrew his hand. The bacon was *hot!* But he didn't have time to let it cool. Instead, he wrapped all the slices in the paper towel on which they rested. It made for a greasy bundle, but he didn't care. He also grabbed an orange from a bowl of fruit in the center of the table.

Juggling the two objects and his weapons, he retraced his steps through the house. He could hear the woman yelling in the distance. The shotgun went off again.

Praying Shadow was still alive, Mato raced through the screen door and out into the open. He heard Shadow barking but couldn't see him. He also heard the woman cursing. Some of the things she said were quite colorful, if not terribly logical. Mato hadn't mastered giant profanity, but he was picking up several new words. The context was tricky, however.

Once he crossed the open ground and reached the relative safety of the sheds near the livestock pens, Mato worked his way closer to the barn from which the barking and swearing emanated. The old woman was poking at the dog with the shotgun, and Mato surmised she had used up the little tubes which made so much noise and caused such destruction.

Shadow appeared to be growing weary of the hunt, and when Mato whistled, he dropped to the ground, dodged around the still swearing giant, and broke for the outdoors. Mato could only hope they moved fast enough that the old woman didn't get a good look at them.

~*~

Josh Langston

Chapter 4

*Most people don't understand how airplanes fly.
They think it's magic, because magic is something
they do understand.*

Helmut Warner, senior flight instructor, or *fluglehrer,* for Zeppelin, had seen all kinds of men and women in pursuit of pilot certification for the new generation of airships. Though the rebirth of the so-called Lighter Than Air (LTA) industry had been stalled for decades, it had finally begun to gather momentum, and there was no shortage of far-sighted individuals who wished to be in its vanguard.

Like most students seeking advanced flight credentials, those who came through the Zeppelin *Flugschule* were universally bright, serious, and dedicated. But almost all of them also had a less focused side. They could relax with a pint of beer or sprawl in a comfy chair in front of a TV screen showing the latest match from the *Bundesliga,* Germany's premier football league.

Klaus Becker, however, seemed out of phase in both respects. His classroom work was adequate, but his performance in the flight simulator earned only a passing grade. Becker's inability to unwind with his fellow students however, struck Warner as distinctly uncharacteristic.

When they went out to celebrate some minor achievement, he stayed in his room. Conversely, when they camped in to study, usually as a group, he would leave the complex only to show up for classes as if he'd been nowhere more distant than the showers.

Though Warner had his doubts about Becker's suitability for command--be it in a hot air balloon, a 100-passenger dirigible or a department store elevator--there was no law prohibiting the uninspired from gaining flight certification. Nor were there any prohibitions about being an *arschloch*. Thus did Klaus Becker, the asshole, approach matriculation from the Zeppelin Flugschule with neither family nor friends in attendance.

Tori approached housekeeping with all the gusto of a condemned man trudging to the gallows. It wasn't that she didn't appreciate cleanliness, she just didn't rank it alongside sainthood. She changed her sheets, towels and underwear on a timely basis, burned the trash and did the dishes as needed. She wasn't a slob. At least, not a complete and utterly hopeless slob.

Still, that left a good bit of work to be done before Nate arrived. She had to restock the larder for one thing, and the liquor cabinet, too. She'd hit it pretty hard lately. Nate would arrive hungry, but she seriously doubted they'd spend anytime at her little dinner table until after they'd gotten *reacquainted.* The mere thought made her blush. She was tempted to try on the fluff and elastic thing--just to be sure it fit.

Then she giggled. Of course it would fit, and if it didn't, she could just Scotch tape the feathery finery in place. It wouldn't be there long anyway.

She hoped.

And, in case Nate forgot to stop and buy groceries, she intended to have enough stuff on hand that they could avoid going anywhere until they were good and ready--or sore, whichever came first. She even texted her editor, Cassy Woodall, to say she'd be unavailable for at least a couple days, maybe more.

She drove into Charm and cruised through Cal's store. He didn't have much of a selection, and his prices were outrageous, but he stocked the basics, and she got most of what she needed without driving too far. Besides, it was good to see the old wrangler. After the scare they'd had in New York, she felt closer to him than ever, and Maggie, too, of course.

By mid-afternoon, she had most everything in order. A bit of shuffling and straightening remained, but she'd get that done soon enough.

Her cell phone rang, but she couldn't find it at first and conceded there might be a teensy bit more stuff to be put away.

Bother! The damn phone had to be there somewhere.

She found it under a pile of clean but

unfolded laundry. When she picked it up, she noticed the low battery signal. "H'lo?"

"Tori! It's me. I'll be on the ground in 'bout half an hour."

She glanced at her watch. Nate was way early, which news couldn't have been more welcome. "Wonderful! When can you get here?"

"Ninety minutes, give or take," he said. "I'll be landing in Worland."

"How'd you manage that? I thought--"

"I'll explain when I get there. Still need me to stop for groceries?"

"No. I mean, hell no! I want you to get yourself out here as soon as you can. No stops along the way, y'hear? None. You can slow down when you go through the driveway. It's still an obstacle course, but as soon as the cabin's in sight, you punch it. Got that?"

"Yes ma'am! I--"

Tori's phone went dead. "Damn!" She was tempted to curse some more, but one overriding thought occupied her mind: Nate would be there soon.

Very soon!

She dropped the phone on her dresser and went back to straightening up. She even hummed. She couldn't remember being so excited, and when Nate got to her door, she'd by Gawd see to it he was happy, too.

~*~

Kwan smiled, but it felt odd. Smiling wasn't

something one did without cause, and it took a great deal to satisfy his requirements. Still, having Bannock in jail worked nicely. Though not as good as sending him back to the mainland, or better still, putting him in the ground, but jail definitely took him off the playing field. As long as the maintenance worker at the hotel stuck to the story they paid him to tell, Bannock would be cut off from the action. Tim Archer would grow steadily angrier as the project suffered still more delays, and it wouldn't be long before Puck put all its eggs in Kwan's basket. Where they belonged.

He already had most of his construction management team lined up. Bannock's senior people would soon be sent home, and Kwan's people could take over. He had no idea how to manage such a large project, but that's what he hired other people to do. He offered them a generous bonus, too. If they performed well, their families would continue living. Such incentives never ceased to amaze him, especially since he had no family of his own.

Kwan himself was the only person he knew who wasn't expendable. Life became far less complicated when a man only had to be concerned about himself.

~*~

Nate had never before flown in a private jet. Riding in Puck's Gulfstream G650ER was like taking a cruise on a very modern, and very well-equipped luxury yacht. Though the aircraft could comfortably seat ten, Nate and Randy Rhoades were the only passengers. A two-man flight crew and a pleasant, young, male steward filled out the manifest.

Nate and Randy had a light lunch while crossing the country at 45,000 feet and at a speed just under Mach one. During that time, Randy explained more about the Puck resort under construction in Hawaii.

"Puck's Paradise will have everything: hotel accommodations, a multi-generational entertainment complex, shopping, and a transportation hub for arrivals by air and boat."

"Nothing by road?"

She shook her head. "No cars. That was one of Mr. Archer's absolutes. Company, employee and delivery vehicles can park up the coast and take a ferry to the complex, but all guests will arrive via cruise ship or air from Lihue or Honolulu. There may be regularly scheduled flights from the mainland if he decides to set up an airline to go with his dirigible. Can you say 'Puck Air?'"

"You've gotta be kidding. He has a blimp--like the Hindenburg? How many people died when that thing blew up?"

"Thirty-five. Two-thirds of them were crew. And it wasn't a blimp; it was a dirigible. It happened in Lakehurst, New Jersey, in 1937 and ended the age of the great airships. That, and the fact that the United States wouldn't sell the Germans any helium. That's why they had to use hydrogen, which--"

"Is highly flammable."

"But has greater lift," Randy added.

"Helium doesn't explode."

"Exactly. It's been used in blimps for ages, pretty much non-stop since World War II. The thing about airships is that they provide a slow, smooth, quiet ride. Perfect for sight-seeing. Which is precisely what Mr. Archer has in mind."

She paused to take a sip of her drink, then continued. "We'll start with just one airship, and if it works as well as we hope, we'll expand the fleet and offer service to and from Honolulu. Originally, Mr. Archer wasn't inclined to enter the cruise ship business, but it turned out to be quite lucrative. He hates to let someone else pocket money that could easily come to us."

"There's nothing wrong with making a profit," Nate said. *As long as it's done legally and without hurting anyone.* So far, his own journey into capitalism had generated more income in a year than he'd earned as a deputy sheriff in the previous five. His expenses had been staggering, but even so, he managed to put a good deal of money into savings. Something he'd never been able to do before.

"So, basically, it's just another big theme park," Nate said.

"Not at all." Randy signaled the flight attendant to refill her drink. He seemed to appear when needed and then disappear just as quickly.

Nate found it spooky.

"Everything is geared toward a complete experience. Guests will eat, sleep, and play all in the same complex. There won't be any need to travel anywhere else. In a traditional park, guests can come and go. They can drive in, spend a few hours, then go somewhere else. Lunch, maybe, or to a movie or a ballgame. That's not how it'll work at Puck's Paradise. Guests will remain on the grounds for the duration of their stay, and if I know Mr. Archer, he'll have them wishing they could stay longer."

"So, why do it in Hawaii? Why not the middle of Iowa, or Pennsylvania? Anywhere for that matter?"

"Because Mr. Archer fell in love with the Napali coast. His cruise ships will feature one of the most stunningly rugged coast lines in the world. The airships will offer views impossible by any other means. They'll also fly right down into Waimea Canyon, another spectacular location. Think Grand Canyon with jungle. And, as if that's not enough, he's even planning some nighttime cruises over the big island."

"Why?"

"So folks can see the volcano and lava flows. It'll be fantastic. And neither Iowa nor Pennsylvania have anything to match it."

Nate readily conceded that.

"The problem is, a lot of people on the islands are unhappy that they won't be getting a piece of the action. It's all self-contained. Very few of those tourist dollars will end up in their pockets. So they're especially keen to get in on construction, and when the resort opens, they'll be looking for employment. But later on there won't be any opportunities to feed off the presence of the resort. No T-shirt and trinket shops just outside the front gates."

"Archer will corner the market on them, too."

"There's no doubt about it." Randy checked her watch. "I'd offer you another drink, but we'll be on the ground soon."

"S'okay. I'm gonna need a clear head tonight."

"You're going to love Hawaii," she said, then winked at him. "You both will."

~*~

Maggie forgave herself for doing what she regularly condemned others for doing: using her cell phone while driving. This, she deemed, was an emergency, and so she dialed Tori's number again. Not that Tori had answered the last three times. Each call went straight to voice mail, but Maggie only left one message.

She had tried very hard to be cagey when she left that message, in case the authorities somehow got their hands on it. The papers were full of stories about dumb crooks who left incriminating evidence in phone and text messages. No way would she record something as stupid as, "Let's hide Mato before the cops find out he killed that guy up in the Cloud Peak."

68

Duh.

So she settled for, "Cal wants to go back to New York. Call me!"

That would give her curiosity a jolt, and Tori was the most curious person Maggie knew, with the possible exception of Daphne Cutter, the journalist. Tori would instantly suspect something was up. Cal had absolutely no desire to go back to the place where he had his heart attack, even if he weren't a homebody. And there were no bigger homebodies than Caleb Jones. His idea of a grand vacation was attending the annual summer music festival in Ten Sleep. And maybe grabbing a beer at the Ten Sleep Saloon.

Tori should have called her back long before now. She was usually pretty good about checking her phone messages. And really, what the hell else did she have to do all day? Sure, she *claimed* to be working on another book, but she never talked about it, and she definitely hadn't asked Maggie to read any of it, which she'd done for her other books.

And, with Nate spending most of his time out of town, there wasn't much left for her to do. It's not like she'd taken up ranching.

Quite the puzzle.

Maggie resolved to check on her friend. It involved a lot of driving, but neither woman had so many friends they could afford to ignore the ones they had. And, she reasoned, it gave her an excuse to swing by Charm, drag Cal out of his stupid store, and spend some time with him. He could bring his harmonica and a bottle of 80-proof anything.

Shaking off her post-massage lethargy, Maggie increased her speed. The road from Buffalo to Ten Sleep was curvy and often crowded with tourists headed to Yellowstone, but there weren't any other options. It wasn't the first time she'd wondered about the cost and availability of ultra-light aircraft. They weren't getting cheap, but the prices had dropped considerably.

She smiled imagining what it would be like to fly to work. Or Cal's house. Or Tori's. Cool shit, indeed!

~*~

Mato kept running even after Shadow whined in protest. But whenever the big dog slowed down, Mato waved the bacon under his nose, and quite suddenly the great canine found a renewed, if short-lived, burst of energy.

When satisfied they'd gotten far enough away from the heavily armed giantess, Mato slowed to a walk. They'd been moving steadily toward Tori's cabin, but it still wasn't nearby. Mato decided they would spend another night in the open then finish their journey in the morning.

He found a spot, sheltered by a low overhang, and halted there.

Shadow sprawled on the ground, panting. The noise surely carried some distance, but Mato no longer worried about it. He gave the dog all the bacon, a nibble at a time, and let him lick the grease from his fingers when it was all gone. Then Mato tore into the orange.

Like many of the foods Tori and the other giants ate, oranges were both rare and exotic. He had tried to describe the amazing fruit to The People, but few believed him. If such things grew on trees, why had they never seen one? They had plenty of trees. Apples and cherries were common, and they'd seen peach and pear trees often enough on giant's land. But oranges? Thick, orange skins with juicy fruit inside? Nonsense.

Mato grinned as he gorged himself on the nonsense fruit. Juice dripped down his chin and onto his chest. Shadow sniffed at it but wasn't interested. When Mato finished the orange, he rubbed his chest and hands with loose, dry soil which absorbed the sticky juice.

Both of the weary travelers remained hungry, but what they'd eaten took the edge off and left them content to pass the night in relative comfort. Mato envied Shadow's ability to lie atop stones and dirt and quickly go to sleep. Unlike the dog, he found it necessary to scrape the ground free of rocks and hollow out a smooth space on which to recline. The exposed soil felt cooler though still unyielding, but Mato had lived with worse.

Running long distances had never presented a problem, but it still took its toll. Mato's back, legs, and feet ached. Nor did the hard ground offer any solace. Rather than dwell on his discomfort, he let his mind wander back to The People. He allowed himself to worry about their safety, especially with giants roaming so close. They would surely relocate as soon as one of the hunters detected them. Indeed, they had probably already moved to a new encampment.

Reyna would have taken their child and gone with them, of course. What other option did she have? Winter Woman would demand that she stay close as the child was almost certain to grow into a Dreamer.

Leaving Reyna and his child had been hard, but he'd been given little choice in the matter. The circumstances evolved slowly. He had come to appreciate many new and wondrous things while living among the giants. But once he'd rescued his pregnant mate and returned from the faraway place the Big Ones called *Po-kip-see*, Reyna wanted only to go home to The People.

And stay there.

Forever.

Mato recalled the warnings of an older warrior who fathered several children. He claimed that pregnancy could alter more than a female's shape. Sometimes it allowed lessor demons to settle within and render an otherwise reasonable mate... difficult. Mato hoped that explained Reyna's displeasure with the giants and their world, for he considered some of them to be good friends, especially those who had helped him save her. But once they finally located The People--an accomplishment no giant had ever managed--Reyna's irrationality grew worse.

Simply being away from the giants was no longer enough; she insisted Mato stay close at all times. She remained adamant in this demand despite the obvious fact The People depended on what its greatest hunter could provide.

Winter months were always the hardest, and life in the mountains made the winter even more arduous. Food stores never lasted as long as the snow, and without Mato and his gigantic dog, the tribe's hunters often returned empty-handed. Mato knew the "greatest hunter" accolade rightly belonged to Shadow, the dog he had borrowed from Tori. Few in the tribe dared to even approach the massive animal which Mato and Reyna had ridden all the way from Tori's cabin.

The search and journey had taken many days, but without Shadow, it would have been impossible. Reyna would have had their baby among the giants, likely right inside Tori's cabin. Such a prospect posed no problem for Mato, but Reyna could not imagine giving birth without benefit of her aged grandmother, Winter Woman, considered the wisest living member of the clan.

With the birth of their child imminent, Winter Woman ordered Mato to move in with the single warriors. Such had been the tradition among The People since time began. If they wished their child to be born healthy, Mato and

Reyna must live apart during the last month of her pregnancy and stay apart until the first full moon after the baby's birth. Though Reyna had long known about the required separation, she argued vehemently against it.

Winter Woman's superior standing among the tribe carried more weight, of course, and Reyna's protests accomplished nothing. Mato had neither the heart nor the stomach to tell Reyna that he looked forward to the solitude such a separation would provide. As the weather improved and signs of spring became obvious even to the least observant, he admitted to himself that solitude wasn't what he wanted either.

He finally realized that life among The People bored him. He'd grown used to the excitement of the giant's world. There, no day passed without a discovery, be it new music, new food, or the amazing magic they called "technology." Mato had hoped Reyna would become equally infatuated with such marvels, but it didn't happen. Her heart belonged to The People and their way of life. It did not belong to him. And that was the saddest realization of all.

Though he tried to hide his unhappiness and mask his disdain for the growing tedium with longer and longer forays into the wild, Winter Woman looked straight into his heart and found the truth. She took him aside as Reyna felt the first pains of childbirth.

"You must go, Black Otter. You must seek your peace among the giants before you can be a father to Reyna's child."

"I do not wish to leave," he'd protested, though without passion.

"Your misery will poison us all," Winter Woman said. "And I have no cure. You must find it on your own. When you do, you will come back to us, and we will welcome you."

"May I not stay until my child is born?"

Winter Woman shook her head. "As long as that mystery remains here, you will have a reason to return. Your child will be cared for. I will see to that. Your hero songs are already being sung, so you will never be forgotten. It is time for you to go."

It was not the first time Mato had relived the discussion, nor would it be the last. He wondered how long it would be until he held his child in his arms. The People witnessed few miracles, he hated missing out on this one.

For the little warrior, sleep did not come easily that night.

~*~

The flight attendant aboard the Puck Productions jet had already lowered the steps, and Nate stood in the open door preparing to disembark when Randy's phone rang. She answered it and quickly put her hand on his shoulder.

He glanced back in surprise as she mouthed

the words, "Hang on."

Striving mightily not to do a Hollywood eye roll and tap dance down the gangway a la Gene Kelly or Fred Astaire, Nate held on. When Randy released her grip on him, Nate followed her back into the passenger compartment to eavesdrop.

"Say again," Randy said, covering her open ear with her palm. The jet's engines hadn't completely wound down. "Who got arrested?"

She listened intently, then said, "For what?"

Another pause followed by, "You've got to be kidding! Of course. I'll be on my way as soon as we refuel."

She shook her head as if the person on the other end of the line could see her, then added, "No, he'll come later. He's got business to attend to here. He'll need at least a day."

Nate frantically waved three fingers at her, which she saw but ignored.

"Yes, yes. Of course I'll explain how urgent it is. And knowing him, I'm sure he'll agree."

Again, listening intently, she bobbed her head, glanced at Nate with her own eye roll, and concluded the conversation with, "About eight hours, I think. What's that? No. A place called Ten Sleep." She repeated the town name twice.

Nate shook his head in silence. They were in *Worland*, the county seat. He wondered if the fancy private jet could land on a dirt runway, assuming there even was one near Ten Sleep. God knew, there was plenty of flat land.

"Yes sir," she said. "I'll tell him."

Nate waited while she put her phone away, took a deep breath, and squared her shoulders to address him. But he spoke first. "I can't leave tomorrow."

"But--"

"Sorry. That's just the way it is."

She gave him a sad smile then reached into her briefcase and extracted the document he'd signed during their flight. "Much as I hate to bring it up, this agreement you signed says you *will* be on a flight out of here tomorrow. I'll push it back as late as possible, but we're in an emergency situation."

"*You* might be," Nate said, "but--"

"We're a team now, so this is your emergency, too. It seems our primary contractor has been arrested and charged with murder."

Nate stared at her. "How in hell did that happen? Bar fight?"

"He says two thugs tried to drag him out of his hotel room, and he merely defended himself. He says someone bribed the only witness to say he started it."

"And you need me to investigate?"

"Ten-four."

Nate grunted. "Please, don't. Not unless you slip into a uniform of some kind."

Randy held up her hands in a gesture of surrender.

"Damn it," Nate said. "I was hoping for some

time off--at least a week. Tori's gonna go nuts if I tell her we have to leave tomorrow. You know how it is. She'll need a month just to get ready!"

"I understand completely," Randy said. "Maybe-- Hold on. Just a second." She didn't wait for an answer but grabbed her purse and unzipped a hidden compartment. Digging inside, she felt around and then extracted a thick wad of cash.

Nate felt his eyebrows slide upward in surprise as Randy peeled off two dozen one-hundred dollar bills and shoved them into his hands. "This ought to cover any incidentals. She can shop in Honolulu while you get busy on Kauai. We'll send a plane for her so she can join you in your room at the resort. I'll handle the details."

"But I-- If-- How'll she--"

"I'll arrange for an escort to drive her around and see that she's well cared for. As one of Puck's elite guests, she'll be treated like royalty."

"Oh."

"You good with that?"

Nate felt as if he'd been run over by an armored car, full of money. "Uh, yeah. That oughta do it. I guess."

"Great! I've got your cell phone number. I'll call you in the morning and let you know what the flight schedule is."

"You're going on to Hawaii, now?"

"Yes. Mr. Archer needs me there. Especially

78

since Mr. Bannock has managed to get himself arrested."

"Bannock?"

"Yeah." She smiled. "He's really a pretty decent guy. You'll like him. But if we don't get him out of jail, we'll have some even more serious problems to deal with."

"Like what?"

"Like an unhappy Mr. Archer." She made a face. "He doesn't do 'unhappy' very well."

"Oh."

"Say hi to Ms. 'More-than-a-girlfriend' for me."

"I will," Nate said as he exited the aircraft. "I most certainly will."

~*~

Chapter 5

One can't help but wonder who Lewis Carroll had in mind when he wrote "The Hunting of the Snark (An Agony in Eight Fits)."

Joe Bannock had never been given to fits of despair. If anything, he took pride in leaving emotion out of virtually all aspects of his life. He'd yell at the television if a football game didn't go his way, but beyond that he remained remarkably steady. Much of the credit for this went to the people he hired. For his top level employees, he sought out three qualities: competence, work ethic and loyalty.

A person's looks, personality, education, disposition and politics didn't matter. At all. He needed work done, and he needed people he could trust to do it, whether he looked over their shoulders or not. Good work he rewarded handsomely. In special cases, extravagantly. Promotions were based solely on merit. He knew his own limitations and leaned heavily on the expertise of his staff. Those who chose to appease him rather than give him honest, accurate assessments quickly found themselves unemployed.

His approach yielded a cadre of dedicated professionals, some of whom even looked the part. His attorney clearly didn't, but when she strolled into the KPD detention center, Bannock felt a wave of relief. The cavalry had arrived in the person of P.S. Jackson, Esq.

Ms. Jackson presented an imposing image. Garbed head to toe in flowing fabric of purple and gold, she strolled into the interview room as if she were going on stage. In sandals she stood six feet, three inches tall and massed well over 300 pounds. She'd competed in field events in college, but only because she wasn't allowed to wrestle or box. Her Ivy League *alma mater* didn't have women's teams in either sport. The football coach had shown interest in her, but several of the linemen claimed her presence would be bad for morale. The unspoken consensus: none of them cared to risk losing a starting position to someone named Princess Shaniqua.

She had confided in Bannock that when she was a coed, she thought it was funny. Stupid, but funny. And when she laughed, those near her grew wary, as if in the presence of a lioness. A hungry one.

Bannock had seen her in action, feeding on the opposition. All too often her unsuspecting prey would be taken in by her name, her appearance, and her speech. Assuming she was all mouth and no brain left them vulnerable, because despite the ghetto-bred impression she worked so hard to present, a sharper legal mind was hard to find. Moreover, she knew how to work the system. She hadn't graduated at the top of her class by being stupid, or lazy, or bashful.

"The hell you done this time, homeboy?" she asked, her voice crashing off the walls and causing the other inmates, their visitors, and the guards to shake their heads and consign the gigantic black woman to limbo--the place where white noise lives and dies. Precisely where she wanted to be.

"It was self defense," Bannock said.

"Like I couldn't figure that out?" Shaniqua shook her big head. "You th' only man I know carries a goddamn golf club instead of a nine-mil like any normal dude."

Bannock smiled. It felt good. He hadn't done much smiling since they cuffed him in his hotel room.

"What'd you tell the cops?"

"Just my side of the story."

She grimaced, then broadcast: "Whut part of 'keep yo mouth shut' don't you unnerstan?"

"I--"

"Shut the fuck up!"

Bannock closed his mouth. Shaniqua leaned close and dropped her voice to a whisper. "Here's the good news: the two asswipes you put in the hospital will probably both live. They're in Honolulu, under police guard. I had to raise a stink to make that happen, believe me. It helped that they both had rap sheets as long as my boyfriend's boto."

"His *what?*"

"Puh-leeze. Have you no imagination?"

"I didn't know you had a boyfriend, much less one with a boto."

She twisted her lips at him, then smiled. "The word's not even Hawaiian. It's Samoan, or Tahitian, or some shit. Very strange."

"So what's the bad news?"

"Havin' yo' ass in jail ain't bad enough? I figured you already knew that."

"Right. So, when do I get out?"

The head shake she gave him wasn't completely unexpected. He'd seen it before, and he'd never been a fan.

"Honey, you ain't goin' nowhere. The man wants a piece of yo ass."

"A man named Danny Kwan set all this up. You know that, right?"

"Yeah. He tried to hide his connection with Kamaka and Kapule, the two punks that came to your hotel room. Proving he paid 'em to do that may be--" she paused, "--difficult."

"What about the handyman?"

"Haven't connected with him yet, but I will. Soon. Funny how these guys go to ground when the shit starts to fly. I'll find him. But I 'spect Kwan's got something on him. Getting him to tell the truth might cost you a chunk of change."

"Sitting in *here* is costing me a bigger one."

"Your arraignment is set for tomorrow, but I doubt we'll get the chance to post bail."

"Kwan owns the judge?"

"That'd be my guess."

"We need that custodian to tell the truth."

She nodded in agreement. "I'll focus on him, then, but I could use some help. A private investigator would be nice. I don't have any connections here."

"Reach out to Tim Archer. Surely he'll--"

"What? Connect Puck Productions to a murder case? Not likely. I put in a call to his assistant, and she says help is on the way, but she didn't give me any details or a timeframe."

"Then I'm stuck here."

"For now, yeah. So here's some advice: stay quiet. Don't complain about being here; don't try to make friends. Don't talk to the cops; don't trust the guards, and for God's sake, don't trust anybody who looks like an inmate."

"That doesn't leave many choices."

"No shit. If there's a nurse in here, you can be nice to her. Or him. Whatever. But that doesn't mean you can trust 'em. Got it?"

"So, keep to myself?"

"Right. Try not to piss anyone else off. And don't be surprised if Kwan has someone in here on his payroll. My guess is he'll be happy just keeping you in jail, but ya never know. He might send someone after you. Sleep lightly."

Bannock felt his world collapsing.

Shaniqua punched him on the shoulder. "Cheer up. It could be worse. You could be dead, or in the hospital instead of those other two guys.

One of them may never be the same." She followed that with an extraordinarily insincere tsk-tsk.

"Don't leave me lonely," he said.

"I'll check on you every day. I promise."

"Thanks, Shan. I owe you."

She chuckled. "Baby, you have no idea."

~*~

Maggie got Cal to close his shop early, mostly on the strength of their mutual concern for Mato. If Tori didn't know where he was, no one did. She also talked Cal into bringing along a bottle of the booze he wasn't licensed to sell. The drive to Tori's cabin wouldn't take too long, and she planned to give Cal a special thank you for her spa trip when they got back to his place.

"She was just in the store, y'know," he told her. "Bought a bunch of stuff on account of Nate comin' home."

"That's tonight, right?"

"I think so. Or tomorrow. Hell, I don't know for sure. He ain't comin' to see me. But Lord howdy, Tori was sure fired up. Talkin' a mile a minute--you know how she gets when she's excited--so I mighta missed a detail or two."

"Really?"

"Well, yeah."

"You're hopeless."

He shrugged. "Want me to drive?"

"What, go in that big ugly van of yours? Hell no. We'll take my car. C'mon, get in."

85

Her cell phone rang as she pulled away from Caleb's store. Daphne Cutter's name appeared in the screen below the number. Maggie answered with a stab of her thumb.

"Got those names for me?" Daphne asked.

"Still haven't been home," Maggie said. "Feels like I've been on the road for days. Tourist traffic on top of a busy day. Makes me so happy."

"I get it. I just thought I'd let you know, the police found a match for the fingerprint they lifted off the arrowhead."

Maggie felt herself blanch. "That's uh-- amazing. Whose is it?"

"There's no ID, but here's the thing, the matching print was found at a crime scene near Poughkeepsie, New York! Cops figure the killer is a tourist, but I'm workin' a different angle. I'm gonna squeeze a couple stories outta this, at least. Maybe a series. If so, I'm really gonna need those names."

"No problem," Maggie said. "I know right where they are. Although--" she paused.

"What?"

"If you've got contacts at the university, they probably know the same folks. Paleo fans and back-to-nature types tend to hang together. At least, they seem to group that way in the park."

"Is that your way of tellin' me you aren't going home to get those names for me?"

"Well, not tonight, anyway. I've got a late shift tomorrow, so I can swing by the house in the morning."

"I hope your boyfriend treats you right." Daphne chuckled. "Lemme know if he doesn't."

"Why, you gonna beat him up? He's a tough old bird."

"Nah. Think Twain. 'Never pick a fight with people who buy ink by the barrel.'"

"Gotcha," Maggie said. "I'll keep that in mind. Talk to you tomorrow."

"Who's a tough old bird?" Cal asked.

Maggie patted his leg. "Nobody you know, sweetheart."

He didn't appear convinced but let the topic drop. Maggie filled him in on the latest from Daphne. "This could easily get out of our control."

"Yep."

"That's it? That's all you've got to say about it?"

He glanced at the wide open spaces all around them. "You really think anybody could find Mato if he didn't want to be found?"

"Probably not," she said. "Trouble is, he doesn't know anyone's looking."

~*~

Tori went through her CDs looking for something appropriate to have playing in the background when Nate arrived. After selecting a Zac Brown album, she checked her watch for the tenth time in ten minutes, realized she was obsessing, and then tried to find something else to do.

Josh Langston

Time sloughed by, and Tori's thoughts shifted from practical to prurient, as if the fluffy thing in her bottom dresser drawer was calling to her. Or *beaming* something at her. A wanton wave! Just like an alpha or a beta wave, only it acted on one's basest instincts--a horny wave.

She giggled as she unwrapped the naughty lingerie. Only, there wasn't enough material in it to qualify as lingerie. Testing the elastic which connected the fluffy bits, she discovered that time had wrought some damage: the bands stretched but wouldn't snap back to their original shape. She went looking for the Scotch tape before she tried it on.

With "Chicken Fried" blaring on the stereo, she began her search. The tape was her sole back-up plan, and finding it gave her something to do while waiting for Nate. An unbidden thought crept out of hiding as the hunt went on: some little part of her wanted Nate to get there before she actually shimmied into the sex cloth.

She shook the thought off. He needed it. More than that, she needed him to soak up the image and hang onto it the next time he found himself alone in some big city with time on his hands. She knew how powerful a force one's imagination could be, and Nate's was no exception. She wanted him to remember this evening for many nights to come.

The elusive sticky stuff turned up beneath a pile of papers she'd printed off from the internet:

parts of web pages, excerpts from news articles, even some of her own writing. In her mind, the various chunks of text would eventually develop some continuity; she just hadn't quite grasped the right links. But when she did, she intended to tape the relevant pieces together in a reference mosaic and hang the whole thing on a wall, assuming she could find one big enough.

For now, however, she needed to focus on getting ready for Nate. Shedding her jeans, T-shirt, and underwear, she faced the big mirror beside her bed and donned the top. Or tried to. Her ex-husband's estimate of her chest measurement greatly exceeded reality. Fortunately, the one-size-scandalizes-all design allowed her to make an adjustment.

Some of the feathers showed evidence of an early molt, and she carefully trimmed them which left a dainty cloud of yellow fuzz drifting on the air currents in the cabin.

Then she slipped into the panty portion of the ensemble which consisted of two formerly elastic bands and an arrangement of yellow feathers loosely attached to a tiny, triangular scrap of fabric. Once again, the scissors came into play, this time artfully pruning an area the garment failed to cover.

Standing tall, Tori sucked in her tummy, thrust her shoulders back, and watched as the bands holding her top in place gave way. Another glance at the clock proved that the universe was conspiring against her, and that Nate was already overdue.

Once again she brought out the scissors, snipped off the failed elastic bands and filled the interiors of the two remaining triangles of fluff with balled up Scotch tape. She placed one over each nipple and pressed down until they appeared to be safely affixed. The effort cost her additional bits of bright yellow flotsam which mingled casually with that already drifting around the room.

But, despite everything, she was *ready*. And best of all, she could hear a car rumbling down the long, rock-strewn path Nate had once described as more of a tank trap than a driveway.

She gazed down, pleased with the look, until she reached her bare feet. That wouldn't do. At all. She needed heels. Nine-inchers. Except she didn't own anything like that. The pair she did have hardly qualified as stilettos, but they'd have to do. If nothing else, they were black, and they'd help give her bottom a bit more shape. But she had to hurry.

Leaping to her closet, she dug frantically for a few seconds until the footwear appeared. She slipped her feet into them and posed once again before the big mirror. No doubt about it. She looked *hot*. And more--she felt powerful, sexy, and more than anything else, impatient.

"I'm coming--ready or not!" she called when she heard the knock on her door.

With a broad smile on her face and a joyous spring in her step, she waltzed toward the door to open it.

~*~

Mato awoke with a start and a vision in his head that wouldn't go away. He clearly saw a giant towering over a woman, threatening her. The female was not a giant, but rather someone his own size. It could have been Reyna, but she appeared in silhouette. She seemed to be young and slender, so it definitely wasn't Winter Woman.

There were several young females among The People, but he had never had much to do with them once they all passed childhood. Pairing off was common, and he'd paired with Reyna. He assumed for life, though recent events challenged that.

He tried to determine if he had seen the giant somewhere, but instinct told him this was someone new--someone evil. If only he had his drawing tools, he would have sketched the man from memory. It wouldn't be difficult; Mato was both an artist and a dreamer. He had already proven his ability. Still, he wished he could record the image in case he failed to have the dream again. Sometimes, dreams were merely dreams. If he had the dream again, he would know for certain he'd glimpsed the future. One in which he would surely play a part.

He would discuss it with Tori when he

reached her cabin. She had impressed upon him the need to avoid killing giants without a valid cause. That issue remained unclear to him. Why else would he kill one? The problem, he presumed, was with the word "valid." Giants used too many words.

~*~

Nate reached the bottom of the gangway when it dawned on him that he'd left his car in a parking lot at the airport in Sheridan. There might be a rental car company in the terminal, but from the looks of the place, he'd landed after normal working hours. He hated to call Tori and ask her to drive all this way at the last minute.

As he began to curse his own shortsightedness, Randy called to him from the door of the Puck Productions jet. "There's a car and driver waiting for you," she said. "Or did you intend to walk to Ten Sleep?"

"You arranged for a car while we flew here?"

"It's what I do," she said, smiling. "It's better that you focus on important stuff, like making your girlfriend happy."

Nate grinned back. "She doesn't live in Ten Sleep. And I really don't need a driver."

"Then drop him off at a hotel and pick him up on your way back to the airport tomorrow."

"I don't know--"

"Yes, you do. I'll text you with the estimated departure time. Now get outta here. Time's a-wastin'!"

The flight attendant had already set his two suitcases on the tarmac and sealed the luggage compartment prior to takeoff. He waved at Nate as he grabbed one bag in each hand and hurried toward the terminal building.

As he suspected, normal operations had been completed, and the tiny airport was nearly deserted. A maintenance man pointed toward the front entrance where a lone man in dark slacks and a white shirt held a sign with his name on it.

"Mr. Sheffield?"

"Damn, son," Nate said with a smile. "How'd you know it was me?"

"I'm a good guesser." He took the two bags despite Nate's reluctance to let them go and loaded them into the trunk of a big Lincoln. He held a rear door open, but Nate stepped past him and took a seat up front.

The driver climbed in beside him and brought the engine to life. "Where to?"

"Find yourself a motel," Nate said. "My treat."

"I--"

He paused to answer his cell phone, listened, then stared from it to Nate and back again. "Will do," he said into the device and clicked off.

"I can suggest a good one," Nate said.

"It's already been arranged." He sounded slightly mystified, but aimed the limo north, toward Worland, and quickly put the airport behind them.

"Anything I need to know about this car?"

Nate asked.

"I just filled the tank," the driver said, "and there's a fully stocked bar in the back. TV, too, but the reception's probably not too good outside of town. I guess you've got a license and insurance?"

"Yep."

"I gotta tell ya, this is the strangest run I've ever made."

"I'm sure you'll be well paid."

"Oh, no doubt about that. They told me to be ready to go around noon."

Nate grunted. "Certainly not before noon, anyway." He punched Tori's number on his cell phone, but she didn't answer. It wouldn't be the first time she'd forgotten to charge the damned thing. He'd be sure to tease her about it.

When the driver pulled into the motel, Nate gave him some money for dinner, and the young man strolled toward the lobby. Nate left before he reached it.

In his rattletrap pickup, the drive from Worland to Tori's cabin would've taken about an hour. In the big Lincoln, Nate figured he could do it in forty minutes. He pushed the envelope anyway, and reached Tori's infamous driveway in thirty-eight. A dusty haze floated above the rock-strewn path as if another car had very recently traveled the same route.

Nate couldn't imagine who that might be.

~*~

Maggie's purse had fallen over in the back

seat during the bumpy ride down Tori's driveway. The contents lay strewn across the floorboard. "You go ahead," she told Caleb. "I'll be along in a minute."

The old cowboy left the car, walked up to Tori's door, and knocked. He heard Tori yell something about "Ready or not," and then she threw open the door in a grand theatrical gesture.

Scant seconds later, as Maggie reached his side, Cal's jaw still hung loose, and his eyes bulged as he stared at the all but naked novelist standing in the doorway with bits of bright yellow fluff orbiting her chest and hips. Her eyes and mouth were opened wide, too.

"Jesus, Cal!" Maggie squeaked as she covered his eyes with her palm.

Tori made a similar squeak as she slammed the door.

"You can move your hand now," Cal said.

Maggie gave him her End Of The World glare. "Don't you say a word. Not a damned syllable."

"Like you could stop me." He started laughing, then gently patted his heart. "Man, oh man! Ya know, a fella needs something like this every now and then to keep his ticker clickin'."

Crossed arms and a concerted effort not to laugh were all Maggie could muster. She could only imagine how embarrassed her friend must feel. "Why don't you go sit in the car. I don't think Tori's gonna want to talk to you just now."

"Aw hell, I didn't do nothin'," he said. "but I

Josh Langston

never knew she had a thing for Big Bird."

"*What?*"

"I sure hope it was consensual."

"Get. In. The. Damned. Car. Cal," she said.

Amid considerable muttering and head-shaking, Cal retraced his steps.

A pair of headlights cut through the early twilight as a car bounced down Tori's drive toward them. Caleb scratched his chin, clearly puzzled.

"It's prob'ly Nate," Maggie said, undecided about going inside to talk to Tori.

The other vehicle, a Lincoln Town Car, slowed to a stop beside Maggie's, and Nate climbed out, lean, tall, and smiling, as usual.

Cal shook his hand and Maggie gave him a hug. "I'm afraid our timing sucks a little bit," she said. "Maybe more than a little bit. Sorry."

"It's great to see you," Nate said, "but I sure didn't expect a party. What's this all about?"

Maggie grimaced. "Mato."

"Is he okay?"

"Probably. I can't say for sure, but I'm afraid he's in big trouble. I tried to call Tori to explain, but--"

"But she didn't answer her phone."

"How'd you-- Oh. Right."

"Let's go inside," Nate said, "and you can tell us all about it."

"Thing is," Cal said, "Tori may not-- What I mean to say is--"

96

"She was expectin' *you*, not us," Maggie said. "She came to the door wearin' this little, uh... I dunno, it was sort of a nighty thing."

Cal started grinning again. "That's what that was?" He stopped grinning when he saw Nate's expression.

"It was fluffy," Maggie said. "And yellow. Adorable. Really!"

Cal knew better than to utter a sound.

"Stand by," Nate said. He pushed open the cabin door and went inside.

"That Big Bird is one lucky sumbitch," Cal said.

Maggie slugged him.

~*~

When Nate walked in, Tori ran to him. She wanted nothing more than to have his arms wrapped around her. She'd never in her life felt like such a complete fool. She confessed as much, though she blubbered her way through it, and he probably couldn't make out a word she said.

He gently pried her loose and held her at arm's length. She'd thrown on a floor length bathrobe with long sleeves, a garment as revealing as a hazmat suit.

"I did it to please you," she wailed. "I just wanted to make you happy. It's been so long, I--"

He pressed his lips to hers, firmly, and kept her from chattering further.

"I--"

"Hush," he said, his smile stretching from ear

to ear. "Let's see this outfit."

She stepped back, her hands on the fabric belt around her waist. Before doing a grand reveal, she rubbed a palm across her face, probably streaking her eyeliner. She followed that with a blubbery sniff. So romantic.

"C'mon, Tori. Don't keep me in suspense."

She smiled at that, then unknotted the belt and pulled the robe open. Even though the music had long since stopped, she wiggled her shoulders free of the heavy terrycloth and let it fall to the floor.

Nate stared at her in undisguised rapture. When the fluffy wad of feathers at the end of her left breast came loose and floated to the floor, he only smiled harder.

"I'm so sorry, Nate," she said.

"For what? Making me happy?"

"I didn't--"

"You're incredible. I'm the luckiest man alive. And you know what? I want to marry you. Right now. Tonight!"

"*What?*" She looked directly into his eyes. "We've been talking about it for months, but--"

"But you still want to, right?"

"Yes. Yes! Of course, it's just--"

"Then let's do it. If not tonight, tomorrow. Early. *Real* early."

"We can't! I'm not-- I haven't-- Geez. There are things I need to do first."

"Like what?"

"I dunno. Find a church? Figure out how to get my Mom out here. Hire an organist. Order flowers. Mail invitations. There's gotta be a thousand things to do."

"I've got a better idea," he said, his smile as broad and bright as ever. "Let's fly to Hawaii and get married there. We'll pay somebody to take care of the details. What d'ya say?"

She looked very closely into his eyes. That's where one looked when they had suspicions about a person's sanity. At least, that's what she'd read. Somewhere. But all she could see was his ridiculous smile. His bright eyes. His-- adoration. "You're serious."

"Yep."

~*~

Chapter 6

Why do bad guys always get the best parts?

"Klaus Becker" made his final report to his Europe-based contact on the eve of his graduation and the award of credentials allowing him to pilot the NT50 airship. The contact, a beardless man of average size, middle age, and limited intellect, displayed a partial set of yellowed teeth with every smile, something he did far too often. His breath reeked of cigarettes, and his clothes needed laundering.

They met in a tiny restaurant featuring Mediterranean cuisine. Unlike the music, the food was tolerable. Someone with no discernable skill had painted a mural on the walls. The figures in it might have been belly dancers, as conceived by someone who could neither see nor paint. The eatery filled the basement of a building on the far side of Friedrichshafen where no one from the Zeppelin factory or flight school was likely to go.

"Congratulations, Kapitän," the contact said in badly accented German.

His companion waved him off. He had no time for banter. "I will be leaving with the airship next week."

"How long a flight is it?"

The former student stared at him, his dark eyes barely visible beneath his drawn brows.

"The airship will be transported--by boat--to Hawaii."

"Of course. Someone there will be in touch with you."

"They'll have the cargo?"

The contact nodded. "It's already been shipped. The box itself has been designed to look like others already delivered, except for a few critical details. I've seen it. It's quite-- colorful. Once it arrives, our people will move it to a more uhm-- *convenient* location."

"I won't have much time to get it loaded."

"Don't worry about that. When the time comes, just make sure you have complete control of the airship. You'll have to deal with any other crew members on your own."

"No problem."

"I've enjoyed working with you," the contact said.

His colleague neither smiled nor offered a similar sentiment.

The contact concluded with a whispered, "Allahu Akbar," which his dinner companion repeated, albeit without emotion.

~*~

Daphne Cutter liked Maggie Scott, even though the park ranger hadn't lived up to her end of their arrangement. Yet. Even so, when it came to investigating a government system--whether a national park or Roswell New Mexico's Area 51-- it was better to have someone on the inside you could rely on for details than it was to hang around the perimeter poking at and nagging potential informants who rarely knew anything.

The fingerprint linking two unsolved crimes in two different places came as a gift from the heavens. Who wouldn't be intrigued by the tale of a midget murderer who roamed from East to West with evident abandon? The headline writers could feast on that topic for months.

She'd talked it over with Conrad Stokes, her editor, but he didn't think she had enough material. They both knew she could fluff a couple facts into a feature piece, maybe two, but this had the potential for a series. And yet the whole thing could just as easily die for lack of new data. "Stonewalling" wasn't merely an expression; for many potential information sources, it became a way of life.

Though she hadn't mentioned it to anyone, she'd begun to think of the suspect as "Little Foot." The tongue-in-cheek homage to the hairy beast which allegedly roamed the woods of the great northwest gave her plenty of rhetorical room to theorize the existence of an equally deadly, if inexplicably small, counterpart.

From what she could remember hearing or reading, Big Foot didn't use weapons other than a club of some kind, but no spears and certainly no bow and arrow.

But why couldn't he use something like that? Primates had been throwing things for as long as they'd had hands and arms. Primitive man came up with the idea of putting a point on a stick--the first crude spear--then trumped the invention by adding a throwing device called an *atlatl*. No one knew how long ago that happened, but then, no one had a complete family tree for all of man's ancestors either.

Apes and monkeys came in a huge variety of shapes and sizes. Why couldn't there be other-sized, human beings, too? And why couldn't they throw spears?

Her imagination thus fired, Daphne rearranged the files on her computer's hard drive. If she could get a newspaper series out of it, why not a syndication deal? Hell, why not a book deal? Well organized notes would go a long way toward making such a thing possible.

Fortunately, she knew better than to let her dreams overtake her grip on reality. She needed *content* in order to write anything, and she believed Maggie's suggestion that she look into the fans of primitive man at the university was a good place to start. What had Conrad called them? "Paleo junkies." She looked the phrase up on-line, but found nothing about fossil hunters or flint tool makers. Instead, she got advice about how to eat like a cave dweller from 10,000BC. Yum.

Not terribly helpful. So, she hit the road.

As she steered toward the Southern Montana State campus in Billings, she activated the recorder app on her cell phone and began to free associate. It wouldn't be the first time she came up with a story subtitle or a new theme. Besides, it was harmless and helped to pass the time.

"Who put the 'pal' in 'PaleoIndian?'" she mused aloud for the benefit of the recorder. "If I were Little Foot, where would I live?" And finally, "How the hell did he get from the Hudson River Valley in New York to the Bighorn Mountains in Wyoming--without being seen?"

The simplest answer came unbidden. Someone, somewhere, had to have seen him. She just needed to find out who that someone was, and then convince them to talk to her.

Easy-peasy.

Right.

~*~

Cal rubbed his shoulder where Maggie clobbered him. She suspected it didn't hurt nearly as bad as he made it look. One didn't spend that many years with the rodeo and not build up *some* muscle. Still, the more he rubbed it, the guiltier she felt.

Or maybe she just felt bad for Tori who *clearly* had no idea who came knocking on her door. The poor girl's face had turned a deeper shade of crimson than Maggie thought possible, so she felt considerable relief when Tori opened her door once again--fully clothed--and motioned them in.

Cal bobbed his head as he crossed the

threshold, but kept mercifully quiet.

Nate had a smile on his face, but Maggie couldn't fathom where it came from. She expected him to be pissed off, but pleased? That didn't compute.

Tori's expression stayed utterly neutral, as if she had just arrived, too. But that didn't last long. She waved them to seats in the tiny cabin: Maggie and Cal at the kitchen table and Nate in the easy chair. Tori sat on the end of her bed.

"Mags, Nate suggested I listen to your messages," she said. "I did, and now I understand why you thought it necessary to drive all the way out here when I didn't respond. That was my fault."

Nate cleared his throat, and Tori continued, "I also missed a call from Nate who has something he'd like to discuss with you. But first, I'd like to hear what's going on with Mato, because as far as I know, he's kept himself out of touch since we got back from New York."

All three heads bobbed at once.

"You already know about what I read in the paper," Maggie said, "I called because I got some more information from a reporter friend."

"And that is-- what, exactly?"

Maggie gave a quick recap: a man, whose name she couldn't remember, had died from an allergic reaction to something presumably on the tip of a spear thrown by a person assumed to be very small. Further, crime lab techs found

Josh Langston

fingerprints on the murder weapon, and when they searched the fingerprint databases, the same extraordinarily small prints turned up at a crime scene in New York state.

"Well, just damn," Nate said. "I wonder what set him off? Do we know anything about the guy he attacked?"

"Not much," Maggie said. "The dead man and another guy were prospecting up in the Cloud Peak Wilderness area. I imagine that's where Mato's people live."

"Wait," said the former deputy sheriff. "Prospecting is *allowed* in a national park?"

"Sure," Maggie said.

Cal stopped rubbing his arm and scratched his head instead. "Even in a wilderness area?"

"Yep. But there's a big difference between prospecting and mining. Using gas engines or operating other machinery in a wilderness area is a big no-no. That's what got my attention about the guys Mato ran into. When one of 'em got hurt, they both drove out on an All Terrain Vehicle. ATV's are prohibited. It's hike in, hike out. Some horseback riding is allowed, but there are strict rules for that, too."

"So, these two may not have been completely on the up and up?"

"Beats me," Maggie said. "There's no proof they were doing anything wrong."

"Other than messing with Mato," Tori said. "I wonder where he is?"

106

"He's got a newborn to look after," Maggie said. "There's no way he's going to leave a little one. He's not going anywhere."

"Sounds logical to me," Nate said.

Cal and Tori agreed.

Maggie checked her watch. She and Cal had already stayed too long. It felt like an excellent time to leave the two lovebirds on their own. She nudged Cal as she got to her feet, and he followed her example. "That's it, I suppose. You two look like you could use some privacy."

Tori smiled at her. "There's just one more thing." She turned to Nate.

He broke out in a broad smile. "You both know I asked Tori to marry me a couple months back. She said yes, and fortunately for me, she hasn't come to her senses yet, even though we haven't been able to nail down a date or--"

"Or any other details," Tori said.

Nate reached for her hand. "Anyway, there've been some big changes in our lives, and I don't want to put our wedding off any longer."

"That's great news," Maggie said. She turned and looked Cal straight in the eye. "It's about time you two got hitched."

Cal seemed perplexed.

"We'd like you two to be there when we do," Nate said. "I need a best man."

"And I need a maid of honor," added Tori.

"So," said Nate, "how would you feel about taking a little trip?"

Cal shrugged. "As long as it's not back to New York, I'd be interested."

"I've got some vacation time," Maggie said.

Nate grinned. "Good! How are you fixed for swim suits?"

~*~

Shaniqua's advice on how to survive in jail was easy to understand but difficult to follow. Not that Joe Bannock entertained any thoughts of finding friends in confinement, nor did keeping his mouth shut and his thoughts to himself prove to be a challenge. The problematic part had Kwan's scent all over it.

The guards were just as likely to hurt him as the other prisoners, a point his Amazonian attorney took pains to point out. Fortunately, she made an important, albeit casual, contact before she left the interview room.

While Joe watched in envy of her confidence, Shaniqua approached a prisoner who appeared to be just her size. He stood up when she stopped beside him resulting in eye-to-eye contact between two people roughly the size of meat lockers. The man, whose Hawaiian pedigree needed no documentation, smiled every bit as broadly as she did.

She whispered something in his ear, and they both had a good long laugh. With practiced skill, Shaniqua pulled a pad and pen from her briefcase and made a few notes. Her new friend seemed genuinely appreciative, and when she left he moved to Joe's side.

"You okay, bruddah?" the huge man asked.

"I think so," Joe said, trying to hide his uncertainty. Terror had a way of making that tricky.

"Funny ting: we gots da same lawyer."

Joe swallowed. "No kidding?"

"And you gonna pay my bill. Dat's good, no?"

"Uh... yeah. Very good."

"But, you gotta stay close. Den nobody give you trouble. We all go home happy."

"And if I don't stay close?"

"Bad idea, brah. Lemme do my job."

Joe began to breathe a little easier. "You don't, by any chance, know someone named Daniel Kwan, do you?"

"Sure. Everybody know Kwan."

"It's his men I'm worried about."

The gigantic Hawaiian patted him on the head like a puppy. "I tol' you, just stay by me. You be fine."

"What's your name?"

"Ku`u Maka, but jus' call me Ivan. You know, like 'Ivan the Terrible?'" He flexed both massive arms. "I be mo' terrible."

"Uh, okay, Ivan. I'm Joe. If this works out, I'd like to talk to you about a real job."

"On da outside?"

"Yeah."

"Doin' what?"

"Pretty much the same thing you're gonna do

in here. Keep me alive. You interested?"

The big Hawaiian appeared to consider the offer. The effort required some serious facial contortions and one prolonged fart. "Any fringe benefits?"

Joe nearly laughed, but caught himself in time. "Like what--tuition assistance?"

Much to his surprise the big man's eyes lit up. "Yeah!"

"I guess. Sure. Plus insurance and profit sharing--the works."

"And I don't haf to kill nobody?"

Joe almost smiled, then realized the man was serious. "Hell no! I don't want anyone killed. No way. I'd never ask you to do anything that wasn't legal."

"Great! Now, tell me 'bout dis lawyer of ours. She any good?"

"She's not just good," Joe said. "She's incredible. They don't come any better, or smarter."

"Aw right," Ivan said, beaming. "'Cause I'm in a whole lotta trouble."

~*~

Unable to go back to sleep after his dream, Mato lay awake looking at the stars. Shadow would grunt from time to time or exhale heavily. The sounds reminded Mato of life with The People. They would often crowd together for warmth. The snow in the high ranges never melted, and there was a great sheet of ice near the tallest peak. Mato had been there often, but the hunting was terrible, and giants too often came to visit.

Everyone knew it was best if giants never saw The People. Still, it happened from time to time, and nothing had yet come of it.

Mato's stomach growled. Shadow rolled over and put his great head next to the little Indian's stomach. The dog's breath felt like steam, not unwelcome in the coolness of early morning.

"Time to go," Mato said, rolling easily to a standing position. As he stretched, he surveyed the land around them and satisfied himself there were no threats. Using the sun and a distant mountain to orient himself, he set off on the final leg of his journey to Tori's cabin.

Traveling was easier knowing she would have plenty to eat.

~*~

"What do you mean, the judge was too busy to see you?" Kwan found it increasingly difficult to mask his rage. Yet another incompetent stood in front of him with excuses rather than reports. This one's name was Clark *something*. He'd been yapping for an opportunity to prove himself.

"Did he know I sent you?"

"I think so. You told me never to use your name."

Kwan's glare caused the man to shrink. "I should cut off your nuts and have them pickled. Put in a jar, on display, so everyone can see what happens to those who fail me."

The man paled, and Kwan wondered if he would further dishonor himself by fainting or shitting his pants. "Go," he commanded. "You disgust me."

Kwan summoned Paku, his long-time aide, with an impatient wave. Though smaller than his employer, Paku had a reputation every bit as fierce. He stood facing Kwan. "Clark Cho failed you."

Cho! Such a common name. Fit for swine. "Yes, he did," Kwan said.

"I should not have suggested him. I should have seen his weakness."

Kwan nodded. "It seems our associates have lost their enthusiasm. The last two jobs I ordered went undone. What's wrong with our people?"

"They have lost their fear," Paku said. "They no longer believe it is in their best interest to serve you."

"And yet I still pay them. I still see to the needs of their families. Am I not a good friend? A generous employer? What have I done to warrant such disrespect?"

Paku responded with a feral grin. "You have been too nice to them."

Kwan reflected on Paku's words, then broke into a grisly smile of his own. "Let's have a luau. See that everyone who works for me is there."

"Including Clark Cho?"

"Especially him." Kwan leaned closer and

whispered more instructions. Paku nodded, then left his office immediately.

~*~

Tori opened her eyes to the sound of bacon frying. Nate, clad only in boxer shorts, stood before her tiny stove fixing a late breakfast. The coffee pot burped and gurgled as two slices of toast erupted from the toaster.

"That's your cue, sleepyhead," he said. "Rise and shine."

Tori slithered out of bed and crept up behind him where she could press herself against his warm back. She stood on her tiptoes and kissed the nape of his neck.

"Easy now. You'll make me burn the eggs."

Without responding, she ran her hands across his chest and down into his boxer shorts. His response was hands-free, but profound.

"Okay, I'm switchin' the burners off."

She yanked his boxers down to his ankles, then twisted away and dived back into the bed.

Nate leaped after her, and they landed in a giggling tangle of arms, legs and sheets. The writhing and fondling continued for a time before Tori sat upright with Nate beneath her. "Wait," she said, panting, "the toast will cool off."

Nate grunted. "I'll make more."

"I'd rather you made something else."

"Like what?"

"Make me as happy as you did last night."

"Both times?"

113

Josh Langston

She giggled some more. "Yeah."

"Slave driver!"

In an instant they forgot the eggs, the bacon, the toast, and pretty much the rest of the universe. They'd been together enough to be completely comfortable, but apart long enough to experience a whole new kind of desire.

Afterward, Tori lay beside him, love-weary and smiling. Nate lay on his back with his eyes partially open, a dazed but contented look on his face.

She spoke first. "I can't believe you want me to drop everything and fly to Hawaii. Today!"

"You're right; it's a terrible thing to do," Nate said, his voice low. "I mean, really--who on Earth would want to get married in Hawaii when they could get a justice of the peace in Ten Sleep to do the honors?"

"Nate, that's--"

"Who needs all the exotic flowers, the fabulous beaches, the gorgeous sunsets, or--"

"Nate!"

"What? I'm just gettin' warmed up."

"I know. I want to go, and I'm amazed that Maggie and Caleb agreed to go, too. But--"

Nate scrunched his eyes shut. "I hate the 'but' part."

"But I could've used a little more time to get ready."

"I know, and I'm sorry. I explained all that, didn't I?"

114

"You did. I still need more time."

Nate glanced at the clock on the stove. "Unfortunately, we've got to be leaving soon."

"I-- I can't."

He held her in his arms. "Yes, you can. If you love me, none of the rest matters. Anything you need, you can get when we get there."

"But--"

"Tori," Nate held her tight, "listen to me. I want you. Now. Forever. Nothing else matters. Come with me. What's so hard to understand about that?"

"It's kinda scary."

"Of course it is."

"For you, too?"

"Not really. I get to marry the girl of my dreams. I get to marry her in the most exotic place on Earth. I get all that, and someone else pays for it. Pinch me, I'm dreaming. Only, I'm not! It's all true. Fly away with me. C'mon, Tori. I love you. I don't want to be apart any more. Come with me."

"You really mean that?"

"Yes!"

She couldn't believe what she was agreeing to. She needed time. She needed to make phone calls. She needed to make plans--call her Mom, call her editor, call--"

"Tori!"

"What?"

"Brush your teeth. Get dressed. We have to

115

go. Now."

"But--"

"Now."

"Okay," she said. She even smiled, but something wasn't quite right. Something was missing.

~*~

With Ivan's help, Joe Bannock survived imprisonment and showed up for his arraignment in good health. He went into it with low expectations, and Shaniqua gave him no reason to hope for a positive outcome. So it came as a shock when the judge set his bail at a level he could afford--without help from Puck Productions.

"How in hell did you pull this off?" he asked.

Shaniqua bowed. "You don't ask a magician to reveal his secrets, do ya?"

"I guess not. So, where do we go from here?"

"Nowhere, I've still gotta get your little friend out."

"Oh, right. Ivan. What're his chances?"

"Way less than yours were. That boy's done some really stupid stuff. He may never get out."

"Listen," Bannock said, "I don't care what it costs. You do whatever it takes to get him out."

"That's really touching."

"Bullshit. I need him. I know what Kwan's capable of, and I aim to be ready. Ivan can run interference for me. And nobody's gonna run over him."

Shaniqua sighed. "I'll do what I can, but I won't promise anything. I had a little chat with the judge yesterday. Turns out his granddaughter is a big Puck fan. Imagine that. Anyway, they're gonna let you out today. The redhead that makes life easy for your pal, Tim Archer, has already found you a new place to live. She had your stuff moved, too. Be nice to her, she's good people."

Bannock opened his mouth to say something, but his huge black attorney gave him a silencing head shake. They escorted him back to his cell before she could say any more. She waved to him as he left the hearing room.

~*~

Mato came to a halt at the top of a rise in view of Tori's cabin. Shadow lay down beside him, panting. They'd been running most of the morning, and the dog showed signs of fatigue.

Lack of food and water were constants Mato had come to live with. Dogs had no capacity for planning ahead and thus depended on their human companions to supply such essentials. Mato knew he'd let Shadow down.

They both sprawled out on the ground, breathing heavily, and wishing they had something to drink when they heard a car engine crank.

Squinting into the distance, Mato could make out a huge gray automobile parked beside Tori's cabin. He'd never seen it before and felt certain it didn't belong to any of the giants he knew.

Josh Langston

At such a distance it seemed unlikely that anyone in or near Tori's cabin could see him, so Mato made no effort to hide. Instead, he concentrated on the car and the two people getting into it.

He felt certain it was Tori and Nate, but they were leaving. Mato waved his hands above his head and yelled to get their attention. Shadow stood and looked around, but obviously couldn't understand what all the fuss was about.

If only they were slightly closer, Mato might have tried to hit their vehicle with an arrow. Alas, the distance was too great. He didn't have time to gather materials for a fire, so smoke signals were out.

"Run," he said, slapping Shadow smartly on the hindquarters.

The dog whined then took off running toward the cabin.

Mato considered chasing after him, but the odds of reaching the two giants before they made their way to the end of Tori's treacherous driveway were too slim to consider.

Instead, he decided try and cut them off. It meant traveling overland, but since he had no other choices, he jumped to the task.

~*~

"You do *want* to go to Hawaii, don't you?" Maggie asked as she followed Cal through his house. Since they got up that morning he had managed to locate his suitcase and pack his

118

toothbrush, razor, and prescription meds, but nothing else.

"Well?" she asked.

"Sure," Cal said. "It sounds like fun. But--"

"But what?" She pushed him aside and pulled underwear, socks and shirts from his dresser which she piled on his bed next to the open suitcase.

"There's no way I can be ready to go this afternoon. If nothin' else, I've gotta find someone to mind the store while I'm gone, and I don't even know how long that'll be."

"Nate said we could go with him today on Puck's corporate jet, or he'd buy round trip tickets for us to fly out later." She stalked to his closet and grabbed two pairs of slacks and some sandals. She took a long hard look at the latter. "These are ancient. Did you take 'em off a disciple's corpse?"

"Huh?" He looked up from the task of transferring the piled clothing from bed to bag. "I was young once."

She bypassed him by throwing everything into the suitcase. "C'mon now, we've gotta hurry. I've never been in a private jet. I can't wait."

"It's just--"

"Are you sayin' you'd rather fly in a big commercial plane than a private luxury job? If so, you're even crazier than I thought."

"I've got responsibilities."

"So do I," Maggie said. "But I know an

119

opportunity when I see one, and this is it. I called in and arranged to take my vacation." She slammed the lid on the suitcase, then paused before she latched it shut. "Where's your swim suit?"

"Swim suit? Uh-- This whole packing thing requires more time. I--"

"Wake up, Cal! I don't have time to pack *anything*. I'm going just like this. No suitcase, no clean underwear, nothing."

"Nate said you could pick up all that stuff in Honolulu."

"Well then," she insisted, "so can you!"

"But the store! Who's gonna take care of it?"

"You'd best figure that out quick, stud, 'cause it's time we went to the airport."

~*~

Chapter 7

Be ~~with~~ someone who makes you happy.

On the morning the aviation class was set to graduate, *fluglehrer* Helmut Warner stood waiting outside the door of Klaus Becker's quarters. Breakfast for the flight instructor had been light, but it lay in his stomach like a slab of runway. He had one unpleasant task left before the ceremony at which he would bestow on the class the documentation proving they had met all the requirements for certification as Zeppelin airship pilots.

Becker's door opened, and the sallow-faced student stood inches from his instructor. "Herr Warner?"

"Good morning, Becker. I'm afraid I have some bad news."

"What do you mean?" the student asked. His voice remained steady, but his face registered surprise. It was the most emotion Warner had ever seen in him.

"As you know, performance data from all students is double-checked and tallied one last time before graduation. Usually, this is a mere formality, a final check to ensure that we haven't made any mistakes in our administrative duties."

"And?"

Warner took a deep breath before continuing.

Josh Langston

He wanted to get it all out in a single breath, as if that would somehow reduce the severity of the news. "For the first time in my career, such a mistake has been found. Unfortunately, it lowered your over-all grade to a point slightly below the allowable minimum."

Becker stared at him without speaking.

"It pains me to advise," Warner said, "that Zeppelin will not be able to certify you today as one of our airship pilots."

Becker remained silent.

"I hope you will accept my apology on behalf of the flight school. If this mistake had been caught earlier, there may have been time for you to re-take the portion of the program you failed. I'm truly sorry."

"I see," Becker said, his voice flat and his face once again a mask.

"I insisted the bursar put your name at the top of the next class list, however. Once you've paid the basic fee--we'll waive all the rest--you'll be able to resume your studies. I'm sure you'll make it through a second round with no trouble."

"That won't be necessary," he said.

Warner frowned. "Don't be hasty. I understand your disappointment."

"I doubt that," the student said. "You obviously overestimate it."

~*~

Daphne arrived at the Southern Montana State campus with visions of tiny cavemen dancing in her head. They resembled sugar plum fairies to a degree, but their outfits tended toward bones and feathers, and several of them carried spears. So, all in all, not terribly fairy like, except in size.

The realization she'd abandoned a goodly portion of her imagination to cartoon animators saddened her. Fortunately for her self esteem, it was unlikely that whoever speared the prospector looked like a Smurf.

After a number of inquiries, Daphne landed in front of the unimposing office of Simon Dole, associate professor of paleoanthropology. Beside an otherwise nondescript office door, a modest corkboard displayed a few announcements, the schedule for an upcoming conference, and a handful of notes signed by various females, presumably students, requesting appointments to discuss fellowship opportunities.

As she raised her hand to knock, the door opened, and a dark-haired man in his early 30's, most likely a model for aftershave or beachwear, emerged. He exposed an astonishingly healthy set of teeth in a Hollywood smile and apologized for practically running over her.

"I'm on my way to an engagement," he explained.

Daphne wondered who was lucky enough to be engaged with him. She quickly introduced herself and launched into an explanation of the sort of experts she needed to find.

"I can think of a couple people you might contact," he said, "but at the risk of sounding unbearably pompous, I'm probably your guy."

Oh, if only that were true.

He continued, "That's not much of a brag. When it comes to Paleo-Indian studies there aren't that many experts. At least, not around here." He glanced at his watch and frowned. "I have this faculty thing I can't get out of, but if you'll walk with me, perhaps I can establish my *bona fides* and answer a question or two."

"Great!" she said, digging into her purse for the photo she'd printed before leaving home. She thrust it into his hands as they walked, and he dutifully examined it, even putting on a pair of wire rimmed glasses designed to look more sexy than studious.

She couldn't help but notice the stares she got from many of the females on campus while they walked. Daphne felt a bit smug but tried not to let it show.

"It's definitely a Clovis point," he said at last. "But I can't tell you if it's authentic. You'd be amazed at how many people sell 'artifacts' they've manufactured in their basements and garages. I don't have a problem with the ones clearly marked as replicas. Problem is, amateur collectors are often taken in by well-made fakes."

Daphne pointed to the photo. "So, this one could be either old or new?"

"If I had to guess, I'd say it's new. Try to

imagine how long it took for a Paleo era craftsman to fashion good, useable spearheads. When a point became dull, or broken, it wasn't discarded. It was re-purposed. Spearheads became scrapers or were cut down to become knives or arrowheads; worn or damaged arrowheads and knives were turned into needles. If--"

"Needles?"

"Sure. Those animal skins the people wore didn't come off the rack in different sizes."

Daphne felt herself blush, something the reporter rarely allowed herself to do. "Sorry, I--"

"No apology needed. *I'm* supposed to be the expert, remember?"

"Feel free to ask me something about journalism," she said as they drew to a halt in front of an administration building.

"It's a deal," he said. "Do you have a business card? I'd be happy to discuss this further, but my meeting is about to start."

She produced a card, circled her cell phone number, and handed it to him. "I'll be around for awhile. It's a bit of a drive back to Cheyenne."

"Perhaps we could meet for dinner?"

Are you seriously playing me? "That'd be great."

"I know a couple good places."

I'll just bet you do. "You've got the number. Call me when you're done, okay?"

"Will do," he said, slipping the card in his

shirt pocket. He opened the door of the building, then stopped and turned to look at her. "Do you like sushi?"

"I--" How could she admit she hadn't eaten anything lately that didn't come on a sesame seed bun, with fries? "Uh--"

"Greek? Thai?"

"I'm good with almost anything," she said. "You choose."

"Done. Ciao!" he said, and then he was gone. With the photo.

That didn't bother her overmuch. She was suddenly more concerned with how her hair looked, and what she smelled like.

But dear Lord. Sushi? *Yuck.*

Then again, "sushi with Simon" had a nice ring to it. She wouldn't have to eat much. And afterward-- She let the thought drift. Maybe they'd look into Paleo recreation. Just what did those cave boys and girls do during long, lonely nights, especially when they weren't turning spearheads into nail clippers?

She paused to mentally replay her morning, smiling when she remembered which bra and panties she'd selected. Professor Dole wasn't the only one capable of looking sexy.

~*~

Tori leaned back in the posh front seat of the big roadster. She'd ridden in big, luxury cars a couple times, most notably when she visited New York, and her editor took her to some of her

126

favorite watering holes. Limo rides were definitely something she could get used to. Although, given the option, she'd have preferred to sit in the back seat with Nate and snuggle.

Sadly, he was all business. Wearing his customary Stetson, he looked the part of the uncompromising western lawman, sans badge. He didn't seem to miss it, however. When he talked about his new security business, his eyes lit up, and a measure of pride crept into his voice. He was a professional, by God, and he knew it.

Yet, that didn't answer a question which nagged Tori since he first mentioned Hawaii. What in the world did Puck Productions need him for? She conjured an image of Stinky, a bearded heavy who represented the dark side of life in countless Puck cartoons. Stinky led a gang of black-hatted bad guys who never got away with their crimes. Oddly enough, they never seemed to be convicted of any either. They were always available for the next assault on the irrepressibly plucky Puck. That, she supposed, was life in cartoon world.

She fiddled with the car stereo which came equipped with satellite radio and found a setting that featured the Zac Brown band, a fairly new indulgence. She turned the volume to a comfortable background level.

Nate, though fully engaged in driving, nevertheless had a look of faraway concentration on his handsome face. Clear-eyed and level-headed, he never seemed at a loss for what to do. It came as no surprise that he waltzed through the high intensity world of crime fighting in the Big Apple and emerged from it both honored and respected.

"I thought we were runnin' late," she said.

"Mm hm."

"So, why are you driving so slow?" If pressed, she would admit her eagerness to climb inside the fancy-schmancy private jet the Puck people sent to collect them.

"Just 'cause this isn't my car doesn't mean I can drive it into the ground," he said. "There are still quite a few boulders in your uh--. driveway. They're big enough that you could have 'em mapped."

Bang!

Tori instantly sat upright. "What the hell was that?"

"A stone, I think. It hit the side of the car."

"Oh, crap! Another rock slide?" She twisted to look out the side window, then bent forward for a better view of the steep-walled canyon on one side of the dirt track.

"Don't think so," he said. "Not enough dust and debris. It was just--"

The second rock bounced off the back window, and Nate jammed on the brakes.

"You're *stopping?*" Tori asked, her voice rising to a squeal. "It's a slide!"

"Nah." He shifted the limo into park,

unbuckled his seatbelt, and climbed out.

Tori did the same and rounded the back of the vehicle to stand beside him.

"I'll be damned," Nate said, looking up at the top of the cliff.

A grinning Mato waved down at them from above.

~*~

"Joe Bob?"

Bannock smiled at the tall redhead standing in the middle of the waiting area outside the Puck offices in Waimea, Kauai. Joe had spoken with her on the phone, but this was the first time they'd met in person, and he immediately regretted the delay.

"Miss Rhoades! We finally meet." He advanced to shake her hand. "I'm delighted."

"Likewise," she said, though her expression suggested an altogether different emotional state. "I thought you were, uhm-- with the police."

"I was." He gave her a theatrical shrug. "A terrible misunderstanding. My attorney's taking care of it."

Randy nodded. "Your Miss Jackson is really--" she paused, "--something."

"That she is," he said. "One of the finest legal minds in the business. But, please, don't mention her to Mr. Archer. He might try to hire her away from me."

"Mr. Archer's quite happy with his legal team," Randy said. "He's big on image and first impressions. I'm not sure she would fit in very comfortably."

"I'd say that's a good thing! So, I hope my little problem hasn't put us any further behind schedule."

"Honestly, Mr. Bannock--"

"It's Joe."

"I thought it was 'Joe *Bob*.'"

"Only for politicians and the media."

"I see. About that--" she waved to an easy chair beneath a large oil portrait of Puck dressed as Julius Caesar. For reasons he couldn't explain, the interior designer made it work in the lavishly appointed foyer.

"Is there a problem?" he asked. "I assure you, I acted solely in self defense. And, by the way, I can't thank you enough for finding a new place for me to stay."

She walked to a large desk near the entrance to the room and retrieved a folded newspaper which she brought to him. "I'm guessing you haven't seen the papers."

"No," he said. "I went to bed as soon as I got to my apartment. I didn't go out for breakfast. This whole thing has been extremely stressful."

"I can only imagine."

He doubted it, but didn't comment. Instead, he glanced at the banner headline:

**Puck Paradise Boss Under
Arrest for Attempted Murder**

After an initial gasp, Bannock's lungs refused to take in air. *Kwan!* Even though Bannock had been released, the conniving bastard made sure the papers dragged his name through the mud. "Aw, hell. Has Mr. Archer--"

"Oh yes. He gets copies of anything the wire services put out which even mention Puck Productions. The cable news stations are treating it as a big deal, too. Which, I hate to admit, it is."

"But I was only protecting myself."

"That's precisely what Mr. Archer is doing, too."

"I don't understand."

"We can't be associated with a murder trial. It's a public relations disaster. Puck Productions is all about entertainment--family fun and family values. Having our prime contractor under indictment for murder is simply not acceptable."

"It's not murder, it's *attempted* murder, and I haven't been indicted. I've only been arraigned."

"For now."

"But I'm being set up!"

She looked genuinely sympathetic. "Try to see this from our perspective. No matter what we do, publicly, the media will tie us to the charges."

"Puck had nothing to do with it!" Joe said. "Well, no. That's not true. They had everything to do with it. Daniel Kwan wants to take over my contract, and he's making me out to be a bad guy. But only so he can clear the way for himself."

"That may be true," Randy said, "but there's

not much we can do about it."

"You could start by standing by me! Isn't loyalty a family value, too?"

"We're not abandoning you," she said. "In fact, there's a man on his way now to conduct a private investigation. He'll also be responsible for overseeing security at Puck Paradise until it opens. He'll be here later today."

"So, what am I supposed to do, direct my team from off-site? That's not very practical, or efficient."

"Actually," she said, clearing her throat, "though McCutcheon Engineering will still be involved in the project, you won't."

"What? I have a contract!"

"Yes, you do. And right now, you're in violation. Our contracts all stipulate strict compliance with local, state and federal laws. You've been accused of breaking a big one, and whether or not you're guilty isn't the point. We must avoid bad press, and this is one of the main ways we do it."

Bannock stood speechless.

"I'm sorry," she said. "Please understand, it's nothing personal."

He left the office wondering two things: where Kwan might be hiding, and where he could get his hands on a lob wedge and a hack saw.

~*~

Mato didn't waste time catching his breath. Once Tori and Nate emerged from the car and saw him, he began his descent down the steep canyon wall. The nearly vertical journey involved too much falling, but he reached the lower level without injury.

Tori swept him off the ground and hugged him, while Nate pressed close and patted him on the back. Had he not trusted both giants completely, their actions would have terrified him. As it was, he was just as happy to see them.

"Where's Shadow?" Tori asked.

"Cabin," he said, pointing back the way they'd come. "Hungry."

He hadn't given much thought to what he might say to them when he finally reached his destination. Their language had been difficult to learn and relied upon much knowledge he had not yet acquired, so he stuck to basics. Fluency would come later.

Tori faced Nate. "We've got to get him something to eat."

He looked at his watch. "I told the driver we'd be there around noon."

"Well, then, call him back and tell him we're gonna be late."

Mato paid little attention to their conversation. He found their vehicle to be of much greater interest. Slipping out of Tori's arms, he dropped lightly to the ground and squirmed through the open door onto the front seat.

The air inside remained cool, and he gazed with admiration at all the buttons and dials on the dashboard. He had actually driven a giant's vehicle once. It belonged to Nate's friend, Caleb. A good man, but very old, much like Winter Woman. He had provided controls just for Mato to use, and he made the big machine go exactly where he intended. It was a short trip, both in time and distance, but it taught him a valuable lesson: giant magic could be his, too.

Nate and Tori climbed in on either side of him. Mato straddled an armrest between them which put him at eye level with the giants.

Tori appeared upset. She would look first at Mato, then at Nate, then close her eyes and shake her head. Mato thought she might be possessed. The demon spirits sometimes had that effect on females. She would recover soon.

"This changes everything," she said.

"What does?" Nate asked.

She waved at thumb at Mato. "He does."

"Why?"

"Well, duh. There's an arrest warrant out for him."

"And you think we should turn him in?"

She twisted away. "I don't know what I think."

Mato tried to process her remark, but it proved extremely difficult. How could someone *not* know what they thought? Perhaps it was something peculiar to giants. Or females. He did not claim to be an expert on either.

"What is warrant?" Mato asked.

"You care to explain that to him, Mr. Security Consultant?"

Nate remained silent until he'd turned the car around, then headed back toward the cabin. He glanced at Mato. "Do you remember something that happened up in the mountains?"

"Yes. Many things."

"Something that didn't involve your people?"

Mato nodded. "Giant try hurt Shadow. I stop."

"Who tried to hurt Shadow?" Tori asked.

Mato shrugged. "Giant. Have weapon, like Nate."

She paled. "A gun? Somebody *shot* my dog?"

"No."

"Mato stopped him," Nate said, then asked, "Did you use a spear?"

"How you know?"

"Was there something on the spearhead? Poison or something?"

Mato shook his head, no.

"None of that stuff you use when hunting?"

"All gone. Long winter. No snake." He looked at Tori. "You no have food? Mato hunt?"

"What? No, there's food. I--"

"Mato want peanut butter."

"Sure."

"And orange."

"No problem."

"And music."

He reached for the controls on the car stereo, but Tori intervened. "I can probably save you

135

some time." She turned up the volume on "Chicken Fried," and Mato bobbed his head to the tune.

After a few minutes he leaned back, closed his eyes, and went to sleep.

~*~

Danny Kwan had just finished an elegant dinner in his crystal and chrome dining room. Paku had offered to hire a girl to dine with him, or just satisfy his physical needs, but Kwan brushed the suggestion off. He was happy just contemplating his domination of Puck's redneck construction boss. Gloating, perhaps over an expensive glass of wine, would have been better, but that would have meant meeting Bannock somewhere, or worse--allowing him into Kwan's inner sanctum. Not a likely proposition. He paid a fortune to insure that the location of his retreat was known to a very limited few, and they risked the most severe punishment if they let the knowledge slip.

Thus far, no one had.

Paku entered the brightly lit room in complete silence. He brought some of Kwan's private stock of brandy and cigars. Kwan rose and walked to his study with Paku in tow. He settled into an overstuffed leather chair and watched while his aide poured a postprandial beverage and lit Kwan's cigar.

"Help yourself," Kwan said, knowing full well that Paku never indulged. Kwan had no idea why.

It never occurred to him to ask.

"The luau has been arranged?"

"Yes. Everything's ready, including the guest of honor."

"Good. I look forward to tomorrow night. Everyone will attend?"

Paku's teeth gleamed. "No one would dare miss it."

It was precisely what Kwan wanted to hear.

~*~

Nate tried not to grind his teeth too hard while Tori played the role of doting mother over Mato. His reasoning was simple: of all the people on Earth--of any size--very few needed a mother *less* than Mato. Shadow, on the other hand, occupied the other end of the spectrum.

The huge dog sat waiting for them at the door of Tori's cabin. Though he barked at the unfamiliar car, he morphed into a wiggly mass of puppy stuff the moment Nate and Tori emerged. How a dog so large and fierce could instantly turn into a big, loveable pillow was beyond him. But Shadow managed and recaptured both his and Tori's hearts anew.

Nate squatted on the ground, and Shadow wedged his big head between Nate's knees. His tail wagged so hard it raised a small dust cloud. The whimpers of joy were most unbecoming of a guard dog, not that anyone cared.

Mato stumbled out of the limo and stretched, then followed Tori into the cabin and climbed up on one of the two chairs parked at her petite kitchen table.

"You know we don't have time for this," Nate said, trying very hard to suppress his impatience.

"We should just let them both starve?"

"No, but they're hardly in any danger of that. Do you see any ribs showing on either one?"

Tori ignored him and slathered peanut butter and strawberry jam between two slabs of whole wheat bread, dropped them on a paper plate, and sent it sliding toward the little Indian. Mato tore into it as if he hadn't eaten in a decade.

Shadow exhibited a similar degree of hunger. He danced and rumbled the whole time Tori poured dry food into his bowl. Nate had no idea where she'd stored either while the dog was with Mato. The animal devoured all of it in seconds then whined for more.

"What are we going to do with them?" Tori asked, refilling the dog bowl. "I've left Shadow with Cal and Maggie from time to time, but they're going with us."

"Have you got a leash?"

"Somewhere."

"Find it. We'll have to bring him with us. If nothing else, we can put him in a kennel in Hawaii."

The look on her face told him she didn't like the idea but couldn't think of a better one. "And Mato?" she asked.

Nate pursed his lips. Mato would be much

trickier. "I suppose he could go, too." *Lord, please tell me I didn't just suggest that.*

"What about the-- You know. The incident in the Cloud Peak? Are we going to hide a fugitive?"

"He's not a fugitive, yet. You won't see his face on a wanted poster in the Post Office. The law doesn't know who to look for, or where for that matter. Besides, all Mato did was protect Shadow from an unwarranted attack. It was his responsibility to look after the dog."

"What about the poison-tipped spear?"

"I believe his explanation. He knows the stuff better than anyone. There's got to be something else at play."

She smiled, and he realized it had been awhile since he'd seen her do that.

"Well then, how do we get him on the plane?"

They could always tell the crew that Shadow was a service dog, but how would they explain Mato? Nate brightened. "Maybe he'd rather be with his own people."

Tori shrugged. "Ask him."

Nate did.

"Mato stay with you," he said. "Go home later."

"But we have to go on a trip," Nate said. "Far away. Many sleeps." *Great, now I sound like Tarzan, too.*

Mato grinned. "Mato go, too."

"I will have work to do."

"Mato help," he said, his tone matter of fact.

139

"I may have to deal with some very bad people." Nate said, reverting to the King's English, but his words had precisely no effect. Mato finished his sandwich and licked his fingers. *Had he even wiped off his hands before he ate?* Nate doubted it.

"Mato ready." He dropped to the floor in a single fluid motion then ambled to the door.

"I found the leash," Tori said.

"How're we going to hide Mato?"

"I could wrap him up in a little blanket and carry him like a baby."

"And what happens when he shoots the pilot with an arrow or opens the doors at 30,000 feet?"

"He wouldn't do that," Tori said.

"Really? How do you know?"

She produced a prescription bottle she'd retrieved from the bathroom. "I'll give him half of one of these. He'll sleep for a solid day." She tossed him the amber-colored plastic bottle.

Nate examined the label with surprise. "Where'd you get pain pills?"

"They're left over from when I was in the hospital after Shane hurt me." Nate had been investigating the assault of her crazy ex-husband when they first met.

"Oughta work." He tossed them back to her. "Have you got anything we can hide his bow and arrows in? I didn't see his blowgun."

"We can wrap them in a little blanket, too. I picked up a couple when Mato and Reyna stayed here." She looked up at her exposed rafters. "I had to store their mattress up above. It took up too much space."

Nate checked his watch for the umpteenth time. "We're late."

"Have you called the driver to explain?"

"Not yet. I'll do it now."

"Fine. I'll get those blankets and meet you in the car."

"Don't forget to give Mato his 'night-night' pill," Nate said, but she was already grinding it up to go in his orange juice. A tiny paper cup would handle that. He could drink it in the car on the way to the airport.

And, Nate thought, if he doesn't go to sleep, we can always just dump him out somewhere along the way. He smiled. *Yeah, like Tori would agree to that!*

~*~

Chapter 8

Your dog may think you're amazing and
wonderful; that doesn't mean anyone else will.

Daphne knew she was attractive, if not drop dead gorgeous. A realist, she had few illusions about her ability to attract someone as magazine ad hot as Simon Dole, but she could usually spot a player when she saw one, and the associate professor of paleoanthropology sitting across from her in the romantic little bistro seemed a likely candidate. Though he kept talking about the case, his actions seemed courtly, as if he were trying to prove himself worthy of continued interaction.

"And the fingerprints the authorities found are about the size of a child's?" he asked.

"An infant's, actually."

"Interesting. I don't suppose a child could have merely touched the binding or whatever it was that yielded the prints."

"Possibly. But what I'm hearing is that the prints also reflected scar tissue."

He lifted his wine glass, swirled the contents, and then sniffed. Daphne had seen something similar during a winery tour. She'd tried it herself, but felt silly. Simon certainly looked silly doing it, but she stifled her giggles.

"I don't have a photo of the prints," she said.

"But I'm hoping to talk one of my contacts into making a copy for me."

He nodded professorially. "I'd like to see them. I'm having a hard time with the idea of such a tiny human being surviving in the wild."

"There are plenty of little people in the world," Daphne said, having spent some time studying the issue on the internet. "But I suspect there are damned few adults under two feet tall."

"That's probably true, even among the so-called Pygmy peoples, of which there are a wide variety. But, that's not my field. I'm more interested in the folk who populated North America ten to thirty thousand years ago."

"And made stone tools."

"Indeed." He refilled his wine glass and offered Daphne more as well.

She accepted, then edged toward her real goal. "Let's assume, for the sake of argument and because we have evidence to support the idea, that a very small person actually did this, and further--that he or she is currently living in the Bighorn National Forest. How could that person survive undetected?"

"You're assuming no one's seen them."

"True, but I'm going to do an article for my paper in hopes of luring someone out of the woodwork who will claim a sighting." She sipped her wine and shrugged. "Someone might even have a photo or two."

Simon swirled the wine in his glass and

contemplated it in silence. A moment later he said, "I don't believe a single individual could survive without a community of some sort."

"A tribe?"

"Okay, yes. A tribe."

"So, there could actually be a village full of little people living in the Cloud Peak Wilderness?"

"As preposterous as it sounds, yes."

Daphne grinned. "How would one go about finding them?"

Simon's expression slowly changed until it matched hers. "I suppose one would have to mount an expedition of some kind."

"Would that be expensive?"

He laughed. "What isn't expensive these days?"

"Seriously, what would it cost?"

"I wouldn't venture a guess without giving it a great deal of thought. However--"

"Yes?"

"One of the advantages of working for a university is access to an educational grant system and a great deal of free labor."

She gave him a puzzled look.

"Students," he said. "They'll do damned near anything for extra credit, and participating in a summer expedition would, I'm sure, draw a crowd of volunteers."

"I wish I could say my paper would help cover some of the expenses," she said, "but my editor would never go for it. But if given an exclusive, I can guarantee you'd get amazing press coverage. And if you actually found something up there--"

"Let's not get ahead of ourselves," he said, finishing his wine and reaching for the check. "Why don't we go back to my place and explore the idea some more?"

She felt reasonably sure that wasn't the only thing he wanted to explore, but she was up for it. "Sure."

When he offered his arm, she accepted it and flounced through the crowded bistro at his side, drawing looks from envious coeds all the way to the exit. *Eat your hearts out, girls.* Sometimes one had to go a little above and beyond to get a story. Daphne knew exactly where she'd hang her Pulitzer Prize certificate and how she'd spend the money that came with it.

~*~

Maggie and Cal waited for Nate and Tori at the Worland airport. Cal seemed anxious, but Maggie couldn't understand why. She felt nothing beyond a mounting sense of excitement. Cal's hand had grown so clammy she let go of it.

"What's wrong?" she asked. "Please don't tell me you're having another heart attack!"

He shook his head and gave her a rueful smile. "I'm okay. No need to worry."

She tried to read his expression, but he'd put on his poker face. *Men could be so damned stubborn!* "Talk to me, Cal. What's going on?"

"I'm worried 'bout the store."

"The Franconi kid's going to look after it. Everybody knows him. His mom runs the only restaurant in Charm. He's a good guy. Besides, you don't get more than one or two customers a day. Or is that per week?"

"Funny," he said, without a smile.

"C'mon. What's really buggin' you?"

"*That* damn thing." He nodded at the sleek Gulfstream jet sitting on the tarmac. The fuselage bore an illustration of Puck in a typical action pose. The tail of the aircraft bore the company logo. There was a smiley face just beneath the cockpit window.

"What about it?"

"It's an airplane."

"It's a jet, actually," she said, trying to loosen him up. "Would you rather fly in some jumbo commercial job?"

"I'd rather stay on the ground."

She looked at him in a whole new light. It never crossed her mind that Caleb might be afraid to do anything, let alone fly. "You've flown before, haven't you?"

He shook his head, no.

"Oh." *Crap.* "Listen, it's no big deal. Flying is safer than riding in a car."

"Cars rarely fall out of the sky."

"C'mon, Cal! How often do they go up *into* the sky? Be real."

"I just need a little time to get used to the

146

idea."

Maggie spotted the limo Nate had driven the night before as it pulled in front of the terminal. "Hope you don't need too much time. Nate and Tori are here."

She didn't wait for him to respond. Instead, she pushed through the doors and hurried to the car as Tori emerged. Cal trailed behind. The two women exchanged a quick hug before Maggie asked if Tori needed help with anything. "As it turns out, I don't have anything of my own to keep up with. Including luggage."

"All I've got is one small bag, one large dog, and--" she leaned back into the car and extracted a toddler-sized bundle "--this."

"Mato?"

"Yeah."

"Is he dead?" Cal asked in a whisper.

"I gave him a little something to help him sleep."

Cal raised an eyebrow. "Got any more o' that stuff?"

Tori nodded, and Cal looked relieved.

Maggie bent close to Tori's ear. "If he's going to die, he'd rather do it in his sleep."

Tori snapped her head back in alarm. "He-- What?"

"Doesn't like to fly."

"Oh. Okay then, I guess."

Nate tried to tip the driver, but he wouldn't accept it. "Just make sure you call for me when you're gettin' ready to come back," he said. "You wouldn't believe what they're paying me."

They shook hands, and the limo pulled away.

Nate had Shadow on a leash which the dog didn't like at all. He kept trying to pull free. Nate just shortened the leash and kept the dog even closer.

A man in a white shirt and dark slacks approached them. Maggie thought at first it might be another limo driver until she saw the epaulettes on his shoulders. He introduced himself as the first officer and walked them through security and out to the aircraft where they met the pilot, a woman with a pleasant smile and a firm handshake.

While a baggage handler stowed Nate and Tori's luggage, the travelers followed the flight crew up the stairs and stepped into a small world of luxury. Maggie decided she wanted to live there forever--with or without Cal. "This is amazing."

Tori parked the sleeping Mato in a seat and joined Maggie in gawking at the interior of the Puck Production's corporate jet.

"Our flight attendant had to arrange for food and drinks and will be back on board in a few minutes," the first officer said. "Make yourselves comfy, and we'll get under way as soon as we can. He reached down and patted Shadow on the head.

Maggie hoped he wouldn't take the man's hand off, but he seemed fairly calm.

"Since we've got a little bit of time, you might want to take him outside. Our lav isn't equipped to handle service animals." He smiled. "I promise we won't leave without you."

Nate thanked him and took his advice while Cal settled into a recliner. "Tori? About those pills?"

She dug the bottle out of her purse and tossed it to him. Maggie watched while the old cowboy helped himself to two and choked them down without water.

A few minutes later, Nate re-boarded with Shadow and a flight attendant. She secured the hatch, made sure everyone was strapped in, and then disappeared. A few minutes later they were airborne.

"That was fast," Tori said.

Maggie, sitting beside Cal, gave him a quick inspection. His face looked pale and tense, which she did not interpret as a good sign. "Just lean back and close your eyes," she told him. "You'll be fine."

"Buh-- Buh-- Bourbon," he said.

Maggie shook her head. "Puh-- Puh-- Pills." She plucked the bottle from his hand and returned it to Tori.

When they reached cruising altitude, the flight attendant reappeared and handed Nate what looked like a plastic briefcase. A yellow sticky-note from Randy Rhoades said merely, "A little light reading. (Skip the movie.)"

The case contained several file folders including a copy of his employment contract, general information about Puck Productions, a thick packet of diagrams and information on the construction project in Hawaii, and another folder simply labeled "Bannock." Nate saved that one for last.

Curious about the plans for the resort on Kauai, Nate opened that folder first. It contained several photos of artist's renderings of what the resort would look like when completed. Maggie and Tori crowded closer so they could see them, too.

The property consisted of a ring of mountains surrounding a variety of Polynesian style buildings, several small lakes--fed by waterfalls and connected by streams--and a number of other features. These included a tunnel through one of the mountains and a broad walkway which led to a white sand beach. The mountain with the tunnel also housed the Transport Terminal to and from which passengers would be guided either to the tenders which serviced the Puck cruise ships or to the Puck airship which ferried passengers to a variety of locations in the islands.

"I don't see any hotels," Tori said.

Nate glanced through the notes until he found the explanation. "All the hotel rooms and club villas face inside the ring of mountains. Puck cut a deal with the state to get the property and had to leave the seaward side of the mountains as they were. The exteriors of the rooms on the inside are designed to hide windows and balconies. If you look closely at the renderings you can see them, but they're camouflaged."

"That is *so* cool," Maggie said. "Is that where we'll be staying?"

"I doubt it," Nate said. "I don't know how much construction remains, but it's definitely not complete. We'll stay on Kauai, somewhere. Randy will handle all that."

"Who's Randy?" Maggie asked.

"She's Mr. Archer's--"

"*She?*" Tori stared through his forehead into the depths of his cerebral cortex. "Randy is a she?"

"Well, yeah. She works for Mr. Archer."

"She's the one who flew out to Wyoming with you?"

"Uh huh."

Tori waved her hand at the jet's interior. "In this?"

"Yup."

Maggie looked at the aircraft cabin with new eyes. Though roomy and comfortable, none of the seats were sleepers. She glanced in Tori's direction and noticed her doing her own survey.

"Oh, here." Nate handed Tori an envelope containing a pre-paid bank card. "Randy stuck this in the folder, too. For when you go shopping."

Tori looked at the accompanying note, and her eyes expanded to roughly twice their normal size. "Two *thousand* dollars?"

"I told her you wouldn't have time to pack much. And Maggie didn't bring anything at all."

"You want me to hold that for you?" Maggie asked.

"It oughta keep you both in bikinis," Nate said.

Tori smiled as she slipped the card into her purse. "I'll keep it safe." Then she looked back down at the drawings Nate had unrolled. "What are those?" She pointed to a number of small, Puck-like figures which appeared throughout the designs.

Nate shook his head. "Beats me. It's the first I've seen of 'em."

The flight attendant rematerialized, took their drink orders and asked if they'd like to watch a movie while they dined. Maggie and Tori said yes while Nate took Randy's advice and settled in at a desk near the back of the cabin where he could review the files he'd been given.

One in particular cried out for his attention-- the one labeled "Bannock."

~*~

Joe Bannock swirled the ice cube in his single malt Scotch as he watched Ivan, the great hulking Hawaiian, march up the sidewalk to the front porch where Bannock sat. The view sucked, but he stayed comfortable in the shade, and he had damned little else to do.

"I got da scoops," Ivan said. "Yo' buddy,

Mistah Kwan, gon' have a party tonight, a luau. All his troops be dere."

Bannock winced at the "buddy" reference. "You said, 'All his troops.' Is that a lot?"

"Could be. I nevah worked fo' him. He can be scary."

"That runt?" Bannock laughed.

"He da boss. Some a' his people not very nice. Like Paku. 'Specially Paku. He like to scrap. Fight dirty."

"Last time I checked, street fighting didn't have any rules."

Ivan frowned. "Paku the kinda guy brings a gun to a fist fight."

"You know where this party will take place?"

"Shoots! I tol' you I got da scoops, brah! We gonna go?"

"I just want to observe. I don't want to take part."

"You wanna see the dancers, no? Island girls. Ono wahine! They can shake it."

Bannock shook his head. "I can see girls anytime. I want to see Kwan. I want to see who's protecting him, and more importantly, who isn't. I want to find his weakness."

"I can tell you dat already," Ivan said. "He never have enough."

"Of what?"

"Any damn ting! He nevah happy wit what he got."

"That'll make one hell of an epitaph,"

Bannock said. "I'd even pay for the engraving."

"Party start late," Ivan said. "After dark."

"I need binoculars. The night vision kind if they're available."

Ivan shrugged. "I know da place. Plenty of light. I used to work da imu."

"The imu?"

"Oven in da groun'. To cook kalua pig. Solid grinds, man."

The smile on Ivan's face made up for the language barrier.

~*~

The Puck Productions jet landed in Honolulu only slightly behind schedule. A car and driver were waiting for Tori, Maggie and Cal. Mato was still sound asleep. That concerned Nate, but his breathing was steady, and his heartbeat was strong and regular.

"He probably just needed rest," Maggie said. "God help him when he wakes up. His internal clock is going to be completely out of whack."

Nate agreed to take both Mato and Shadow with him. Tori claimed she and Maggie would have their hands full keeping track of Caleb. She waved the prepaid bank card as if she were leading the Rough Riders up San Juan Hill.

"You've only got a few hours to find what you need," Nate said. "After his long nap, Cal should be up to carrying anything you buy."

"We'll be fine," she said, eyeing the Hawaiian shirted driver and his sleek limo. "I may not be able to handle going back to my old life in Wyoming."

"Enjoy this while ya can, darlin'. I'll meet you at the airport on Kauai," he said. "Have fun!"

He watched the three of them depart then hurried back to the Puck jet. Shadow had not been happy about being left behind, but fortunately had not taken his frustration out on the airplane. It remained intact.

The pilot smiled at him as he dropped into a seat and buckled himself in. "We'll be leaving soon," she said. "It's a very short flight. I took the liberty of calling Ms. Rhoades to let her know when you'd be arriving."

"Thanks."

"Mahalo."

True to her words, the captain had him back in the air in minutes. The flight seemed to be half ascent and half descent. They touched down in Lihue without incident. Nate deplaned with Mato in one arm and Shadow pulling on the other. The leash only seemed to frustrate the animal as he continued to struggle with it.

"Give it up, dog," Nate growled, then to the man unloading his bags, "I'm outta hands. How'm I gonna haul my stuff?"

The man smiled and pointed at a stretch version of a golf cart headed their way. "Someone's coming to take care of it."

A smiling young man brought the cart to a halt, loaded Nate's bags and helped him coerce

Shadow into climbing in, too. Nate kept Mato in his lap in case the little Indian woke up.

"We didn't realize you were bringing a child with you," the driver said as he zipped by commercial aircraft to reach a distant part of the field where a helicopter sat waiting for him.

"I--" Nate closed his mouth rather than try to make up something on the spot that might sound reasonable. He settled for, "Unusual circumstances. I hope it won't cause any inconvenience."

"Not at all," said the driver. "We know how to handle kids."

Probably not this one.

"Here we are," the driver said, pulling to a stop beside a helicopter.

Nate had last ridden in one while in the service, and he'd hoped never to repeat the experience.

Randy stepped out to greet him. "Hey there!"

Nate looked from the chopper to the redhead.

"Who are your friends?" she asked.

Shadow's tail went into overdrive while Nate shifted the blanket-bound Mato and his similarly wrapped weapons. "This is my, uh, nephew. Matt," he said, "and my fiancée's dog. I'm sorry, but we didn't have enough time to make other arrangements."

"It's okay. The pilot told me you were bringing guests, but she didn't give me any details. I can arrange a sitter for you."

"No need. Tori, my fiancée, and her, uhm, sister, can watch him. He doesn't do well around strangers. Plus, the dog's pretty protective of him."

She looked perturbed despite her assurances to the contrary, but gave in with a shrug. "Seems like a lot of distractions, but as long as none of it gets in the way of your job--"

"It won't," he said. "Promise."

"Fine. Climb in. I'll have your bags stowed. It's going to get noisy. I doubt the little guy will sleep through it."

I hope like hell you're wrong. "We'll see. His meds really knock him out."

"He's ill?"

Oh crap. Answer that, smart ass. "I'm not sure what the deal is. He's not contagious. I know that much. You can ask his mom when they get here."

His "mom?" Oy.

Randy raised an eyebrow at him. "I'll be sending someone to escort them. But I'm concerned about the child's welfare. What if he needs a doctor?"

"There are doctors on the island, aren't there?"

"Well, yes, but not too many specialists."

Nate shook his head. "He'll be fine. You'll see."

The pilot shut the door and told everyone to strap in.

Randy was right about the noise, though

157

neither the sound of the rotors nor the vibration they caused matched Nate's memories of flying in a Huey. Neither did the size or the furnishings. The Huey could haul a dozen heavily armed men, and offered no creature comforts. The Puck Productions chopper seated four passengers in relative comfort--assuming one had faith in the physics of rotary-wing aircraft.

Nate didn't.

~*~

Tori heard her cell phone but had no idea how many times it had rung while they were shopping. Their driver had dropped them off at a mall close to Waikiki and the ocean, and the ambient noise level seemed high, especially for someone used to the solitude of the Wyoming outback.

"Nate!"

"Hey. How's the shopping?"

"Fabulous," she said. "I can't wait to show you what we got."

"That may happen sooner than you expected. I need your help."

"Lemme guess. Mato, right?"

"Yeah. I didn't realize Randy would meet me at the airport. I figured she'd send a car and driver, and I'd have time to wake Mato up and get him settled before I went to work. She wants to show me around the development as soon as possible."

"What did you tell her about Mato?"

"I said his name was Matt, and that she was your sister's kid."

Tori felt a moment of confusion. "But, I don't have a sister."

"C'mon, Tori! Roll with it. I was referring to Maggie."

"Oh." She turned to look at her friend who was trying on a sundress. "She's gonna love that."

"Tell her I'm sorry, but I couldn't think of anything else."

"Where are you now?"

"I'm in one of the finished villas in the resort."

"I thought you said--"

"I was wrong. They fixed several of 'em up for visiting dignitaries and Puck VIPs. It's pretty snazzy: three bedrooms, three baths, a hot tub and a phenomenal view of the construction."

"Sounds-- I dunno, odd."

"Could be a lot worse. The place is fully stocked with food, too. So, no grocery shopping required. For a while anyway. Thing is, I need you to get here as quick as you can. Randy's sending a chopper to pick you up."

"So, back to the airport?"

"Nope. Tell your driver to take you to Kuakini Medical Center Heliport. I don't know what kind of strings Randy pulled to get access, but she did it. You and the Puck helicopter should both get there about the same time."

"Okay," Tori said, unable to hide the

Josh Langston

disappointment in her voice. She hadn't come
even close to spending up to their limit.

"Sorry about this," Nate said. "I'll make it up
to you."

"How?"

"I was thinking about a beach wedding.
How's that sound?"

Tori brightened considerably but kept her
excitement under control. "That sounds amazing.
Let's talk about it."

"Tonight," he said. "After dinner. I love you."

"Love you, too," she said and almost cut the
connection. "Wait!"

"What?"

She had him repeat the name of the helipad
which she jotted on one of her shopping bags.
"Okay. Bye."

Tori explained the change in plans to Maggie
and Cal. Maggie took the news in stride, but Cal's
reaction surprised her.

"A helicopter?" he asked. "I-- It's not-- Is
there some other way I can get there?"

"Like a train?" Maggie asked. "It's another
island, Cal. I suppose you could charter a boat, but
I doubt Puck will pay for it. How good a swimmer
are you?"

"You did fine on the jet," Tori said.

"I slept most of the way."

"I've got more pills."

Maggie squeezed his arm. "C'mon, Cal.
Cowboy up. It's a short ride. If you could handle

bulls and broncos, you can handle this."

He grumbled but offered no further resistance, and the trio began their trip to Kauai.

"I could arrange for *you* to ride a bull," Cal said to Maggie. "I guarantee it'll be a short one. Best of all, the ground will be real close."

As Tori guided them toward the exit where their driver was waiting, she wondered how best to break the news to her friend that she'd suddenly joined the ranks of motherhood. "Uhm, Mags?"

"Yeah?"

"Do you have any strong feelings about adoption?"

~*~

The man calling himself Klaus Becker was not the least bit surprised when the publicity department of Zeppelin Luftschifftechnik, GmbH announced that the newly christened NT50 *Puck One* would make its debut in Hawaii. That had been his next destination for quite some time.

Everyone on Earth was familiar with the inane cartoon character called "Puck." His name appeared on countless products aimed at the offspring of idiots living on every inhabited continent. His face and chubby likeness had even been pressed into service by Middle Eastern religious fanatics bent on convincing children that Allah wanted them to sacrifice themselves in the war on Israel.

Puck Productions Inc., legendary in its

Josh Langston

willingness to protect its trademark name and characters, had opted not to pursue those radicals, however. Doing so would only invite reprisals of a violent and deadly nature. So, instead of filing suit or even denouncing the usurpation of their products, they purchased additional insurance on their amusement parks and studios and sided with most of the rest of the world in letting the Jews take care of themselves.

"Becker" didn't give a damn about the Jews. Nor did he care about the religious crazies who were paying him to do their dirty work. His only concern was contract fulfillment and his looming--and extremely comfortable--retirement.

With his goals firmly in mind, he once again reviewed the steps remaining in his final job. This he accomplished while seated in the first class cabin of a Lufthansa jet en route to Los Angeles where he would board another flight on another airline under still another alias. By the time he set foot on land again, Klaus Becker would finally cease to exist.

~*~

Chapter 9

"To succeed in life, you need two things: ignorance and confidence." --Mark Twain

Daphne woke up feeling disoriented. She lay in a strange bed and heard breathing beside her. It took a moment to regain perspective. She and Simon had managed to seduce each other, although not as smoothly as either would have liked. Daphne figured an encore would help them iron out the rough spots. As partners, they needed more time to learn signals and build trust. They might not always get by on whatever lust-fired energy motivated them a few hours earlier.

She slipped out of bed and crept toward the bathroom. Sunlight leaked past the edges of the curtains, but that alone didn't tell her the time. Her internal clock chimed "breakfast," a cue she'd grown to trust.

Borrowing Simon's toothpaste, she brushed her teeth with her finger, took a quick shower, threw on the same clothes she'd worn the day before and made her way into his kitchen. She felt a momentary tremor of satisfaction noting that his was no messier than hers. If anything, Simon's kitchen lacked her organizational touch, and she guessed his cooking skills might be limited to boiling canned soup and reheating leftover takeout.

Josh Langston

She, at least, knew how to cook eggs. Sadly, he didn't have any. Or bacon. She checked the fridge and the freezer for bread and struck out in both places.

He did have an abundance of wines and cheeses, an excellent selection of mixers for cocktails, and a giant, economy-size jar of maraschino cherries. The veggie drawers held lemons and limes, and there were chilled glasses by the score. She thought for a moment she'd stumbled into the prep room of a fern bar.

"Can I help you find anything?" he asked from the doorway.

She turned away from the open fridge. "Breakfast stuff?"

"Hm." He frowned. "I have coffee."

"I need food."

"I need a shave."

He did, but he didn't need anything to enhance his magazine ad looks. Still, she wasn't a big fan of cheek rubs when the other cheek felt like the prickly side of Velcro. "Go. Shave. And get dressed. We're going out for breakfast."

"I have class in just over an hour."

"Then you'd better move your ass," she said, "or I'll leave without you."

A short time later they reached a diner just off campus. Daphne insisted they drive separate cars.

"So," she asked when they were inside and seated. "Are you going to ask for volunteers from

164

your classes today?"

He looked puzzled. "Volunteers?"

"To hunt for 'Little Foot.'"

"Oh! That. Yeah, I guess I could. Normally, I'd have to run something like this past the administration. An expedition is kind of a big deal."

"But--" she prompted.

"But if we make it voluntary, then the school wouldn't necessarily have any financial or liability issues."

"Nor could they claim credit for any discoveries we make," she said as her meal arrived: a sausage and cheese omelet, hash browns, toast, and coffee. She let the aroma resolve her suspicions about the quantity of grease used in her meal's preparation.

Simon nibbled at a cheese Danish.

"How many people would we need?" She asked.

"I have no idea."

"Five? Fifty?"

"A smaller party would be easier to manage," he said through a yawn. "Four should be enough for starters."

"Does that include us?"

"Depends. You plan to give up your job and move to the dig?"

"There is no dig. At least, not yet. All I'm really looking for is some sort of proof that little people are living up in the Cloud Peak."

Josh Langston

"That's a long shot. Don't get your hopes up."

She ignored the suggestion. "How soon can we get started?"

"In a day or two, I suppose. It depends on people's schedules. I teach three days a week, so--"

"That leaves four you can devote to the search. We can start tomorrow."

He groaned. "I've got a life, y'know."

"Me, too," she said. "But this is important."

"To you, maybe."

She took his hands in hers and stared into his eyes. "Tell me you don't want to be credited with an amazing discovery--a whole tribe of tiny people, living in the wilderness. Their technological level is probably stone age, which is what really should be firing your imagination."

He still looked dubious. "If they exist, and I'm not saying they do, their level of advancement would be of great interest."

"Said like a true professor. A really old and sedentary one."

"Hm. You never answered my question. If you're not quitting your job, how often will you be visiting?"

"A lot," she said. "Count on it. We can start tomorrow."

"But--"

"I'd have suggested this afternoon, but I've got a deadline to meet. After that I'm free for a couple days."

166

"Did you not hear me say I had a life?"

Smiling, she cupped his freshly shaved cheek with her palm. "I did. I also heard you say last night that you wanted to spend more time with me. Is that true?"

"Yes!"

"Well, here's your chance."

"Does that mean we'll be together again tonight?"

"Sure. Provided we leave in the morning."

He surrendered.

~*~

Reyna had refused to speak with Winter Woman ever since she learned the elder had told Black Otter to leave The People. She had no doubt he would return as quickly as possible to Tori's cabin on the far side of the settlement the giants called Ten Sleep. It made no sense to her. He had his own people--normal-sized people--he didn't need to live with the big ones.

She tried to explain this to Winter Woman but failed.

"He must satisfy himself about which world he will live in," Winter Woman said. "No one else can do that for him."

"But he doesn't even know he has a son," Reyna cried. "A father deserves to know."

Winter Woman cast a weary eye upon her granddaughter. "The woman bears the burden; the man deserves whatever he gets. Your Mato knows he has a child, but he must come here if he wants to become a father. If he does, we will rejoice. If he does not, we will say no more about it. Either way, The People will go on living as they always have."

Reyna felt no better for having heard her. "Nothing changes?"

"Not really. We have our place in the world. The giants have theirs."

"But every year we see more giants walk these mountains. Every year it becomes more difficult to hide from them."

Winter Woman chewed her lip. She stayed quiet for a long time, much longer than usual, though she never spoke without thinking first. "Perhaps I was wrong. Some things *do* change. Sometimes we learn new truths. You have special knowledge of the giants."

"Not as much as Black Otter."

"That is true, but you lived with them, too. You've seen their magic. You know more about them than you think."

Reyna doubted that very much. Where Mato found learning the giants' language to be a welcome challenge, she had found it boring and difficult, with too many words based on things and ideas she didn't comprehend. Where she feared the giants' magic, Mato sought to understand it and bend it to his will.

"The People need your knowledge," Winter Woman said. "When the giants come, you must be ready to help us understand what they are doing, even if they merely hunt. We must be ready to save ourselves should they decide to hunt for us."

"I don't know how I can help," she said. "Do you want me to go with the hunters and leave my child behind? I can't do that! I would never do that."

"You are a dreamer," Winter Woman said. "Just as Black Otter could see into the future, you can, too. I hope that some day your child will be able to do so as well. From now on, I want you to come to me and tell me your dreams."

"All of them?"

"Until you can tell which ones are about the future, yes."

~*~

Bannock let Ivan drive, and he parked the car a short distance down an unmarked dirt road. They walked until they saw people gathered at the far side of an open area. There, a tree line separated the field from a wide expanse of beach. The star laden sky provided enough light for them to find their way through dense foliage at the far edges of the clearing.

For such a large man Ivan moved quietly, and Bannock struggled to emulate him. Several times the Hawaiian cautioned him about making too much noise. If Kwan discovered them, they would almost certainly be turned over to Paku. And that would not end well. Bannock redoubled his efforts to move in silence.

Once they reached the tree line, Ivan crept

Josh Langston

behind dunes and a downed palm, sometimes crawling on his enormous belly. Bannock followed him, mindful of crabs, shells, and driftwood. Somehow they reached a vantage point Ivan deemed satisfactory.

Bonfires blazed at strategic spots on the sand while traditional island music played in the background. Roughly two dozen party goers congregated there--all male, and all heavily engaged in beer consumption. Empty cans and bottles littered the beach. There were too many conversations going on for Bannock to pick out words from anyone in particular.

"Do you see Kwan?"

"Chill, brah. He come. You see."

Both men used binoculars, though Bannock worried it might be too dark to see anything useful. He lay close to Ivan behind a dune and concentrated on the scene unfolding before them.

"Dey got da pig. See?"

Bannock turned his glasses to follow the progress of the two men hauling the meat toward a central table. As they worked their way through the crowd, the conversations ground to a halt. Several men turned away.

"So strange," Ivan said. "Dat no way to luau."

"What's wrong?"

"Shhh! Kwan talking."

Kwan must have used a microphone and speaker system, for his voice carried well beyond his guests and boomed over the waves. No one

170

bothered to turn down the music.

"Paku tells me everyone is here," he said. "Everyone who can still walk."

That generated some scattered laughter, mostly among the back of the crowd.

"That's good, because I have an important message for you."

The guests fell silent. No one moved.

"I am a generous man. I pay all of you well. Do I not?"

There was widespread agreement emphasized by nods and high fives.

Kwan smiled broadly. "As my long term associates already know, I do not like to be disappointed." He shook his head slowly from side to side. "But lately, that has happened all too often. I send messengers, but the messages go nowhere. Two of our associates are in the hospital now. A redneck *haole* put them there before they could deliver my message to him. Another failed to even talk to the man I sent him to. He gave up at the first sign of resistance."

Bannock toyed with the focus ring on his binoculars. He could hear Ivan breathing as he looked through his own.

"Many of you know him. I'm talking about Clark Cho," Kwan continued, "but I do not think of him as a man. Because of his failure, I think of him as a pig. He's our guest of honor this evening." Kwan made a sweeping gesture with his arm and pointed to the main course steaming on the table.

Josh Langston

Bannock swung his binoculars back that way and zeroed in on the meat. It didn't look like any roast pig he'd ever seen.

"Oh, God," Ivan said as he turned his head away and threw up.

"What the hell is that?" Bannock asked in a harsh whisper.

"It's a man. Or was."

The reality finally hit him. A man's body had been bound with wire in a tight tuck, like that of a spinning acrobat. He had been posed on his knees, face down, with what appeared to be a fish stuffed in his mouth. The tail hung off the edge of the table.

Paku stepped toward the body with a carving knife. The heavy blade caught a sliver of light as he freed one of the man's arms and hacked away at the wrist. When the appendage came free, Paku waved it at the retreating crowd and yelled, "Let's all give Clark a big hand!"

Kwan laughed as Paku took a bite out of the palm and chewed with his mouth open.

"Remember one thing," Kwan roared as his guests backed away. "*Never* disappoint me. Unless you want Paku to take a bite out of you!"

"I've seen enough," Bannock said, his words tasting acidic. "We should go."

Ivan shook his head. "Dey see us."

"It's dark. We'll blend in."

The big Hawaiian grunted. "I'm too big. You're too-- white."

172

"Oh, yeah. Guess we'd better stay here then."

"No shit."

~*~

"I had hoped to get an earlier start," Randy said. "I didn't mean to keep you out so late."

Nate assured her it was his fault. "I should have told you I was bringing extra guests. But, to be honest, I only planned to bring my fiancée."

"She sounds like a great person. Her sister and brother-in-law sound nice, too. I wish I'd had a chance to meet their little one."

Nate nodded. He'd threatened Mato with dire consequences if he didn't stay hidden while Randy was there. He'd avoided making introductions when Tori, Maggie and Cal arrived, and left them to deal with Mato.

Randy took him on a tour of the facility via golf cart and pointed out the many features which would make the resort not only world class but unique in an amazing variety of ways. She also pointed out how where additional work was needed.

"And Mr. Archer thinks enough of this will be completed to open by the end of the month?" Nate asked.

"That's one of his goals, but I don't think it's very realistic, especially in light of Mr. Bannock's problems."

"I thought you said he was out on bail."

"I did. That doesn't mean he can return to work for us. Too much bad press."

Josh Langston

Nate's experience with the media remained sketchy, despite his work with New York police forces who all had heaping helpings of face time with reporters. "Still, losing one guy shouldn't hold things up much. Surely he has someone who can step in for him."

"He has a collection of subcontractors who've been with him for ages, but not all of them are still on the job."

"Where are the rest?"

"That's something we'd like you to look into as well as Mr. Bannock's problems. It seems a number of the primary subcontractors have received threatening phone calls. They've been told to leave the islands or suffer the consequences."

"What are the consequences?"

"Presumably the same sort Mr. Bannock faced. Unfortunately, he seems to have over-reacted."

Nate examined Randy's expression for some hint of her feelings about Bannock's predicament. He found none. "I thought he claimed self-defense."

"He did."

"The write up you gave me says the men he put in the hospital were both armed."

"And licensed."

"Hm." Nate resolved not to reach an unwarranted conclusion. "I'd like to talk to him."

"Of course," Randy said. "His contact

information is in the file. I imagine his attorney would like to see you, too."

"How well do you know the guy?"

"I've met him in person once, but we talked on the phone many times. He always seemed like a reasonable man despite his occasional cornpone accent." She shook her head. "I've spent my share of time in the south. Enough to know a phony accent when I hear it."

"So, you think he's a fraud?"

"I think he wants people to believe he's less sharp than he is. It gives him a tactical advantage with business adversaries if they continually underestimate him. But I assure you, if he wasn't capable of doing his job, Mr. Archer never would have kept on hiring him. We don't care if he gives orders in pig Latin or refuses to bathe until a project is finished. We don't care if he only hires left-handed transvestites to get it done. If the finished development meets specifications, gets done on time and with no bad publicity, we'll be happy."

"So," Nate said, "the ends justify the means?"

"Don't overlook the 'no bad press' proviso."

He grinned. "Anything goes provided it does so under the radar."

Randy turned the golf cart toward Nate's villa. He didn't realize they'd come so close. "Have you ever seen what goes into a hot dog?" she asked.

"Can't say I have."

Josh Langston

"Trust me when I say you probably don't want to know. Business can be like that. Sometimes, the less you know the better off you are."

Nate nodded. "I suppose the same can be said for lots of things."

"Probably."

She pulled to a stop in front of his quarters, and he got out. "One last thing," he said. "I noticed on the artist's renderings and throughout the areas we just drove through, there are some cartoon characters I've never seen before. I haven't seen all the Puck movies, but between advertisements and what-not, I figure I've seen most of the major characters in 'em."

"Mr. Archer had them designed. They're an imaginative rendition of Menehune, Hawaii's version of leprechauns. They're also the official hosts and guardians of the resort. We even have some robotic versions planned for face-to-face interaction with guests."

"Menehune," Nate said, wrapping his tongue around the syllables.

"There should be a notebook in your villa with maps, schedules and general information about the resort. They're all prototypes, of course, and subject to change, but there should also be one in there that goes into the history of the Menehune. The legends are charming."

"I'm sure."

They parted ways and Nate walked to the

176

front door. He knocked once, and Tori yanked it open.

"I'm so glad you're back!" she said, panic in her eyes.

"What's the problem?"

"Mato's gone."

~*~

Kwan could not have been more pleased with the luau. It had opened eyes-- wide--and confirmed Paku's role as his nightmarish lieutenant. None of his associates would dare fail him now.

Paku drove him back toward his home, and though Kwan normally sat in the back seat, he rewarded his able assistant by riding next to him up front. "I didn't expect you to take a bite of the hand."

"It seemed like the right thing to do at the time," he said.

"It certainly got their attention." Kwan waited for Paku to add something, but the man remained silent. "I have to ask," Kwan said. "What did it taste like?"

Paku gave him a wolfish grin. "You really want to know?"

"Yes."

"It tasted like shit."

They both had a good laugh at that, then continued on to the estate without further conversation. As Kwan exited the car, he looked back at his man. "Make sure no one mentions the

Josh Langston

luau to anyone who wasn't there."

"Everyone will know you want it kept secret."

"Excellent. And what about our guest of honor, Mr. Cho?"

"He'll be cooked the rest of the way, as you wished. I sent two men to handle it at the mortuary you selected."

"Bring me the ashes," Kwan said. "I want to flush them down a toilet."

"As you wish. Is there anything else?"

Kwan had been thinking of how best to follow up his triumph over Bannock. "You have served me well, Paku. Several of the people you contacted have decided to stop working for the disgraced manager of the resort project. I want you to take his place. You'll be in charge of everything. I know your experience in construction is limited, but you are a great motivator, and I believe all you need is a schedule and a list of the people responsible for the tasks on it. I trust you can convince them to work quickly and efficiently."

Paku smiled again. "I can do that."

"I know. Archer will have no choice but to put the project in our hands. I'll arrange a meeting with him to confirm it."

Saying that, however, didn't make him feel as good as it should have. He wanted more, and suddenly he realized he'd been going about things all wrong. Why be content with the scraps Archer might give him for building the resort

178

when the real money would come from the resort itself. Over time, he'd earn vastly greater sums from the hordes of tourists sure to flock to the place once the word got out. And if the project was as spectacular as Archer claimed, it wouldn't even need to be a part of the Puck empire to generate phenomenal cash flows.

At last Kwan could smile. He knew what he really wanted--he wanted it all.

~*~

Mato tried not to remain angry, even though his supposed friends had done something to him to make him sleep. He remembered riding in their car and then-- nothing. No dreams--nothing--until he woke up in a strange building with Nate. It had taken him some time to regain his senses. His brain felt as if it were wrapped in fur. Eventually, however, he began to feel normal.

Nate tried to explain where they were but it made no sense to him. How could they be so far from home? And how could they be on an island? When he looked through the windows, he could see only nearby mountains and some construction. Piles of materials and great hulking machines sat everywhere. Yet, he saw no one working. It all seemed to have been arranged to look like a busy place when, in fact, very little went on.

"Tori will be here soon," Nate had told him, and then some other female giant would arrive, too. Mato was supposed to hide from her. He knew Nate only meant to protect him, but the day would come when he could no longer hide. If he intended to live in the giant's world, he had to make his peace with it. And more importantly, the giants would have to make their peace with him.

"What is this place called?" he asked.

"Kauai, Hawaii," Nate said.

Mato repeated the words, which while new, did not feel as uncomfortable as so many others the giants used. "How long we stay in Kauai, Hawaii?"

"Just Kauai," Nate said. "Hawaii is the bigger place. There are several islands, not just this one."

"I see mountains, not water. Island have much water. All around."

"It's a big island. You'll see more of it tomorrow with Tori, Maggie and Cal."

Mato had waited patiently for them to arrive, and during that time Nate did not stop talking. He talked as much as Reyna had, and Mato ignored him as he had ignored Reyna.

Yet, thoughts of Reyna saddened him. Despite her constant chatter, the rules she tried to impose on him, and the boredom of life with The People, he missed her. He missed sleeping beside her, and he missed their lovemaking.

When Nate left with the red-haired female giant, Mato spent some time with Tori, Maggie and Cal. They explored the building, which Mato had already done, and chatted among themselves as if he weren't with them. Tori paused once to ask him if he wished to eat, but the last time he'd done that she'd given him something to make him sleep. It wasn't magic, for Winter Woman, too, had ways of making someone sleep. Nevertheless, he didn't think it right or proper for her to do that to him without telling him first.

He could get his own food, he decided, and so while Tori and the others talked and talked-- giants could talk for hours without doing anything else--he unwrapped his bow and arrows and went out.

The building he'd left behind had been quite cool, and it felt good to be outside in warmer air. He took a moment to look around, but his view was badly obscured by buildings and machines, so Mato climbed to the roof of the building he'd just vacated. From there he could easily see the surrounding mountains. There were two breaks-- one led to a great body of water, the other to what appeared to be forest. He had no difficulty choosing a destination.

As he walked toward the forest, he guessed at the functions of various machines he passed. Some seemed obvious--digging machines and machines for pushing earth for instance--others mystified him. He would ask Nate. Nate knew everything. It explained his incessant talking. All that knowledge kept trying to escape. Mato vowed not to let it fill him up, too.

The end of the construction area turned into the beginning of a wasteland. Everything in it had

181

been knocked down. The larger trees and boulders had been cleared away leaving only weeds, sticks, and rubble.

Mato searched for small animal tracks, but found none. He continued into the forest, stopping first to get his bearings so that he could find his way back. He wished he had brought Shadow with him, but it was too late to return for him. No doubt, the giants would want him to stay. They tended to be fearful of moving about at night. For all their cleverness and their machines- -*not magic* he reminded himself again--giants were generally superstitious, predictable and easily frightened.

Mato straightened with pride. He was none of those things. No one questioned his bravery or his cunning. He was Black Otter, and he could go anywhere he wished to go. He needed no one's permission, whether they were man-sized or giant.

The forest he entered was unlike any he'd ever seen. The trees and bushes, while dense, held none of the usual leaves. Many had flowers. This, too, seemed odd. The different fragrances baffled him, too. He wondered if he might have been confused about more than just flowers. Perhaps he was confused about being awake. Maybe he had dreamed everything!

He poked himself with the tip of an arrow to assure himself he was awake and in control. He welcomed the slight sting from it as he welcomed his freedom. In time he would learn the smells of this forest. He would understand the animals it housed, and he would become its master.

Instinct, and senses tuned to the vagaries of nature, forced him to an abrupt halt. Something moved nearby. Mato dropped silently to the ground, tense and alert. As he listened for telltale sounds and smelled the air for the scent of danger, he also surveyed the nearest trees to see which might offer protection from a predator.

And then he saw something at the edge of his field of vision. It had moved quickly and without making the slightest sound, disappearing as fast as it had appeared. He hadn't seen enough to identify it, or even to know if he should run.

Mato did not like running away.

Unless he absolutely had to.

~*~

Chapter 10

What you see isn't always what you get,
and what you get isn't always what you deserve.

The first class passenger who deplaned from Lufthansa's non-stop flight to Los Angeles bore little resemblance to the man who boarded in Munich. His hair had changed from a closely cut blond to a full brunette that fell over his collar, and his complexion had darkened considerably from its original Teutonic white. His clothing had also undergone a dramatic change: the drab solids worn by the former flight school student had been exchanged for a colorful Hawaiian shirt, flashy Bermuda shorts, and sandals. The image screamed "tourist," and no one paid him any attention.

The name on the U.S. passport he presented to customs on his arrival said "Lewis Cass, Jr." He thought the suffix provided a nice touch, and he'd insisted on it over objections of the counterfeiter who produced the document. Indeed, he'd obtained all the "Cass" paperwork for free since he'd garroted the forger and disposed of his body in a New Jersey landfill.

Pushing a pair of newly purchased sunglasses to the top of his head, Lewis "Lew" Cass, Jr. strode confidently into the Delta Air Lines Sky Club lounge where he would pass the time before boarding. First Class certainly did have its privileges, and after everything he'd suffered through at the Zeppelin flight school, he felt justified in any pampering the airline would provide.

After his second Scotch--neat, no ice--he flagged down the hostess, an attractive young woman of Asian descent.

She gave him a broad smile. "Yes sir? Can I get you something?"

He tried to appear slightly timid, though it was an unaccustomed role. "Is there any chance you can tell me if the seat next to mine will be occupied?"

She shook her head and apologized. "I wish I could, but I don't have access to the flight manifest."

"I don't suppose there's any chance the seat will be empty."

Again, she shook her head. "First class almost never goes out empty, sir. Folks are eager to purchase upgrades, and if they don't, there is usually a standby passenger who will qualify for the seat."

"I had hoped to sleep during the flight," he said, "but I always seem to attract the sort of people who like to chat."

She nodded in sympathy. "In that case, you should ask the flight attendant for eyeshades, a pillow, and a blanket. Curl up and go to sleep, and if you can't sleep, just pretend. You're not required to talk to anyone, you know."

"That's true. I just hate to be rude." *And the authorities hate it when I shoot people to keep them from being annoying.*

"About the only recourse you have is to pay for the open seat. Even then, someone is liable to make a fuss over it. I'm sorry. I wish there were some other way around it."

"I'm sure I'll survive," he said, though he wouldn't have given the same assurances about anyone overly talkative who might be seated beside him.

~*~

"I knew this would happen," Tori said. "The minute we turned our backs on him, Mato took off."

"Did he say anything before he left?" Nate asked.

"Like what, 'Adios?' No."

Nate winced. *Prob'ly not the right question, podnuh.*

Tori sat at one end of an over-sized sofa. Maggie patted her shoulder. "Nobody could guess he'd leave. I don't know him as well as the rest of you, but he seemed out of sorts. Not angry, exactly, but--"

"He was pissed off," Cal said. "Knockin' him out may have made life easier for us, but he didn't like it at all. Probably scared the little fella."

"Nothing scares him," Tori said. "Trust me. He's tough. Tiny, but tough."

"Maybe in his own backyard," Nate said. "But out here? I'm not so sure. It's hard to be one with nature when you've never experienced the nature."

"He'll be fine," Maggie said. "He's smart, and resourceful. And he'll be back. Where else does he have to go?"

"We should do something," Tori said. "Look for him, at least."

"Why not let Shadow try and find him," Cal said.

Nate didn't know the dog well enough to say if that might work. He deferred to Tori. "You think he might track our little friend?"

She shrugged. "I have no idea, but it's worth a try."

"Then let's saddle up," Cal said. "Let the pooch do his thing. We don't need to sit around jawin' all night anyhow. Mags? You see my boots anywhere?"

Tori grabbed the leash, and Nate hooked it to the dog's collar.

"Let's go," Maggie said and led the way outside into the dark, expansive construction zone.

"Hang on," Nate said. "I'll be right back." He ran inside and rummaged through his suitcase until he found his service flashlight. His gun and holster lay right beside it. He brought them along, too.

~*~

Bannock and Ivan returned to the construction manager's recently acquired quarters. Neither man spoke much, and Ivan still looked pale.

"We've got to report this to the police," Joe said.

Ivan held up his hands. "Not my job, man."

"Right."

"Jes don' call from here, and don' give your name."

"Hello, police?" Joe said, pretending to hold a phone to his head. "Some poor shmuck got himself grilled on the beach. Medium rare. I thought you should know."

Ivan shook his head. "Gotta tell 'em *which* beach, brah. Dey too many."

"How the hell am I supposed to know which beach it was?"

"Dat's why you pay me," the big man said. "Anyway, bones on da beach be bad. *Ujee.*"

"Don't you mean disgusting?"

"Whut I just said, brah."

"C'mon. Let's go."

Bannock had rented a car, and the two reversed course to go back to it. Ivan had volunteered his own vehicle if Bannock covered the cost of a "few minor repairs." Joe declined despite Ivan's protests that the car was a classic and truly *nokaoi*, whatever the hell that meant. He did, however, let Ivan steer him to a local rent-a-car dealer rather than one of the chains which regularly fleeced the tourists.

The cell phone in Bannock's pocket chirped, and he stopped to answer it.

"Joe? It's me, Shaniqua. Where you at?"

"My apartment. We were just about to go out."

"You've *been* out, Kemosabe. I called your place like a million times. And who said you could turn off your damned cell phone?"

"Had to. We've sorta been under cover, trying to keep an eye on Kwan. He--"

"You stay away from that crazy son of a bitch, y'hear?"

Bannock imagined the gigantic woman in her purple and gold toga, or dashiki, or whatever it was. She'd be waving her arms and making one grand gesture after another. "Listen," he said, "this isn't a real good time."

"You're outta jail, bubba. That oughta count for something."

"It does! Absolutely. Thing is, Ivan and I need to check something out."

"You deaf, son? I said don't mess with Kwan. You'll be stepping in a massive pile of bad juju. You got enough trouble already."

"We've gotta do this. You won't believe what we just saw."

Shaniqua groaned. "Please tell me you saw it on TV."

"It was on a beach."

"Maluhia Beach," added Ivan over the top of

the car.

"Go on," she said.

"Kwan had a luau, and--"

"Don't tell me you ate with him!"

"Of course not. Lemme finish. The main dish at this shindig was a man. Kwan had the poor bastard cooked."

"Like kalua pig," Ivan said. Bannock waved him off.

"Kwan had someone *barbequed*?"

"Yes."

"You can prove this? You've got pictures?"

Bannock clenched his jaws. "No. But--"

"Then stay the hell away from him. Puck's hired an investigator--a pro. Let him look into it."

"But--"

"Damnit, Bannock! Why won't you listen to me? God knows you pay me enough for my advice. Why waste the money?"

"We can do this, brah," Ivan said. "Don' lissen to her."

"Joe? You tell that big knucklehead to shut up, or I'll rip his boto off and beat him with it."

Bannock put his hand over the phone and looked at Ivan. "Shaniqua's worried you might get hurt. I think she likes you." Then he uncovered the phone and spoke into it. "All right. We'll back off. Who's this security guy, and how do I get in touch with him?"

"We both need to talk to him," she said. "I'll set it up for tomorrow and let you know when and where we'll meet. Okay?"

"Yeah."

"Stay home. You hear me?"

"Okay."

"I'm serious," she said. "It's too damn hot on this island for me anyway, so I'm down with putting my happy ass on a jet back home. And that's exactly what I'll do if you keep ignoring my advice. Got it?"

"Got it."

Click.

"What now, brah?" Ivan asked.

"We try to find out what Kwan did with the body."

~*~

Daphne recalled her hikes in the Big Horn mountains with park ranger Maggie Scott. Two things stood out clearly: Maggie was in vastly better shape for hiking, and the mountains got damned cold at night, even in the summer. She doubted either of those things had changed.

Rather than drive all the way home and back, she dipped into her limited savings and bought toiletries and other necessities. She also splurged on a pair of good hiking boots and appropriate clothing to keep her cool in the daytime and warm at night, just in case. Even though Simon insisted they limit their preliminary efforts to day hikes, she aimed to be prepared.

They made the drive in Simon's car, which had four-wheel drive. He wanted only to survey the terrain and, if possible, locate the spot where the attack on the prospector had taken place. He made it clear he had no desire to go camping there.

"What if we find something?" she asked.

"Like what?"

"I dunno. Artifacts or something."

"You have no idea what you're talking about, do you?"

She conceded the point on technical grounds.

"For now," he said, "we're just looking for garbage--cast off materials from your hypothetical tribe of pygmy pygmies."

"And if we find some?"

"I'll make a note of the GPS coordinates so we can find it again later."

"This is gonna be fun!"

"Oh, yeah," he said. "Loads."

They drove in as far as they could. Daphne had worked out their first destination based on a few hints gleaned from a contact she had in the sheriff's office. Though merely a dispatcher, he had ambitions, and she had no qualms about using them to ferret out a detail or too. In this case she found out where the detective and crime scene techs had entered the park.

It was a good start, and they only followed three false trails before they found one the investigators used. They hiked in on it, a seemingly all uphill, until Daphne figured they had reached the Arctic Circle, or Saskatchewan, whichever came first.

"Is this the place?" Simon asked.

"Could be. I expected to find crime scene tape. You know, that yellow stuff."

"They probably weren't too worried about random visitors contaminating the site."

"Or maybe they finished already and took it all down. Doesn't matter. I'm pretty sure we're close. The prospectors said they were working in a ravine." She pointed to the nearest one. "Let's start there."

Simon agreed, and they worked their way up the hill from the creek into which the channel emptied.

"It might be helpful if you told me what to look for," Daphne said.

"Anything that doesn't belong."

"Like what?"

"Signs of human activity: tool marks, arrowheads, dead bodies."

Daphne stared at him in surprise.

"Just kidding. I'm only interested in *sincerely old* dead bodies--bones."

"Your sense of humor needs work."

When they reached the top of the ravine they took a break. Daphne expected the dapper young professor to break out champagne and strawberries. Instead, he found a spot in the sun and stretched out on the ground.

"What? No picnic stuff?"

"Too heavy. I'm content to carry a canteen, a

camera and digging tools. What did you bring?"

"A notebook and my personality."

"You're going to get thirsty."

"But you brought water!"

He took a swig. "Yep, and it's good, too."

"May I have a sip?"

"I guess. If you think you've earned it."

She frowned, and before responding took a moment to look around. They had come a good distance uphill, or more accurately, up-mountain, and had seen many patches of late snow on the ground, especially in the shadows of trees.

"I could always eat snow," she said.

"True. Mind the yellow-tinted variety."

She walked away with an audible huff and headed toward the nearest patch of white. That's when she spotted tracks.

"Don't see any yellow snow, but I've found some dog tracks."

He sat up and looked at her. "Probably wolf tracks. Suddenly I'm not keen on hanging around here."

"Well, I'll be damned," Daphne said. She knelt closer to the snow. Melting and refreezing had left it hard and smooth.

"What is it?" He asked.

"There are some other tracks, too."

"What kind?"

"I dunno. You tell me."

Simon got up and approached, then knelt beside her and took a hard look at the dual sets of marks. "These have to be from a wolf or an extremely large dog," he said, pointing to the first set. "Whatever made the others is two-legged. I'd guess some kind of bird."

"Why not a small person?"

"They're just holes in the snow," he said. "They're not distinct enough to say more. I'm guessing bird tracks. "

"But wouldn't bird tracks be wider? The ones I've seen always had three toes. Well, four actually--three in front and one in the back. These tracks look like they were made by very small shoes. Maybe very small *moccasins*."

Simon crossed his arms and shook his head. "Doesn't seem likely. They could've been made by almost anything."

She gave him her don't-be-an-asshole look. "Aside from birds, name some other kinds of two-legged critters roaming around out here."

~*~

Mato nocked an arrow. He didn't think the animal in the bushes had smelled him, but that wouldn't last much longer. The wind favored his suddenly discovered quarry. He moved quietly, hoping to catch a glimpse of whatever had been watching him. His senses keenly attuned, he strained for signs in the dark woods. *Something* had sensed him, he wished to return the favor. Provided, of course, it didn't eat him.

The snap of a twig or the rustle of leaves in an otherwise windless area was all he needed. A sound, a smell, movement--he'd welcome anything that offered a hint about which of them was in danger. Animals, though better equipped to move quietly and smell at a distance, lacked his profound patience. Like them, he could stop all movement, save for the beat of his heart. Unlike them, however, he could hold such a pose for hours, if necessary, and all the while his eyes, ears and nose would be alert for anything out of the ordinary.

This time, however, his adversary seemed to have similar talents. Indeed, if Mato hadn't detected a bit of odd motion earlier, he'd be tempted to shrug it off and go on about his business. But the woods told a different story. It remained unnaturally quiet, something that rarely occurred without the presence of a human.

He refused to believe the giants in this new place could move around with any more stealth than those he encountered elsewhere. For a giant, Nate had great skill, but even at his best, Mato could track him as easily as Nate could track a bear in Tori's cabin.

Whatever shared the thick cover with him also shared his skills. The game of waiting had begun. Whoever made the first sound would lose. Mato dropped to a comfortable squat and settled in, content to stay immobile until he saw, smelled, heard, or felt more.

It took time, but eventually the natural sounds of the forest returned. At least, he assumed them to be natural, for he had no expertise in these woods. *That*, he promised himself, would change.

Though the forest floor remained dark, a few breaks in the trees allowed a bit of moonlight to penetrate. A clear sky and abundant stars helped. At last he saw movement once again, but not in any fashion he'd anticipated.

The creature was small and moved in a fitful manner, pausing often to turn its head this way and that. It even made noise. But how could such a silly thing have kept him on edge for so long? And what was it doing in the forest? He knew precisely what it was, and more importantly, he knew how it would *taste*.

Mato pulled back the string of his bow and took careful aim. He wouldn't get a second shot. He let the bowstring slip from his fingers as he had done countless times before. The arrow tore through the light underbrush and knocked his prey to the ground with a squawk, a thud, and a puff of feathers.

Hurrying after the arrow, Mato quickly came upon his prize, though it turned out to be a rooster rather than a hen. After thanking the spirit of the dead bird for its sacrifice on his behalf, he dressed the carcass and left the entrails on the ground.

With any luck, Tori would still be awake. She could cook the bird for him while he played with the machines in the house where they would all be staying. The giants used two main devices for entertainment. One produced music while the other provided pictures *and* sound. The People hadn't believed him when he tried to describe them. Fortunately, Reyna had chimed in that she'd seen them, too, but she had never grasped the difference between magic and what, for the giants, were merely toys.

Thoughts of Reyna saddened him. She may have become crazy, but he still missed her. To dislodge her from his mind, he focused on the amazing rooster. Had it truly been stalking him? Why wasn't it in a cage where a giant could easily catch and kill it? He'd never seen a chicken before he ventured into the giant's world. *Perhaps this island is where they came from!* It made sense. And if such stupid birds could wander around freely, there must not be many predators to harvest them.

On the other hand, perhaps he had already encountered the predator, one whose skills *exceeded* his own.

Nonsense, he thought. *No one has skills like mine!*

The rooster proved heavier than he thought. Dragging the bird through the forest was likewise turning out to be more difficult than anticipated. Fortunately, he hadn't traveled too far from the giant's construction area, and with the presence of so much hard cement, the opportunities for the bird to get tangled in scrub diminished to nothing.

He saw a beam of light not far ahead and scrambled for a place to hide. A stack of paint cans provided a reasonable spot, and he crammed the rooster into the shadows before joining it.

Voices came soon after, and he had no trouble recognizing them. Tori and Nate had come looking for him. As well they should, he thought. It was their fault he'd been dragged so far from home. He tried to remain angry with them, but concluded that they'd actually given him an opportunity to see a new place and hunt new animals--*chicken isle!* A descriptive name if not melodic.

"Mato here!" he called out when they drew close.

Tori hurried to him and picked him up. Mato hung on to the rooster, and Tori screamed when she saw it. She let go of Mato *and* the bird. They hit the ground at the same time.

"It's just a chicken," Nate said. "No need to freak out."

"It startled me, that's all," she responded, then to Mato, "Where'd you get it?"

He brandished his bow and said, "Woods." Then pointed back the way he'd come.

"They're all over the islands," Maggie said. "Feral hens and pigs are a real problem here, or so I've read. The pigs are especially nasty. We're lucky in Wyoming. I haven't seen any signs of wild hogs, but other states have been deluged."

"Eat now," Mato said, lifting the rooster off the ground with both hands.

Tori chuckled. "Don't you want to cook it first?"

"You cook," he said, extending the bird in her direction.

"I'll take it," Cal said. "It won't be the first one I've plucked."

Mato didn't take his eyes from Tori.

"You're serious," she said.

"Mato hungry."

"That's not the word I'd have chosen."

Mato ignored her. He couldn't get over the thought that something had gotten the better of him in the forest. And whatever had accomplished that feat certainly wasn't a rooster or a pig.

~*~

Bannock and Ivan drove back to Maluhia Beach, hoping to find something that would tell them what happened to the dead man's body.

"We shoulda stayed until we saw dem move it," Ivan said.

Joe nodded. "My mistake. But there's nothing we can do about it now. We just need to check out the area in case they left something behind."

"Like da body?"

"Maybe. They might have tried to burn it down to ash right here," Bannock said. "If so, there'd be something left of it. A piece of bone, at least."

"Den what?"

"We'd get the cops to investigate." He kicked at one of the many beer cans abandoned on the sand. "If we call 'em now, the only thing they could charge Kwan with is littering."

A voice from the tree line behind them broke the calm. "Move and we shoot!"

Despite the warning, both men turned in the direction of the voice.

Boom!

A single gunshot convinced them to mimic statues.

"I said *don't* move!"

"Okay!" Bannock yelled, though the shooter's command was confusing. In any case, his own voice sounded like a scream.

"Chill," whispered Ivan.

Bannock glared at him and whispered back, "You're a bigger target than I am, buckaroo."

They watched as two men approached from the darkness. Both held flashlights, so Bannock couldn't make out any details.

"Dey need get close," Ivan said, his voice low enough to blend with the sound of the surf.

"Why?"

"So I can reach 'em."

"Wha--"

"Shhh!"

"Who are you, and what're you doin' here?" The speaker and his partner remained indistinct behind the bright lights.

Josh Langston

Bannock smelled burnt gunpowder, but he hardly needed a reminder about who was armed. "Who wants to know?" he asked. "This is a public beach."

"The access isn't. It's private, and it's the only way in. We saw your car, asswipe. You're trespassing."

"Sorry," Bannock said. "I didn't realize that was a hangin' offense."

"Shut up." The gunman nudged his partner. "Check 'em out."

The second thug stepped behind Bannock and patted him down then shifted sideways to do the same to Ivan.

"Careful, brah," Ivan said. "I'm ticklish."

"Fuck off," the man grunted back.

"Now," continued the first gunman, "what are you really doing here?"

He hadn't quite finished the question when Ivan twisted around and grabbed the second gunman. Moving with astonishing speed, he hauled the man off his feet and into the space between himself and the first gunman.

Boom!

Bannock grabbed the gunman's arm with both hands and pushed him away from Ivan. He meant to drag him to the sand but only managed to end up there alone, looking toward the stars.

He watched as Ivan tossed the second man into the first. The shooter got off another round which did nothing to stop the landing of his

202

airborne accomplice who did what Bannock had failed to do: knock the gunman down.

Ivan pounced on top of both men, but only the one on the bottom made a sound--like a badly built whoopee cushion.

"I can't breathe," he wheezed.

"Sucks for you," Ivan said. "You could die."

"Please!"

"Where's da gun, brah?"

"It's-- Between me and-- and him. And oh, shit. He's bleedin'--bad."

"Dats 'cause you shot him, dumb ass. Twice."

"Get-- off-- me. I--" The shooter went silent.

Bannock crawled to the compressed punks. "Geez, Ivan. You squished him to death."

"Nah. He jes' pass out. Seen it befo'." He chuckled. "When I roll off, you get da gun."

Bannock did as instructed. As soon as the weight came off, the man on the bottom took in a great shuddering breath. By the time he came fully awake, Joe had the gun, and Ivan had inspected the second thug.

"You sure he's dead?" Bannock asked.

"Plenny sure. He took two inna chest."

The surviving gunman let out a groan.

"You should be happy," Joe told him. "You're still alive."

"For now," he grumbled. "Mr. Kwan--"

"Go on," Joe said.

"Nuthin'."

Ivan poked him. "He gonna fry your ass, too?"

Joe stared into the man's eyes. "Were you at Kwan's party?"

"Whut party?"

"Lemme sit on 'im," Ivan said, shifting his bulk toward the downed man. "He talk."

Bannock waved him back. "Don't bother. I've got a better idea."

~*~

Reyna was nursing her baby when the elder bearing Winter Woman's summons arrived. The elder insisted Reyna come immediately. She knew better than to ignore her grandmother, and so with her child still at her breast, she went.

When she reached the council space Winter Woman claimed, the other elders had already gathered. It wouldn't have taken long. The clan spent the winter in a warren of caves and tunnels dug out and expanded by uncounted generations of The People. Torches supplemented the limited light from concealed openings in the ceiling.

"Come," Winter Woman said, patting a deerskin covering the cave floor. "Sit."

A hard-featured brave leaned back against a cavern wall, his face unreadable. The People called him Stone Fist, and he had once been Mato's rival for her favors.

Reyna leaned toward Winter Woman. "What is this about?"

The old woman nodded at the hunter. "Tell her."

"The giants have returned," he said. "They

are in the high meadow."

"What are they doing?" Reyna asked.

Keeping his eyes on Winter Woman, he merely shrugged.

Another elder chimed in, "How many are there?"

He held up two fingers.

"Were they hunting?" Winter Woman asked.

"Could be," he said. "They were looking at tracks in the snow."

"Whose?" asked the elder.

"It had to be Black Otter and the dog," he said. "No one else would walk so close to such a beast."

Reyna shifted the baby to her shoulder and burped him. Winter Woman waited until she finished. "You must go with Stone Fist," she said.

"Why?"

"Because no one else knows the language of the giants."

"Neither do I!" she protested. "Besides, who will take care of my son?"

"I will," Winter Woman said. She held out her arms to receive the child.

"But--"

"Now!"

Reyna reluctantly surrendered her baby.

"Go," Winter Woman said. "Learn what you can. Do not let them see you."

Stone Fist stepped forward to take her hand. "And don't step in any snow!"

~*~

Chapter 11

You can either cowboy up,
or lie there and bleed. It's your choice.

Nate turned the kitchen in their resort unit over to Tori and Maggie who declared it astoundingly well-equipped. They even found a couple culinary gadgets which baffled them. Neither appeared to be potentially useful as weapons, so Tori made no effort to hide them from Mato.

"That thing there is a pineapple corer," Caleb said. "It'll slice 'em, too."

"Is that based on your vast knowledge of Polynesian fruit and veggies?" Maggie asked.

"I've had a cooking magazine or two in the store," he said crossing his arms defensively. "I may have ordered 'em by mistake, but that didn't mean I couldn't read 'em." He cleared his throat. "I'm not a complete Palestine."

"Or a philistine, either," Maggie said.

Tori shook her head and shoveled an embarrassment of scrambled eggs onto five plates, and a bowl for the dog. Maggie followed that with bacon and biscuits. The coffee pot was already on the table.

"I would've done cheese grits," Tori said, "but whoever stocked this place didn't include any."

"That's just awful," Nate said, contorting his

face like a four-year-old contemplating escargot. "I can't imagine a breakfast without grits."

"Him," Cal said, stabbing his thumb in Nate's direction. "He's the philistine."

"On the other hand," Tori said, "there's a lifetime supply of Spam."

"That's like what, one can?" Nate asked.

"All comments are welcome, gentlemen," Maggie said, "especially since you're fixin' breakfast tomorrow. We'll likely be too tired to do much around here."

Cal frowned. "Why's that?"

"'Cause we've got a wedding to plan," Tori said. "Oh, Nate? How do we get outta here? We've got lots of shopping to do, among other things."

"Yeah," Maggie said, "We've got Puck bucks left over!"

Cal appeared crestfallen.

"What's the problem?" Maggie asked.

"There's a dandy beach out there. Don't you wanna go for a swim? I wouldn't mind gettin' a look at you in your new bikini."

"Who said I bought a bikini?"

"Oh, well, actually-- I think Mato was lookin' at it."

Mato had been ignoring them all morning, concentrating on the food they'd provided instead. He consumed it with a passion--and an occasional grunt.

"Is nothing sacred anymore?"

"Prob'ly not to Mato, if it comes in a fancy

bag," Nate said. "But, I do like the beach idea. We'd have the whole thing to ourselves. The construction workers won't be using it."

Tori looked at her fiancé with a coquettish smile. "I still need to find something to wear on the beach." She flushed a bit. "You know, other than a smile and half a canary's worth of feathers."

"Just don't go overboard," he said. "I like that fluffy stuff." He would have said more, but his cell phone rang. Randy Rhoades' name showed on the screen.

"S'cuse me," he said and left the table to answer it.

"Nate," Randy said, "I've got something else for you to work on, in addition to what we discussed last night. It seems someone's been in contact with several of Bannock's remaining staff--not just the top people."

"And?"

Randy sounded far more tense than he'd ever heard her. "They're bailing out. But only a couple admitted that either they or their families had been threatened unless they quit and went back to the mainland."

Nate stepped outside his luxury resort unit and looked across the construction site where activity appeared minimal. "Who's behind it?"

"I'd guess Daniel Kwan," she said. "Though I can't prove it. As far as I know, his name hasn't come up in any of the threats."

"Why's he trying to sabotage the project? What's in it for him?"

"My guess is he wants to secure jobs for his people. I don't know how he does it, but he's got his hooks into just about everything--the law, the courts, the unions. Lord knows who else."

"I presume you want me to figure out what he's up to and why?"

"Yes."

Nate looked out on the vast project area with all its pools, canals, underground facilities and mountain facade accommodations. The transportation center and administrative offices were housed in a separate mountain, the top of which appeared in the distance. Based on his conversations with Randy and the plans she'd given him, only about half of the complex would be visible to guests. Puck planned to put the rest underground or camouflage it so heavily no one would know it existed. The result would truly resemble a paradise. "All by my lonesome?"

"We have security guards who can keep an eye on construction. You need to concentrate on Kwan."

"And if it's not him?"

"It's him. You've got to prove it."

"I'll do my best," Nate said, wondering where to start.

"Mr. Archer wants regular reports."

"How regular?"

"Daily."

"Swell. I'll type 'em up in my spare time."

~*~

"There's going to be a change in plans," Kwan announced to Paku the next morning.

"You no longer wish me to manage the resort project?" Paku asked. Nothing in his words or demeanor betrayed the slightest emotion. He would have looked the same asking if Kwan wanted jelly with his toast.

"What I'm planning won't be easy," Kwan said, "but it should be immensely profitable. I want Archer to complete his project, but I want the cost to be so high that his board of directors will lose confidence in him. If he ever opens the place, it needs to lose money from the very first day. I want him to curse himself for ever thinking he could make it work."

"You hate him that much?" Paku asked.

"I don't care about him at all! I just want his resort, and I want him to sell it to me cheap, but only after he gets it up and running. That means things will have to go terribly wrong at every turn."

Paku nodded, and Kwan imagined what could be going through the man's mind. "We can't harm tourists," Kwan cautioned. "We'll want them to keep coming once Puck Productions abandons it."

"Would it even work without their cartoon characters running around?"

"We'll create our own! We don't need Puck. Besides, they've already invented new characters of their own based on the Menehune."

"Menehune?"

"Little people of the islands. You're not Hawaiian, are you?"

"No."

"Doesn't matter. I just need you to make life miserable for anyone working on the resort. We need to slow them down, make them do things twice, three times maybe. Costs must go up, and productivity must go down."

"Bleed them but not kill them," Paku said.

"Exactly."

As Paku cleaned away Kwan's breakfast dishes, he said, "There's something you need to be aware of."

"What?"

"Two of our men were found by the police on Maluhia Beach. One was dead, and the other was tied to a palm tree."

Kwan realized he was grinding his teeth and made a conscious effort to stop. "Who did it?"

"It appears one shot the other."

"And after calling the police, he tied *himself* to a tree? There had to be someone else involved."

"That's all I know, sir. Our contact at KPD didn't have any more details."

"Then get them," Kwan growled. The mere thought that someone dared to come after him made his blood pressure spike. *Whoever you are, you'll regret it.*

~*~

Mato watched as the giants finished breakfast and prepared to go their separate ways. No one asked him if he wished to accompany them, which was fine with him since he had already made plans of his own.

Nate arranged transportation for the two women who wouldn't be back until later in the day. They seemed oddly excited and left without saying a word to him.

Caleb offered to assist Nate, but he declined. "Why not go to the beach? It's about the only place that isn't under construction."

They talked about palm trees, hammocks, and drink coolers--things which meant nothing to Mato, but all of which were supposedly available if Caleb needed them. Mato had seen the sand and the shore. He was convinced both were clearly meant for giants. Many of the waves were taller than he was, and his swimming skills were limited at best. The water extended far beyond the horizon and doubtless played host to fish who could eat him in a single bite.

The ocean and the beach would have to get along without him. Besides, he couldn't wait to return to the forest, only this time he'd take Shadow with him.

Nate was the last of the giants to leave. "I need you to stay here and take care of the dog," he said.

"Dog sick?"

"No, he's fine. I want you to make sure he

stays that way."

Nate must have had too much of the giant's special drink. What did Tori call it? *Bourbon!* Dangerous stuff. It could make giants do stupid things. Like asking him to watch Shadow. Such a waste of time! He didn't bother to respond.

"I don't know when I'll be back. But we'll all have dinner together and figure out what we're doing tomorrow."

Mato didn't care what the giants planned to be doing today or tomorrow. He was already planning his own activities. This time, however, he wasn't going alone. He'd have Shadow. If he tired of walking in the jungle, he could always ride.

"So, you'll stay here? The TV works. I hope you like soap operas."

"Soap?"

"Never mind. Just stay here--out of trouble and out of sight. Don't go near any of the construction."

"Con-- stru..."

"Construction. Buildings and workers. Stay away, okay?"

Mato nodded agreement. He had no interest in what the giants were building. At least, not until they were done. Then he might look at them. But now? Now he had things to do.

"Good. I'll see you tonight," Nate said.

Mato doubted Nate would see him at all, unless he followed Mato into the jungle, and even then, Mato knew he could hide so well the giant would never find him.

Silly giants.

~*~

Daphne insisted that Simon take as many photos of the tracks in the snow as she did. He complied, but only because she promised to raise even more hell if he didn't. He grumbled the whole time, and when they finished he demanded they head for home. He claimed he'd accomplished enough for the day. She let that slide knowing full well she had to badger him into offering his "professional" opinion. She would have preferred that of a professional tracker. Unfortunately, she didn't know any.

She wanted to keep looking, but none of her arguments succeeded, and that felt doubly odd. She almost always won arguments with men. But then, she usually cheated, and he didn't appear interested in anything she might offer to sweeten the deal. Trading a bit of intimacy for a little more research time didn't violate her personal code of ethics. Unfortunately, he'd become obstinate. And abruptly chaste.

What made it even more annoying, she wasn't demanding "real" research. At least not to her way of thinking. And even if it was real, it didn't *feel* like it. It felt more like hunting--like they were on the trail of something. But Simon held his ground.

She had to make do with noting that the

tracks appeared to be heading down the mountain, which was good. Except that the ground was rocky and hard, and when the snow ran out, so did the tracks. Whatever--or whoever--made them could have turned in any direction, and they'd never be able to tell.

Daphne's choices were to give in and hike back down the mountain with Simon, or find a place in the wilderness to spend the night. Without a tent. Or anyone to protect her from the wolf Simon insisted had made the larger tracks.

Unwilling to spend the night in the company of wolves, she opted instead to spend it with an asshole. In addition to discovering the tracks in the snow, she found out that after a hard day in the field, Simon snored at night.

In the morning she changed tactics. She'd appeal to his managerial side, and for that they needed accomplices.

"Maybe now we should enlist the aid of your students. Those tracks will probably still be there. If we had a few more people out looking, maybe we could pick up the trail again, only farther up the mountain."

Simon acted as if he hadn't heard the suggestion. Instead, he loaded the photos he'd taken into his desktop computer and enlarged them to full screen. The result astonished him.

"I may have been a bit premature in my guess that the second set of tracks were made by a bird."

Cradling her breakfast coffee in both hands, Daphne fought the temptation to say, "I told you so."

"This may sound strange, but I think the tracks were left by a monkey."

She stared at him and suffered an extremely rare moment of speechlessness. Sarcasm eventually wormed its way from her hindbrain to her vocal cords. "Well, of course! Any particular species? Wait. I know! The Montana mountain monkey!"

"I'm serious."

"Ah. Then you must mean arctic banana monkeys. I hear they're awful this time of year, attacking tourists in swarms--completely unprovoked!"

"Hear me out," Simon said, his eyes aimed at the ceiling. "It makes sense."

"Okay. Enlighten me."

"The cops say they found fingerprints on the murder weapon, right?"

Daphne nodded.

"But they're too small to be made by an adult human."

"True."

"Why couldn't someone train a monkey to shoot a bow and arrow?"

She frowned. "I suppose they could. But why would they? I mean, who needs an armed monkey, other than the Wicked Witch of the West?"

216

"A murderer might."

"It'd be a lot easier to teach a child to use a bow."

Simon pushed back from the computer. "Probably, but a child that small wouldn't be as strong as a monkey."

Daphne's mind had already shifted into overdrive with story possibilities. She examined a number of them as she nursed her coffee. Eventually, she returned to the original topic. "This gives us even more reason to go back up there with a team of students."

He looked at her as if she'd sprouted fur and a prehensile tail. "Why?"

"To either prove or disprove your theory. And besides, we need some evidence that isn't frozen--something that won't melt."

"You're relentless."

She grinned. "My editor thinks so, too. He says it's cute."

Simon shook his head. "All right. I give in. We'll give it one more day, and this time I'll recruit a few kids looking for extra credit to help us."

"Great!" she said, pushing him out of the way and taking control of his computer keyboard.

"What are you doing?"

"Checking the internet. I want to be sure monkeys have fingerprints."

"Is that what you call research--cruising the internet?"

She turned away from the screen after a brief search, smiling. "How 'bout that? Monkeys *do* have fingerprints!"

~*~

Randy Rhoades introduced Bannock to Nate Sheffield. Bannock, in turn, introduced the former deputy sheriff to his attorney, Shaniqua Jackson. They filled all the available seats in Ms. Rhoades' office.

Bannock tried to read Sheffield, but he had difficulty getting past the man's cowboy hat. He doubted anyone not engaged in cattle ranching or rodeos would ever take him seriously. He nudged Shaniqua's arm and whispered, "Can you believe this guy?"

She squinted at him but kept her thoughts to herself.

Randy had spent a few minutes bringing everyone up to date on conditions at the construction complex. "People are quitting left and right. Someone is threatening them, but so far no one has been harmed. We think Daniel Kwan is behind it, but there's not a shred of evidence to back that up. I've asked Nate to look into it."

"Kwan is a sick, sick man," Bannock said. "I've seen what he's capable of." He told them what he'd seen at Kwan's so-called luau.

"That's disgusting," Nate said.

Randy turned even more pale than usual for a redhead.

"Unfortunately, we can't prove any of that,"

Shaniqua said. "It's all hearsay. And, since it's coming from someone accused of a major crime, no one's going to pay any attention to it, no matter how grotesque the alleged act is."

"I have it on good authority," Bannock continued, "that two of Kwan's henchmen were found on the very same beach where the luau occurred. One of them had killed the other."

Nate frowned. "And the killer didn't leave the area? That's odd."

"Someone tied him to a tree," Bannock replied.

"Who did that?" Randy asked.

Shaniqua glared at Bannock so hard he wondered if she could check his spine for alignment.

"Beats me," Bannock said.

Nate seemed to be peering at his spine, too.

"Hey, I'm just relating facts here."

"That best be all you doin'," Shaniqua said, her voice low.

"I hate to ask this, Joe," Randy said, "especially since you're no longer officially connected to the project, but it might be helpful if you spoke with some of the people you brought on board to see if they'll ignore the threats and continue working."

Though tempted to suggest she go pound sand, Bannock swallowed his pride and agreed. "After all, I intend to get my job back as soon as my name is cleared."

"Helping us in the interim would certainly be taken into consideration later," she said. "As for any further investigations, neither I nor anyone else from Puck Productions can be involved in anything that isn't directly linked to the resort."

"Understood," Bannock said.

Nate also nodded agreement.

She smiled at both of them. "Of course, what you choose to do on your own time is a different matter."

~*~

Careful to stay out of sight, Mato walked Shadow to the edge of the construction area. Fortunately, there were few workers on the job to spot them, and Shadow had learned to follow Mato's lead, especially while he maintained a firm grip on the dog's ear.

When they reached the open space separating the development from the jungle, Mato waited for the right moment and then raced Shadow across the open area to the thick foliage on the other side. Mato lost the race, but only by a step or two. Their entrance through the undergrowth and into the heavily shaded forest was quick but noisy.

"We must move quietly, my friend, if we wish to find out who lives in these woods before they discover we're looking for them."

Shadow paid rapt attention, as if he understood everything Mato said, then began noisily sniffing his way forward. Mato shook his head, resigned to having a companion with so little understanding of the need for stealth. If it weren't for the huge dog's unwavering loyalty and willingness to defend Mato and his loved ones at any cost, he would have been killed and eaten long ago by The People.

Mato let Shadow continue on his own but moved a reasonable distance away. This allowed Mato to proceed in relative silence. Hopefully, the noisy dog would draw the attention of whatever had been observing him when he ventured into the wild previously.

Though alert to any sight, sound or movement that might indicate they were not alone, Mato tried to absorb his new surroundings. Some of the plants seemed familiar, but most of them he'd never encountered before. The jungle teemed with animal life, and like the vegetation, most of it seemed strange and new. The sheer variety of new birds amazed him. Their colorful plumage and unusual songs kept him entertained for hours.

He stopped from time to time to make sure Shadow remained nearby. The dog seemed better at locating fresh water, and as the temperature rose during the day, frequent water breaks proved welcome.

During their foray, Shadow disturbed a handful of deer and several feral hogs. The excited pigs crashed through the underbrush to get away and made even more noise than the dog.

The farther they moved into the jungle, the more Mato felt sure he could reach out and touch anything they might encounter. Shadow, of course, guaranteed nothing stayed around long enough for him to find out.

They found an abundance of fruit growing in the wild, but the only one Mato recognized was the banana. He'd seen several in Tori's cabin. Here, however, they grew in massive bunches. Mato helped himself and gorged on them. Shadow, however, merely turned up his nose.

"I'll find something for you, too," he advised his four-legged companion. "But you must be patient. This land is full of food just waiting to be taken. You won't go hungry for long."

They rested beside a small stream for awhile, then continued their trek through the shaded woodland. Tall trees with thick, dense leaves made determining their direction difficult, but not impossible. Mato felt sure he could find his way back to Nate and Tori, but he was in no hurry to do so.

All during their trek, Mato expected to find some sign that they weren't alone. He had yet to meet a giant who could move quietly enough to surprise him, but he allowed that such a thing might possibly happen. Maybe. Perhaps once in his lifetime. Navigating in the wilderness felt natural to him. He could not imagine any giant feeling the same way, even Nate.

So it came as a complete shock when a knife

whizzed past his head and sank into the trunk of a tree behind him.

Mato dropped to the forest floor as if a trap door had opened beneath him. His first thoughts were about Shadow and whether or not the big dog had been hurt. He remained quiet, and Mato prayed he did so by choice.

Moving with practiced skill, he crept away from the base of the tree and tuned every sense to detect the slightest hint of another's presence. A dark tangle of wood and brush offered better cover, and he slithered toward it in complete silence. A snake would have envied his stealth.

Though he'd had only a moment to examine the blade which so narrowly missed him, he knew from its size a giant hadn't thrown it. But being made of metal meant the user dwelt in the giant's world. The People had made tools from metal discarded by giants, but the process of grinding and shaping took longer and was far more tedious than simply making something from bones, antlers or stone.

He didn't dwell on such thoughts then. Staying alive meant concentrating on unfolding events and seizing whatever advantage he could find. His adversary remained invisible, but he didn't move as quietly as Mato did. Subtle sounds let Mato know his stalker intended to flank him.

A low, menacing growl emanated from somewhere near his flanker and brought a smile to Mato's lips. Shadow was still in the game. Since

Mato had only detected the sounds of a single entity, he drew comfort knowing his enemy was now outnumbered. So Mato began his own approach.

Still moving soundlessly, he abandoned his cover and pulled himself up into a tree. The improved vantage point allowed him to see Shadow advancing like a cat, his nose and belly both touching the ground.

Mato strained to see through the heavy cover but eventually spotted his antagonist, and the sight sent a shock wave coursing through him. A member of his own tribe--another son of The People--was on his trail!

His mind reeled with the impossibility of what he saw, and it took a moment for him to collect himself.

"What do you want?" he called out.

Shadow's bark ripped through the dense, wet quiet of the jungle, but Mato's stalker said nothing.

"Speak up, now, or you'll sleep with the Spirits tonight."

When Shadow ignored his hand signals, as usual, Mato yelled at him to stay put. For once, the dog complied, but his continued growl made his unhappiness clear.

"Talk to me, or I'll let the dog eat you!" Mato yelled.

A high voice responded, and for a moment Mato worried that it came from a giant's child.

Perhaps one who had wandered alone into the wilderness. But then he remembered the knife which had whistled by his ear. Toddlers didn't throw knives that well.

"What did you say?" he demanded.

The words came through better the second time, and some of them even made sense, though the language used could not have come from anyone who grew up among The People.

"Who are you?" he asked.

"I am Makani."

Wind? His name means wind? What a stupid name! "What do you want?"

The response did him no good. Too many of the words sounded familiar but not quite right. Mato drew his bow, took aim, and let an arrow fly. It sank into the ground between Makani's feet, and he leaped backwards against a tree.

"Don't move," Mato said, a second arrow already nocked. He whistled for Shadow who bolted toward their quarry as if he'd been summoned to a meal. Mato climbed down from the tree with just one hand.

The warrior and the dog converged on a trembling boy holding a leather sling. Shadow barred his teeth at him, with profound effect. Young Makani appeared ready to cry.

~*~

"Lewis Cass, Jr." checked into the Sheraton Waikiki hotel under yet another assumed name, John P. Hale. He had a credit card with the same

225

moniker that would be good for the duration of his stay. Though he'd managed to sleep through much of the flight, he still had to make up for the time difference between Germany and Honolulu. One's internal clock was a great deal more delicate than a dime store watch. It couldn't be reset simply by twisting a knurled knob or moving tiny clock face limbs into new positions. Acclimation required effort.

Fortunately, he had arrived ahead of schedule and wouldn't have to attend to ground preparations for some time, as the MK50 *Puck One* was still en route. So, after having his bags sent up to his room, he wandered outside and camped on a barstool with an unrestricted view of the hotel's massive pool and the magnificent beach beyond.

Though he had no one to admit it to, his prolonged stay in Friedrichshafen had been wearing. He actually liked people, but he knew better than to become friendly with anyone he might have to kill at some point in the future. Hence his reluctance to socialize with his fellow students at the Zeppelin flight school. No such problems existed for the bar staff at the Sheraton, however. He made sure that both the bartender and a particularly fetching cocktail waitress knew he was a big tipper.

The waitress even accompanied him to a more comfortable spot closer to the beach where he could watch the amateur surfers maim themselves under the watchful eyes of bikini-clad "admirers." He loved tourists, especially Americans, so many of whom assumed that by wearing the right style swim trunks and renting the proper surfboards, they could somehow magically transform themselves from cubicle dwelling desk jockeys into wave riding athletes.

"Aloha! We're here to take you to Honolulu General."

He never tired of the show.

The barmaid's name was Sally, or maybe Suzie, and she hailed from Bucyrus, Ohio. Or maybe Akron. He neither knew nor cared. She had a lovely dimpled smile and her own pair of Zeppelins which the outfit she wore featured prominently.

After an hour or two of intermittent banter, she told him she'd been first runner up in a beauty contest. When the winner turned up pregnant, the coveted title of "Zucchini Queen" went to her, along with some scholarship money. She used the funds to get to Hawaii where she signed on with the hotel.

"The tips aren't bad," she claimed, "but they could always be better."

Who was he to argue with the Zucchini Queen? Especially one so well-endowed. He responded accordingly which brought her back to his little window on the world even more frequently. Eventually, he invited her up to his room at the conclusion of her shift.

She gave him a long look, as if she might poke around a bit within his soul, and then began to decline, so he sweetened the deal with the offer of a five hundred dollar "gratuity."

"Okay, Mr. uhm--"

"Hale," he said, "John Parker Hale. My friends call me 'Johnny.'"

"All right, Johnny. I'll see you a little after ten."

~*~

Chapter 12

Everything you want is on the other side of fear.

At Randy's request, Nate remained in her office until Bannock and his attorney left. She settled into a chair beside him and appeared to be gathering her thoughts before she spoke.

Nate beat her to it. "Bannock's an interesting guy."

"So's his lawyer," she said. "Think you can work with them?"

"Shouldn't be a problem."

Randy fiddled absentmindedly with the hem of her skirt, and Nate waited patiently for her to resolve whatever inner turmoil had captured her attention.

"There's something else going on here that you aren't aware of," she said at last.

"I've found that's the case more often than not," Nate said. "For some reason, folks just don't like to give up the extra details."

"I imagine," Randy said, "that while sometimes they won't tell the whole story, sometimes they can't, for one reason or another. I'm facing just such a situation now."

"How's that?" Nate tried to maintain a neutral expression hoping she would open up.

"My connection to Puck Productions isn't what it seems."

Nate squinted at her. "I don't understand."

"Tim Archer, the President and CEO is my uncle," she said. "My job here is merely a cover for what I really do."

"So, you're not Archer's direct contact with the resort project?"

"Not in any meaningful way. He's dealt directly with Joe Bannock for years. My presence hasn't changed much other than to add a layer of contact between them. Whatever Joe reports to me goes straight to Uncle Tim. Unedited."

After removing his hat, Nate brushed the hair back from his temples. "So, what's the point? Why complicate things?"

"I made the arrangement because I needed to be close to the project. There's been some chatter in the intelligence arena which--"

"You're a *spook?*" Nate asked, then went on without waiting for an answer. "Which agency? CIA? NSA? Homeland Security?"

"My group operates as part of the National Security Agency. We interface with Homeland Security, but our tasks are more tightly focused, and we have a much shorter chain of command. My boss reports directly to the Director; she reports directly to the President."

Several jokes came to mind, but Nate limited himself to just one. "Lemme guess. You're afraid someone's out to kidnap Puck. Right?"

She didn't smile. "Actually, it *is* something like that. We've been hearing rumors about some sort of incident that's in the works. We don't know exactly what's involved, but it has something to do with the new Puck Resort."

"You're talking about a terrorist plot?"

"Yes."

"To do what? Blow up the resort?"

"We have no idea, but rumors like this have circulated before, sometimes weeks and months prior to major attacks. The World Trade Center disaster is a good example of one that didn't get enough attention. Then there were the London bombings in '05 and many others--in India, Pakistan, and Russia, to say nothing of countries in the Middle East."

Nate felt distinctly uncomfortable. "And you're here, all on your own, to stop something from happening in Hawaii?"

"Sort of. We don't have enough staff to follow up every lead with a platoon of agents. Until something more substantial turns up, I'm it. Unless, of course, you'll work with me."

"To hunt for terrorists."

"Hunt? No. But be vigilant. I need you to be mindful of anything that's way out of the ordinary."

Nate grumbled, "Doesn't our friend Daniel Kwan fits that description?"

"He's a well-connected crook, that's all," Randy said. "He's not crazy enough to get in bed with terrorists."

"You hope," Nate said.

She stared at him for a moment. "That's exactly what I hope."

~*~

Reyna had known Stone Fist since infancy, and while she became an adult in the eyes of the tribe by virtue of giving birth, he had done nothing to confirm his own readiness to be declared a man. This, she believed, explained his insufferable attitude. He fancied himself a great hunter though he'd never provided as much game, nor as swiftly, as Mato had.

Before she and Mato mated, Stone Fist tried to win her over, but his gifts of food and skins paled in comparison to Mato's. The young seer, whose spirit name was Black Otter, had carved her likeness in the trunk of a tree, and the image he created drew everyone's praise. They said he captured her beauty, and in so doing he also captured her heart.

But with Reyna's mate gone, Stone Fist stepped forward to serve as her guide and protector. The elders gave the arrangement their blessing without consulting her. Had they done so, she would have suggested that she spy on the giants all by herself. The plan to send her with Stone Fist smelled of Winter Woman's meddling, but Reyna chose not to make an issue of it. Winter Woman owned more years than anyone else in the clan, and Reyna would surely take her place when she died.

Until then she would abide by the wishes of

the elders, though it pained her to do so.

"You move too slow," Stone Fist said as they left the entrance to the clan's burrow behind. "Has childbirth also made you clumsy?"

Reyna cast about for something to throw at him, but since he would likely be ready for it, she decided to wait. Hitting him with a rock when he least expected it would make her feel better, and more importantly, would keep him on edge.

"I have a child," she said. "Someday you may have someone who depends on you. When that day comes, you may not move with such abandon. A wise man knows where he puts his feet."

"A smart man can do that and still move faster than the seasons change."

"Feel free to travel as quickly as you like. I won't have any trouble following your trail."

"I'm not leaving a trail!" he cried, his face flushed with indignation.

Reyna sniffed the air. "Some trails cannot be seen. That doesn't mean they aren't obvious."

He growled something which she ignored. Nothing he said would interest her unless he spotted Mato returning and reported it. That would be welcome news indeed.

They moved on, slower than he wished, but at a pace which brought them all too rapidly in sight of the giants. They expected two, but that's not what they found. From a hastily occupied position amid some boulders, Reyna counted five giants in the meadow. "Forget numbers. You should stick to hunting," she whispered.

He ignored the slight. "There were only two yesterday."

"Is this what they were doing then?"

He pointed to a stand of fir trees where the last snow of the year could still be seen beneath the lowest limbs. "They were looking at some tracks in the snow. Mato and the dog left them. How could he be so stupid?"

"Do you see any other cover available?" she asked. "Perhaps he had no choice."

"He could have chosen to stay away."

Reyna squinted at the intruders, then at Stone Fist. "That would be the coward's way."

"Then he chose the way of the fool."

"It must give you great comfort to know everything," she said. "How did you get so smart? Certainly not by saying little and hearing much."

He didn't respond, which Reyna counted as a minor victory. They watched in silence for a long time. The giants seemed to be inspecting the ground, but neither of them could fathom what they might be looking for. Eventually, they tired of their task.

"We should go back," Reyna said. "I cannot hear them from so far away, and I can't get any closer without being seen."

"I could," said Stone Fist.

Reyna sighed. "Fine. Go. Get close and listen carefully, then come back and tell me what they're saying."

He shifted uneasily, as if he'd begun his advance on the giants before he realized how futile such a mission would be. "I don't--"

"Know their language?" she said, completing his thought. "We will come back tomorrow. They seem to be moving toward the other end of the meadow where there are more trees and rocks."

"And closer to our path into the mountain," he added. "They'll find the caves."

"We must caution The People to hide and stay silent. Those who can't will have to be moved--either deeper into the caves or farther into the forest."

"The elders should move everyone to a new camp."

"There's no time for that," Reyna said.

Stone Fist crossed his arms and said with conviction, "That is not our decision to make."

Though she hated to, Reyna agreed with him.

~*~

In the huge, wood-paneled area Kwan used for an office, his chief subordinate gave him an update on the situation involving his two associates found by the authorities on Maluhia Beach.

"It was Bannock," Paku said. "But he wasn't alone. He had help from a local, a big man named Ivan."

Kwan stared at him. "A Russian?"

"Hawaiian, I think. Our guy said he used to be a professional wrestler."

Josh Langston

"An actor, in other words."

Paku shook his head. "He wrestled *Sumo*. You don't wanna mess with them."

"Bah! It's all fake. Wrestling is crap. What's wrong with you?"

"Sumo is different," Paku said. "It used to be pretty big here, back when guys like Akebono, Musashimaru and Konishiki were involved. Now, it's small time. But in Japan, where I grew up, it's still very popular."

"You actually like that stuff?" Kwan asked. *How could anyone be so gullible?* Perhaps Paku was not the right man to serve at his side after all.

"It's the national sport of Japan!"

"It's still crap."

"You prefer ping pong?" Paku asked.

The growl in his voice served as a warning, and dredged up a mental image of Paku munching on a hand. Kwan backed off.

"Obviously, I know nothing about Sumo. If you say it's for real, then it must be." He gestured with his head in the slightest of bows. Paku acknowledged it by lightening up immediately.

"So," Kwan continued, "what did Bannock have to do with it?"

"I only had a few minutes with Puanani, then he had to go back into the holding cell."

"And?"

"He said Bannock and Ivan jumped them. Ivan made him shoot Hoku, his partner. Then they tied him up and left him with his gun just out

236

of reach."

Kwan rubbed his chin. "Why would they do that?"

"Puanani didn't know. Maybe they were just snooping around."

"But why there, unless someone told them about the luau." He stared hard at Paku. "I thought you told everyone I wanted it kept private."

"I did. And after what they saw, no one would dare say a word to anyone."

"Then how did Bannock find out?"

Paku shrugged. "Maybe someone talked *before* the luau."

Kwan turned away in disgust.

"Boss?" asked Paku.

"What?"

"Puanani wondered when you'd send him an attorney."

Grinding his teeth once again, Kwan digested the request. He had little choice. Without showing support for yet another blundering idiot, the fool might tell the police what happened at the luau. He couldn't afford to kill off every bungler on his payroll. He wouldn't have anyone left to do his bidding, or even attempt to. "Make the calls. See that he's taken care of. If it looks like he might talk, have someone arrange a tragic accident for him."

"Yes sir," Paku said.

"Oh, and what about the two in the hospital?"

"One of them has already been released."

Kwan grunted. "See about having the other one terminated." Hospital bills these days were insane, especially when he had to pay for the mistakes of his unappreciative subordinates. He might not be able to remove all the incompetents, but it wouldn't hurt to thin the herd.

Mato took pity on the teen and helped him to his feet. Shadow stopped growling when it became evident the threat had been eliminated. He stuck his huge nose in the youth's face and sniffed. The lad did not return Mato's smile at the dog's curiosity, nor did he back away when Shadow licked his cheek.

"He won't eat you," Mato said. "But he enjoys your tears. Now wipe your face and go get your knife." He pointed at the tree with the blade still in it. "Why did you try to hurt me?"

Makani seemed to have less trouble understanding Mato. "I wanted to scare you."

"Why?"

The teen shrugged. "To make you go away."

Much of the boy's language Mato understood, especially if Makani used short, simple sentences. It wasn't the People's language, but it felt familiar. When Makani spoke at length, Mato often lost track of the thread. The People didn't use any words but their own. When Makani spoke, Mato recognized a number of words he'd learned from Tori, Nate and a few other giants he'd listened to.

"You could have just asked me to go away," Mato said.

Makani muscled the knife free and slipped it into a sheath at his side. He tucked his sling in his belt. "The People do not welcome strangers."

Mato stared at him in surprise. *The People? Here?* "But," he stammered, "I *am* of The People. We live in the high mountains, as far from the giants as we can get."

Makani's eyes narrowed as he looked into Mato's. "That's not true. You and the great dog live with the giants. I saw you."

"Ah," Mato said with a nod, "now I understand. The giants you saw are friends. They brought me here, but my home is with The People."

"Then how come I've never seen you?" the teen demanded. "I know all The People."

Mato laughed. "I could say the same of you. Obviously, there must be two clans."

"That's impossible!"

"Then you explain it," Mato said with a shrug.

Makani groped for an answer but came up empty. "I must ask the elders."

"Good. I'll go with you."

A look of consternation clouded the youth's face. "I-- You-- No! I must go alone."

"You do that," Mato said. "Just remember, sometimes the elders are full of shit."

"*What?*"

"It's a phrase I learned from the giants. It

239

translates well, I think." He reached up to scratch Shadow behind the ear. "Would you have me wait here?"

"I must think on this."

"Or, you could just start walking and pretend you don't know we're following you."

Makani's uncertainty made Mato impatient.

"Listen to me, boy. It is hot, and I am tired and hungry. So is the dog. I won't stay here and argue with you any longer. Either you lead me to your clan, or I will find them on my own. It doesn't matter to me."

"I will melt into the jungle."

"And I will follow you with my nose," Mato said, patting the dog's head. "I might lose the scent, but Shadow won't."

Though clearly unhappy about it, Makani gave in. "Follow me," he said. "It's not far."

~*~

After several polite suggestions, and a couple which were downright rude, Daphne decided she couldn't make anyone happy. No matter how she tried to conduct herself in the field, someone--if not Simon, then one of the three students they'd brought with them--would complain that she was disturbing the terrain, or that she was leaving tracks which would obscure what they sought, or simply that her humming and/or chatting disrupted their concentration.

So, she relocated.

While they labored in the area between the

ravine and the fir trees where she'd first spotted the tracks in the snow, Daphne sauntered a good hundred yards away.

"Don't go too far," Simon said. "Lotsa bears up here." He held up a metal whistle suspended from a chain around his neck. "I never go into the woods without something to scare them away."

Daphne reached into her fanny pack and extracted two items she had purchased the evening before, while Simon phoned his students looking for searchers. The first was a party horn connected to a can of compressed air. She'd tried it in the store and brought a great deal of unwanted attention to herself. It sounded like a cross between a fog horn and a robotic fart. She liked it. She also liked the pepper spray she'd bought to go along with it. Though tempted to try it on Simon, she resisted the temptation.

"I should be okay," she said, holding up her arsenal. "If I see a bear, I'll either deafen him or give 'im a snoot full of this stuff."

"Just be careful."

"I will."

She didn't mind putting some distance between herself and the students, one of whom kept looking at her with a creepy smile on his face. She couldn't tell if he was leering at her or preparing to sneeze. Either way, she didn't like it, and she hoped that if anyone found something of interest, it wouldn't be him. The last thing she needed was to feel obliged to interview some horny college snot over a find that she had made possible.

Convinced that she'd never see tracks or traces of little people in the dirt, she choose to simply survey the area in general. There could be game trails or other signs that might prove interesting.

As she moved closer to the trees at the edge of the broad clearing, she noticed something near the base of an old, old aspen. The smooth white bark of the broad tree had provided some outdoor artist with a convenient canvas.

Daphne knelt on the ground for a closer look at the carved image. The artistry proved astonishing. The lines of the image had been done in a minimalist fashion, suggesting rather than detailing, yet the end result captivated her. Whoever carved it had ample and obvious talent. The visage rendered on the tree was clearly happy. A few bold strokes suggested long, straight hair that framed an oval face with soft features--the face of a truly beautiful young woman.

She looked back across the meadow, wondering if she should interrupt Simon to show him what she'd found. He was busy talking to one of the two female students, a girl in jeans that appeared to have been spray painted on. If she was engaged in any study at all, it was centered on Professor Simon Dole. What bothered her more was his evident interest in the student.

Daphne abruptly stood, no longer worried that she might bother the good professor in his role as a mentor. She was driven by the need to remind him of who he'd spent the last couple nights with. And the carving provided a dandy reason for dragging him away from Miss Tight Pants.

"Simon!" she called as she hurried across the field.

He looked up and smiled, then dismissed the student who looked none too pleased about it.

"Come with me," Daphne said. "There's something I'd like you to see."

After taking a last look at his trio of assistants, Simon joined her. "What is it?"

Daphne told him about the carving.

"You'll see carvings all over the place," he said. "Aspens are good for that. I've seen dated signatures going back seventy or eighty years."

"How many have you seen with faces carved in them?" she asked.

He shook his head. "I've seen a few hearts with initials in them. Nothing more involved than that."

"Wait'll you see this!" She grabbed his arm and pulled him toward the tree.

Like Daphne, Simon dropped to the ground for a better look. "It's amazingly well done," he said. "The face has interesting features. She's lovely."

"Do you notice anything peculiar about it?"

243

Daphne asked.

He examined it from several angles before answering. "Not really, although it's certainly remarkable. I've never seen anything like it. So, from that perspective, the whole thing is peculiar."

"That's not what I meant," she said.

"Well then, tell me!"

She pursed her lips. "Why is it so close to the ground?"

His head snapped back to look at the carving again. "I have no idea."

"Do you suppose it's because the artist was extremely short?"

Simon pulled out his camera and started taking pictures. "You may be on to something."

"Thank you."

"Now, kindly move away," he said as he put his whistle in his mouth. He blew two short blasts, and Daphne covered her ears in case he did it again. The three students looked his way immediately, and he signaled for them to join him.

"Why should I move?" Daphne asked. "I found the damned thing."

"Yes, you did. And now I want to scour the ground around here to see if we can find out anything about who carved it."

"Or who may have come to look at it?"

"That, too," he said.

~*~

244

Nate caught up with Bannock and his attorney in the parking lot outside Randy's office. Nate thought he'd seen all kinds, but P.S. Jackson was in a class by herself. For one thing, he had never seen a woman so big. Her demeanor, and the way she spoke, made Nate question Bannock's credibility. He could not imagine what had possessed the man to hire her as anything other than a bodyguard.

"I'll see you later," she said to Bannock, then offered her hand to Nate. It felt like shaking hands with an oven mitt.

"I'm pleased to meet you," she said. "I hope you'll keep an eye on my client. He doesn't seem to understand advice, especially mine."

"How's that?"

"I told him to stay the hell away from Daniel Kwan. I might as well have told him not to shit, or breathe." She turned to face Bannock head on. "I oughta bail the hell outta here now, before you get yourself killed. I don't do estate settlements."

"I didn't--"

"Shut yo' lyin' mouth, Joe. That shit won't fly wi' me."

Nate marveled at her rapid descent into a black patois he'd heard in New York. The angrier she got, the faster her words parted company with the language of the court, or the tea room.

"I can't guarantee anything," Nate told her, "but since we have a mutual interest in Mr. Kwan, I'm sure I'll have an opportunity to look out for him."

She grunted something as she backed into the driver's seat of her rented Cadillac and swung one massive leg after another under the steering wheel. Somehow she got the door closed and then lowered the window. A thick, black elbow slid through the opening like the prow of a nuclear submarine. Shaniqua Jackson's face peered out from what would have been the conning tower. "Don't do anything stupid, Joe. I'm warnin' ya."

Bannock leaned toward her. "I--"

She stabbed his chest with a beefy index finger that put him back on his heels. "My bad. Make that: don't do anything *else* stupid."

The two men watched her back up and then leave the parking lot.

"She's-- Wow. Sumpthin' else," Nate said. He removed his hat and wiped his brow. "Where'd you find her?"

"Harvard Law. She finished near the top of her class."

"You're kidding."

Joe Bannock's smile seemed excessively broad. "Nope. She's as good as they come."

"She sure knows how to administer a ration of crap. Hope you had enough." Nate put his hat back on. "So, what's your involvement with Daniel Kwan?"

Bannock filled him in on all three incidents: the abortive attack at his hotel, the bizarre main dish at the luau, and the incident with two more of Kwan's goons at Maluhia Beach. Along the way, he explained where and how he'd teamed up with a former wrestler named Ivan.

Nate credited his law enforcement experience for his ability to keep it all straight. "But basically, you just want your old job back, right?"

"Yep. Listen, I've put a great team together. We've worked on almost all the Puck properties. We know how demanding Tim Archer can be, and we know how to make him happy. We do that by giving him exactly what he wants. If he has to change his specs, we don't argue. He tells us what he wants, and we build it."

"And this Kwan character doesn't like it?" Nate asked. "What's he want?"

"At first I thought maybe he was one of those environmental types who hate all development, no matter what it's for. Then I thought he wanted the project for himself. Lord knows, there's a lot of money to be made."

"But now?"

Bannock scratched his head. "Hell, I don't know what he's up to. All I'm sure of is that he's crazy. I wouldn't put anything past him."

"Would that include making good on his threats?"

"Absolutely."

~*~

Reyna and Stone Fist arrived back in the camp as The People were preparing their evening meal. Low fires of seasoned wood produced little smoke, but Reyna worried that it would be too much. If the giants in the meadow saw it, they might be tempted to investigate. It was better, she reasoned, to not arouse their interest at all.

She argued as much to Winter Woman who listened intently to what Reyna had to say. Instead of answering the younger woman, the elder gave her back her baby son and hurried off to gather up a few more elders.

They had an urgent gathering at which Reyna and Stone Fist gave their opinions of what the giants were doing in the meadow.

"It means nothing," said a wizened old man who moved with the speed of the dead. Reyna had no doubt he hated moving anywhere.

"If they find us, we are doomed," Stone Fist said. "We must go. All of us! And quickly."

Reyna urged caution. "There is as much danger of exposure in moving as there is in staying here. I say we smother our fires and hide in the deepest parts of the caverns. If they can't see us or hear us, they will go away."

"And if they find our tracks? Like those Mato left behind? What is to keep them from finding and enslaving us. Isn't that what giants do?"

"Not always," Reyna said. "Mato and I lived among them for a time. Not all giants are evil. Some are worth knowing."

Stone Fist snorted. "Then why didn't you stay with them? Mato has gone back to them. You should, too."

She turned on him in a fury. "I wanted to raise my child as one of The People. Who are you to tell me to go away? You who haven't even mated yet! Prove yourself before you speak of others."

"Silence!" barked Winter Woman. "Bickering will do us no good." She surveyed the faces grouped around her, and when no one contributed anything else, she spoke. "We have been at this camp too long. There is no more game here anyway. We must prepare to move to another site. The elders will select one and let everyone know where we will be going. For now, you must pack anything you wish to take with you. Bury what's left. We cannot risk any more fires until we reach the new camp."

Several complained that they had not eaten, and their food needed more time to cook. Winter Woman waved such complaints aside. "If the giants see the smoke from our fires, they could find us. And then there would be no more cook fires. They would bring their magic against us."

"You've seen this?" asked a life-weary old woman. "You've had a dream?"

"Reyna is the only dreamer we have left," Winter Woman said. She turned toward her granddaughter, but her face betrayed no emotion. "What have you seen, girl? What have you dreamed?"

"Nothing, Grandmother," she replied. "But I

sleep badly these days. The baby keeps me awake, and my husband is gone. Mato--" She paused, but whether fearful, frightened or angry she did not know. "The dreams-- They do not always come."

Winter Woman put her hand on Reyna's head. It felt warm and comforting.

"We will sleep one last night in the caves," the elder said aloud, then she gently patted Reyna's cheek and spoke in a whisper. "The People need you to dream tonight, child, and you must. You cannot disappoint them."

~*~

Chapter 13

Texas small: No bigger'n moles on a chigger.

Tori and Maggie returned to the resort tired and hungry. They'd had enough shopping and wanted only to be pampered and loved for their efforts. Regrettably, Nate had not yet returned, and the two women were greeted by a different redskin than the one they'd left behind: a shirtless, part-time grocer from the Wyoming hinterlands.

"Aw, geez, Cal. What the hell happened to you?"

"I fell asleep on the beach."

Cal's sunglasses left him with a mask of pale skin in an otherwise puffy red face. Distinctively raccoon-like. She tried not to laugh, but once Maggie started giggling, Tori did, too. Somehow, she managed to gasp out a few words. "We leave you alone for one day, and you burn yourself to a crisp on the beach?"

"Didn't have any sunscreen," he mumbled.

"Good thing you thought of that before you ventured outside."

"Yeah, well, sue me. I forgot."

"No need to get touchy," Maggie said. "We bought some lotion today just in case. Come into the bedroom, and I'll get you smeared up."

When he turned and walked toward their

room he revealed the pale white skin of his back, which only made them chuckle more.

"I'm sorry," Tori said. "I know I shouldn't laugh. I'll see what I can scare up for dinner. Did Nate say when he'd be back?"

"Soon," Cal said.

"Did Mato go to the beach with you?"

"I think he and Shadow went with Nate. They were all here when I left." He and Maggie walked into their room and closed the door.

Tori felt a twinge of jealousy imagining how Nate would react if she were massaging something cool and soothing on his bare skin. He'd likely return the favor. *There'd be some playful tickling, followed by some gentle fondling, followed by some serious necking, followed by some urgent--*

"Hey! Anybody home?"

Nate's voice boomed through the house, and Tori hurried to him, her mind still awash with an imagined tryst. She hugged him fiercely, knocking his Stetson to the floor. Her mouth locked on his, and she pressed close enough to merge with him.

Eventually they came up for air.

"Whoa, babe," he said. "You sure know how to make a fella feel welcome."

"This is our home away from home. I aim to make it memorable."

He wrapped his arms around her and pulled her close again. "Ya know what? I can't imagine home without you. Hell, I can't imagine *life* without you. I hope you know that. You mean everything to me."

"Aw. I bet you say that to all the girls."

He shook his head. "Nope. I might tell 'em they've got really nice boobs or something, but--"

She squeezed his cheeks into fish lips. "Shut yo' nasty mouth, you crude thang!"

"You just can't muzzle that little magnolia blossom you call a heart, can ya?"

Tori hugged him more fiercely than before. She put her mouth close to his ear and whispered, "Shut up, hoss. Take me into our bedroom and make love to me."

"I--"

"Now!"

"Yes'm," he said.

Thirty minutes later Tori caught her breath. With her head already resting on Nate's arm, she rolled toward him and put her hand on his bare chest. Life was good. In fact, life was better than just good. Life was awesome. Then she recalled that life was also occasionally burdened by the unexpected, the activities of miniature Indians for instance.

"How'd Mato do with you today?" she asked.

Nate turned to look at her. "How'd he do what?"

"You know--work out?"

"Mato stayed here all day."

Tori glared at him. "Here?"

"Yeah."

"Oh. Shit," she said.

~*~

Joe Bannock had never seen one human being eat so much at one sitting. He had heard about hot dog eating contests and the like but didn't consider such events dining. Ivan, however, devoured one plateful after another as if he were defending a title, and he had been only too willing to point out that since he'd saved Bannock's life, the construction boss had an obligation to pick up the tab.

They occupied a corner table in a Red Lobster restaurant, and the wait staff seemed nearly as impressed by Ivan's capacity as Bannock was. He assumed they anticipated a four figure tip.

"Good grinds, brah," the wrestler said when he eventually stopped eating long enough to breathe.

Bannock could only marvel at the destruction he'd just witnessed.

Ivan belched, a world class window rattler, the likes of which Bannock had not heard since a childhood stroll through the lion exhibit at a zoo in Cape May, New Jersey, where one of the big cats startled him so badly he'd crapped his crisp, new BSA-issued Cub Scout knickers.

"Oops. Sorry, brah."

"Classy. I s'pose you want dessert?"

"Nah. I'm full."

"Good. Next time, we go to a buffet."

"I like dem places," Ivan said.

"Who knew?" Bannock waved for the check and tried not to blanch when it arrived.

"You want I fine out where Kwan stays? I kin shake up some boys I know. Dey tell me plenny quick."

Bannock shook his head. "Lemme check public records first."

"He won't be in dere."

"You think he's smart enough to disguise his property?"

Ivan probed for a bit of food lodged near a molar the size of Mount Etna and said, "Nah, but he'd hire someone smart enough to do it for him." Then he sucked down the morsel skewered on his fingernail.

"You're probably right," Bannock said, "but it's worth a try."

They left the restaurant in Bannock's car. He hoped the suspension system was up to the challenge.

~*~

Mato followed Makani through the jungle. Shadow seemed content to stay near them, and they eventually reached an area which gave evidence of habitation. Grasses appeared either cut low or packed down; shrubs had been arranged for both aesthetics and security, and native fruits and vegetables grew in abundance nearby. In short, the location seemed idyllic, except for the lack of people.

"Where is everybody?"

255

"Watching," Makani said. "It's a good thing your weapons aren't drawn."

"Why?"

"'Cause they'd probably have killed you by now." He waved both arms over his head and yelled a few words Mato couldn't translate well, but he got the idea.

Men and women materialized at the edges of the open area. None of them were smiling, and many—mostly males—bore pointed instruments clearly not intended for gardening.

Mato stood motionless while Makani divested him of bow, arrows, and knife. No one appeared interested in approaching Shadow, but the dog seemed to have enough sense to know he was outnumbered.

"I still have teeth," Mato growled.

"Then shut up, if you'd like to keep them," the teen replied. "I tried to warn you not to come here. The People don't like strangers."

"I see," Mato said. He looked at Shadow and commanded him to sit. Sometimes he would, especially if he was tired. Fortunately, this appeared to be such an occasion.

An unhappy warrior who stood a hand span taller than Mato approached and spoke briefly with Makani then demanded to know Mato's name and intentions. There was more, but Mato struggled just to glean the essentials.

"Makani says you're a slave of the giants."

Mato grimaced. "Makani is a child. And not a

very smart one."

The warrior drew back his hand as if to strike him, but Mato merely smiled. "Go ahead. The last one who tried that is now food for worms." The claim was utter fiction, but the man confronting him had no way to know that, and where Mato came from, a boast delivered with conviction was often enough to sidestep a fight.

"I'm not stupid!" Makani yelled.

The warrior lowered his arm and stared at him. "I'll decide that."

An ancient man came forward slowly, his knees and back both bowed. His sallow skin appeared ready to drip from his bones, yet his eyes glowed with vitality. "Silence," he said, his voice reflecting none of his physical decay.

The tall warrior gave way quietly, and Makani shuffled even further back.

"I am Koki," the old man said. "Welcome to our village."

Mato looked around but couldn't see anything that looked like a dwelling. "Thank you," he said and introduced himself. "My spirit name is Black Otter."

Koki squinted at him. "Black what?"

"Otter," Mato said. He briefly considered trying to explain what an otter was then gave up.

"We no longer have spirit names," the old man said. "They are only for dreamers."

Mato brightened. "I am such a one."

Koki seemed not to have heard him. "There

are no dreamers," he declared. "We've not had one for generations, and look--" he waved his arm in a broad arc that encompassed the group surrounding them "--our numbers dwindle. When I was young, there were twice as many of us. My father knew twice as many more."

"What happened to them?" Mato asked.

"The giants came," he said, his sadness profound. The more he heard the old man speak, the easier it became to understand him. Mato had picked up the giants' tongue without great difficulty, and as he had discovered listening to Makani, many of the words this clan used were taken from the giants.

"They plague the land of my own people," Mato said. "But the giants have never hunted us."

"They don't hunt us, either. But they kill our way of life. They have filled our land with buildings and destroyed the woods. Many animals no longer live here, and the noise--" His voice tapered away to nothing.

That much Mato understood completely. The giants had also come to the mountains where he grew up. The greater their numbers grew, the more often The People were forced to find new encampments, farther and farther from the places they preferred—the places where life was less of a struggle.

Koki straightened a bit, his back creaking in protest. "I fear we have waited too long."

"For what?" Mato asked.

"To strike back."

Mato blinked at him.

"You say you are of The People," Koki continued. "Are you willing to fight with us?"

"Against the giants?" *What kind of madness was this?*

"We know the giants have magic," Koki said. "It is clever, but it can be defeated. We have even captured some of it for our own use."

That explained the metal blade Makani had tried to use on him. Knives, however, would be of little use against the long-distance killing tools the giants had in variety and abundance. Mato had seen some of them, and they were frightening indeed. Doubtless there were many more whose effectiveness he could not even imagine. Such was the stuff the giants called "technology." If only they applied it solely for noble purposes. But such was not their nature, nor, he suspected, could The People claim any moral superiority. Given the same kinds of tools, his kind would have long ago brought the battle to their over-sized foe.

Koki went on as if convincing Mato to join them was his mission in life. "Our biggest advantage is our size. The giants don't even know we exist. Only a few have ever seen us, and they think they're dreaming. They call us 'Menehune,' and say we come and go like the mist."

"Menehune," Mato said, tasting the word like bad meat. He briefly considered Koki's claim that The People's strength lay in their size. Truly, the old man's years had left him with little brain, and what remained testified to his lunacy.

"So, you'll join us?"

Though he had not yet forgiven Tori and Nate for making him sleep and bringing him to this place without consulting him, he had to admit the area intrigued him. He had Shadow, and now he'd found more of his own kind, something he'd never considered possible. He understood their mistrust of him—in their place he'd feel the same way—but this elder had already abandoned his suspicions and offered Mato a place alongside them. True, it was a place in a line of madmen running to their own deaths, but the invitation meant he could become a part of something. Perhaps he could even turn the tide of their suicidal rush. It was worth a try, and they had as much right to live as the giants did.

Mato could not risk angering Koki. He dared not treat the old man as if he had asked him to join in a march to the moon, but the elder deserved an answer. The wrong one could prove fatal. Once again, Mato put his faith in boldness.

"I'm curious," he said. "If I should assist you in this, how will you dispose of the bodies?"

~*~

It wasn't that Paku had a great deal of respect for Daniel Kwan. In truth, he didn't like the man at all. On the other hand, he did have great respect for the man's power and influence. It rivaled the kind of underground authority the

Yakuza wielded in his homeland. He had no desire to suffer the scrutiny of the authorities the way they did. And even on Kauai, where island life was calm and laid back, the cops had their good days, and he knew it would only be a matter of time before his boss tripped up. When that happened, Paku had no intention of stumbling with him.

Until then, however, it suited him to work with the insatiable Kwan. If for no other reason, the job paid well. Usually, it involved holding up shipments of much-needed goods: machine parts or supplies not produced in the islands. These would be set aside for "special" handling, code words for extortion. Pay the extra "storage" and "cartage" fees, or the stuff went *sploosh*--into the ocean, somewhere deep. They'd been doing it to Puck Productions since the project began. It was still going on. Last he heard, they'd waylaid a carton that, according to the manifest, contained goodies just too valuable to ignore.

There were bonuses, too, for tasks deemed particularly difficult or dangerous. The bite he'd taken out of Clark Cho's hand had earned him the use of a shiny new sports car, a cherry red BMW Z4 roadster. Kwan paid for the lease using one of his many companies, most of which existed in name only.

The car made Paku smile. It practically drove itself. He felt sure it would be a *wahini* magnet, if only he had the time to experiment.

261

Josh Langston

Unfortunately, Kwan kept him busy with his stupid war on the Puck resort. The latest installment of which called for the establishment of a camp in the jungle bordering the massive development. Kwan expected him to stage attacks from there as if the cops wouldn't be able to track them. He wasn't happy about giving up such things as electricity and flush toilets in order to avoid detection by helicopter or drone.

Still, the bright red, payment-free Z4 proved to be an irresistible incentive. And so, under his direction, a half dozen unhappy campers took up residence in the jungle. They hauled in tents and cots and enough food, water and beer to last a couple weeks. Hopefully, it wouldn't take any longer than that. Paku wasn't about to give up cable forever.

Now that he no longer had to waste his time frightening Bannock's workers, he could concentrate on a different form of sabotage. Kwan had given him free rein in choosing targets, and Paku picked the first one with practically no thought at all.

The job would entail risk, but then, so did life.

Besides, he had the Z4.

~*~

"You may find this hard to believe," Simon said over a pitcher of margaritas slightly smaller than an inverted Liberty Bell, "but I can't determine the height of an artist simply by looking at one of his canvasses."

262

"And yet, with no evidence at all, you assume the artist is a male." Daphne drained her glass.

"What? No. Of course not. That's just a figure of speech." He slurped the last bit of frosty lime perfection from the bottom of his glass. "How many of these have you had anyway?"

"Not enough," she said, pouring herself another. The three students crammed into the all-too-intimate booth with them were hard at work on their own Three Tequila Wonderz. She was willing to give the bar a pass on their spelling since they didn't stint on the alcohol they put in their drinks. At least, not in their allegedly infamous "TTWs."

Their waitress earned a giggle from the younger set when she recited the all but obligatory "One tequila, two tequila, three tequila, floor" line. That, however, was before Daphne had tasted their signature concoction. Now she believed like a cultist whose pilgrimage would surely end in temporary oblivion. She was quite willing to accept such an outcome, especially since Simon refused to admit the creator of the work they'd spent the afternoon admiring *had to be* tiny.

"There's absolutely no proof of that whatsoever," he whined.

"Stop whining."

"Stop making shit up!"

Daphne poured them both another round. The bucket barely registered the reduction. "We

Josh Langston

keep this up, we're gonna get hammered," he said.

"I certainly hope so." She took a long sip and promptly gave herself a Slurpee tumor.

Simon laughed at her as she pressed her palm against the center of her forehead.

"Serves ya right," he said.

"Wait'll I dip your *cajones* in that bucket."

"Interesting thought."

She glowered at him. "Whoever carved that image had to be little. *Had to be!* Think about it-- why else would it be so low to the ground?"

"Maybe the artist was lying down. It worked for Michelangelo."

"Actually," she said, "that's bullshit. It's not a good idea to get your information from Hollywood. Charlton Heston made a pretty good Michelangelo, but the genuine article painted the Sistine Chapel standing up."

"He did?"

"Yep. And he hated it. Wrote a poem about it, too. A pretty funny one."

"You're making this up," Simon said.

"True fact. I wrote a term paper 'bout it in college. Memorized it, too." She cleared her throat and began to recite in a voice pitched lower than her own and surprisingly free of tequila-induced stutters and slurs:

"I've already grown a goiter from this torture,
hunched up here like a cat in Lombardy

264

(or anywhere else where the stagnant water's poison).
My stomach's squashed under my chin; my beard's
pointing at heaven; my brain's crushed in a casket;
my breast twists like a harpy's. My brush,
above me all the time, dribbles paint
so my face makes a fine floor for droppings!"

"That's it?" he asked.

"No, there's more, but I like the first part the best."

Simon tilted his head as if to get a better look at her. "He sounds-- I dunno, kinda like the head of my department. She likes to complain, too."

Daphne took another pull at her drink. "Ol' Mike had reason to complain."

"Yeah, I guess so." Simon saluted her with his glass, careful not to spill any of its contents. "I had no idea you studied Art history."

"I didn't. This was for Journalism. An advanced feature-writing class. Tough course. Had to cite references, and the asshole instructor actually checked 'em. He thought I was fulla crap, too. But I showed him, the pompous little butt monkey. There's a lotta them these days: smarmy professor types leading dumb ass college kids down the garden path."

Simon's smile dissolved into a semblance of pique. "You takin' shots at me, too?"

Josh Langston

"Nah." She shook her head, but only briefly. The room didn't like it. "You're dif'runt. You just wanna get laid." She managed to follow the comment with a wink.

The three students drinking beside them started laughing, but didn't look their way.

"Are they even old enough to drink?" Daphne asked.

"I guess so. They're all grad students."

She waved at them to get their attention. "Gotta ask you guys a question."

They didn't look terribly happy about the interruption.

"'Member the carving we were looking at?"

They nodded. In unison. Graduate bobble-heads, Daphne thought, then giggled. "How tall do you think the artist is?"

None of them answered her directly, but the consensus was clear: no one gave a barking rat's ass.

"Something tells me they won't be going back to the Cloud Peak," Daphne said.

"Can't blame 'em." Simon polished off his drink then pressed his own palm to his forehead, and Daphne laughed at him.

"I'm not going back either," he said.

"Why not?"

"'Cause there's no reason to. We haven't found anything to substantiate your theory. We haven't found anything the cops would even be interested in, assuming they'd care about anything we might tell 'em. Professional pride gets in their way."

Daphne couldn't believe he was giving up so easily. But the very fact that he'd said it had a sobering effect. "You're serious? You aren't going back?"

He shook his head, no.

"And you still think you're gonna get back in my pants?"

He tried to shush her and tilted his head toward the students.

"There's only one girl over there," Daphne said, "and she appears to have her hands full. You're not going to have any luck there unless you're prepared to exchange grades for gratification."

"That's ridiculous," he said. It came out "ridiculush."

"Not that I care," she said. "You can screw anyone you like, including Little Miss Levi-skin over there. But if you're not willing to help me up in the Cloud Peak, there's no way I'll help you down here on the kiddie campus."

He exhaled heavily, as if a great weight were slowly bearing down on his chest. "I've got a lot of real work to do," he said, "but I'll make you a deal."

She pursed her lips and waited.

"If you go back up there on your own--"

"Which I might just do."

"--and you find something somebody can

267

actually study, I'll go back with you."

Daphne crossed her arms on her chest. "Lemme get this straight. If I find evidence of some little people living in the Cloud Peak, you'll go with me to share in the credit? Is that about it?"

"No!" he said, his hands raised in protest. "All I'd do is verify the validity of your findings, and maybe help you draft a research paper."

She laughed in his face. "Dude, I'm a *writer*. Why on Earth would I need your help to do something I work at every day?"

He nodded in what he probably thought was a sage fashion. "I'm talking about *academic* writing."

"You mean stuff that's boring?"

"It's not all boring!"

"How in hell would you know?" she asked. "Do I tell you how to do *your* job?"

"Actually, that's exactly what you've been doing."

That earned him a glare. "Okay, so yeah. Maybe a little."

"I know the difference between a subject and a verb. Geez. You think you're the only one with an education?"

She smiled and slid her hand across his thigh and paused when she reached his zipper. "You're right. Lots of people have educations. But right now, you're the only one here with an education *and* a woodie." She felt around to be certain. "You sure you don't want to go back to the Cloud Peak with me?"

~*~

"Nate? It's Randy. I just got a call from--" she paused, "--from Mr. Archer."

"What's up?"

"His airship is headed to Honolulu."

Nate scratched his head. "Okay. So?" From somewhere deep inside his brain, he dredged up an image of an old Pan Am clipper, the funky-looking four engine machine which the now-defunct airline used to fly across the Pacific. They called it a "flying boat" which seemed like a promise of disaster.

"It's a pretty big deal."

Nate wasn't sure why. "Sorry to be so dense, but what does that have to do with me?"

"You need to make sure everything's ready when it arrives. I'll handle the media. It'll touch down first on Oahu, of course, and then there'll be a relatively short tour of the volcanoes National Park for the media. They'll be clambering for a ride, and this way we'll get 'em all on our side."

Suddenly it clicked. The airship was Archer's prized blimp-thingy. "And you want me to ride along and hold hands?"

"No. I'll take care of that." She didn't say the media would respond better to her, though she could have, and he wouldn't have argued the point. "I need you to make sure the landing area is secured, and that the crew will have everything they need once the airship is secured to the ground."

"I thought I was responsible for security," he said.

"You are, and we want to be damned sure *Puck One* is secure."

"Puck One?" He imagined Randy shaking her gorgeous head.

"Yeah. For now, nobody goes near that thing that didn't arrive in it."

"How many would that be?" he asked.

"There's a two-man flight crew, but they'll be bringing about a half dozen others to guarantee the ground facility has everything needed for the long term. I'll make sure they have adequate housing close to the transportation terminal. You need to make sure they have everything else."

"Like what?"

"Like I don't know! Sweet Jesus, Nate. Get with the program!"

"It would help if I knew what the program was, Randy. Last I heard, I was looking for Daniel Kwan. Now you want me to babysit some blimp jockeys?"

"It's not a blimp. It's an airship," she said. "A dirigible. A rigid frame airship. Fortunately, it doesn't need a ground crew. I don't understand the particulars, but it has something to do with the ability to compress helium to control lift. The crew is all German, but I'm told most of 'em speak English."

"Das ist gut," he said.

"Cute."

"When do they arrive?"

"End of the week," she said.

"We'll be ready," he said and sincerely hoped that would be true.

~*~

"Has my shipment come in?" asked the man with many names. He didn't need one for this phone call since the party who initiated the contact proved his identity simply by knowing what number to dial. That number had been provided by their mutual employers long before John Hale arrived in Honolulu. Indeed, it happened long before "Klaus Becker" arrived in Friedrichshafen.

"Yes, the shipment's here, but we've been unable to claim it. There's been a holdup at the port."

"With Customs?"

"No. It has something to do with the union. They're demanding additional storage and cartage fees. The charges are outrageous."

"Pay them." The man who'd spent the night with the Zucchini Queen did nothing to hide his irritation.

"We don't have enough money. We're willing to negotiate, but we're having some difficulty finding the right person--"

"Nonsense. Grab someone and squeeze. They'll give you someone else. Grab them, and

271

squeeze. Keep doing that until you find whoever's holding up the shipment, or until you've choked the life out of everyone in the way."

"It's not that easy."

"Of course it's that easy!" Hale roared. "Just do it, and call me when it's done. Or--"

"Or?"

"Or we scrap the mission. You can explain it to the people who're paying us."

"They-- They wouldn't understand." Fear dripped from the caller's voice like syrup on pancakes.

"And neither do I."

"But--"

"Just find out who's standing in the way, then call me."

"But--"

Click.

Hale put the phone in his pocket and went out by the pool to see if anyone new was working the bar.

~*~

Chapter 14

You don't really live longer in the city;
it just seems that way.

Reyna slipped away from the encampment after nursing her baby and talking a friend into keeping an eye on him for a while. The People had been busy preparing for the move to their next camp. The exodus would begin soon, and she had one last thing to do before they left. She had no idea how long it might be before they returned to the area, but knowing Winter Woman, they'd be gone a long time.

She had already left a message for Mato: a symbol scratched on the wall of the cave where she and the baby had been sleeping. Mato was clever enough to understand. The People had no need for the curious array of marks the giants used. A message could be told in pictures. Who needed a language of scribbles?

Leaving the cave network was easy enough, but doing it without being observed required skill. As an adult she had the right to travel wherever she wished, but Winter Woman's edict--that everyone must pack up and leave--implied that Reyna's mission, in the opposite direction, had to be approached covertly. If giants lurked nearby, the chances of being spotted multiplied. Winter Woman would not be pleased to learn

Reyna had tempted fate.

Her short journey therefore took on an aura of secrecy, and her movements became furtive. It made the trip longer, but once she left the caverns behind, she picked up speed. Trading the shelter of the rocks for the shelter of the trees, she hurried to the white-barked aspen on which Mato had carved her likeness. She wished he had carved an image of himself, too. No one knew his features like Reyna did, but the more time they spent apart, the more she worried she might forget his face. Worse still, he might forget hers. The thought caused her to feel the world grow cloudy, though nothing but blue sky stretched between the mountains at either end of the wide clearing.

She sat on the ground at the base of the tree and looked at herself. A smiling young woman, captured in a moment of mirth, looked directly back at her. Alas, she no longer felt that happiness. Even when holding her precious little one, she remained sad. And nothing would change that short of Mato's return.

Under normal circumstances she could absorb the sounds and smells around her, and know instinctively if danger lurked nearby. Now, however, she was consumed by sadness, and her heart's need confounded her senses.

She had no idea she had been observed.

~*~

"What are we going to do about Mato?" Tori

asked Nate, Maggie and Caleb over a lasagna dinner they'd found in the freezer and cooked in the microwave. According to the packaging the gourmet offering included Italian sausage in a meat sauce with "real" tomatoes.

"I hate it when they use phony tomatoes," Cal said.

"'Cuz then you have to break out special dentures?" Maggie asked, hoping to lighten the mood. Sadly, Tori's question had an opposite and lingering effect.

"I don't think there's much we can do about Mato," Nate said. "He can take care of himself." He made a noise low in his throat that might have been chuckle. "Haven't we had this conversation before?"

"Yeah, but this time he's got Shadow with him," Cal said.

Tori frowned. "I'm not sure that's an advantage."

"We need to keep in mind that he's an adult," Maggie said. "He may not look or act like us, but he's old enough to care of himself. He's no child, despite his size."

Nate agreed. "We can't think of him as a child, much less treat him like one."

"But in many ways," Tori said, "he most definitely is a child."

Maggie frowned. "Child-like, maybe. I'll give ya that much. Child-like."

"As long as he's not trying to kill somebody,"

Josh Langston

said Cal. "We mustn't sell him short. No pun intended."

Despite a consensus that Mato would be fine, none of them felt comfortable with the idea of just leaving him on his own.

"We can't very well launch a search party," Nate said. "What if someone else found him? They might think he was the genuine article instead of one of those little guys the Puck cartoonists have plastered all over the resort."

"The Menehune?" Tori asked.

"Yeah."

"Ya know," Cal said, "there's probably some truth behind the little people legends. What if he really is some sort of lost descendant of the Menahymies?"

"Menehune," Maggie said, pronouncing each of the syllables carefully.

"Yeah, them."

"I dunno," Nate said. "I guess it's possible."

Tori looked at the other three in surprise. "You think his ancestors swam across the Pacific and then hiked a zillion miles to reach the middle of nowhere in Wyoming?"

"Who knows how long ago it might've happened," Nate said. "The Polynesians were great sailors. Who's to say they never reached North America?"

"I still think it's a stretch."

Nate yawned. "I doubt anyone believes the Menehune really existed."

"Who would've believed Mato existed? Or that he came from an entire tribe of two-foot tall people?" Tori said.

"We don't really know there's a whole tribe of 'em. We've only seen two: Mato and Reyna."

Tori laughed. "And you think they sprang to life, fully formed, from a box of cereal or something? No. Wait! They appeared during a full moon underneath a cabbage leaf in Mother Freakin' Goose's garden."

"C'mon, now. Relax. I'm willing to go looking for him in the morning," Cal said. "I'm sure as hell not going back out to the beach."

"I'll go with you," Maggie said.

"You're not leaving me out." Tori gave Nate a look that issued a silent, "What about you, Mister?"

"Sorry," he said, "I can't, much as I'd like to help you catch the runt and wring his neck. I've gotta spend the day at the transportation terminal, where according to the brochure, 'Sea and sky meet adventure.' Randy says we've got some big gas bags comin' in, and I'm supposed to make sure nobody messes with 'em."

"Sounds like fun," Cal said. "Almost as much as sand and sunburn. Maybe they should work that into a slogan. Like: 'Where sand and sunburn chafe yer ass.'"

"I'll pass it on to the marketing weasels," Nate said. "I'm sure they'll love it."

~*~

277

Mato cataloged Makani's clan as The Island People, though truth to tell, he'd seen nothing to convince him he was really on an island. But since his giant friends believed it, as did Makani, Koki, and all the others who melted in and out of the jungle like spirits, Mato did, too.

Though he was given a seat of honor beside Koki, few of The Island People regarded him as a comrade. He looked from face to face during the preparations for a communal dinner hoping to find someone willing to return his smile. There was only one, and try as he might, he couldn't stop admiring her at every opportunity.

Shorter than Reyna, but about the same age, she displayed none of the shyness which had originally attracted him to his mate. This girl sparkled. It was a word he'd learned from the giants, but it seemed perfectly fitting. She had high cheekbones and long, black hair, neither trait unusual among either tribe, but she wore both like gifts from the Spirits.

Instead of furs or animal skins, she wore a lightweight wrap of cloth. The fabric contained a clever floral pattern that allowed her to blend at will with the nearby jungle, but did not disguise the feminine curves within. Her eyes seemed especially large, her lips soft, and her smile as inviting as a cool drink on a hot day. The only issue that concerned him was the attention so many other males paid to her, and yet, she seemed to have eyes only for him.

It made him sit straighter. But it made Kiko's words even more difficult to grasp. He had no interest in what the old man said; all his instincts were focused on the amazing beauty of the nameless maiden sitting too far away to touch, but too close to ignore.

"What do you think of that?" Koki asked, bringing Mato's ruminations to an end.

"I uh-- I think the giants will be difficult to uhm-- defeat."

Koki frowned at him. "I asked if you liked roast pig."

"Oh! Of course. Doesn't everyone?"

"We used to eat fish every day. They were easy to catch, and the giants never bothered us. Now it's difficult to reach the sea without tripping over them or their machines."

Mato tried to appear interested, but the girl who'd caught his eye was busy talking to one of the local males. Mato couldn't imagine why she'd waste her time on such a poor specimen. He had nothing to offer. "I like fish," Mato said. "Especially trout."

"Trout?"

Mato wondered if he'd said something stupid. He didn't think so, but there was much about this language he didn't know. "You might call it something else," he added.

"Like humahumanukanuka'apuapa?"

Mato stared at him as if a set of male genitals had suddenly sprouted from his forehead.

279

"It's a fish," Koki said. "Pretty, but not very good to eat. The giants think it has value. We don't."

Mato struggled to find something to say, and failed.

"We're going to eat some pig now," Koki said, "and drink some nakuah, and then we're going to talk about killing giants."

"What's nakuah?" Mato asked.

It was Koki's turn to stare. "It's tradition. Our warriors drink it before battle. If they get enough, they can't feel pain."

Mato wondered if they'd be able to feel anything else. He turned his attention back to the girl and saw her for the first time when she wasn't smiling. It was all he needed to recognize her from his dream. In it, she was the one threatened by a giant.

~*~

Daphne wasn't happy about returning to the Cloud Peak on her own. She tried to think of someone else she might talk into going with her, but even if she had dredged up a name, getting them to make the drive to the northeast corner of the state from Cheyenne seemed unlikely.

Instead, she packed her air horn, her pepper spray, two bottles of water and a half dozen power bars in the camera case with her aging Nikon and began the trek one last time. Knowing the route helped; knowing it was mostly uphill didn't. But that's where the carving was, and it seemed to be as good a place to start as any other. Better, in fact.

Though no bears had been spotted during their previous trips, that didn't mean there weren't any lurking nearby. She proceeded slowly, air horn in hand. She also proceeded quietly because, she reasoned, it was better to sneak past a bear without disturbing it than to offer herself up as a meal. Stealth meant health. And that would make a pretty good tag line for her articles, assuming she ever got the chance to write them--with or without input from Simon, the co-ed hunting college prof. She'd show him, by gawd.

Caution also dictated that she move through the perimeter of the clearing rather than hiking up the middle. Though certainly a longer route, it was also cooler. She liked the shade better anyway. At that altitude, fair-skinned folk pinked up a whole lot quicker, and Daphne was definitely fair-skinned.

She worked her way forward without paying much attention to anything. Instead, she let her mind wander, thinking just how unbelievably cool it would be to find some sort of evidence that the little people were real--something profound, which Simon and his snotty, pet grad students had completely overlooked.

How sweet that would be!

And then she noticed something at the base of the carved aspen tree, and her heart went into overdrive. Her breath came in short, shallow gulps, and she lowered herself to the ground lest she fall on her butt. The thing at the base of the tree looked like a person. An incredibly small one. But it wasn't moving, and she realized why.

Simon, you asshole. You left a goddam doll at the base of the tree, didn't you? What a pointy-headed weasel needle you are! I'm so going to--

And then the doll sat up.

Daphne swallowed to keep her heart from leaping free of her chest.

The doll was alive!

Daphne rolled sideways to hide behind a thick pine. Once under cover she fumbled with her camera bag. The bear-scaring paraphernalia slid out, as did the water and power bars, not that she cared. She had to get her hands on the Nikon, without alerting the whatever-it-was sitting by the carving.

Moving with infinite care, Daphne bent, twisted and leaned around the tree, her telephoto lens already mounted. She aimed the heavy optics at the person--it had to be a human, no matter how small--and started snapping photos. The click of the shutter had never seemed so loud, but her subject didn't flinch. Daphne twisted the barrel of the lens for a close-up and got yet another shock. The diminutive girl on the ground must have modeled for the artist, though only one of the two continued to smile. But rather than empathize with the tiny female, Daphne switched her thoughts to the last male she'd dealt with and snapped yet another photo.

Suck on these pix, Simon, you mega-weenie! You had your chance to add your name to the Scientific Breakthrough Hall of Fame, but you blew it, bub. Blew it right out your uptight little academic sphincter.

The urge to give him a Bronx cheer possessed her, but she managed to resist the temptation. Instead, she clicked another half dozen frames in case something unforeseen happened, like having a bug crap on her lens. The thought gave her pause, and she backed away to check the zoom. No poop. Bug or otherwise, thank heaven.

But when she shifted around to get still more shots, she discovered her subject had disappeared.

Just like that.

Not there.

At all.

~*~

Paku had no friends among the men in the jungle, which suited him perfectly. As long as they remained more fearful of him than the cops, he'd be satisfied.

The men grumbled and whined about sleeping outdoors, but Paku told them it made their advance on the resort much shorter. The only road began at the resort's dock, otherwise no one could drive to it. Paku couldn't imagine a more foolish way to design a resort. How would anyone arrive? All by boat? Parachute? There were no flat clearings long enough for airplane landings. The whole project was doomed by stupidity.

Yet, Kwan remained confident the complex would become not just a money tree, but an orchard of them, and Kwan was rarely wrong. So Paku ignored his instincts and followed Kwan's general directive for serious but not fatal sabotage.

The most obvious target seemed to be the transportation center, which struck him as a heavily trumped up name for what was essentially a warehouse. Supplies arrived by boat, were transferred to trucks and delivered to the carved out interior of a mountain. And it wasn't even a side of the mountain facing the complex. That was reached via tunnel through to the other side. Paku had never been near it, but Kwan had obtained plans and shared them with him.

Paku unrolled the oversize printed schematic for his men. "The important thing is: we can't be seen. We sneak in, leave our surprise packages, and sneak out. But before we can do that, we need to know how many guards there are, how often they make their rounds, and if we need to create a distraction of some kind in order to get in or out."

"Why not just bribe a guard to let us in?"

Paku slapped him, hard. "Idiot! How stupid do you think we are? We've already thought through that idea and discarded it. Now shut up."

That put a speedy end to creative thinking on the part of his subordinates, but it also made him wonder if Kwan had tried to bribe a guard. It would've made things easier. Paku assumed the worst. When dealing with Daniel Kwan that usually proved to be the wisest course. It cut down on disappointments, and as the madman had already proven, disappointments were to be avoided at all costs.

"You're probably wondering why we can't just knock a guard over the head and walk in whenever we want," Paku said, and two of the men were bold enough to nod their heads.

"It's because we don't want to leave any evidence that we were even there." He went on to explain their mission in greater detail. The explosives they had were crude, but they weren't intended to knock the building down, just make it unstable. He dwelt especially hard on the fact that the destruction they wrought had to be carefully balanced. Repairs had to be expensive, but not ruinously so. And no one was to be hurt, especially tourists, though that wouldn't become a problem until after the resort opened for business.

"When'll that be," asked a gangly member of the crew, a kid named Murphy.

"Not for another couple weeks," Paku told him.

"And you want us to blow up the docks n' shit? It'd make more sense to do that when

285

there's a crowd around. You know, like at a Grand Opening or something."

Paku grunted. His attempt to inoculate the men against creative thinking had failed. Miserably. He found it particularly galling when a subordinate's ideas were better than his own. In such situations, most underlings had enough sense to keep quiet. Those who didn't often went missing. If God wanted to fool with them, Paku was only too willing to arrange the meeting.

"Actually," he said, mentally revising his plans as he spoke, "we're only going to do a little damage now. The big stuff will come later."

Kwan had told him that at some point the Puck people planned to fly a big blimp into the area. He wished he had paid more attention, but the idea of flying a blimp all the way to Hawaii for a publicity stunt struck him as totally irrational.

What the hell would they do with a damned blimp? Kwan had said something about flying tourists around, but the only blimp Paku had ever seen advertised life insurance or something and floated above a stadium or a racetrack. It was huge, but he doubted it could haul more than a dozen people, tops. So, why bother?

And even if it was worth the trouble, didn't they often explode? He'd seen something about that once. Big fireball. Dead bodies fallin' like rain. Totally fucking stupid.

Maybe he should blow up the transportation center completely. Think of the lives he might save. Then he chuckled to himself. Paku? Save lives?

Right.

~*~

Just as Bannock feared, the public record contained no recent traces of Daniel Kwan, though he was mentioned as a principal in dozens of corporations and LLCs, all of which listed post office boxes as their "official" addresses. Many of those boxes served double duty. Evidently, Kwan had no desire to harvest his mail from too many places.

Joe had been reluctant to set Ivan loose, even if it was on a mission as benign as finding an address. It was never a good idea to do a skip-trace on a mobster, especially one who hadn't been convicted of anything let alone the sorts of crimes for which he knew Kwan was responsible. But he had little choice, and now Ivan had been gone for hours.

Of course, since Ivan had driven his own vehicle--Bannock's was likely too well-known among Kwan's henchmen--there was a better than even chance the piece of crap had broken down somewhere. Ivan had a cell phone, and Bannock had seen him enter his employer's number, but that didn't mean the phone had a charge, or that Ivan had actually turned it on, or that he hadn't left it somewhere.

When he didn't have something big to build, Bannock tended to focus on little things--usually the annoying ones he couldn't do anything about. It wasn't that worrying made him feel better, because it didn't. But it gave him something to occupy his mind. Counting sheep had gotten way too boring.

He was, therefore, quite excited to hear from the former Sumo wrestler.

"Got it, brah," Ivan said as he entered Bannock's condo.

"Kwan's address?"

"I tink so, yeah."

"Great! Where is it?"

"Edge of de island," Ivan said, "but no road. Need a boat. Only way we gonna get dere."

"And I'll bet you just happen to know somebody with a boat."

Ivan flashed his choppers in a sharkish semblance of a smile. "You know it, brah! How big a boat you want?"

"I have no idea," Bannock said. "I don't even know if I want to go near him."

"Oh yeah, da lawyer lady. She got you inna fix. You mess wi' her; she quit."

"She only gives me advice. I can take it or leave it."

Ivan shrugged. "So you say. Jes' give me enough time to find da boat. Big, little, it don' mattah."

When his cell phone rang, Bannock answered, thinking it was Shaniqua. She seemed to have some sort of bizarre radar that alerted her to anything stupid he might attempt. Instead, it was Tim Archer's fetching assistant, Randy, the gal who'd given him his walking papers.

"We have a situation," she said.

Joe felt a moment of deep satisfaction. How nice that things were going all to hell without him. "I'd guess you have several."

"Work on the complex has all but stopped. None of your people are willing to stay on in light of the threats. They say the only way they'll continue is if you, personally, manage the entire project."

"And since you fired me," Joe said, "that puts you in a pickle, doesn't it?"

"To be more accurate, it puts Mr. Archer in a pickle. I never would have dismissed you in the first place. That wasn't my decision."

She sounded genuine, but Joe hadn't forgotten the cool manner in which she followed Archer's orders. He reflected on the situation, briefly, then responded. "I'm willing to return, but I have a few conditions."

"Such as?"

"We revise the target dates for completion based on the work stoppage suffered during my absence."

"That's reasonable," Randy said. "Mr. Archer won't like it, but he doesn't have much choice."

"I also want my bonus doubled if we hit the new goals."

She hesitated briefly before agreeing. "I'll

Josh Langston

have to confirm it with Mr. Archer, but I think he'll go for it."

"And I want Ivan, my new aide, put on permanent payroll."

"Permanent? Like on the resort payroll?"

"Yes."

"We're going to hire a lot of wait staff and maint--"

Bannock cut her off. "Security. And I'm not talking about guarding parking lots. He doesn't need to run the show, but he has some, ah, unique talents."

"Does he have a record?" Her voice suggested she might be cringing as she asked.

"Several, I imagine," Joe said. "You may have to overlook a few things."

"We have strict corporate policies which--"

"Which might get in the way of finishing the resort? I doubt that. You're already ignoring a couple just to hire me back. Might as well toss a couple more in the dust bin while you're at it. You won't regret it."

"If we do," Randy said, "it'll be your tit in the wringer, not mine. We clear?"

Joe smiled. He liked this gal. *I wonder if she'd jump Archer's ship and become my personal assistant?*

~*~

Chapter 15

*Alabama wisdom: Don't skinny dip
with snapping turtles.*

Nate's trip to the Transport Terminal took longer than it would in the near future when the guest trams were fully operational. Once Puck's Paradise officially opened, visitors would have access to all the above-ground shuttles, lifts, sky cars and moving sidewalks. Few would be aware of an even larger, underground system used to deliver food, laundry, supplies and personnel to and from all parts of the vast resort. Recently, the delivery and distribution of furniture to all the guest rooms and cottages had stressed that system to its limits. There was no room for the casual transport of individuals, even those charged with the task of keeping the entire complex secure.

So Nate drove a golf cart on a meandering route through the complex and into a tunnel at the far end which led to his destination. He left the vehicle in a restricted area and used a passcode to access the heart and brain of the resort.

Randy had told him about the Command Center, located in the Transport Terminal, which monitored, according to her, "everything equipped with a motor and designed to move." It also managed Puck's fleet of cargo and passenger tenders as well as the planned operation of the Puck airships, the first of which was due to arrive soon.

Joe Bannock met him in the Command Center.

"Randy told me you were coming," Bannock said. "It's official, I'm now back in Puck's good graces."

"Does that mean your legal issues have been resolved?"

"Not entirely, but it's looking better. It turns out the two hoods I ran into had lengthy records in other jurisdictions. Their concealed weapons permits were forged, and Shaniqua spent some time with the hotel employee who backed their story. He now claims he only went along with them because they threatened him."

"So, who's seeing to his safety now?" Nate asked.

"You are!" Bannock grinned. "He got a job with the resort. His expertise seems to be in demand."

Bannock took Nate around to the various subsections within the Control Center. Each had a bank of monitors, dedicated radio channels, and staff whose uniforms were color-coded by area of responsibility.

"Dock operations are over there," Bannock said, pointing to one obviously busy corner. "The airships will be handled across the room." Two men in that area appeared hard at work testing equipment.

"Where's the garden variety security done?" Nate asked. He knew it was in the Command Center somewhere, but he didn't have a clue where to look.

"It's across the hall," Bannock said. "We'll pop in there shortly so you can look around. I'm surprised you haven't been there before."

Nate chuckled. "Randy's kept me busy, mostly off-site. She assured me the existing staff could handle day-to-day stuff."

A buzzer sounded, and red lights blinked overhead. Conversation in the Command Center stopped momentarily, then picked up again as the various crews recognized the warning had been issued by security. A disturbance of some kind had been detected outside the Terminal.

"Let's go see what's up," Bannock said. He strode quickly toward the hall.

Nate hurried to catch up, and Bannock waved him through a steel door on the other side marked "Sec. Ops." Inside, several uniformed guards were gathered around a collection of TV monitors.

"What's going on?" Nate asked.

They all turned to look at him, though only one responded, a man wearing captain's bars, and a nametag marked "Odom." He addressed Bannock. "Who's this?"

"Your boss," Joe said. "This is Nate Sheffield."

"Oh! Sorry sir," Odom said. "We had no idea what you looked like. We were wondering when you'd stop by."

"No problem," Nate said. "We can catch up over a beer sometime. For now, just bring me up to speed on this alarm."

"Sure." He pointed at the screens. "We've got uninvited visitors. We thought maybe they were wandering tourists at first, but they're acting suspiciously, and they sure don't look like hikers or backpackers."

"I agree," Nate said. "Is anyone going to intercept them?"

"We thought we'd just keep an eye on them for now," Odom said. "They can't get in, even if they have the passcode. We changed that the minute we saw 'em."

"That's one of the reasons for the red lights," Bannock added. "It lets everyone in the Command Center know the code's been changed."

"How often has this happened?" Nate asked.

"Outside of security drills? Never."

"Well, it's your show," Nate told him. "Don't let me get in the way."

"Captain Odom?" a younger man called out. "It looks like they're using a crowbar on the door."

Bannock grabbed a phone from his belt and speed-dialed someone with whom he had an abbreviated conversation. He looked at Odom and said, "Ivan's on his way. He'll meet you near the exit."

"Good." Odom turned to Nate. "You're weapons certified, Mr. Sheffield?"

Nate nodded and unfastened the strap securing his automatic in its holster.

"On second thought, why don't you leave that the way it was." He reached into a cabinet and extracted a pump action shotgun with a bright green stock. "Use this first. We don't want to kill anyone unless we have to. You okay with that?"

"Absolutely." Nate had seen beanbag guns before and knew how to use them. Fortunately, he'd never been on the wrong end of one.

"Excellent. Let's go see what those guys are up to."

~*~

Reyna moved as swiftly and silently as she could, berating herself with every step for being so stupid that a wandering giant had spotted her. The knowledge was every bit as galling as it was frustrating. No giant had ever seen one of The People unless he or she allowed it. Even Mato, as casual as he was with the giants, had held to that principle. She had, too.

Until now.

She'd made it halfway back to the cave entrance when she realized her calamitous return had only compounded the problem. What would she report when she got home--that one giant had seen her? They never came alone! How many more were there?

Cursing herself anew, she turned around and carefully made her way back, over and around the great rocks, through the high grass of the meadow, and into the sheltering woods beyond. With every step she listened for any sound the giants might make. Only after she'd traveled part way down a mountainside did she hear a voice.

Reyna moved even more cautiously. She had to know how many there were. Dropping low, her body barely off the ground, she crept toward the sounds coming from a deep ravine ahead of her. It angled down steeply, cut by winter run-off. Only a fool would try to descend the mountain in a ravine. Loose stones and snakes provided a wealth of opportunities for injury.

She stopped and listened intently. The voice she heard had to be a giant's although it sounded more like that of a wounded animal.

Or someone crying.

Perhaps the giant had injured itself! Surely the spirits smiled upon her, and if they did, Reyna would dance and sing their praises every night for a full cycle of seasons. She would dance until her child no longer cried at night, and then she would dance some more.

The closer she came to the giant, the more pitiful the sounds it made. Reyna stopped moving when it dawned on her that if more giants lurked nearby, even if they hadn't come with her target, the cries of the wounded one would surely draw them in.

Reyna backed away, shifted her direction to approach at a wider angle, and once again crept forward. The weeping had grown quieter and now consisted of deep sobs and only occasional sharp cries of anguish.

What had happened, she wondered. How could anyone blunder down a mountainside so precipitously that they incapacitated themselves?

Eventually Reyna reached her goal, and the assumptions she'd made proved correct. The giant was alone, and she was injured. She lay sprawled in an angular shift in the ravine, her foot wedged between a pair of boulders.

Reyna looked to see if suitable rocks lined the ravine above the giant. If so, she might be able to dislodge enough of them to cause a landslide. If done properly, the giant would not only be killed, but covered up as well.

A perfect solution!

Abandoning most of the caution she'd exercised before, Reyna scrambled upwards in search of unstable ground. She needed rocks big enough to cause a slide, but small enough for her to move.

"I see you!" screamed the giant. "I know you're there. Please, please help me!"

The words were simple enough for Reyna to understand, even with her limited grasp of the giant's tongue. And even if she hadn't lived among them at all, she could have accurately guessed the giant's meaning, so pitifully was it delivered.

But Reyna had to be strong. The giant had to die. The very existence of The People depended on it. A landslide was the only way.

"I won't hurt you," the giant moaned. "I just need a little help. Please!"

Reyna ignored her, but the cry of someone injured, even if they were a giant, tore at her heart. She remembered how concerned for her Mato's giants had been when she emerged from the river in Po-keep-see. They seemed truly happy that she survived.

And now, here she was, contemplating how best to murder one of them.

"Please!" the giant female cried. "Please. Help me!"

Reyna squeezed her eyes shut. A greater need existed--that of The People. She had no choice. As much as it would pain her to do it, she had to kill the giant. And finally she found just what she needed: the right sized rock to start an avalanche.

A tree branch lay wedged beneath the big stone. She had no hope of moving it, but she could dig away the soil holding it in place. And, if she moved out of the way quickly enough, she might even survive the rock slide.

Moving carefully once again, and ignoring the anguished cries from below, Reyna angled toward the precipitating boulder.

~*~

Tori, Maggie and Cal searched the grounds all

day but found no trace of Mato or the dog.

"They're off in the jungle," Cal declared. "Otherwise we'd have seen 'em."

"Not Mato," Tori said. "We'd only see him if he wanted us to see him."

"Yeah," said Maggie, "but we brought left over lasagna, which I'm pretty sure Shadow could smell from a couple zip codes away. And if he did, he'd break cover in a skinny minute. That dog loves to eat."

By day's end, the trio gave up. "We can look again tomorrow," Cal said. "Once we're rested."

"I'm not sure we should," Tori said as they returned to their sumptuous Puck-provided quarters. "Mato is his own guy. If he wanted to come back, he would. He's obviously found something more interesting to occupy his time. What right do we have to hunt him down and make him do what we want him to do?"

"Which is what, exactly?" Caleb asked.

Tori laughed. "Ya know, that beats the hell outta me."

"We'd be better off planning your wedding," Maggie said, to which Cal gave an exaggerated amen.

"Darn right! Folks get married in the islands all the time. All we need to find is a beach, a preacher, and some flowers," Tori said.

"You need music, too, hon'," Maggie added.

Cal said, "And booze."

"Agreed." Tori smiled at her friends. "You

want to help with the arrangements, Cal? Or would you rather go back out to the beach?"

"I think I'll poke around the outskirts of the resort," he said. "There are a couple places where the jungle gets pretty close. I'm guessing that's where Mato and the dog went. Who knows, maybe I'll find a paw print or something."

"Suit yourself," Tori said. "Let's hit the bar. I aim to be nice and mellow by the time Nate gets home. Who's turn is it to cook?"

~*~

Nakuah, Mato discovered, had two primary effects. When consumed in quantity, it turned relatively peaceful folk into vengeful killers bent on blood and mayhem. If, however, the original dosage proved insufficient to incite bloodshed, only a little more induced a coma-like state.

After feasting on roast pig and chicken, with a sumptuous array of fruits and vegetables, and slurping down a prodigious volume of nakuah, most of the warriors lay in disorderly clumps where, between snores, they communed with the spirits. Koki had led the charge and now lay slumped across the plank table on which the feast had been served.

Most of The Island People had followed suit. There were some exceptions, notably most of the children, but chief among the conscious adults were Mato and the female who had so captured his interest. The girl from his dream introduced herself as Li, and when they appeared to be the only ones still mobile after the meal, she gestured for him to follow her away from the banquet carnage.

He trailed her into the cool darkness of the jungle.

"It's up to us now," she said.

"What is?"

"An attack on the giants."

Mato scanned Li's head for some sign of injury, since only someone of unsound mind would contemplate such a course of action. He found no wounds, only a lovely head of thick, dark hair decorated with a pair of brightly colored blossoms. He craved to smell their fragrance to see if it differed from hers.

"Well?" she said.

"Have you ever been close to a giant?" he asked.

"Many times."

"Did you not notice how large they are?"

"Of course. So what?"

"How do you propose to attack creatures so big? Will you make a terrible face and frighten them to death?"

She shook her head, which sent waves of dark hair cascading around her soft shoulders. It was enough to melt Mato's heart. Somehow, he stayed alive.

Li produced a long plastic straw, similar to the kind Tori kept in her cabin somewhere on the other side of the world.

301

"A straw?"

Li shook her head again, though less dramatically than before. His heart only melted a little. "We use them to shoot poison darts."

Mato felt a smile tug the corners of his mouth. "You know about the sleeping paste?"

She smiled and held up a tiny harpoon.

"Only the women of my clan know how to make the paste," Mato said. "Hunters make the darts."

"The same holds for us," Li said. "We use the poison from the pupu poniuniu." When Mato stared at her, she added, "It means 'dizzy shell.' If you find one on the beach, it can make you sick. Some of The People have died from its sting. It is but one part of the recipe."

"And you know the rest?"

"Of course! Would you like to test it?"

Mato backed away, his hands raised in protest. "I believe you!"

"Then come with me. You and I will attack the giants, put them all to sleep, and return in time to embarrass Kiko and all the warriors when they wake up. We will do what they only dreamed of."

Mato felt fiercely attracted to the woman. He wanted to reach out, pull her into his arms, and make love to her right there in the jungle. Li, however, was focused on the poison darts in her grasp, and gave no sign that she desired to mate. Her heart was set on a different sort of conquest.

"Do you plan to attack any giants in

particular, or were you going to go after them all at once?"

"You're funny," she said. Her smile warmed his heart, despite the bouquet of deadly darts. "I know a place where a few giants hide from their own kind. We can start with them." She handed him several straws and a narrow leaf with half a dozen darts threaded into it.

"The blowguns I use at home are bigger," Mato said, "and longer." He slipped a dart, point first, into the straw and held it to his lips, took a breath, then expelled it through the tube. The tiny missile streaked away and stuck in the trunk of a palm tree twenty feet away.

Mato grinned. "A longer tube might improve aim."

"Get close enough," Li said, "and you don't need great aim."

"Why not just reach out and stab them?" He meant it as a joke, but she didn't smile.

"Save one or two for that purpose. Just to be safe," she said. "But don't stick yourself. I won't be able to carry you back here."

Mato wondered how far he could carry her if he had to. And what Reyna would say if he carried her all the way back home.

~*~

"It's me," the caller said.

The man registered at the Sheraton Waikiki as John P. Hale looked toward the heavens as if solace would soon be on its way. Alas, the idiot on the phone proved otherwise. "What do you want?" Hale snapped.

"I have the name of the guy who's holding up our package."

"Keeping me in suspense is a terrible idea."

"It's Kwan. First name Danny or Daniel. Something like that."

Hale clenched his jaws as he jotted the name on a cocktail napkin. "Address?"

"Somewhere on Kauai. We couldn't get any details."

"Why not?"

"The guy is extra careful. Only a couple people know where he lives."

"Naturally. And you couldn't convince anyone you spoke with to release the shipment?"

There was a pause on the other end of the line, then, "No. They're more afraid of this Kwan guy than they are of us."

Hale made a conscious effort not to grimace. "Do you *really* want me to do your job for you?"

"Uh, no. That's not--"

"Then get the damned shipment! I don't care who you have to kill to do it. Is that clear?"

"Yes. But what about Kwan? He's bound to make trouble. If--"

"If you're careful, he won't know who to punish, and by the time he figures it out, we'll be long gone." Hale smiled. *One of them would be long gone, anyway.* He would have another name by then and another address somewhere and probably another barmaid, too. He'd be enjoying life and all the money he'd earn from this job, the last half of which would be paid on completion. What happened to the people he left behind was of no concern to him.

~*~

Paku and his men had searched in vain for a guard anywhere near the Transport Terminal. The mountain structure had no windows and few doors. Of those, none were unlocked. Their mission seemed doomed from the start, a condition Paku was loathe to report to Kwan. Breaking in seemed unavoidable.

At Paku's insistence, the men stayed in the thicket of jungle which had grown back toward the facility since it had been originally cut back. He assigned a man to specifically search for surveillance cameras, but he hadn't spotted any. Thus it came as a shock when three men burst through the door they were trying to force open.

Two of them waved guns, while the third, who was easily as big as two or three men, brandished a baseball bat as if it were a bandmaster's baton. Paku's men retreated in panic, stumbling over each other in the process.

"Who are you, and what do you want?" asked a uniformed man in the open doorway.

Paku, whose skill set favored smash and grab over smile and gab, played dumb. His men followed his example and edged nervously toward the jungle.

305

"You're trespassing," the uniformed man said. "And we have the right to hold you until the police arrive."

So, Paku reasoned, the uniform meant nothing. This was no cop. The knowledge made him feel better immediately. "There are eight of us, and only three of you. What makes you think you can hold any of us?"

One of the three, a man in a cowboy hat, aimed his weapon at Paku's face. Though he stood thirty feet away, the muzzle of the shotgun he held looked as big around as an oil drum. Nor did the man holding it appear the least bit nervous, unlike Paku's crew in which the condition ran rampant.

"I can drop you and three of your pals before you even get close to us," the cowboy said. His accent and demeanor reminded Paku of a Hollywood movie hero. But if nothing else, the shotgun was plenty real.

"I'll take out the two on the left," said the man in uniform.

The huge man with the baseball bat just smiled. Paku assumed he was the Sumo wrestler Bannock hired. The man looked all too eager to test his club against the oddball array of guns Paku's men carried, the biggest of which was only a 9mm, hardly enough to stop a man built like Godzilla.

"There's no need to get crazy," Paku said. He recognized futility when bludgeoned by it. "We'll just go now. Sorry to have bothered you."

"Not so fast," said the uniformed man. "I asked what you were doing here. I want an answer. The authorities have already been--"

Crack!

One of Paku's handful of halfwits had fired his gun, and the man in the cowboy hat jerked sideways, violently. But just as quickly, he stood back up. Worst of all, he started firing the damned shotgun. Three of Paku's men went down, hard. The uniformed man returned fire, too, blasting away as Paku's survivors fled.

As if that weren't enough, the big man charged. He raced down the steps, his baseball bat poised for slaughter.

Paku had no desire to be a target. He fled into the jungle after his men. Behind him, the firing stopped, but the bruiser with the bat didn't. He broke through the woods like a bulldozer, which only made Paku move faster.

Leaves and branches whipped him, lacerating his face and hands as he surged through the thick foliage. The only time he looked back, someone in front of him released a bough that nearly took his head off. After that, he kept his eyes to the front.

Rather than go directly back to camp, Paku circled around and approached from the far side, as quietly as he could. Still gasping for air, his heart beating like a sewing machine on steroids, he dropped to his knees and crawled toward the tents. The adrenalin coursing through his system made his hands tremble, and sweat from his forehead bathed his eyes. Everything hurt--head, hands, arms, legs. All exposed skin was raw; everything else was bruised, including his ego.

Forcing himself to breathe normally, he leaned into the base of a tree and waited until he recovered some semblance of calm. It came slowly.

From his wretched vantage point, he tried to examine the campsite, which seemed oddly quiet. His men had to have reached it before he did, and yet nothing moved. There were no sounds. Alas, the thick brush prevented him from seeing any details, and he hesitated to give his position away lest the three Puck defenders were waiting for him.

Eventually, however, he pulled himself upright and surveyed the scene.

His memory was crippled by fear, but he felt reasonably sure at least three of his men went down during the shooting. After that, it had been every man for himself, and the jungle had been more of an obstacle course than an escape route. Everyone fell during the melee away from the abortive raid. Paku turfed himself more times than he cared to count. He doubted the club-wielding maniac had caught up to anyone; he was simply too big to maintain the kind of speed needed to overtake someone running from a nightmare.

Moving closer, he saw bodies. Two at first,

then another. And finally, near the far edge of the camp, a fourth: the skinny kid, Murphy. Paku wasn't close enough to make out any wounds, but none of the downed men leaked the volume of blood he associated with a gunshot wound or a clubbing.

So, what had taken them out?

The slightest of sounds alerted him to nearby movement. Paku swung toward the sound, his gun cocked and ready. Still shaking from his ordeal, he grasped the weapon in both hands to steady it. His heartbeat had returned to dragster speed, and the blood pounding in his ears made it difficult to hear anything, but he tried.

Wiping sweat from his eyes, he squinted into the gloom. Dusk was at hand, and someone was out there.

He looked down just in time to see the strangest damned thing.

~*~

Chapter 16

You can catch more flies with honey than vinegar,
but hopefully, you can find something better to do.

When she first saw the tiny woman staring down at her in the ravine, Daphne recognized her as the girl from the carving--the same one she'd photographed. It never occurred to her that she might be hallucinating. The pain of having her foot jammed between a pair of boulders provided all the stay-awake stimulus required.

Crying out to the elfin female seemed logical, though she was hardly big enough to do anything useful. Nor did it seem likely that someone who'd been hiding from the civilized world would be willing to expose herself to help a stranger. But all that aside, surely she had *some* sympathy for a fellow human in distress.

Instead, the little imp scampered up the ravine and away. Crawling over and around the rocks and debris uphill, she managed to dislodge pebbles and dirt which rolled downhill and peppered Daphne like rain. She covered her head and neck to avoid the worst of it.

What the hell is she up to?

And then the tiny vixen stopped moving. She seemed fixated on a particular patch of rock and deadfall near the top of the incline.

Once more, Daphne yelled for help. The little

woman wasn't so far away that she couldn't hear her, unless she was deaf, but that didn't seem likely. She'd looked directly at Daphne the first few times she begged for assistance. Now, her unlikely liberator didn't react at all, except to start clawing at the soil.

The view was far from clear. Daphne shifted to improve it, but only managed to twist her ankle. Pain lanced upward from her foot to her brain like a needle of acid. Choking on a rising tide of bile, Daphne gritted her teeth and waited for the agony to subside.

A noise worked its way downhill.

Grunting?

Daphne tried to reason it out but failed. *What was she up to?*

The drizzle of dirt and debris had continued, on and off, while the miniscule woman went about her work. The grunts and groans of heavy effort by a small but determined laborer increased to a muffled crescendo and then stopped. A louder, more ominous noise replaced it, and suddenly Daphne realized what was coming.

And from somewhere inside the rumble of displaced rocks, Daphne heard a scream of terror which hadn't come from her own lips.

~*~

The timing could not have been worse. Though everyone in management at the resort had been expecting the airship, *Puck One*, to arrive, few people were actually ready for it. Bannock had counted on Nate and Randy to handle the details; he had enough on his plate simply trying to complete construction of the sprawling complex. The list of things still to be done was staggering, despite the nearly complete appearance of the property.

Like so much of everything at a Puck development, a very great deal of it was illusion. The biggest single problem was the bottleneck presented by the Transport Terminal. What they really needed was a big-ass highway, but Tim Archer made sure that wasn't available. And, to be fair, he could count on one hand the number of people who might favor having a road bisect the heart of the island. Hell, he'd have fingers left over.

So, everything from washing machines and bulldozers to crystal chandeliers and toilet paper had to be shipped in, transferred to a cargo tender, and brought to the terminal where it would again be transferred to one of the ubiquitous underground shuttles for transfer to its final destination. Thank God for temps!

For now, most of it seemed to be working well.

Unless, of course, Kwan managed to waylay a shipment somewhere. And now the goddam airship was about to land, and everyone in Puck's employ seemed to have emptied their brains in unison. Except Nate Sheffield. He'd simply gotten his cowboy ass shot. And Captain Odom. Somehow, the latter had managed to continue functioning more or less normally.

What a mess. Someone had once described such a situation in faux German as a "klüster fücken." He couldn't have agreed more. Still, Nate had shown he had some serious balls. Bannock had watched it all on a color monitor in the security suite of the Command Center. After being shot in the side, Nate had managed somehow to get back on his feet. He brought the beanbag gun into play and pumped out three rounds so fast, his hand on the slide became a blur.

Three punks went down as if poleaxed before Nate dropped the weapon and slumped back against the wall. Odom fired, too, but he must not have bothered to aim, since he didn't hit anyone. Ivan raced after the retreating goons with his makeshift war club, but they were running for their lives, and he had little chance of catching them.

Captain Odom tended to Nate outside as someone within the Command Center announced the arrival of *Puck One*. It was set to land in minutes.

Bannock raced out of the security area and back across the hallway to the Flight Ops suite. "Tell that damned blimp to stay right where it is!"

A man in the stylish uniform of a Puck Air official gave him a look that suggested he dine on excrement and perish.

Josh Langston

"We need the chopper over here, now!" Bannock roared. "We've got a gunshot victim, and I'm not wasting time with your silly ass blimp. Keep it out of the way."

"First, it's not a blimp. And second, we can't stop it or--"

Bannock charged the man and grabbed him by the shirt front. He didn't lift him completely of the ground, but he got close. It was a move the "airman" had likely never experienced before. The growing stain on the front of his slacks attested to that. Bannock, however, had thirty years of experience motivating men who shoved steel beams around and rearranged mountains for a living. Getting a piss ant in a fancy uniform to follow his lead was child's play.

"Tell the pilot to back the fuck off and wait," Bannock said, his voice steady, though he could feel a vein in his head pulse as if ready to blow.

"Yessir."

"And get the chopper over here. Now."

"It normally lands--"

"Put it out there," Bannock said, his voice as low and menacing as he could make it. He nodded toward a monitor focused on the landing site set aside for the airship. "Our guys are waiting."

"Yessir."

When Bannock let go, the man all but merged into the console. No one else spoke.

"As you were," Bannock said. It was something he'd heard Charlton Heston or Sam

314

Bronson or some other badass say in a movie. He loved that kind of shit.

"Chopper's on its way," someone advised. "The landing zone is clear."

Another anonymous voice added, "*Puck One* is holding at two thousand feet, three miles east of the LZ."

It was time to report back to Randy. Ivan would see to it that Nate got to the hospital. Bannock prayed that a higher power would see to it the former lawman survived.

~*~

From the first moment Li vetoed his suggestion that they bring Shadow with them on the raid, Mato knew things would never go according to plan. But then, Li didn't really have a plan. Nevertheless, the dog had been left behind, tied up, and Mato had willingly followed the island girl through the jungle. At times he struggled to keep up with her. Much as he hated to admit it, she moved with even greater stealth than he did. And that said a great deal. Among The People, nobody out-stalked Mato.

Li slowed as they approached the giant's camp which seemed unnaturally quiet. The reason soon became evident: Li and Mato were the only ones there.

Mato checked the remains of a campfire which still contained enough embers to be easily rekindled. Garbage had been strewn in all directions, and only by moving cautiously had

Josh Langston

they avoided stepping in places where the giants relieved themselves.

How could anyone live this way, Mato wondered.

Holding their noses, Li and Mato searched the tents and made sure the area had only been temporarily deserted and not abandoned altogether. Clothing and other gear convinced them the giants would return at some point.

"We should just wait for them," Li said. "We can hide close by, and when they least expect it, we'll attack."

Mato found Li's attitude disturbing. He'd spent enough time with giants to know that while they were certainly eccentric and universally hard to comprehend, most of those he'd met seemed reasonable and merely wished for lives of peace and well-being.

"Tell me again why we should attack them." Mato tried to say it without inviting the kind of scorn Li had shown for her inebriated clansmen.

"Because they deserve it. They've ruined our island. Look around! This is what they leave behind everywhere they go."

Mato had seen similar things in the mountains where The People lived, but it never got as bad as what they saw here. Tori's house, and Nate's, too, were both tidy and pleasant, to say nothing of being vastly more comfortable than anything Mato had lived in before he met them.

"I agree they've made a mess of things here," he said, "but--"

"Sh!" She waved him to silence. "They're coming. Hide!"

The giants made no attempt at stealth. Four of them crashed through the trees and bushes as if pursued by demons. When they reached the camp they raced into their tents and began packing their gear as quickly as possible.

They made so much noise Mato and Li could have marched through the camp blowing horns and pounding drums, and the giants would not have noticed.

Mato freed a dart from the stiff leaf where they were stored and poked it into his straw. He assumed Li had done the same though from where he sat, she was out of sight.

Two of the men occupied the same tent, and both were on their hands and knees as they scraped their belongings together. The sight of two rumps, so close together and barely moving, proved irresistible. Mato took aim and sent a dart into the nearest cheek. He was rewarded with a sharp cry as the giant he'd hit went to his belly inside the tent.

"Whassa mattah?" growled the second man.

"Sumpin' bit me!"

Mato fired another dart.

"Damn!" yelled the second man, as he also dove into the cramped shelter.

It would take a few moments for the sleeping

paste to work its magic, so Mato slipped quietly away and closer to his next target. Li had a similar idea and had already moved well away from her first prize. Like the others, he lay on his belly, groaning. His movements had already grown sluggish.

While Mato watched, Li ducked between two tents to get a better shot at the only giant remaining. He stood up and turned to look at his companions.

"What the hell? You guys sleepin? We gotta git outta here!"

Li sent a dart straight for his navel, but the giant moved, and the missile became tangled in his shirt. It never touched his skin. Dropping out of the giant's line of sight, Li frantically examined both her remaining darts and the plastic tube with which she fired them.

Mato knew there was nothing wrong with her weaponry, but he had no way of telling her without giving himself away. The giant had already drawn his weapon, and he looked frantic. Mato wanted no part of becoming a target.

Instead, he took his time and waited for the giant to look away. As soon as he did, Mato let loose a dart which lodged firmly in the man's neck. Like the others, he yelped, and then he slapped at the stinger, driving it deeper.

Too late, Mato realized he had nowhere to go if the giant fell toward him unless he moved while his prey remained awake. The giant made the decision for him and began to topple. His eyes widened as Mato stepped into the open and tried to get out of the way.

Displaying an amazing strength of will, the falling giant managed to move one of his arms in Mato's direction even as his world grew dark. Both arm and giant hit the ground at the same time. Mato, his lungs emphatically emptied of air, lay pinned beneath an enormous elbow.

Li broke her own cover and approached cautiously.

Mato rolled his eyes at her. It was the closest thing to communication he could muster. He knew if he didn't get air soon, he would black out, too. Or die.

That's when yet another giant entered the fray. Mato saw him rise from hiding and stand as Li charged him with a dart in her hand.

The giant looked down and spotted her as she leaped toward his leg to stab him. Mato struggled to stay awake and managed to do so long enough to see the giant kick Li with the toe of his boot. The blow sent her tumbling backwards like a doll hit by a train.

And Mato passed out.

~*~

Tori answered the condo phone without having noticed that the condo even had a phone. She chalked it up to the interior designer who managed to find a place for everything in quarters that lacked nothing.

Josh Langston

"H'lo?"

"I need to speak to Nate Sheffield's fiancée," said a woman on the other end of the line.

"That's me," Tori said, parking her bourbon and cola on a coffee table.

"This is Randy Rhoades. I work with Nate."

"He's talked about you." *A lot, actually. Redheads. Geez.*

"I wish there were some other way to say this--"

Tori's heart stopped.

"--but there isn't. Nate's been shot."

"Oh my God!" Tori shrieked. "Is he all right? Where is he? What happened?"

"He's alive, and he's being flown to the hospital in Lihue. I'm told their emergency room is equipped for--"

"How do I get there?"

"Well, actually, there's--"

"I have to go there *now*. This instant!"

"I understand," Randy said, her voice surprisingly calm. "As soon as our chopper delivers Nate to the hospital, the pilot has orders to come back and get you. It won't take long. Gather whatever you need and go directly to the helipad."

"How do I get there?"

"Follow the blue line painted on the edge of the walkway; that'll take you toward the Transport Terminal. The helipad is on the resort side of the tunnel. It's where you landed when you first arrived. There's a waiting area enclosed in Plexiglas. You can't miss it."

"Thanks," Tori said, trying to sound less resentful, but one thought occupied center stage in her thinking: if Randy hadn't dragged Nate to Hawaii, he wouldn't have gotten shot.

"I presume all four of you will be making the trip." Randy phrased it as a question.

"Four?" Tori asked.

"Unless you'd like me to find someone to look after your little nephew. Hospitals usually frown on child visitors, and visiting hours are already over."

Mato! Tori had forgotten all about him. "That's okay. My uhm-- sister and her husband will stay here. Like you said, it's after hours."

"I'll be happy to arrange transportation for them tomorrow."

"Thank you."

"It's nothing, really."

"Do you know how badly hurt Nate is? I mean--"

"He was hit in the side," Randy said. "That's all I've got."

"Who shot him? And why?"

"Thieves were trying to break into the Transport Terminal. Nate and two other security officers intercepted them."

"But--"

"You need to get moving, Miss Lanier. The helicopter will be there soon."

321

~*~

Though he'd never admit it, Daniel Kwan missed having Paku around. He had plenty of people to do his bidding; that wasn't the problem. What he missed more than anything was Paku's *attitude*. The man obviously didn't give a shit about Kwan's wealth, his power, or anything else, but he was a consummate pro. Kwan paid for his loyalty, and Paku delivered it. In spades. On time, and without excuses, delays or--most importantly--repercussions. Kwan liked that.

He also liked that Paku was utterly ruthless. Kwan fancied himself to have the same attribute, though he'd never actually had to dirty his own hands. He'd always managed to have a layer of subordinates between himself and anything that might go wrong.

He was reflecting on these very issues when a substitute for Paku disturbed his evening meal to announce that a boat had tied up at Kwan's private dock. The guards on duty had reported its arrival, but they had sent no further word to the main house.

Kwan had established a protocol for handling such situations, though this was the first time anyone had ever breached the security of his estate.

"Make sure my safe room is prepared," Kwan ordered.

The subordinate looked at him blankly.

Kwan threw his linen napkin on the table. "In

my study, you moron! Make sure I have provisions in case I must lock myself in."

The man still didn't look like he had any idea how to comply with Kwan's orders, but he bowed his head and backed out of the room as if he knew what he was doing. Kwan assumed he could survive for a few days, even without fresh food. He had a well-stocked bar and plenty of snacks. It would have to suffice.

Besides, he thought, no one's ever tried to get in before. The whole thing is likely overblown. With that, he returned to his meal.

Long before he reached the dessert course, three men wearing ski masks and carrying machineguns entered the dining salon. Kwan stabbed the buzzer at his elbow to summon help. Alarm bells went off throughout the house alerting everyone on his staff that an intruder had reached his inner sanctum.

By that time, however, they were all dead, though Kwan didn't know it.

"You're Kwan?" one of the masked men asked.

"Of course I am, you idiot! Who else would--"

Three prolonged bursts from the guns carried by the masked men halted Kwan in mid-sentence. Many of the rounds missed, but enough made contact to throw the local kingpin's body around like a feather in a wind tunnel.

He came to rest in a jumble of limbs and torso that bore little resemblance to the man who had been dining mere moments before.

The gunmen left the building the same way they came in.

~*~

Paku had kicked the tiny bitch reflexively. He'd have done the exact same thing if it had been a rat attacking him, or a snake, or anything else. The fact that his attacker was a miniscule female human only entered his brain as an afterthought.

But once it lodged firmly in his gray matter, he couldn't shake it.

I found a miniature person!

The revelation was followed immediately by another thought. What the hell would he do with her? Kwan would claim her for himself the instant he heard about her, so obviously, saying anything to him was out of the question.

A quick look at his associates convinced him that none of them were in on the secret. Hell, none of them were even moving, so he assumed they were dead, and further, that the little female he'd just kicked into oblivion had most likely done to them what she intended to do to him.

But he was alive, and she was-- *Crap. Was she dead, too?*

He hurried to her, and after making sure she had nothing in her hands with which to stab him, he put his head to her chest and listened for a heartbeat. It wasn't easy to hear, especially since his own heart was still beating at a pretty good clip, and the blood pumping through his veins made it damned difficult to focus on something as faint as the heartbeat of a real live Barbie doll.

Which is pretty much what she looked like. Or would have looked like if the iconic plaything had dark hair and Polynesian features.

"Whatever," he muttered to himself. The important thing was that she seemed to be alive. He'd kicked her pretty hard, but evidently not hard enough to kill her. At least, not yet.

Shit! What if he'd messed her up pretty bad? He'd hit a dog with his car once. It had gone flying, and when he went to look for it, he discovered it had dragged itself a good distance from where it landed. And then it died there.

When she moaned, he took it as a good sign. He carried her into his tent and set her down on his pillow while he gathered his gear. He had no intention of leaving any trace of himself behind. When the cops came--and he had no doubt they'd find the camp eventually--they wouldn't find anything to tie it or the bungled break-in to him. They'd blame it all on the other guys.

He paused to look back at them. Dead. Had to be. The observation gave him a heightened appreciation for the micro-midget in his possession. He didn't know exactly what he'd do with her, but her size alone made her valuable. He inspected the tiny, sleeping beauty more closely. It sure as hell didn't hurt that she was gorgeous. It almost made him wish he was small enough to--

Josh Langston

He slapped himself. He was a badass, not a pervert. He'd look after the little hottie. At least until he figured out what to do with her.

He decided he didn't really need anything he'd had his men carry in for him. He picked up the girl and set her aside while he piled his stuff in the middle of the tent and set it on fire.

Then, with the girl cradled in his arms like a newborn, he began the hike out of the jungle. He'd figure out what to tell Kwan as he walked. Or maybe he'd just drive his hot little Z4 to the airport and leave Hawaii forever.

Maybe he could hide the little babe in a carry-on bag or something.

~*~

"We got rid of that Kwan character," the caller informed Hale as he lounged by the pool admiring a fetching lass in a bright orange thong.

How I love tourists in America! He pulled his eyes away and spoke into the phone. "That should save us a few dollars."

"Those guys you sent--"

"Spare me," Hale said. "As long as they got it done, and didn't leave anything incriminating behind, I don't care about the details."

"There is one little problem."

Hale closed his eyes and exhaled in disgust. "Go on. Tell me."

"It's about the shipment. Somehow, our guys got the wrong crate. Either that, or whoever was supposed to supply the spores sent us coffee

326

makers instead."

"Please tell me you didn't just make a joke." Hale visualized the man on the other end of the line sweating heavily--something he had every reason to do.

"Sorry."

"Where is our shipment now?" Hale asked.

"We think it went to the resort."

"You *think?*"

"Okay, it's got to be there. The crate had Puck cartoons stamped all over it, and the resort is the biggest construction project in the state. But we're okay. We can load it in place, right before you take the blimp."

"It's not a blimp, you moron!" Hale's voice caused the girl more or less wearing the orange swimsuit to look his way, concerned. He pointed at his phone, glanced up to the heavens, and shook his head dramatically. She laughed.

"We'll have to. We don't have any other choice," Hale said. "There's no time to make other arrangements. The game is this weekend, and it's sold out."

"Poor bastards," said the man on the phone.

"Get your head straight," Hale snarled. "It's just business."

~*~

Chapter 17

Life is not about how fast you run, or how high you climb, but how well you bounce.

Reyna knew it wouldn't be easy, and she knew that unless she worked with care, the rockslide she meant to start could crush her just as easily as it would the giantess further down in the ravine. But she couldn't let that slow her down. She dug anyway--as fast and as hard as possible.

And when the debris finally shifted enough to let gravity send the boulder above her it on its way, Reyna found herself in exactly the wrong place.

Screaming did nothing to change that, but she screamed anyway. The giant screamed, too, though only the ground beneath Reyna had turned liquid. It would take a moment before the same thing happened to the ground beneath the giant.

Reyna was moving fast. And worse than that, she was *gaining* speed. She had no control over her direction and no way to stop. She'd become a very soft bit of debris in a very hard stream of rubble.

She would soon be dead. At least, she hoped it would be soon. She had no desire to lie bleeding in the sun until the coyotes and buzzards came to finish her. The notion raced through her mind only to be replaced by terror. All coherent thought ceased.

Rocks and boulders bounced all around her. She tried to shield her head, but the blows to her limbs and body came harder and harder until something grabbed her leg. The dust was too heavy to see through, but that suddenly didn't matter. Nothing did. She went limp, and the world faded.

~*~

Tori reached the emergency room at a dead run, and someone directed her toward a desk marked "Information."

"I'm here about my fiancé," Tori said. "He's been shot. They brought him in a little while ago."

The clerk looked at her over the top of her glasses. "Name?" she asked, bored.

"Sheffield, Nathan."

"Nathan is his last name?"

Tori glared at her. "No."

"Sheffield then. One 'F' or two?"

"Two!"

"He hasn't been assigned a room yet."

On the verge of climbing over the desk to choke the life from the idiot on the other side, Tori felt a restraining hand on her shoulder. It was a huge hand, and she experienced a blindingly short-lived epiphany about what Mato felt when she touched him.

"He in surgery," said the person attached to

the big hand. "He gonna be fine."

Tori looked slowly past the big hand, up the equally massive arm, and into the huge, round face of the largest human being she'd ever encountered.

"Come," he said, in a voice whose gentleness belied his size. "I work wit' him. Security." He tapped his chest for emphasis, then led her to a chair in a waiting area.

"You wan' a soda?"

She shook her head, not quite willing to speak. His question made her wish she'd brought her drink with her from the condo.

The big man settled into a loveseat beside her and filled up most of it. Though he didn't wear a uniform, Tori had the sense he was on the level. If anything, he seemed a little nervous.

"I'm Tori Lanier," she said, offering her hand. "Nate and I are--"

"Gettin' married. I know. He tol' me to look for you. I'm Ivan."

She stared at him. "*Ivan?*"

He grinned. "Dat's my Sumo name. Real name is Ku`u Maka, but mos' haoles can't say it."

"How-lays?"

"White people. Like you. Not from 'roun heah."

"Right." She shook her head a bit to clear it. "Can you tell me what happened to Nate?"

Ivan's expression quickly grew intense. "Yeah. I was dere. Some mokes try to break in. I know one: Paku. Japanee. Bad guy."

"Did he shoot Nate?"

"Nah. Dat some uddah moke. Ah din' see it. Oh, man. So jam up; happen so fast! Bang! Nate go down. Den he get back up and boom, boom, boom! He drop tree uh dem boys. Wit' bean bags. De uddahs, dey run. Could'n catch 'em."

Tori pulled a tissue from her pocket and dabbed her eyes with it. "How long's he been in surgery?"

Ivan shrugged. "A while." He squinted at the clock on the wall. "Half hour." He reached for her hand and patted it. "He gon' be fine. I know it. He tough."

She tried to smile but broke down instead. Ivan put his arm around her but didn't squeeze. It felt like a half ton of blankets had snuggled up to her.

"Do you know what your name means?" she asked after a while.

"Ivan?"

"No. Your real name. Say it again."

"Ku`u Maka."

"It sounds pretty," she said. "I'll bet it means 'big brother' or something."

Ivan chuckled. "You gonna laugh."

"Maybe not. Try me."

Somehow, he made four hundred pounds of fleshy muscle look timid. "It means 'apple of my eye.'"

She couldn't help but smile. "That's

331

wonderful!"

"So, what's yo name mean?"

"I have no idea. Tori is short for Victoria. I think it means 'my shoes are too tight,' or something."

Ivan's laugh rumbled like a volcano. It felt as good as it sounded. The next hour passed with little conversation until a doctor appeared, his surgical mask dangling from one ear. He looked as tired as Tori felt.

"Mrs. Sheffield?"

"Yes?" She stood but didn't bother to correct him.

The surgeon introduced himself, then said, "Your husband is stable, for now. The bullet did a great deal of damage. If he makes it through the night, he's definitely going to need more surgery."

"*If* he makes it?"

The surgeon grimaced. "I won't sugarcoat it. He's in very bad shape. It doesn't look good, and I don't want to get your hopes up."

"When can I see him?"

"Soon. They'll take him up to ICU. Someone will let you know."

"Thank you," she said.

The doctor reached for her shoulder and gave it a gentle squeeze. "I just wish I had better news."

"Yeah," she said. "Me, too."

~*~

Mato felt something warm and wet on his

face. Though decidedly unpleasant, it wasn't nearly as bad as the cloud of bad breath which followed.

Shadow? How did you get here?

The dog licked him again, then set about moving the arm of the giant which lay across Mato's thighs. The little Indian's chest hurt, and he felt sure he'd broken some ribs, but being able to suck in air made up for it, even if every breath made him wince.

Shadow wagged his tail so hard, Mato feared he might hurt himself. The dog shoved his huge nose under Mato's back and nudged. He eventually rolled free of the confining limb and staggered to his feet only to have the dog knock him down again in his excitement.

Mato grabbed the remains of a rope hanging from his collar and let the dog lift him back to a standing position. Other than the added presence of Shadow, nothing had changed. The four giants he and Li had put to sleep would stay that way for some time, and Li--

The memory of her predicament came rushing back to him. Twisting around, as if she might still be in view, he looked for her and the remaining giant. They were both gone, of course, though he had no idea how long ago they departed. Mato couldn't believe he'd been sleeping while Li fell prey to the giant in his dream. The image remained fresh in his memory.

But, he reasoned, as long as the giant didn't

have too great a head start, Mato could not only track him, but catch him. Once he did, though, he'd need to be prepared. He needed a weapon.

While Shadow poked around looking for something to eat, Mato concerned himself with retrieving his blowgun, such as it was, and darts.

After a brief search, he located one end of his straw. The rest of it was pressed beneath the unconscious body of the giant who'd nearly crushed him. He tugged on it, but made no progress at all and abandoned the effort in favor of finding Li's.

Moving as quickly as he could, he studied the space between the tents where he'd last seen her. Li's straw was gone, but he found the leaf she'd used to transport her darts. It had been stepped on by a huge shoe. The darts were ruined--surely the handiwork of the giant who now had Li in his possession.

Cursing his luck, Mato returned to the area where he'd last had his own gear. A familiar looking leaf stood on end next to a tree trunk. Mato inspected it and found the remains of his own dart supply. Two still appeared useable, but the sharp points on the others had been broken off.

He pulled the darts out of the leaf and threaded them carefully in the thin fabric of his shirt, points out. Moving his arms experimentally, he made sure he wouldn't accidently stab himself while he pursued Li and the giant.

Then he whistled for Shadow.

The dog responded quickly, and Mato climbed up on his back. "Just like old times," he said. "Now, let's go catch a giant."

Shadow laid back his ears, and farted.

~*~

Maggie clicked off her phone after talking to Tori.

"How's Nate?" Cal asked.

"Bad. The doctor doesn't think he'll make it through the night."

Cal appeared stricken. "Aw damn. Poor Tori. She must be a wreck."

"She is. But she hasn't given up. She wants us to track down Mato and bring him to the hospital."

"His blood!" Cal exclaimed. "Geez. I'd almost forgotten. A transfusion from him will cure damn near anything."

"We don't know that," Maggie said.

"Well he's got a helluva track record. How many times has he pulled that stunt?"

"Often enough. Trouble is, he doesn't know Nate's hurt, and there's no way to tell him without finding him. He could be anywhere. There's a butt load of forest on this island, and he's most likely sittin' in the thick of it."

"Could we get that redheaded gal to loan us the chopper?"

Maggie pondered the idea, but only briefly. "You know how thick the woods are and how little Mato is. We'd never see him from the air."

"Then it's back to hunting for him on the ground. Maybe we could hire bloodhounds."

"That's a thought. I'll go ahead and call Ms. Rhoades. Might as well tell her about our 'child.' If there's an APB out on him, she'll discover he's no babe in arms anyway. I'd rather she heard it directly from us."

"Did you run this by Tori?" Cal asked.

"No. I probably should have, but all she can think about is Nate. I can't imagine what she's going through."

As Maggie reached for the phone to call Randy Rhoades, Cal stayed her hand. "Let's stop and think for a moment, okay? What are you gonna tell her, the truth?

"Well, yeah."

Cal didn't need to say more. Maggie fully understood the problem. "She's not going to believe me."

"She'll think you're high on Maui Wowie or something."

"*Maui Wowie?*"

"It's mari--"

"I know what it is," Maggie said. "I'm just surprised that you do."

"I've got cable, y'know. I've seen Cheech and Chong." He paused to reflect then said, "Why not say Nate needs a transfusion, but he has a rare blood type, and Mato--I mean, our little Matt--is the only one with a match?"

"And we need to bring him in right away, only he's gone missing? And, oops, we didn't mention it earlier? Great idea. They'll arrest us for dope *and* negligence."

"Damn. It's up to us. We've gotta find Mato on our own," Cal said. "And pronto."

Just then the condo phone rang. Maggie answered, assuming it would be Randy Rhoades, or someone else from the resort. It wasn't.

"Hi, this is Cassy Woodall, Tori Lanier's editor. Is she available?"

"She's not here right now, Cassy," Maggie said. "Can I take a message? This is Maggie Scott. We met last year."

"Of course! You and Cal were so nice to me."

"Can I put you on speaker?"

"Sure. So, tell me--how are the plans for Tori's big wedding?"

Maggie exhaled as if punched in the stomach. "Not so good."

"Tell me about it," Cassy moaned. Her voice sounded tinny through the little speaker in the handset. "I tried to buy a ticket to Hawaii, but they're all gone! I called three different airlines and got the same message. There's some sort of big football game scheduled for this coming weekend, and none of the carriers have any seats left. Even the cruise ships are booked to capacity. And the regular season doesn't start for ages! I don't understand."

"I read about it," Cal said. "Pro football wants

more distance from the college schedule. They've got all their pre-season games, as usual, plus this super special one here in Hawaii. The stupid game doesn't even count. I don't understand what everyone's so excited about."

"I never understood why anyone got excited about football, period," Cassy said. "Although the cheerleaders are fun to watch."

"You make an excellent point," Cal said.

Maggie burned him to cinders with a scornful look. "Listen, Cassy, there's something you should know. There's not going to be a wedding. Not this weekend anyway."

"Why?" she asked, suddenly concerned. "I thought Tori and Nate were madly in love."

"They are," Maggie said, then she went on to tell Cassy about the shooting and their need to track down Mato.

"Is there anything I can do to help?" Cassy asked. "I can send money if--"

"Prayers," Cal said. "That's what we need right now. And help. If you know somebody in law enforcement who could give us a hand, we could sure use it."

"I only know one person," Cassy said, "and I don't know her all that well. She's Nate's ex-fiancée."

"We probably don't need to go there," Maggie said.

"Hold on. She has connections to cop shops all over the country. From what I heard, she got

Nate the security job with Puck. If anyone has ties to the law in Hawaii, it's Beth Torrence."

"It's worth a try," Maggie said. "Call her. Please. Meanwhile, we're headed out to look for Mato on our own."

"Good luck," Cassy said.

"Thanks. We're gonna need it."

~*~

Paku tried to remember how long it had taken to hike in to the campsite. *How long ago had that even been?* It felt like forever, and the need to leave it all behind had grown like a mushroom cloud. Now, all he had to do was concentrate on hiking out. Fortunately all he had to carry was a flashlight and a sleeping girl about the size and weight of a house cat. Or so he supposed; he'd never owned one.

So, despite blundering through a jungle in the dark, he made decent progress, mostly due to the swath of trampled vegetation his crew had made during their journey in. That progress continued until the micro-babe woke up.

And bit him.

Paku dropped the girl as if she'd burst into flames. She hit the ground hard and bounced, apparently dazed. Yet, when Paku reached for her, she leaped up and bit him again.

When he reacted to the pain, she bolted into the dark.

"Damn you!" he screamed. "You'd better hide good, 'cause when I find you, I'm going to beat the shit out of you."

He followed this logic-challenged threat with additional warnings, each more grisly and specific than the last. When he exhausted all the ways he could think of to harm her physically, he described the sexual crimes he intended to visit upon her.

"And when I'm done, I'll feed what's left of you to the pigs!"

He didn't own any pigs, of course. Nor did he even know where he might find some, but he'd heard that pigs would eat people, and he assumed the vicious little midget had heard the same things. She'd be paralyzed by fear. And that's when he'd find her, cowering beneath a jungle shrub, shitting herself.

And then, by God, he'd make her pay. Dearly.

But after a prolonged period of shrub shaking, misogynistic curses and finally, self-recrimination, Paku gave up. The bitch was gone, and he had no more time to search for her. Because of the monumental fuck-up at the Transport Terminal, to say nothing of all the dead bodies in the camp, Paku had ample reason to vacate not only the jungle, but the whole damned state.

He turned his attention toward escape, his focus limited to nothing beyond climbing into his magnificent little crimson speedster. He had parked it, along with the vehicles of the other men, at the end of a service road that snaked through the national park property which comprised a great deal of the island.

The dirt track through the interior had been hard on the low-slung Z4, and he knew the others had laughed at him for using it. Now, however, he was glad to know it was waiting for him--dirt road be damned!

Focus, he reminded himself. *It can't be much farther.*

~*~

Bannock met Randy at the helipad. Most people crouched down as they moved out from beneath the swirling rotors, even though the clearance was more than ample. Randy didn't, nor did she bother trying to keep her dark red hair from being blown around. When they entered the tunnel to the Transport Terminal, she merely shook it back in place, a gesture he'd consider suggestive under other circumstances, then went on about her business.

In this case, her business was him. With Nate unavailable, Bannock had inherited security oversight along with everything else already on his plate. It fit right in with a dream he'd had recently in which he worked as a reservations agent, booking rooms while simultaneously building, furnishing, and servicing them.

"So, who tried to break in?" Randy asked.

"Local punks," he said. "We turned three of 'em over to the police, and they're looking for the rest."

341

Josh Langston

Randy nodded. "An acquaintance of mine--who knows Nate, too, by the way--said she'd spoken with the Governor about making additional law enforcement personnel available."

"That explains all the extra chopper traffic," Bannock said. "Our Flight Ops people have been bitching about it."

"I'd rather they focus on the airship," Randy said. She seemed reluctant to say more, then leaned closer, as if for emphasis. "We need to increase security for *Puck One*."

Bannock laughed. "You think those assholes will try again? I'm not worried about them--at all. Their weapons were a joke, and the explosives they brought hardly live up to the name."

"There may be more going on here than meets the eye."

"How so?"

She shook her head, and Bannock couldn't help but admire the effect.

"I'm not sure," Randy said. "But I need you to trust my instincts. Beef up security, and do it as soon as possible."

"That's going to be difficult with Nate in the hospital and Ivan standing guard over him."

"Then bring Ivan back, and put everything we've got into securing the airship."

"I'll get Captain Odom on it right away."

Her eyebrows went up. "The *cops* will handle it?"

"Odom's a security guard. Supervisor type.

Former military I suppose." Banock didn't bother to mention Odom was a lousy marksman.

"Oh," Randy said. "Fine. Now, kindly take me to the airship."

"Yes'm."

~*~

Mato had no trouble tracking the man who'd taken Li, even in the dark. Both Li's scent and that of her captor lingered on the path he'd taken, but neither Mato nor the dog needed it. The path itself provided the most direct route imaginable, and Mato took advantage of it, urging Shadow to move faster.

Mato had some doubts about taking the giant down, but that and rescuing the Island girl had become his only objectives. He had to get close and work fast.

By the time he heard distant shouting, the sky had begun to lighten with the early morning sun. Little of it penetrated the thick canopy of vegetation, but enough came through to cast the darkness in lighter shades of gray.

Rather than let Shadow give his presence away, Mato secured him to a small tree and proceeded on foot. The dog gave in gracefully, and flopped down for a much needed nap.

The yelling continued. Mato recognized the tone more than the words, though he'd heard some of them on the magic box Tori called a "TeeVee." And then they stopped.

Mato wondered if Li had managed to subdue

343

Josh Langston

the giant on her own, but he knew she had no weapons left. After being kicked so viciously, she would probably find moving difficult, assuming she survived at all.

He quickly shunned such thoughts as unproductive and continued his search as before, following the path and listening for his quarry.

A short while later he heard the giant again. Mato pressed harder. Ignoring the need for silence and caution, he broke into a run, racing along a path which grew easier and easier to see.

Eventually, he left the heavy cover of the forest and burst into an area the giants had scraped clean. They obviously hadn't finished the job, as the ground remained uneven and rock-strewn. Nor had the giants covered it yet with the thick black material they used to keep the plants from growing back. Mato smelled only the one giant he'd been chasing, but several of their vehicles cluttered the area. Only one of them, however, had an occupant: a small, red car streaked with mud.

Mato hurried closer, even though his intended target had already closed the doors and started the engine. A cloud of vile-smelling fumes erupted from it as the wheels spun and sprayed him with dirt and pebbles.

Then it raced off, into the distance.

With Li.

Mato hung his head in shame. He'd failed, again. Fighting giants, one-on-one, was futile.

Fighting them two-on-one, or a hundred-on-one would be equally pointless, and not simply because of their superior size. They also had machines and *technology*. All Mato had were two poison darts. He didn't even have a blowgun with which to launch them.

It occurred to him that he wasn't entirely empty-handed. He wasn't utterly bereft of tools and tricks. He had Nate. And nobody could hunt down the man Mato needed to find better than Nate.

No one.

All Mato had to do was go to him and tell him what happened. He'd know where to look for the man who took Li. He'd know what to do with him when he found him. If necessary, Mato could show him the hole in the ground under Tori's cabin where her first mate lay rotting. It would be a fitting place for this new giant, too. Let him also commune with the Spirits, and trouble Mato no more.

All he had to do was go to Nate and ask for help.

He thought briefly of returning to The Island People to let them know about Li and the attack on the giants. But they could do nothing. They had already proven that. They would suck down more of their stupid nakuah, tell themselves what great warriors they were, and then go to sleep. He'd tell them later, when they woke up. With a little help, Li might be able to tell them herself.

345

Josh Langston

Turning, he walked away from the cluster of parked vehicles and once again entered the thick woods. He needed Shadow. They had a long way to go to reach his friend.

No, he corrected himself. He needed *all* his giant friends. And he needed them now.

~*~

Chapter 18

A bumble bee is faster than a tractor.

Daphne spotted the murderous little snot who started the landslide tumbling toward the boulder Daphne used for shelter. She grabbed a leg and pulled her into her lap, then curled up with her eyes closed until she either woke up, or died.

Waking up came as a surprise, but not a terribly pleasant one.

The slide had caused the rocks that trapped her ankle to shift, and she was able to extract her leg from the geological vise, but she was reasonably sure she'd broken something in the process. The pain subsided when she held still but never completely went away.

Sitting motionless gave her time to examine the elfin body she had plucked from the rolling mayhem. The inspection generated more questions than answers, not the least of which centered on where the tiny human had come from, and why she felt compelled to commit murder by avalanche.

Rather than risk the pain that would come with leaning forward, Daphne raised the limp body to her ear and listened for a heartbeat. Finding one in a hummingbird might have been easier, but she persevered and eventually heard

347

something. The tiny body remained warm, and although it was covered with scrapes and bruises, there didn't appear to have been much bleeding. The most telling evidence of life was a slight rise and fall in the girl's chest when she breathed.

"I hope you've got an aspirin or two hidden away somewhere, lady. You're gonna need 'em," Daphne clucked over the unconscious girl. "Come to think of it, I could use a couple myself."

She tested her leg again only to wince and then give up. Looking down at the body in her lap, Daphne shook her head. "Ain't this a pickle?"

Which is when the girl opened her eyes.

She stared directly into Daphne's face, a look of fear spreading across her own. Daphne held her firmly in place. She wasn't about to let her go until she got some answers.

"Relax," Daphne said. "I won't hurt you."

That earned her a sneer of contempt.

"You don't seem to appreciate the delicate position you're in."

The girl squirmed and kicked her legs, but Daphne hung on.

"Calm down, damn it!" she said. "In case you hadn't noticed, I just saved your miserable life." She nodded her head at the rubble below. A thick cloud of dust hovered over it like smoke. "Or would you rather be underneath all that?"

Daphne couldn't tell if the doll-sized girl understood her words, but at least she stopped thrashing around like a fish on a line.

"Much better," Daphne said, and she followed that with a smile.

It wasn't something she meant to do; it just slipped out. She had every right to be pissed off, and she should have been struggling to resist the urge to toss the little bitch into the pile of rocks and tree limbs and God-only-knew what else at the bottom of the ravine.

Instead, she smiled.

The girl responded with a clearly puzzled look, as if she, too, expected Daphne to chuck her down the hill.

They both remained silent while the world around them seemed to settle. Daphne located her camera bag and fished out one of her two bottles of water. She helped herself to a sip, then offered some to the girl, holding the bottle at an angle so she could drink without drowning or bathing in it.

The girl wiped her mouth then looked directly at Daphne and said, "Thank you."

Daphne was so startled she almost dropped the girl *and* the water bottle.

"You speak English!"

The girl only shrugged.

~*~

A man bearing an Oregon driver's license and credit cards in the name of Rufus King stood in a security line at Honolulu International Airport. He had burned his John P. Cole documents and checked out of his room at the Sheraton hotel on

Josh Langston

Waikiki beach in plenty of time to catch a commuter flight to Lihue, on the island of Kauai. However, he had not anticipated that a tourist running behind schedule would try to save time by entering the gate area without passing through security. This maneuver required the tourist to sneak past a sleepy, uniformed guard assigned to watch over the exit *from* the gate area.

Though the guard failed to apprehend the culprit, he did sound an alarm, and the Transportation Security Administration responded by locking down the airport.

With a level of efficiency only possible by a federal government bureaucracy, the TSA spent the next seven hours sweeping the concourse for suspicious packages, enemy agents and/or religious extremists. Other than an intoxicated Alabama football fan and a rowdy punk rocker from Saskatchewan, no serious threats were discovered.

Rufus King was informed that it could take hours before all the delayed flights were cleared. Including his.

The irony of the situation wasn't lost on him. His employers had been instrumental in bringing about the kinds of security arrangements virtually all western countries had adopted. It didn't alter the fact that he hated waiting. He had only a narrow window of opportunity to accomplish what he was being paid to do.

If the delay lasted too long, the project he'd spent almost a year preparing for would have to be abandoned. And if that happened, he'd not only never see the rest of his money, he'd have to repay what he'd already received--assuming they let him live at all.

~*~

Maggie and Cal had just stepped outdoors to begin yet another hunt for Mato, when they spotted something huge floating above the mountain enclosing the inland side of the resort.

"Is that what I think it is?" Cal asked.

"It's a blimp, but it's got a funky shape."

"Or it could be a really slow spaceship. Maybe it's an invasion!"

"I doubt aliens would decorate their ships with pictures of Puck," Maggie said.

"Prolly not," he admitted. "But damn, that's a big sucker. And it's comin' down!"

The huge double cylinders of the craft dropped slowly behind the mountain.

"Nate said something about an airship," Maggie said, "but I didn't realize it was so big. Guess I didn't fully understand what he was talkin' about."

"Let's check it out," Cal said.

"We don' t have time. We've got to find Mato."

Cal slipped behind the wheel of the golf cart. "C'mon. Get in. I was thinkin' of starting our search in that direction anyway. If Mato went anywhere, it was deeper into the mountains, not down toward the ocean."

Maggie climbed in beside him. She put a bag of sandwiches and a small cooler full of beer behind the seat. "How far do you think we can go in this thing?"

"I don't know, but I reckon we'll find out."

"I wish this thing had four-wheel drive," she said.

Cal looked up at a rapidly darkening sky. The airship wasn't the only thing casting broad shadows. "I'd be happy if it had windshield wipers."

~*~

Tori hadn't slept much. A constant stream of hospital personnel came through Nate's room as if it were a central corridor. Most of them stopped to check a dial, adjust a tube or update a chart, but none of them seemed able to work in the dark. As a result, the overhead light went on and off like a Vegas marquee, and no matter how pleasantly any of the staff behaved, Tori hated them all. Not because they bothered her, but because they *might* bother Nate.

However, they kept coming back, and that meant Nate hadn't given up on life. Tori wouldn't give up either. She vowed to stay by his bedside, praying, or crying, or begging. She would do anything necessary to keep her man alive.

Her back hurt from the way she'd had to twist her body to try and sleep in the room's only chair, which, she was quite certain, had been designed by Torquemada or some other monster of the Spanish Inquisition. She stood and stretched hoping her bones might find their way back to the proper position.

A tall woman with dark red hair entered the room. Tori looked at her with suspicion since she wasn't wearing hospital attire. She assumed it was someone from the business office come to talk to her about who would pick up the tab for Nate's care.

The woman had just finished a conversation on her cell phone and slipped the device into the pocket of her tailored slacks. She then smiled and extended her hand. "I'm Randy Rhoades. We spoke on the phone last night."

"Oh, right. Of course," Tori said. *She's gorgeous. No wonder Nate talked about her so much.*

"How's he doing?"

Tori reached out to touch him. "He must be doing better. He's still--"

"I know. I talked to the medical staff. He's a strong guy with a strong will to live. There's plenty of reason for hope."

Neither woman mentioned the fact that life support gear was the only thing keeping him alive.

Tori sniffed. Her face ached from all the crying she had already done. She didn't want to turn the tears on again. Not with Randy Rhoades standing there.

"I arranged for someone to come here and give you a massage," the redhead said. "It won't make up for the lousy accommodations, but hopefully, it'll make them a little easier to endure."

"Thank you," Tori said. *Maybe she's not so bad after all.*

"As soon as Nate can be moved out of Intensive Care, he'll have a private room, and I'll see that you'll be comfortable there, too. You'll have a decent chair and a decent bed. The food here isn't too bad, but--"

"You don't have to do all this," Tori said, feeling slightly overwhelmed. "I'm sure Nate's got some kind of insurance, and if he doesn't--"

Randy waved her off. "We'll take care of all that. The only thing that matters is Nate's recovery."

"That's very generous of you."

"Nonsense. It's company policy. Besides, you need to be with him, and he needs you here. It's that simple."

"Again, thank you," Tori said.

Randy hesitated before continuing. "There's something I need to ask you about, even though circumstances have changed drastically. But I'm still required to follow up on it."

Tori didn't feel like discussing much of anything, but she had little choice. She couldn't very well throw the woman out. "Okay, shoot."

"We always run background checks on prospective employees, and while the resulting file focused on Nate, it also listed those close to him. Like you."

Tori tried not to squirm. "And?"

"According to the report, you don't have a sister, or a brother-in-law. And you certainly don't have a nephew or a son. So, would you please explain to me what you're doing with a small child?"

"I--"

"You have to understand my position. I was the one who hired Nate. If there's something shady going on here--and frankly, I can't imagine how or why Nate *could* get caught up in something like that--I need to know about it."

"Mato is--"

"Nate said his name was Matt."

"It's complicated."

Randy pursed her lips and waited.

It didn't take long for the moment to become awkward. Tori thought about making something up, but she knew Randy would see through it-- sooner rather than later. So instead, Tori told her the whole story. How she met the little Indian; how he saved her life and that of several others; how his mate had been kidnapped and taken to New York, and how after they all came home again, he reappeared under unusual circumstances.

Tori went on to explain the fears she and

Nate shared about the world discovering Mato and his people, and how their lives and culture would be destroyed if, for no other reason, people just came to gawk at them. The reality would be far worse. Everyone would want some of Mato's blood. And even if they managed to keep that secret, his people would be subjected to academic studies, TV exposés, and the worlds of entertainment and advertising. They'd never be left alone, and they'd never be the same.

"But Mato's blood is the biggest thing," she said. "I know it doesn't make any sense, but it works. If we could find Mato and bring him here--"

"I thought he was with you."

"He was," Tori said, "but he took off on his own. The rest of us were busy with other stuff. Stupid stuff. And now we don't know where he is. Maggie and Cal are out looking for him now."

During most of Tori's story, Randy said nothing, though her eyes widened in surprise from time to time. When Tori finally paused for breath, Randy said, "You mentioned unusual circumstances' concerning Mato's return. What's that all about?"

"He may have been involved in a homicide," Tori said.

"He *killed* someone? How's that possible? You said he was only two feet tall."

"I said he was little. I never said he wasn't tough as nickel steak. Besides, we're pretty sure

356

the whole thing was an accident. He was just trying to protect my dog. His dog, really. The poor thing's spent way more time with him than me."

"And?"

"Some asshat aimed a gun at the dog, and Mato stabbed him."

"To *death?*"

Tori gave her head an intense shake. "No! He uses something on his arrows that'll put whatever he shoots to sleep. It doesn't kill. Only, in this case, the cops think the guy Mato attacked had an allergic reaction. Mato says the stuff was all dried up and shouldn't have had any effect at all."

Randy stood silent and motionless for some time, as if allowing Tori's tale to sink in. "This whole thing is so bizarre, I doubt you made it up." She paused again. "But there's no way in hell I can put any of this into a report."

"Thank God," Tori said.

"I have no idea what to do with it!"

"Just keep it under your hat, like we've been doing."

"I'll see what I can do about helping your friends find the little guy."

Tori felt a bit of hope. "That would be wonderful."

Randy nodded and turned toward the door, then stopped and looked back. "There's one more thing. I thought you'd want to know that the police have arrested all but one of the hoods

357

involved in the attempted break-in."

"Did they shoot any of 'em?"

"I don't think so," Randy said.

Tori frowned. "Too bad."

~*~

Just about everyone who lived on Kauai knew about Mount Waialeale, which many residents claimed was the wettest place on Earth. Paku had heard it rained there almost every day. He'd never paid much attention to such talk, but reminders of it marched into his awareness as he drove closer to the peak.

His little car had handled the extreme challenges of the service road he'd been traveling. He'd followed instructions provided by Kwan when driving in, but he'd burned them along with everything else he left behind. Now, he wasn't sure where he was. Everything looked the same.

He passed a few turn-offs, but tried to stay on what he thought was the main road, though the term was debatable. When two dirt roads intersect, which is the "main" one? Without the guidance provided by Kwan, Paku had no clue.

What he did have, however, was better than half a tank of gas. If he couldn't get two hundred miles out of it--or more--no one could. Two hundred miles! That was like a round-trip flight to Honolulu. Sooner or later he was bound to reach blacktop. All he had to do was keep driving.

And ignore the rain.

All too often he'd seen choppers overhead,

and he knew they weren't providing a field trip for TV weathermen. Those were cops up there. So, whenever he caught sight of a helicopter, his first reaction was to find a tree big enough to hide under. This caused him to leave the road on several occasions, and it was only through great good luck, and the superiority of his self-proclaimed driving skills, that he didn't get bogged down in mud while waiting for the law to fly away.

Instead, he grew cocky.

He was Mario-goddam-Andretti. Dirt road? Pah. He could handle it. So what if the back end of the Z4 tended to drift a little? Who cared if he kicked up a little mud?

The rain kept falling.

Paku kept driving.

And much to his surprise, a trio of wild hogs trotted across the muddy, rutted road in front of him.

Paku jammed on the brakes, which did nothing to slow the scarlet Z4 down. Instead, it began to spin and hurtled sideways toward a massive banyan tree.

Paku's legs stiffened as he reflexively tried to push both the brake pedal and the accelerator through the floorboard. The engine screamed in protest.

Paku screamed, too.

And then the banyan tree put an end to it all. Several of the many snaking roots of the tree were scored by the impact, but the trunk absorbed the worst of it. Paku's lifeless body blended wetly with the Z4's crumpled exterior.

The rain could hardly reach the wreckage which remained well hidden from the view of anyone flying by overhead.

~*~

Kiku and the rest of The Island People were delighted to see Li. She wandered among them, proud of the wounds she'd received in her battle with the giants, chief among which was a bruise that darkened her entire torso and limited her movements.

A scouting party was dispatched to ensure the enemy had indeed left the area. They reported back that while they watched, giants had flooded the camp, trampling much of the jungle and despoiling it with their enormous flying machines. They didn't stay long, however. They gathered their fallen comrades and loaded them into their vehicles. Then, with great noise, and the usual measure of destruction, they departed leaving not a soul behind.

When asked by the youngster, Makani, about the stranger who'd accompanied her, Li dismissed him as irrelevant. He had done nothing to assist her in the battle, and while he may have landed a surreptitious blow or two, his disappearance spoke to his lack of bravery.

Kiku ordered another feast. Alas, they would have to make do without nakuah as they had recently exhausted their supply. Kiku said it didn't matter. Li's victorious return was reason enough to celebrate.

~*~

No one batted an eye at Maggie and Cal when they drove their golf cart through the tunnel leading to the Transport Terminal. When they reached the far side, however, they were unable to go anywhere near the airship which filled up the field on the far side of the complex. Low windows had been provided for future passengers, but the doors were all locked and sealed. A couple security guards wandered the area but once they'd inspected room keys and identification, they had no further interest in the pre-opening sightseers.

Lacking other options, Maggie and Cal turned around and drove back to the resort area, then took their chances off-road. The woods near the base of the sharply rising mountain had been cut back at some point, but now reasserted itself.

Cal tried to avoid the thickest vegetation and drove a tortured route through to the far side. There they encountered an area marked by yellow police tape and assumed it was where Nate had been shot. The reason for putting up tape baffled them since one couldn't get there unless seriously determined to do so. Nobody would wander by casually.

As they weren't interested in the crime scene, they focused on the route leading away from it

Josh Langston

and into the forest. Several vehicles had recently traveled the same route and left an obvious path for them to follow.

"Would Mato have come this way?" Maggie asked.

Cal shrugged. "Fact is, this is the *only* way we can go. Unless you want to try walking."

She didn't. "Maybe if we make enough noise, he'll hear us."

Bouncing and crashing through the jungle generated plenty of noise, which Maggie and Cal augmented with groans and curses. The route had definitely not been carved by a road grader.

Though the sun had moved to a position nearly straight above them, they saw little of it through the canopy of green overhead. Maggie focused on the woods around them while Cal maneuvered down the misbegotten "trail."

Both of them were shocked when Mato jumped on board from behind and tapped them on the shoulders. "Find Nate," he said, "now."

Shadow appeared, too, and jumped up on the seat pushing Maggie firmly against Cal.

"Mato!" Maggie gasped. "Where'd you come from?"

He pointed vaguely in the direction which lay ahead, then began to inspect the bag of sandwiches with a mumbled, "Hungry."

Though she was a little late, Maggie told him to help himself.

Cal appeared slightly wounded as the little

Indian grabbed one sandwich and handed another to the huge, black dog. Both quickly disappeared.

"There's beer and water in the cooler," Maggie added.

Mato grabbed a bottle of water while Cal tried to turn the golf cart around. He soon discovered the implausibility of that and gave up. "Looks like we're going to have to back outta here."

"Where Nate?" Mato asked.

Maggie explained that he had been gravely injured. Mato frowned, clearly concerned. He understood what it meant to be gunshot. He'd seen plenty of people wounded on the "TeeVee" machine in Tori's cabin.

"We'll get you there as quick as we can," Cal promised, though their progress in reverse was even more torturous than it had been on the way in.

"We had no way to tell you about Nate," Maggie said. "I wish you had a phone." Then she looked at Cal. "Why not give him yours?"

"Why mine?"

"'Cause you rarely use it, and as long as we're in Hawaii, we'll probably be together, so anyone who needs to call can reach me. Besides, your dumb old phone will be easier for him to use."

Cal grudgingly surrendered his flip phone, and Maggie went through the basics with Mato. She called Cal's phone with hers to demonstrate the ring tone.

"You can tell who's calling because their photo will appear on the little screen."

"No, it won't," Cal said.

"Why not? I showed you how to do it."

"Yeah, well, I sorta never had time to--"

"Geez, Cal! You didn't do anything with the ring tones, either, did you?" She didn't bother waiting for an answer. Instead, she prodded the phone's keypad and listened to possible tones until she found one Mato liked. She then assigned it to Tori's number.

"Okay. Now, whenever you hear that sound, it means Tori is trying to call you." She fiddled with the buttons again and played another snippet of sound. "When I call, it'll sound like that."

They practiced briefly until Mato mastered it. He slipped the phone into a pouch he wore slung across his chest. Maggie noticed two sharp darts threaded through a fold in the cloth and reached toward them. Mato pushed her hand away. He looked at Cal then, and smiled.

"Phone good," he said.

Cal grunted a "You're welcome" in return.

Standing on the back of the cart where golfers would normally stow their gear, Mato kept a lookout. Shadow leaned into Maggie, panting heavily, and she put her arm around him, completely ignoring the dog's damp coat and disagreeable odor. He appeared worn out.

Mato, however, seemed relatively fresh.

Never one to bother speaking much, he pointed to the sky and said, "Great machine in sky. Big, like cloud."

"The blimp! How in the world did you see that through all the leaves?"

The little Indian seemed surprised that she would ask. "Climb tree. See far." He looked closely at her. "Bah-limp?"

"Yes. It's full of gas. Helium. So it's lighter than air."

Mato pretended to hold something in his hand. "Air weigh nothing."

"I can't explain it," she said. "Maybe Nate can once you help him."

He nodded. "Mato find giant who took girl."

"What girl?"

"Name Li. Very pretty. Brave. But not smart."

Maggie squinted at him. "Who are you talking about?"

"Island People," he said. "Like me. Not giants."

Cal almost rammed the cart into a tree. "You found more little people?"

"Yes."

"Well, I'll be dipped in shit," Cal said.

"And a giant captured one of them?" Maggie asked.

"Li," Mato said. "Her name Li."

They drove on without further comment until the wretched trail opened up near the base of the mountain which housed the Transport Terminal.

365

"Where bah-limp?" Mato said as he stepped off the back of the cart.

Cal pointed at the sharply rising ground. "On the other side of that."

Mato turned away and began to climb the steep slope. Shadow barked at him without attempting to follow, the futility of that obvious even to him.

"We can get you to the hospital," Maggie yelled to him.

"Mato fly. Find Nate," he yelled back. "Bah-limp!"

"But--"

"There's no talkin' to that boy," Cal said.

"They'll never let him board that thing."

"What makes you think they'll even see him?" Maggie fumed. "That's just stupid, Cal! They're not going to the hospital. I don't know if they're going anywhere."

"Best we can do is just go back through the tunnel and see what's going on. We'll straighten it all out then."

Maggie continued to shake her head. "I hope you're right."

"Of course I am," he said. "Aren't I always?"

She looked at him sideways, then switched places with the dog. "The least you can do is turn this damn thing around and drive forward for awhile."

~*~

Chapter 19

*"The two most important days of your life
are the day you were born, and the
day you find out why." --Mark Twain*

The man calling himself Rufus King clambered up a ladder leading to the resort's main dock and dumped a knapsack at his feet when he reached the top. He'd been deposited by the same trio who had heard the last words spoken by the late crime boss, Daniel Kwan.

A man in the uniform of a security guard looked down at the knapsack and then back up at King. "I've already got the crate unpacked and the cylinder loaded. Your parachute and hazmat gear are in bags on the deck beside it. I got everything done last night."

"Good," King said. The man appeared to be waiting for a compliment, but King wasn't in the mood. The airport hold-up had nearly cost him the entire operation. He'd be lucky to reach Honolulu before the mid-point of the game. *What did the Americans call it? Half-time?*

"Do you need me to go with you?" the security man asked.

"Why would I want that?"

"I dunno. Something might go wrong. Ya never know."

"In which case I will be much better off

367

dealing with it by myself," King said. "Your job is to assure the authorities that my flight is proceeding normally. I don't need some idiot in a fighter jet shooting a missile up my ass."

"Of course."

"We follow the plan. Once I've left the stadium behind, you are free to go. And if you have any brains at all, you'll go as far away as you can. You have money?"

He nodded. "Half. The rest will come later."

"You can count on it," King said. "I've dealt with these people before. As long as you don't cross them, they'll live up to the bargain. If you don't, they'll kill you. That has a way of insuring cooperation despite the--" he paused "--*unpleasant* things we're paid to do."

The man appeared uncertain. He swallowed too much. If not for all the cash his employers had surely promised the man, King would never have trusted him. As it was, he didn't trust the people paying him. He had no intention of wearing the protective gear or using the parachute they provided. They might as well have been labeled death traps. He'd found a more elegant solution for finishing the job and insuring his own survival. Everything he needed was in the knapsack.

"The crew is in the briefing room," the security man said, checking his watch. "You've only got a few minutes."

King picked up his gear and stuck his arms

through the shoulder straps. "Then quit wasting my time and take me there."

The guard broke into a trot, and King kept pace, despite the knapsack. He'd been in better shape, but he could still move quickly when he had to. And this was clearly such a time.

~*~

Whatever guilt Reyna felt before she started the landslide didn't begin to compare with what she felt after the giant saved her life. The target-turned-savior not only smiled at her, but gave her water, too.

Who was crazy enough to do that?

And yet the woman holding her showed no sign that she'd been possessed by Spirits of any kind, let alone those which drove people mad. She was in obvious pain, but Reyna couldn't think of anything she could do to help. Winter Woman might have been able to suggest something, but much of what the old woman knew remained a secret.

"What's your name?" the giant asked.

Reyna recognized the phrase. It was one of several Mato badgered her to memorize. She responded by rote. "I am called Reyna."

The giantess smiled again. "I'm Daphne."

Further conversation seemed doomed, and Reyna strained to remember some of the other phrases Mato tried to teach her. Daphne had no such constraints and rattled off so many questions that Reyna's only recourse was to stare at her, quiet as a trout.

Daphne helped her to a sitting position atop the boulder they'd hidden behind during the rockslide. Reyna relaxed, and when it was obvious she wouldn't run away, the giantess tried again. This time she asked questions using simple language. Even so, Reyna had to guess at some of the meaning. The giantess even tried to act out what she meant which made them both giggle.

Daphne reminded Reyna very much of Tori, Mato's first giant friend. She, too, had an easy laugh, and never appeared threatening. She had good food, too, and a warm comfortable home. Reyna suspected Daphne did, too.

From the way Daphne reacted to the pain in her leg, Reyna thought she had broken a bone. The giantess would not be walking home any time soon.

Then Daphne took something out of her bag and held it to the side of her head. Reyna had seen such a thing before. Tori had one and would often talk into it.

Daphne, however, talked *at* it, and she did so in a loud voice. She also shook the device and made angry faces at it. Evidently, the Spirits which made it work had been frightened away. Reyna had forgotten how foolish some giants could be about things that seemed quite obvious. There was no point in being angry at the Spirits. They would do as they pleased and often ignored entreaties put forth by The People. It would be no different for giants.

Daphne then did something truly extraordinary: she offered to share her food. Reyna was shocked. Though the slide had roughed her up, she was still perfectly capable of finding her own food. Daphne couldn't even stand up. And yet, she tried to give away some of what little she had.

Amazing!

Reyna refused the offer, of course. The giantess needed it much more than she did. Reyna doubted she could provide her with enough food to stay alive. If her own people didn't come for her soon, it would be too late. That made Reyna sad.

Worse still, she had to leave. The People had surely packed everything already, and if they hadn't begun their trek to the new camp, they would very soon.

How could she explain all that when they had struggled just to exchange names?

~*~

The climb up and over the mountain didn't prove too taxing. The mountains where Mato had grown up were much bigger and more challenging. He paused at the top to catch his breath and admire the unimaginably huge bah-limp. It was so long and fat it all but filled the valley which the giants had obviously enlarged just to accommodate it.

Mato's mind whirled with the enormity of the

371

machine. He'd never seen anything even remotely similar. And the fact that it could be floated off the ground completely mystified him. Once again, it was giant technology, and once again he found it bewildering.

But, one issue over-rode whatever reluctance he might have had to investigate the machine. Nate needed him. If Mato didn't reach him soon, Nate would die. And since the only way to get to Nate was to fly, Mato was determined to do exactly that. The Spirits obviously approved, since they provided him the means to do so.

With that, Mato began his descent on the far side of the great hill the giants called a "mountain." Going down went much faster than going up, and Mato jumped, skidded or fell most of the way. He hit the ground on his feet, however, and ran directly toward the part of the machine clearly meant for passengers.

The door to the compartment was closed, and Mato couldn't reach the handle no matter how high he jumped. He backed away and searched for another way in. It amazed him that such a monstrous vehicle--one large enough to fill up a valley--was held off the ground by a few small wheels. The ones on Tori's truck were larger, and she said hers was a small truck. Other than the tires, a few thin ropes on each side connected it to the canyon walls, but they did nothing to hold the immense craft up.

Crazy, crazy giants.

Mato then found a different way in: a low entry at the end of a ramp. After a quick look around to be sure no one saw him, he scampered up the ramp into the dark, warm interior.

He waited until his eyes adjusted to the limited light, then looked around. It appeared to be a storage area. Empty racks lined the walls, and when he looked up, he saw a network of beams and crossbars upon which rested what appeared to be a double row of enormous round bladders.

He also saw a door leading to the part of the ship which had windows. He tried to open it, but couldn't. The knob wouldn't budge.

Concerned that someone would soon arrive to close the door through which he entered, Mato searched for a place to hide. There weren't many to choose from since the shelves were empty and only a few items lay on the deck. These included a large, metal tank. It was strapped to a flat wooden stand and was cold to the touch. There were two bags behind the tank, but he could only open one of them. It contained a rubbery material in bright, shiny yellow. Some sort of clothing, he thought. The other bag was larger and significantly heavier. It had a metal ring on one side and several heavy straps on the other. In other words, a complete puzzle.

Neither the tank nor the two bags offered enough protection from view, so Mato climbed up one of the storage racks, confident he could pull himself up into the exposed rafters. Part way up he saw a compact flashlight mounted on the wall. Though a different color, bright orange, it was otherwise very similar to one that Tori had given him. He and Reyna had used it to explore the sacred cavern under Tori's cabin. He grabbed it and attached it to his belt, then continued his climb.

He reached a narrow walkway which went straight through the double row of partially inflated bladders and led toward the front of the ship. It would do. Mato lay down there, and waited.

With any luck, he could climb down and out--unseen--as soon as the flying machine reached the hospital. It never occurred to him the airship might be headed to some other destination, or be engaged on some mission other than the one to which he'd dedicated himself.

The Spirits had smiled on him, after all. One ignored them at their peril.

~*~

Joe Bannock had way too much to do. He certainly didn't need to spend time worrying about the damned airship. He had a construction job to finish, and though he had no one to confide in, he couldn't wait to finish it so he could go home. He was tired of Hawaii, something he once thought impossible.

Unfortunately, Randy had ordered him to manage the operation of *Puck One* on its inaugural goodwill flight. The great airship was set to fly over Aloha Stadium in Honolulu as part of the half-time activities of a pre-season pro football game.

If it had been left up to Bannock, he'd have vetoed the idea as shamelessly expensive. Puck had all the goodwill it would need for the next million years, give or take. One more blimp flight wouldn't make any difference. The decision, however, had come from Tim Archer himself, and no one argued with him, not even the heavenly redhead who represented him.

Bannock made a token appearance in the Security office and was surprised to see only Ivan on duty. "Where's Odom?"

"Doan know." The big man paused in mid-bite of a *malasada*, or Portuguese doughnut. "Boss?" Crumbs erupted from Ivan's maw. "You see dat?"

Eager to look away, Bannock followed Ivan's gaze to a security screen focused on the passenger compartment of the enormous airship. "See what?"

"Somebody jus' climbed up inna blimp. Small guy; keiki mebbe."

"Kay-kee may-bee?" He made no effort to disguise his irritation with Ivan's crippled version of English.

"Keiki. A kid. You know. Little boy."

"There aren't any children around here."

Ivan hiked his massive shoulders up toward

his ears. "'Kay den. Mebbe he wuz menehune."

Right. Just like the idiotic, cut-out cartoon characters Archer insisted they put up all over the resort. "Have you been smoking something?"

"No, brah. Doan do pakalolo. Dis fo real."

"Then go check it out, if it makes you feel better. But don't waste much time. It looks like you're the only one on duty around here."

If he could find an empty office somewhere, Bannock thought, maybe he could get some paperwork done, at least. Not that he liked the stuff, but big corporations lived on it. Paperwork--the mother's milk of industry.

He decided to find some coffee first.

~*~

Captain Odom walked into the Flight Operations area of the Control Center and cleared his throat. The three people in the room, all wearing light blue, Puck Air jumpsuits, turned to face him.

"The captain and crew of the *Puck One* asked me to invite you to a brief celebration in honor of their first flight in service to the resort." He smiled hard, but didn't want to appear as if he was over-selling the invitation.

"I know you're all busy trying to get ready, but I'm told you can probably afford to take a few minutes to meet with the flight crew and wish them well."

"We're already short-handed," one of the men said. "Our boss quit after his uhm--

376

encounter with Mr. Bannock."

Odom nodded. "That was unfortunate. I'm sorry I wasn't here to help. The timing couldn't have been worse."

A woman stood up. "Come on now guys, we aren't *that* busy." She had a friendly smile and made the summons sound celebratory. "Will there be cake?"

Odom returned her smile. "One never knows."

They followed him out of the room like a parade of baby ducks. Odom led them to a sound-proofed meeting room at the end of the hall. Smiling, he waved them in, then closed and locked the door behind them. Since cell phones weren't allowed in Flight Operations, Odom felt reasonably sure no one in the room would be able to summon help.

He checked his watch. He only had to hold out for another 90 minutes. Maybe less. Then he walked back toward Flight Operations. As long as the guy in the airship did his job, Odom would soon be a wealthy man.

~*~

Simon Dole finished his last class and trudged into his office, fully expecting to find Daphne Cutter waiting for him. Sadly, she wasn't. And as he settled into the chair behind his desk, unable to avoid looking at a pile of ungraded research papers, he realized how much he would have preferred to be out tramping around in the

Josh Langston

Cloud Peak Wilderness Area--with her.

Thoughts of Daphne softened the ruggedness of the terrain he envisioned. The woman was simply amazing. She was also frustrating, sexy, demanding, and persuasive. All of that and more. Hell, the things she could do in bed were-- He went limp. She must have done graduate work in Boudoir Arts. And if not, she could teach the whole damned course catalog.

So, where was she? He thumbed her number from the Contact list on his phone, but she didn't answer. That meant she either wasn't getting his signal, or worse: she didn't want to talk to him.

Shit.

He took another look at the mound of research papers on his desk. The grad student working as the department secretary had taken no pains to stack them neatly. An untidy pile always seemed larger somehow.

He turned to his computer and looked up the number of the newspaper where Daphne worked. She was probably there; someone could surely connect him.

Alas, he was proven wrong, again.

He looked out the window. Sunset wouldn't hit for a few hours yet. He had time to reach the Cloud Peak. He could probably hike in while it was still light. But there was no way he'd make it out before dark.

Just... damn!

He tried her cell phone again and got the

same result. For once, he wished he knew some of her friends. Maybe they could tell him where she was.

But he already knew that. And he decided to go look for her.

On the way out of his office he bumped into the girl who had gone with him and the two male grad students the last time he'd visited the Cloud Peak.

She still wore the jeans that so delightfully captured her sculptured curves. Her warm smile and breathy greeting demanded his attention.

"You probably haven't had a chance to look at my paper yet," she said.

"No," he admitted. He hadn't looked at any of them. "Is there something I can help you with?"

"Actually, there is. But I'm afraid it'll take some time to explain. I thought maybe we could talk over a cup of coffee or something."

Simon checked his watch, then looked back at the girl and decided he could always check on Daphne in the morning. He promised himself he'd get an early start.

~*~

King reached the briefing room and stopped to catch his breath. There would be at least two people in there--a pilot and a co-pilot--and possibly an air hostess, although it seemed unlikely any passengers would be on board. One never knew, however. Americans had the strangest ideas about such things. They'd try to make something momentous out of the company's first official flight. Someone might want to be on board just to be able to say they'd been there.

Crazy bastards.

He checked his sidearm. The magazine was fresh. He had fifteen rounds. If he couldn't put down two or three unarmed people, he didn't deserve to live himself.

Time to go!

He pushed open the door, and two men looked up. King recognized them both from the Zeppelin flight school in Friedrichshafen.

"Klaus? Klaus Becker?" One of them said.

King shot him in the forehead.

The other man said nothing, though his jaw dropped open and his eyes swelled in shock.

King shot him in the chest. Twice.

He glanced around to be sure he hadn't overlooked anyone, then hurried toward the exit. Handy windows along one side of the corridor made it impossible to mistake which way to go. Aside from a baggage loading ramp, *Puck One* appeared ready for its inaugural mission.

So was King.

~*~

Ivan lumbered toward the airship and tried to climb in through the cargo door, but the conveyor belt for loading baggage barred his path. He shoved it back toward the terminal then bent low and wormed his way into the dark storage space like a Calypso dancer.

Once inside, he loosened the collar on his aloha shirt and looked around. The little stowaway had to be here somewhere; there weren't that many places to hide.

"C'mon out, you," he said. "Come to Ivan."

There wasn't much to see. A metal gas tank roughly the size of a garbage can sat in the middle of the storage area. He walked around it and discovered a bag with a funny-looking plastic suit, and another bag that looked like a parachute.

He scratched his head. *What the hell was that all about?*

He walked over to the door leading to the main cabin, but found it locked. Overhead a maze of girders and struts led to a double row of odd, partially inflated airbags. Then something clanged off the floor behind him.

Startled, he twisted around and looked down to investigate.

It was a bad idea.

~*~

Maggie worried about Mato. She and Cal flanked the dog on the seat of the golf cart while Cal drove them back around the mountain to the tunnel entrance. Cal had popped open two beers which served as their lunch since the dog and the little mountain climber had eaten their sandwiches. The beer could have been colder.

She didn't complain and kept a firm grip on Shadow's collar even though the stout animal

Josh Langston

showed no interest in leaving. He appeared content just to lean on her. Had he been dry, and a little less smelly, she would have found it comforting.

"I'd have thought there'd be a lot more folks at work around here," Cal said as they drove into the tunnel. "The resort will open soon."

"There's a bunch of 'em working on the guest rooms," she said. "Remember that huge pile of empty furniture boxes we saw piled up in the tiki plaza."

"What's a tiki plaza?"

"You really can't figure that out?"

He compressed his lips. "I saw the boxes. I just didn't know the place had a name. Couldn't see many of them tiki things though. Too many boxes in the way."

She let it go. "Anyhow, that's where I think the workers are."

"Yep, prob'ly," he said, scanning both sides of the tunnel. "Have you seen a restroom anywhere around here?"

~*~

Mato congratulated himself on his clever hiding space, which he hadn't been settled in for long. He'd only enjoyed a few heartbeats of relaxation before he heard something and looked down into the cargo hold. There he saw what must have been the biggest giant who'd ever lived squirming his way into the ship.

Stunned by the sheer size of the man, Mato

hurriedly pulled himself together. He was in no immediate danger. There could be any number of reasons for the man's presence.

"Relax brah," said the man, as if he were speaking directly to Mato. "I know you in heah. You come out now."

Mato held his breath. How could anyone know he was there? It had to be a trick of some kind. Either that, or the giant was looking for someone else.

"C'mon, brah."

The giant moved slowly, as if the floor was slippery, but he soon stopped directly beneath Mato.

"If you doan come out, you get hurt. You awful small."

His words seemed strange, but they were close enough to what Mato learned from his time with the giants at home that he thought he understood. In any case, none of it sounded good.

Moving silently, Mato pulled the flashlight from his belt. The giant obviously didn't know where Mato was, but given enough time, he'd find out.

Mato extracted one of the two remaining darts from his shirt. The sleeping paste Li had coated them with had long since dried, but they might still retain some power. Mato prayed that they did. Without waiting further, he dropped the flashlight behind the giant.

It hit the floor and bounced, causing the giant

to whirl completely around. Mato dropped down from his perch in the ceiling onto the man's broad back and jabbed the dart into his neck, then quickly leaped away to the nearest storage rack.

As the giant straightened and rubbed his neck, Mato climbed back up into the girders and beams above, listening.

The giant mumbled something, but Mato couldn't understand him. Clearly, the big fellow wasn't happy. He leaned against a wall and slid down it to the floor.

Then there was silence.

Chapter 20

*Mississippi wisdom: Never annoy a woman
who can operate a backhoe.*

King left the bodies of the dead air crew where they fell. If his accomplice did his job right, King would be safely away before anyone started looking for him. The gun he'd used would go into the Pacific Ocean along with anything else that might tie him to the crime. They'd be looking for a ghost.

As he approached the airship he noticed someone had left the hatch to the cargo bay open. More than likely one of the two men he'd just killed was responsible for securing it during a pre-flight inspection. King wasn't about to waste time on a complete walk-around and simply closed and locked the hatch, then boarded the passenger cabin through the main entry.

Once inside he withdrew and collapsed the fold-out steps which stowed neatly into the floor. He then sealed the door, made his way to the flight deck. After stowing his gear in a locker beneath the back of his seat, he slipped into the captain's chair.

The ship powered up quickly, and a preflight checklist appeared on his touchscreen monitor. Running his finger down the list, he ticked off every item as "Ready" without bothering to verify anything. This was, after all, a Zeppelin. If nothing else, one had to admire German engineering. Anything that didn't work properly when the airship flew to the resort would have been repaired already. Or so he hoped. Besides, he couldn't waste time on such niceties as checklists.

He did, however, have to wait for the helium to decompress and inflate the gas bags enough to provide the lift he needed. Because he had neither cargo nor crew, that level was achieved in a reasonable length of time. Too slow for King, but quick enough.

The killer glanced at the warning indicator for the cargo hatch he'd closed earlier. It was dark, and would stay that way until he unlocked the hatch from where he sat. He would enter the cargo bay from the main cabin and open it when the time came.

The voice of his collaborator soon came over the radio giving him clearance to take off. King responded with a snort. Since when did he require clearance from a hireling?

He responded with a curt, "Roger." Just like in the movies.

The last thing he had to do was disconnect the tie-down cables securing his craft to its mountain berth. Those fell away at the click of a switch. After that, every light on the control panel glowed green.

With a clear sky and a favorable breeze, the huge airship lifted gently off the ground. As soon as he cleared the sheltering mountains, he brought the outboard engines up to their operating maximum and began to leave Kauai behind.

King took a deep breath and entered the GPS coordinates for Aloha Stadium. The flight would take approximately one hour, plenty of time for the tasks ahead.

~*~

Reyna waited as long as she could before leaving to catch up with The People. Daphne seemed to understand in spite of their limited ability to communicate. Gestures and pantomime only accomplished so much.

A pile of brush and deadfall lay near the giant's feet, the result of much effort on Reyna's part to give her a means to stay warm during the coming night. At first Daphne didn't understand, and may even have thought Reyna meant to set her on fire. Fortunately, she got the idea soon enough but made it clear she had no way to get a blaze going.

Reyna demonstrated chipping sparks from flint, gave her fire starting tools, and urged her to practice. Daphne seemed interested, but something in her expression suggested she would soon give up hope. That gave Reyna a new idea.

Perhaps she could convince Winter Woman that not all giants were bad. If this one survived, perhaps she could even help protect The People from future incursions by other giants.

387

Reyna didn't put great hope in the plan. The People were driven more by tradition than anything else. It had kept them alive since the First Days, about which the elders often spoke. The same words had been repeated by one generation after another. Nothing changed, except the giants.

More of them came every year. Living in secrecy had become the primary task of the entire clan. It overshadowed everything else in their lives. The result was a smaller tribe composed of mostly frightened people--a sad way to live.

Perhaps, if Reyna presented it the right way, Winter Woman would at least consider the idea, and hopefully act on it. If not, Daphne would likely die soon.

And alone.

~*~

Bannock received a call from Odom in security advising that there were unauthorized visitors in the terminal and asking him to escort them back to the resort proper.

"Are you seriously asking me to do your job?"

"We're short-handed everywhere today," Odom said. "If you hadn't tried to strangle the Flight Ops guy, we--"

"Okay, okay," Bannock said with an added curse. "I'll take care of it. Where are they?"

"In the tunnel near the entrance to the Command Center. I don't know what they're up to."

"I'll find out."

"One other thing," Odom said. "They've got a dog. A damned big one. Be careful."

Hoping to get Ivan to handle it, Bannock called him on his cell. Ivan didn't respond, and Joe hung up before the call went to voicemail, which Ivan never listened to anyway.

With another round of curses, he abandoned his overdue reports and walked to the far end of the windowless compound to the tunnel and the civilian-centric boarding area for the airships. There he spotted a middle-aged couple and a huge black dog standing beside a Puck Paradise golf cart. The dog was not on a leash.

"Can I help you folks?" he asked, trying not to reveal his uneasiness around the animal.

The couple introduced themselves as friends of Nate, and the male, a guy in a cowboy hat much like Nate's, claimed he needed to use a restroom.

"If you'll tie the dog up out here," Bannock said, "I'll show you to the facilities."

The woman apologized for not having a leash or a rope but assured him the dog would behave.

"It's not me," Bannock lied. "It's company policy, y'know?"

"Company policy doesn't have to take a pee," the man in the cowboy hat said. "Give me a break. Just think of Shadow as a service dog."

Bannock relented and led them to the building where he entered the pass code. The door, however, didn't open.

"That's odd," he said, reaching for his cell phone. "I'll call someone inside and get them to let us in."

But when he dialed Odom, there was no answer.

~*~

The man in the pilot's seat of the *Puck One* eased back and relaxed. Despite potentially disastrous problems, things were now moving forward smoothly. Even the weather cooperated, providing additional tailwind which would push the colossal airship to its destination ahead of time. The autopilot would make any course corrections needed.

King allowed himself time to reflect. He even lit a joint to insure he'd be able to finish the tasks ahead calmly. It was a vice he'd picked up from the young Swiss who'd taught him how to fly--not in a machine, but using a winged flight suit.

The colorful apparel mimicked the attributes of flying squirrels. Specially designed fabric in the suit stretched from hand to ankle on each side with a third glide surface stretching between the legs.

Though one dropped vertically at launch, velocity combined with skillful positioning of arms and legs generated horizontal momentum. With the proper conditions and training, a wingsuited jumper could travel great distances. He'd read about several such flyers who'd even landed without the usual parachute, on both land and water. But that required a great deal more skill and daring than he possessed. He'd stick with the parachute that came with the suit. He would only get to use it once more before he ditched it in the ocean.

King smiled as he inhaled and anticipated a mild sense of euphoria from the THC in the cannabis. It wouldn't take long, and by the time he finished the weed, he'd be ready to climb into his slightly modified wingsuit. Instead of wearing the hazmat gear provided by his employer, he would rely on the alterations in his suit to protect him from any stray anthrax spores which might be blown back into the airship during dispersal.

He reviewed the tasks remaining: don the suit and mask any exposed skin, then drop to the proper altitude and hover over the stadium. Next: raise the cargo bay door and open the nozzle on the tank letting gravity deliver the spores to the crowd below. Once the tank emptied, he would regain altitude and head for the open water. His team would be waiting for him on board the launch, and he would join them after a pleasant glide back to Earth. The *Puck One* would slowly float out and away over the Pacific until it ran out of fuel or was shot down. It didn't matter to him.

Though fairly certain he'd have to dispose of the three man crew in the recovery vessel, he hadn't quite decided on how to manage it. He had stowed spare magazines in his bag--more than enough ammunition to kill a dozen men--but in all likelihood, his associates would expect him to try something like that. He might have to poison them instead.

That was the wonderful thing about life-- there were always choices.

~*~

Saddened when Reyna left, Daphne knew her departure had to come sooner or later. Other than gather firewood and show her how to light it-- assuming Daphne got the flint to work--there was damned little Reyna could do for her.

She had one bottle of water and two protein bars left. Night was falling, and so was the temperature. Snow wasn't out of the question, though the sky looked clear. Her phone battery still had a decent charge, but the nearest cell tower was way too far away to do her any good. Her advance planning included packing a spare memory card for her camera, a pocket pack of tissues for when nature called, and some cinnamon-flavored chewing gum.

Some survivalist, she thought. The airhorn and the pepper spray might keep her safe from bears for awhile. They'd probably just wait 'til she died of starvation or boredom and then feast on her remains.

Eventually, some curious camper might come along and find her bones. They'd probably steal her camera and maybe even look at the photos she'd taken of Reyna. But unless they knew about the carving, they'd have no real way of knowing how little the tiny Indian girl was. She'd just look like another Indian.

Well, sorta like an Indian, Daphne mused. If she saw her photo somewhere, she'd more likely have assumed the girl to be Polynesian. But that, obviously, couldn't be the case.

A few faint stars showed themselves, and Daphne decided she'd best get started with her fire-making. It would likely take forever.

By the time the sun dipped behind a western peak, Daphne was weary of chipping sparks onto dry grass where they died as if they'd landed in water. But as she sat back, nearly overcome by the urge to weep, her emotions slowly shifted from self-pity to anger.

Life wasn't meant to be a picnic; life was a string of difficulties *punctuated* by picnics. Her current predicament was simply that: a difficulty. And she'd survived plenty of difficulties before now. She'd damn well survive this one, too!

Daphne sat up straighter, got a firm grip on the flint, and sent a new shower of sparks toward the pile of dead weeds at her feet.

~*~

Maggie held on to Shadow's collar and watched while the man who'd met them in the tunnel entered a passcode into the digital keypad for the fifth or sixth time. "It doesn't like you," she said.

Bannock glared at her. "Either there's

something very wrong going on, or someone in the security office is playing a practical joke on me. If it's a joke, his name's Ivan, but I'll change that to 'Mud.' He didn't answer the phone when I called him earlier, and now there's no answer from anyone else in security. I don't like it."

Cal was hopping from foot to foot and looking distinctly uncomfortable. Even Shadow stared at him. "I can't wait much longer."

Bannock gestured toward the grassy field where the airship would be docked. "You can always go out there," he said. "You could leave the dog out there, too. There's a fence at the far end."

"Isn't today when the blimp flies over the stadium in Honolulu? I'd have thought there'd be a lot of people here to make that happen."

"Not really," Bannock said. "There's a two-man flight crew, and we're actually a man or two short on the ground. Everyone else is either working on getting the resort ready, or they're at the stadium to watch the game. The company bought up a ton of tickets."

Cal pointed at a fire axe mounted on the wall beside the door. "There's an emergency key."

Bannock made a face. "I hope it really is just Ivan, but I can't take the chance that something else is going on. And if Ivan is behind this, I'll have the cost of repairs taken out of his paycheck." He grabbed the axe and positioned himself in front of the door. It took three swings to knock the keypad loose. He gave it one more chop to sever the wires protruding from the wall and sent the device clattering on the cement floor.

"Good start," yelled Cal as the echo from the blows diminished.

Bannock started swinging the axe again, taking deep breaths and making long-arced contact with the door like a home run hitter in the major leagues. After a dozen such blows, the door finally buckled.

"Want me to spell ya some?" Cal asked.

Bannock snorted like a rodeo bull. "I'm just gettin' started." He then swung away again while the two civilians and the canine watched.

Eventually, the door folded enough to free the deadbolt from the jam, and Bannock shouldered it out of the way. He dropped the axe in the hallway and pointed down the corridor for Cal's benefit. "The restroom's over there. It should be marked, but I can't guarantee it. We've still got a million odds and ends to wrap up around here. It's going to keep me busy for weeks."

Cal hurried down the hall, checking on doors as he went.

Bannock turned to Maggie. "Would you mind hanging around here for a bit? Your friend won't be gone long, and I'll be back as soon as I've dealt with Ivan."

Maggie would have suggested he delay the tongue lashing he had in mind until he had cooled off, but he didn't stay long enough to hear her suggestion.

She reached down and patted the top of Shadow's broad skull. The dog made a soft groaning sound and leaned into her. She hoped he wasn't planning to make a habit of it.

Looking up at a sound from the end of the hallway, Maggie saw Cal exit one door, and then pause outside another. He appeared anxious, and she called out, "What's up?"

He just made a face and pushed the door open wide enough to look inside, then he quickly stepped away and let the door close on its own.

"What is it?" she yelled, concerned now.

"Where's the guy who let us in?" he asked as he hurried toward her.

"I dunno. He went inside to chew somebody out. Said he'd be right back. Why?" Maggie had never seen Cal so shaken.

"There are two dead men in a room back there."

Maggie's breath caught in her throat. "How--"

"They were shot. One in the head; one in the chest."

"What are we going to do?" she asked.

"Start by calling 911. I'll find the security office. There's something terribly wrong going on here."

"You aren't leaving me behind!" Maggie squealed as Cal bolted back up the hall. She stayed right on his heels, and Shadow stayed on hers.

"Cal, wait," she said after a half dozen steps. "What if that guy is in on it?"

Cal lurched to a stop. "Well-- Just shit! I don't know. I heard Nate mention his name a couple times, but that's not like a front page endorsement."

"I think we should give him the benefit of the doubt. After all, he let us in, and he trusted us enough to leave us alone. Would a bad guy have done that?"

He pushed his hat back on his head and wiped his brow. "I reckon not. Guess we'll find out soon enough. Come on."

They stopped at a spot in the hall marked by two doors: one labeled "Security" and the other designated "Command Center." They ignored the latter and burst into the security office.

Which was empty.

"This ain't good," Cal said. He glanced at a wall of monitors, none of which revealed any activity at all.

"Let's try that other door," Maggie said. She and the dog were both leaning in that direction. "What've we got to lose?"

Cal snorted. "Have you already forgotten those two dead guys I found?"

"Well-- I, uh--"

"We need to do this carefully. I have no idea who or what is on the other side of that door. I don't care to barge into a room full of gun-totin' bad guys." He guided her back out to the hallway.

Josh Langston

"I'd rather you stayed here. If something bad happens--"

"I'm not leaving you, Cal!"

"Wake up, Maggie! There's something bad wrong going on here, and until we find out what it is, we've both got to be careful. If something happens to me, you've got to keep on goin'."

"You make it sound like the damned Alamo."

He kissed her, hard and fast. "Nah. Those guys had way more time to figure things out. We've gotta play it by ear."

"Cal--"

"You stay here. Keep your eyes open. Hang on to Shadow. Don't let him run off half-cocked."

She brightened. "Take him with you! Because he knows you, he'll protect you. He's done it before. Besides, if you need a distraction, he could provide one."

Cal considered the suggestion only briefly before agreeing to it. "Stay safe," he said. "With any luck, I'll be right back."

"Cal?"

"Yeah?"

"I love you."

He broke into a broad grin. "I love you, too. Now stay here until I give you the all clear."

As the door closed behind Cal and Shadow, Maggie's fears grew as furiously as Jack's beanstalk. Cal hadn't been gone more than thirty seconds when she decided she couldn't stand not knowing what was going on, and followed him into the Command Center.

The rooms inside were marked off by half-walls and glass windows. Sections were set aside for various monitoring functions like Trams, HVAC/Guest Rooms, Shows and more, including Flight Operations. Cal was working his way in that direction.

Maggie found the lack of workers disturbing. Even though the resort was not yet up and running, there should have been more people here. As far as she could tell, the tram system alone was operating at or near capacity. Someone had to be coordinating that. What if a car jumped a track? What if two trams occupied the same track at the same time? There had to be a thousand other issues, too.

But other than Cal, she didn't see another soul. So she followed him, as discretely as possible until he stopped.

She could hear the dog growl, never a good sign. Back home, when Tori heard him do that, she headed straight for her shotgun. The dog had an uncanny knack for identifying lowlifes. He'd taken down Tori's ex-husband without so much as a whisper of command. It made Maggie proud to be on Shadow's team.

As she crouched in a corner formed by intersecting cubicle walls, Maggie saw a head rise above the waist-level room dividers. The man wore the uniform of a security guard and held a gun in his outstretched hand. He ordered Cal not to move.

"And shut that damned dog up before I shoot him."

Instead, Cal released his grip on Shadow's collar, and the dog raced toward the gunman as if he'd been launched from a bazooka. Unnerved by such an all-out, full-on, frontal attack, the security guard fired twice, but neither round came close to striking the animal.

Cal raced in right behind Shadow.

The security man might have gotten off another shot or two if he hadn't been unnerved by a bear-sized beast made of teeth and drool racing toward him.

Jettisoning caution, Maggie ran forward too, figuring her presence could only add to the distractions the guard faced.

Shadow reached him first, his massive jaws clamping down on the man's gun arm, dragging it toward the floor. The weapon clanged off the deck and bounced to a stop against a nearby wall.

Cal burst forward and aimed a roundhouse punch at him. The blow missed, and Cal spun around, but it didn't stop him. He followed it up with a jab to the gunman's nose which dropped him like a lead weight and set off a small geyser of thick, red blood.

By the time Maggie reached them, the fight was over. Cal had the man's gun, and Shadow had the man's arm. He hadn't detached it yet, but he looked as if all he was waiting for was permission from Cal.

"Where's Bannock?" Maggie demanded.

The gunman gave her a puzzled look, then tilted his head toward a set of cubicles arranged in a square with the open sides toward the middle. "Over there." Maggie moved in that direction until she found Bannock on the floor, unconscious.

Cal stood over the security guard, and stared down at him through the gun sight. He called Shadow to his side, and the dog reluctantly obeyed. "Now, tell me why you killed those two fellars up the hall?"

"I didn't kill anybody!"

"That's odd, 'cause up 'til a couple minutes ago, you were the only one around here with a gun, and both of those men were shot. How d'ya explain that?"

"You're no cop."

Cal nodded. "True enough. So I don't have the kinda discipline the average killer might expect."

"I want a lawyer."

"Keep that shit up, podnuh, and you'll be in the market for an undertaker."

"Cal!" Maggie called out. "Bannock's comin' around."

She looked around for some place where he might be comfortable and settled for a desk chair. At least the back reclined, and when she finally got him situated, he took advantage of it.

Maggie found a roll of paper towels in a break

area and pulled off a handful to staunch the wound on top of Bannock's head. "You're gonna need some stitches."

Bannock moaned as he held the paper towels in place. He slowly turned to look at the security guard, his face contorting in anger. "Odom, you asshole, what do you think you're doing?"

Maggie hadn't shared the paper towels with the security guy, and his nose continued to leak blood on his shirt. "Like I told Cowboy Bob here, I want a lawyer." He wiped his lips with the back of his hand.

"Mind the furniture, stud," Cal said. "Blood stains are a bitch to clean up."

"Fuck you."

Cal kicked him under the chin and sent him crashing backwards onto the floor. Shadow leaped forward and gave him an up close view of his teeth. Odom's eyeballs blossomed.

"We don't use that kinda language around ladies," Cal said. "Next time I won't be so gentle."

"You can't do this!"

Cal chuckled. "You're not exactly a quick learner, are ya?"

Maggie stared into Bannock's eyes, both of which remained dilated. She didn't think that was a good sign, but it would have to wait until they got some answers.

"Cal found two dead men," she said. "Do you know anything about that?"

Bannock frowned, and his anger boiled up

even more. "Odom!"

Maggie used both hands on his shoulders to keep him in the chair, but he got to his feet anyway.

"I didn't kill anybody!" Odom screamed. "I swear."

Bannock turned to Cal. "Where are the bodies?"

"Down the hall. Third or fourth door on the right."

Maggie accompanied Bannock out into the corridor and urged him to lean on her for support. Together they looked for the victims Cal had first spotted. They found them in the second room they checked.

"My God," Bannock groaned. "It's the two guys who're supposed to operate the airship."

"If the pilots are here," Maggie said, "who's flyin' the blimp?"

"I have no idea," Bannock replied.

Maggie could think of only one person, but he'd be the least qualified human in the world to do such a thing. Mato was too small to drive a go-cart let alone something the size of a soccer field.

Nevertheless, she dug her cell phone out of her jeans and dialed Cal's number. She prayed that Mato not only still had Cal's phone, but that he would answer it.

~*~

Chapter 21

Before you criticize someone,
walk a mile in their shoes. That way, you'll
be a mile away, and you'll have their shoes, too.

Tori couldn't prove it, but she suspected Randy Rhoades had said or done something to the hospital on her behalf. Nothing else explained why they provided her with a comfortable chair in Nate's room. It didn't change the fact that he remained in Intensive Care, and while he mumbled from time to time, he never came fully awake. He seemed to know she was there, however, and that gave her the emotional strength to stay with him.

A smiling man in street clothes peeked in through the door. "May I come in?"

Tori shrugged. What was one more person in the endless parade of hospital staffers? She went back to the magazine she'd borrowed from the waiting room. It wouldn't be missed; there had been two congressional elections since publication.

"Are you Mrs. Sheffield?" the man asked.

"Not yet, but that's the plan."

"Oh." He seemed taken aback. "I thought-- Well, the thing is, I need to speak with his next of kin."

"Then fire away," Tori said. "I'm as close as

404

you'll ever get."

"Right. It's just a little unusual, that's all."

Tori didn't hide her irritation. "If this is about the hospital bill, I--"

"It's not," he said. "I need to talk to you about organ donation."

"Nate needs a transplant? This is the first I've heard of it."

He shook his head. "I'm sorry. I didn't make myself clear. We'd like you to consider donating *his* organs."

Tori blinked. "What?"

"It's common in cases of terminal patients. They often have viable organs which--"

"He's *not* terminal," Tori said, emphatically. " He's going to live. He's going to put his Stetson back on his head, and he's going to walk out of here all on his own. And when he does, I'm going to be right beside him, y'hear?"

The man bobbed and weaved like a boxer. "Of course, we all hope for outcomes like that. But we need to be proactive in case--"

"I think you need to proactively march your ass out the door," Tori said.

"If you'll just hear me out, I--"

She stood up, her nose and his separated by mere inches. "Git out. Now."

"But--"

"While you still can."

He backed toward the door. "How 'bout I just leave the forms here for you to look at?"

If screaming had been an option, she would have screamed. But that would only have brought her more grief. She realized the same constraint kept her from punching his face into pasta. "Fine," she said. "Leave the forms."

He extended his arm toward her, a clipboard held loosely in his hand.

She regarded it like a sidewinder in her sewing basket. "Leave it by the door."

He complied and went away.

Tori stumbled toward Nate's bed and knelt beside it, tears once again flowing down her face. "You listen to me, Nate Sheffield, you *are* going to walk out of here. No stupid little bullet is going to take you away from me. You're going to get well, and you're going to meet me on the beach, and we're going to get married and then we're going to grow old together. You hear me?"

She couldn't see him too clearly because of the tears. Her nose was running, too, and her hands shook. "And another thing," she said. "I want kids."

"I hear ya," Nate whispered.

Tori gasped. "Nate?" She clutched his hand with both of hers. "Nate!"

But he didn't respond. He had already gone back to sleep.

~*~

Without a window or other means to confirm it, Mato couldn't be sure the structure he occupied was, in fact, moving. He could hear the sound of engines, and from time to time a sway made him shift his balance, if only slightly. But such clues were enough. He was on his way to the hospital. It was a word he'd heard the giants use. He knew it to be a place where they brought their sick and injured.

Among The People, healers made the journey, not the sick. Once again, the giants had found a way to surprise him. But, if that's where Nate was, then it was where Mato needed to be.

The talking machine Maggie had given him made its sound. Though not unpleasant, the tone required him to give the device his attention. He fished it out and opened it as Maggie had instructed. He held it near his head and waited for it to say something.

"Mato? Mato! Can you hear me?"

He nodded.

"Mato?"

"Yes," he said. "What do you want?"

"Are you flying that damned blimp?"

"No."

There was a pause, then Maggie said, "Are you *in* the blimp?"

"Yes."

"Can you tell me who *is* flying it?"

"No."

There was another pause, longer than the last. Finally, Maggie spoke again. "Something bad has happened. We think a bad guy is flying the blimp. We don't know what he's up to, but it isn't good."

Mato processed her words as best he could but didn't feel compelled to answer.

"Did you hear me?" she asked.

"Yes."

"Is there any way you can find the person flying the blimp? He must be stopped."

"Giants hard to kill," he said.

"Well, geez! Don't kill him unless you have to."

Just because you have magic doesn't mean I do, too. Foolish giant!

"Mato try," he said. He had one dart left, and the sleeping paste on it had long since dried, but it might bring the bad man down. Perhaps long enough to cut his throat. Mato checked to be sure he still had his stone knife.

"It's important," Maggie said. "Do your best, but be careful."

He wasn't sure how to accomplish such contradictory commands. Stop, but don't kill; take risk, but stay safe. *Make up your mind!* "Mato go now."

"Wait!"

Though frustrated, Mato sat quietly in the dark, waiting while Maggie spoke to someone else, her voice distant. Without warning, her voice grew loud again. "Is there a big man there with you? Bigger than Nate?"

"Yes. Big giant. Mato make him sleep."

"You did? Wow."

Wow?

"He's on our side. His name is Ivan. Don't hurt him."

Mato had no desire to go near him much less hurt him. "Go now," he said, again.

"Good luck."

He wasn't sure what that meant either and closed the device before she could confuse him further.

Since he could already see to the back end of the huge craft, and nothing there looked promising, Mato stood and walked toward the front. Somewhere far ahead, he reasoned, would be the place from which the bah-limp was controlled. With any luck, he'd be able to attack the person flying it before they knew he was coming.

Unfortunately, he couldn't find a way to get into the passenger cabin below. After poking around as much as he needed to, he retraced his steps in hopes of waking up the giant called "Ivan."

He shook his head. Ivan was a *terrible* name.

But friends, however strange their name or size, were always better than enemies, especially in situations like the one in which Mato found himself. He hurried back toward the rear of the bah-limp until he reached the section of open ceiling. There he looked down on Ivan and tried to think of a way to wake him up.

Fortunately, Ivan was already moving. But

Josh Langston

just barely.

Mato called down to him, "Ivan! Look up."

The giant rolled slowly onto his back and looked straight overhead. "Who are you, brah? Can't see. Wait." He reached for the flashlight Mato had dropped earlier, turned it on, and pointed the beam of light in Mato's eyes.

"Oh shit," the huge man grumbled. "Menehune!"

Mato blocked the glare with his hand, stared down and yelled, "Get up!"

Ivan managed a sitting position, but appeared unable to stand. He sat on the deck, patting his cheeks and mumbling.

Impatient, Mato climbed down the storage rack until he came even with the giant's head. "I am Mato," he said. "We help each other."

Ivan stared at him in wonder. "How'd you know my name?"

Mato held up the phone.

"You fo' real," Ivan said in a tone of wonder. "Menehune."

Hearing the word twice didn't help. "We go now," Mato said, dropping lightly to the floor. "Get up!"

"Why?"

"Bad man have bah-limp. We stop him."

Ivan rubbed his temples then staggered to his feet. "Door's locked, brah."

"You little baby now?" taunted Mato. "Break it."

410

~*~

Reyna did not stop running until she reached the caves. Winter Woman and the other elders had insisted that nothing be left behind to indicate The People had been there. Cleaning up must have been an enormous task, Reyna thought. Completely hiding their trail, however, would have been impossible.

Knowing the general direction in which they'd fled, Reyna began running after them again. The journey would have been easier if she had Mato's big dog to ride, but running was something she'd done since childhood. All The People ran, except the sick and the lame. Even the elders did their share. Winter Woman said it would keep them strong despite their years. It seemed to work.

Reyna maintained a ground-eating pace despite doing so under the stars. There was enough light to follow the path, for even very small feet left tracks that eyes close to the ground could see.

In the shelter of distant rocks she saw the glow of campfires. Unless she had accidentally stumbled on the camp of giants, The People were very close. She kept running, though slower, and she stayed near the shelter of trees and brush. If the camp did belong to giants, they would never know she had been there.

Fortunately, the fires were far smaller than those of the giants. The light they cast was minimal, but the warmth was enough to keep The People comfortable.

Reyna burst into the camp and paused only long enough to find the spot where the elders gathered, then she hurried toward them.

Winter Woman greeted her with a frown. Reyna knew a scolding would soon follow. Rather than suffer the old woman's wrath, Reyna jumped into the speech she had been mentally preparing during her race to catch up with them. She delivered it as passionately as she could.

Winter Woman and the other elders listened while Reyna told them of the giantess trapped in the ravine. They were startled to hear that the doomed giant willingly offered to share her last bit of food with someone who had tried to kill her.

"She's crazy," one of the elders said. "Evil Spirits have taken her mind."

Reyna assured them that wasn't the case, and then shared her hope that if The People came to the giant's aid, she might be willing to help them in return.

"Why would she help us?"

"Because we helped her," Reyna replied. "Is that not our first law?"

Winter Woman stayed silent while the discussion went on, but her face betrayed no preference for or against Reyna's cause. Eventually, the conversation wound down to a vote. Those who felt the giantess deserved their help stood with Reyna. Those who disagreed remained seated.

The elders were evenly divided, though Winter Woman had not moved.

Reyna looked at her, but could not read her heart.

"Do you think it is wiser to care for this giant than for your own child?" Winter Woman asked.

"It is wiser to work for something good than to suffer something bad."

"Would you have us give up everything to save one giant?" the elder asked.

"If we lack the heart to save one giant," Reyna said, "then we have already given up everything."

Winter Woman looked deeply into the eyes of the younger woman. Reyna felt as if the elder had exposed her very soul. But eventually she gave a nod and spoke, "Summon the hunters and anyone strong enough to carry food. Go to this giant. See that she has enough to eat and a fire to keep her warm. I will join you when I can."

Winter Woman then turned to the elders. "You will go on to the next camp. Take the young ones and everything you can carry. Leave the rest. I will return with Reyna and the hunters when we are done with this giant. We will soon see if she can change our future."

~*~

Nothing but ocean lay between Kauai and Oahu, so there was little to distract King from his mission. Though the augmented wingsuit limited his mobility somewhat, he had worn it often enough to be comfortable.

As the island of Oahu loomed on the horizon, he prepared to make his way toward the cargo bay and the tank of anthrax spores waiting to be sprayed on fifty to sixty thousand American football fans.

The nearly invisible spores would flood the sky over the stadium and rain down on all those below. Many, if not most, would inhale a sufficient quantity to contract the disease, though the symptoms would not likely appear until after they returned home. Their clothing, and everything they had with them in the stadium would provide a transport mechanism which would deliver spores throughout the country. After all, pro football was *tremendously* popular in America.

Knowing this and caring about it were two different things. King was quite aware of the likely outcome, but he was being paid enough money to dampen any empathy he had for the victims. As he'd told his accomplices, it was business. He didn't care what it was called by those who paid him.

He flipped the switch on the command console which unlocked the cargo bay door. Then, with the airship still operating on autopilot, he exited the flight deck and walked to the rear of the cabin and the door to the cargo compartment.

Before he could open it, however, he heard a

distinct but disturbing sound. The outer cargo hatch was opening. That could only be accomplished by someone outside the airship preparing to unload it--clearly, not a possibility--or by someone *already* in the cargo bay.

King drew his gun and checked the magazine. He still had over a dozen rounds. There was no need to retrieve his knapsack and get more.

~*~

Bannock still felt woozy from the blow to his head, but anger had gone a long way toward restoring his ability to function. He and Maggie checked all the other rooms off the hall to insure there weren't any undiscovered bodies.

They found three live ones, all very grateful, and all quite eager to express their feelings to Mr. Odom. Cal, however, stood in the way.

He had the only gun, and he kept it trained on Odom's chest. The turncoat security man had bandaged his arm with a necktie Cal found in someone's desk drawer. "I'd offer ya something to put on that dog bite," Cal said, "It looks pretty bad. But to be honest, I'm kinda hopin' you get rabies."

Two of the just-released flight ops crew settled for strapping Odom to a chair with duct tape. They made sure he was immobile, but weren't entirely satisfied until they knocked his chair over and removed two of the casters.

Their senior member, meanwhile, went to the radio and hailed *Puck One*, ordering it to respond.

415

He repeated the command several times without effect.

"Who's flying the damned thing?" Bannock asked. Unfortunately, no one knew. "There can't be that many people who even know how."

"They're all trained in Germany," said the crew's lone female member. "I could put in a call to the Zeppelin plant and maybe get a list."

"It's a start," Bannock said.

"Then I'm on it," she said, reaching simultaneously for a phone and a computer keyboard.

"Now what?" Maggie asked.

"I've got to report all this to my boss and the proper authorities."

"Do we even know who the proper authorities are?"

"I don't," he said. "But I'm hoping someone will tell me. I already called 911. The cops can fly out here whenever; there's no longer a threat."

"What can be done about the blimp?"

"It's an *airship*, not a blimp. Okay?"

"What's the difference?"

"One's got a rigid frame covered with some kind of material. A blimp is just a big bag of gas." He smiled. "Kinda like me."

Maggie gave him a short laugh, then turned serious. "You think they'll try to shoot it down?"

Bannock didn't know how to answer that. If it were up to him, he'd have already scrambled enough firepower to put *Puck One* in the ocean.

416

He never much cared for flying anyway.

~*~

Ivan had no idea Menehune could be so hard-headed. But then, the little guy who called himself "Mato" was the only one he'd ever met. No one could blame Ivan for not taking orders from somebody smaller than his forearm.

No way, brah!

All that aside, it was clear somebody else was on board and up to no good. A parachute and something that looked like a rubbery yellow spacesuit convinced him of that. Nobody hijacked a blimp and loaded a tank of something mysterious in it unless they meant to do bad things. Ivan had an idea about how to end that damn quick.

Rather than waste time banging on the door to the passenger cabin, where somebody was likely to shoot his bota off, Ivan chose instead to toss the tank full of mystery shit into the Pacific.

Mato protested, but Ivan ignored him. The little guy didn't represent much of a threat and evidently knew it. He just hung out near the locked door, waiting.

Meanwhile, Ivan thumbed a button labeled "Hatch Activation" and watched the door slide open. He could see the ocean far below and the island of Oahu growing larger as they drew near.

He tried to shove the pallet-mounted tank toward the door, but it was too heavy to move without a lot more effort. As he put his shoulder to it, he heard the door behind him open.

"What the-- Ow!"

Ivan dropped to the deck with the tank between himself and the intruder and peeked out from behind it to see what was going on.

Mato had disappeared, but some guy in a brightly colored suit stood in the open doorway trying to figure out how to stay upright. Moments later he failed the quiz and dropped to the floor as if someone had kicked him in the head.

"Yo, Mato! Did you do that?"

Mato scrambled out from beneath a storage rack and rocked back and forth on his heels, smiling.

It instantly dawned on Ivan that Mato had done the same thing to him. He rubbed his neck where he'd felt what he thought was an insect bite. "You one bad little moke, brah!"

Mato seemed to like that. Which was good. Ivan didn't want to get stung again. He turned his attention back to the tank, this time putting his shoulder into it and shoving as hard as he could.

The pallet gave ground slowly and with an annoying squeal. Ivan paused for a breath and looked for the Menehune, who was nowhere in sight. Though tempted to race after him, Ivan knew his first priority was dumping the tank. Even though the bad guy was down, the tank might be wired to explode, and he had no desire to be anywhere near it if it did.

He kept pushing, and the pallet kept

squealing in protest, but eventually he got it to the edge of the hatch. He had to lift it to clear the lip of the opening, but with sufficient sweating and swearing he got the job done. Once he had it propped on the edge of the open hatch, he felt energized and walked the tank closer and closer to a salt water grave.

Finally, as sweat poured off his head and back, Ivan shoved the tank through the opening and watched it tumble through the air to ocean below.

Dusting his hands in satisfaction, he stepped over the body of the weirdo in the funky suit, and made his way toward the front of the blimp. If nothing else, he intended to borrow the Menehune's cell phone.

He couldn't help but wonder what kind of deal the little guy had on it. Did he have to sign a contract like everybody else, or did he get a discount for being so goddam small?

~*~

Bannock had finally taken a seat. His head hurt like hell, and he'd gobbled down enough aspirin to tie his stomach in a half hitch. Now he had to wait for Randy Rhoades to powder her nose, or piddle, or whatever in hell it was women did when there was an emergency.

"Sorry," she said at last. "I was on the phone with HPD. They're trying to evacuate the stadium."

"Why?" he asked.

419

Josh Langston

"Because that's the biggest target on the whole island," she said. "If we can't shoot that airship down, there's no telling how many people could be hurt."

"You already knew somebody hijacked it?"

"When it didn't respond to air traffic controllers at Honolulu International, they called the Command Center at the resort. When there was no answer there, they called Mr. Archer. He called me. I called the Air Force."

Joe quickly revised his earlier opinion of the redhead on the other end of the line. "I've got an update, of sorts."

"Go," she said.

"We've got a man on board," he said. "He's not terribly smart, but he's strong and quick. Oh, and he's loyal."

"That's all very nice, but is he armed?"

"No."

"Shit."

"We're trying to get in touch with him now by radio," Bannock said.

"Good. Put the phone on speaker and don't hang up. That way you can keep me posted. The air force is scrambling jets from Hickam Field. They'll be in the air in minutes. Get in touch with your guy if you can. He doesn't have much time."

Bannock set his phone aside as instructed and hailed the senior flight ops worker. "Any luck reaching Ivan on the radio?"

"Not yet, but someone's playing with the

equipment up there. We're gettin' a lot of clicks and squeals. It sounds like squirrels nesting in the transmitter."

~*~

Daphne shivered in the dark. She had been told temperatures would drop at night. She believed it, now. After wearing a blister in her hand from trying to coax sparks out of the stupid flint, she had finally gotten a small fire started. If she'd been thinking, before the sun went down, she could have used a spare camera lens like a magnifying glass to get a fire going. If she ever saw Reyna again, she'd have to show her that trick. Although, if Reyna had something similar, she'd probably use it to cook grubs and beetles.

And most likely eat 'em. Bleah!

Finding things to laugh at became harder as the temperature went down. Too resilient to remain morose for long, Daphne concentrated on keeping herself alive until someone came to haul her out of the wilderness. Surely someone would. If not Simon, then her editor. Someone would miss her and call Search and Rescue.

She imagined the banner headline on page one, above the fold:

Reporter's Skeletal Remains
Found in Cloud Peak Wilderness.

Oh yeah, a real triumph. Her editor would probably write the item himself, with maybe a little help from Simon Dole, her last known contact.

She poked what was left of the fire. The deadfall Reyna had collected didn't last long. Daphne theorized that the little people made do with little fires. Their wood lasted longer.

As the temperature fell, so did her spirits. She intended to save the last power bar for breakfast. With any luck, she could get a day or so out of the last bottle of water. After that, who knew?

She saw something moving silently high above. Jet liner, she thought, probably on its way to Phoenix or Miami--someplace warm.

Fortunately, she'd seen very little wildlife. Her crappy vantage point, halfway down a ravine, surely accounted for some of that. Still, other than Reyna, a couple squirrels and some birds, Daphne had no company at all.

She had begun to drift off, despite being thoroughly uncomfortable and unable to move, when she heard a noise. Concentrating, she held her breath and listened. It was definitely something big--a deer, a raccoon, or God help her, a bear.

Reaching into her camera bag, she felt around for the air horn and the pepper spray. If it did turn out to be a bear, she wasn't going down without a fight.

"Bring it, you furry bastard," she growled. "I'm ready."

~*~

Chapter 22

Some of the best moments in life
are the ones you can't tell anyone about.

With the tank gone, Mato and Ivan left the cargo hold and hurried to the front of the main cabin. The door to the flight deck stood open, and they both raced through. Mato got there first and stood in one of the two crew seats. He busied himself examining knobs, dials, buttons and lights.

"Don't touch nuthin' brah," Ivan said, his voice betraying fear.

Mato ignored him. Through the windows in front they could see a great land mass, and they could tell they were descending.

Ivan found an odd clamp-like device which he put over his head. It covered his ears and positioned a blob of something small and black near his mouth. Then he began to stab buttons and talk nonsense.

"Anybody read me?" he asked.

Mato stared at him. Perhaps the sleeping paste The Island People made had properties Mato never saw before. Crazy talk could be one of them.

"Dis da blimp," Ivan said. "We up high, but we comin' down soon."

"Brah," added Mato. "We comin' down soon,

brah."

Ivan gave him a funny look, then turned away and said, "You read me out dere?" Then he turned a dial and went through the same routine again.

Mato figured Ivan would be dead soon. According to his best recollections, though he hadn't witnessed complete madness often, it always ended badly. He mentally prepared an escape route in case the colossal giant came after him.

"Puck One, do you copy?"

Ivan stopped talking when he heard the voice. Mato looked around to see if he could figure out where it had come from.

"Dis Puck One!" Ivan shouted. "Puck One. Puck Two. Don' mattah."

"Ivan, this is Joe Bannock. I need you to listen."

They both heard a new noise: the sound of a bullet being jacked into the firing chamber of a handgun. It was followed closely by a voice which said, "Shut up, and turn the radio off."

While Mato peeked out from the side of his seat, Ivan swiveled completely around to look at the gunman Mato had knocked out with his last dart. Mato thought the effects of the dried sleeping paste would last longer in a smaller man than it did in Ivan. Evidently, they didn't.

"All I want is my knapsack," said the man in the bizarre body suit. "Then I'm leaving."

"Where is it?" Ivan asked.

The gunman pointed to a small gear locker under Ivan's seat. "In there."

"Come get it," Ivan said.

"In that case, I'll have to shoot you first."

~*~

"What happened," Maggie asked. "Where'd they go? Why aren't they responding?"

"I have no idea," Bannock said. "But at least we know Ivan's in the cockpit."

"I just hope Mato's all right."

Bannock squinted at her. "Who the hell is Mato?"

Oops! Damn. Now what do I do? Maggie felt the need to get a drink of water. "He's, uhm-- I guess you'd call him a stowaway."

"Can he handle himself in a fight?"

"Prob'ly better than you'd think."

"Good," Bannock said. "Ivan may need some help, especially if there's more than one hijacker on board."

"If the radio doesn't work, I can always call Mato on the phone."

Bannock's eyebrows went parabolic. "You've been on the phone with him?"

"Yes, but he didn't say much. He couldn't see anyone but Ivan, and Ivan was unconscious at the time."

With a considerable shake of his head, Bannock turned his attention back to the radio. "Ivan, do you read me? Answer, please!"

~*~

Stone Fist made it painfully clear he didn't agree with their mission. He'd been complaining non-stop since Reyna and the clan's hunters had accumulated enough food to feed the entire clan for days and repacked it for travel.

"Why are we doing this for a giant?" he asked again. Reyna had lost count of how often he'd badgered her with the same query.

"Because Winter Woman says we must." She didn't bother to add that it was all happening because of Reyna's desire to effect the rescue.

"It makes no sense," Stone Fist complained. "We have never let the giants see us. We don't talk to them; we don't go near them."

"Some of us do," Reyna said, though she instantly regretted it.

"Some of us are idiots," Stone Fist declared.

"We'll see."

He brandished a spear with an especially long blade. Reyna had no doubt it was sharp. Such weapons brought down deer, causing wounds that bled until the animal lost too much blood to live.

"I will show the giant mercy," he said. "I will kill her quickly. She will feel little pain."

"And you think this will make you a hero in the eyes of The People?"

He stood tall. "Someone must do the right thing."

"Then you had better keep an eye on me," Reyna said. "Because if you go near the giant with your sharp spear, my dull knife will find your heart."

~*~

Rufus King stood looking at the huge man sitting in the pilot's seat of the airship who had single-handedly wrestled King's tank of anthrax spores out the cargo hatch, ending a plan he and others had worked on for almost a year. It seemed almost comical. The man who had ruined everything appeared too stupid to even realize how close to death he was.

One more dead man would make little difference, and King gave him a sad smile as he raised his gun to shoot. Just then an altimeter warning sounded. The airship would soon pass over Aloha Stadium and would quickly descend to the level King had selected for dispersing the deadly spores.

He had no time to waste. Though his target had turned away, King fired three times at the back of his seat. If that didn't kill him, it would at least slow him down, King thought. He grabbed his knapsack out of the locker and raced back through the passenger compartment, digging frantically for a waterproof pouch containing his next set of IDs. He slipped it into a Velcro-sealed pocket on his wingsuit along with two spare magazines for his gun. Those went into a similar pocket on his thigh. He would need his hands free when he jumped clear of the airship.

What he also needed was enough altitude to

make a successful glide. Landing in the cheap seats of Aloha Stadium hardly fit his plans. He needed room to fall, room to gather speed and create lift.

Throwing the knapsack out ahead of him, the man last known as Rufus King dove through the open cargo hatch and plummeted toward Earth.

~*~

Mato saw Ivan lurch forward, driven by the gunshots, and felt the airship tilt more sharply toward the ground. Additional warning tones blared from unseen speakers.

He looked at the giant's back to see where he'd been hit. Blood leaked from two holes near his shoulders. Mato tore off his own shirt and used it to staunch the flow of blood. He could think of little else to do.

With a deep groan, Ivan pointed at a switch on the control console in front of them. Mato flipped it to the "ON" position and Ivan spoke into the tiny black blob in front of his mouth. "Yo. Dis Puck One."

"Ivan!"

"I got shot, but we okay. Fo now."

"Thank God! Who shot you?"

Ivan groaned. "Crazy man inna funny suit. He gone."

"Dead?"

"He crazy, like I said. He jumped."

"*Out of the blimp?*"

"Yeah. He-- Oh, shit," Ivan gasped.

Mato followed the giant's gaze and looked through the windshield at two small but extremely fast flying machines streaking toward them.

"Boss!" Ivan gripped the little black blob in front of his mouth. "Doan let dem mokes shoot us down!"

~*~

Cut off from the world outside Nate's room in the ICU, Tori Lanier finally succumbed to boredom. She'd finished reading the magazine purloined from the waiting room and now knew everything she ever wanted to know about the lives and loves of three dozen "celebrities" she'd never heard of before.

The parade of technicians and medical staffers who formerly hiked through the room had trickled down to a bare few. Apparently, they'd lost interest in the man everyone expected to die.

And so Tori dozed.

Until a harsh beep erupted from one of the monitors connected to Nate. Tori's eyes snapped open, and her heart began to pound as if she'd run a sprint.

But the beeping didn't stop.

~*~

Bannock grabbed his phone and spoke frantically to Randy Rhoades. "Did you hear that? Fighter jets are-- *Randy?* Did you hear what's going on up there?"

429

Josh Langston

He glared at the screen on his phone which indicated they were still connected, but the temptation to hang up and re-dial was overwhelming. As he poised his thumb to cut the connection, she answered him.

"The jets have been ordered to break off. I've been talking to the Air Force. They weren't real keen on shooting down something that big over a heavily populated area."

Bannock wiped his forehead on his sleeve and gave her a weary, "Thanks."

"Problem is," she continued, "your guy doesn't know how to fly the airship."

"Neither does the stowaway," Bannock added, glancing at Maggie as he spoke. "What do we do now? How long does it take for the helium to wear out?"

"Like in a birthday balloon?"

"Yeah."

"Approximately never. And airships aren't designed to leak. Makes 'em easier to fly."

"Mr. Bannock?"

He turned his attention to the woman from flight operations who had been on the phone with the airship factory in Germany.

"I've got Helmut Warner on the line. He's the chief flight instructor for Zeppelin."

The first thing that went through Bannock's brain was a memory of the barely passing grade he'd earned studying German in college. The only words he remembered with confidence involved beer drinking and casual sex.

"Line two," the woman added.

Bannock picked up a phone and poked the appropriate button. "Herr Warner?"

"Call me Helmut," said the man on the other end of the line. He seemed pleasant. "You have some problem, yah?"

And he spoke English! Sort of. "Yes sir, we do," Bannock said. He covered the mouthpiece and waved to the senior member of the flight ops team. "Shouldn't you be taking this?"

The man shook his head. "You're in charge."

"You must find zomvhere to land," Warner said. "Enter the GPS coordinates und set the altitude. Mit autopilot on, the ship vill fly itself."

"How difficult is that?" Bannock asked.

"Finding a place to land, or entering the coordinates?"

"Both."

"The NT50 needs a big space--a football pitch mit no overhead vires."

Vires? Wires! Got it.

"Coordinates can be entered on the video screen. Look auf der Menu under 'Destination.'"

"Thank you, Helmut. Would you please stand by in case we have more questions?"

"Of course," he said.

Bannock put him on hold. "I need GPS numbers for a landing field, quickly! We've got a man with gunshot wounds up there."

Maggie, Cal, and the others in the room just

stared at him. "Is there an app for that?" she asked, holding up her smart phone.

"There is," Randy said, her voice sounding thin on the little speaker in Bannock's phone. "I have the coordinates. They're for a high school football field not far from a hospital."

"Give 'em to me," Bannock said. He then jotted the numbers down and repeated them for Ivan along with instructions for entering them on the computer screen in the cockpit.

"I can't do it myself, brah," Ivan said. "Can't move my arms."

Bannock looked hard at Maggie. "Can your stowaway do it?"

"Let's hope so," she said.

"Mato, this is Maggie. Can you hear me?"

~*~

Suddenly, the parade of personnel came roaring back into Nate's room. Nurses and technicians poured into the cramped space and made no apologies for pushing Tori aside. They all seemed to be talking at once, and no one seemed interested in shutting off the damned alarm. Or a second one when it went off.

Someone finally shoved her out into the hallway and away from the frenzy. She looked around feeling lost, helpless, and afraid.

Until the guy who wanted Nate's organs put in another appearance, and Tori found a new channel for her emotions.

"Just came by to pick up the forms," he said.

"So you can cut out my fiancé's heart?"

"It's not like that!"

"Oh? What is it like, then?"

He backed away even though she hadn't yet punched him. Her ability to restrain herself was fading fast.

"I know I've made a mess of this," the man said. "I don't usually get involved in this stuff, but the regular organ procurement team isn't available, and time's running out. How 'bout I just take the forms and--"

"I haven't filled 'em out yet," Tori said over the noise from Nate's room. "There's no point. He's going home soon."

"I understand what you're going through, and I know this is a terrible time, but--"

Tori crossed her arms and took up a position in front of Nate's door.

"I'm just trying to do my job," he said. "Be reasonable."

"Where I come from, being reasonable means not shooting someone who won't get off my property."

"This hospital isn't your property!"

"The man in that room is," she said, but whether it was the tone of her voice or merely the determined way she stared him down, the man gave up and left.

Though tiny, stupid, and inconsequential, the victory was something she desperately needed. Tori waited outside Nate's room, not wanting to see what the medical personnel were doing to him, but not wanting to leave, either.

Time passed, and uniformed people came and went, but none of them had time for her until one of the doctors finally took her aside.

"I wish I didn't have to say this, but there's nothing more we can do."

Don't tell me that! Don't say those things! It's not true. It can't be true. Tori felt her tears welling up, again.

The doctor held the door for her. "You'd best say your goodbyes."

"Can he *hear* me?" she asked in surprise.

The doctor shrugged. "Maybe. I don't know. You'd better hurry."

~*~

"Shouldn't they be landing by now?" Bannock called to the flight operations crew. "Where the hell are they?"

"Approaching Lihue."

"Lihue? I thought the blimp was near Honolulu."

"It's an *airship*, sir," the flight ops crewman said.

Bannock tried to incinerate him with an atomic glare.

"It turned around and headed back to Kauai when new coordinates went in."

Bannock picked up his phone and dialed Randy Rhoades.

She answered on the first ring. "What's up,

434

Joe?"

"What the hell's wrong with you?" he shouted. "Ivan has gunshot wounds. You knew that, and yet you sent the ship all the way back to Kauai?"

"I had to. A man's life is at stake."

"Yeah, Ivan's!"

"There are circumstances you don't understand," she said. "Ivan will be taken care of right alongside Nate."

"Nate," Bannock said, ashamed that he'd forgotten about the cowboy who'd been shot by Kwan's thugs. "I-- Right. How's he doing?"

"Not well, but if we can get Mato to him--"

"The stowaway?"

Randy didn't respond immediately, then said, "Uh yeah. I guess so. Anyway, he's vital to Nate's recovery."

"How? Is he a surgeon or something?"

"I'm not at liberty to say."

Joe Bannock stared into the distance. "You're shitting me, right?"

"I'm waiting at the ball field now," she said. "I've got an ambulance standing by for Mr. Ku`u Maka."

"Who?"

"Ivan," she said. "The guy you insisted we hire. Remember?"

"Of course."

"Here it comes," she said. "Gotta go."

~*~

435

Tori was still sitting beside Nate's bed when Randy Rhoades burst into the room pushing a laundry hamper. She watched in amazement as Randy shoved folded sheets and towels aside way while Mato climbed out.

"Thank God," Tori breathed.

The little Indian already had his knife out and was sawing away at his wrist. Tori stood up and moved out of his way.

"How does this work, exactly?" Randy asked.

Tori put a finger to her lips and walked to the door to block anyone from entering until Mato had finished his work.

"He's going to give Nate a transfusion," she told Randy. "It's pretty crude."

"And from the looks of it, there won't be much of an exchange of blood."

"It doesn't take much," Tori said. "Which is fortunate, 'cause I don't know how much blood the little guy's got."

Randy looked at her in undisguised wonder. "And I thought *my* life was pretty bizarre."

Tori smiled. It had been too long since she had something to smile about. But for the first time since she'd learned of Nate's wounds, she began to feel something other than forced optimism.

Mato's ministrations didn't take long, and Tori helped herself to surgical tape and gauze to cover the cuts on Nate's and Mato's arms.

"That's it?" Randy asked.

"Yep."

Tori looked down at Mato. "Is this going to work?"

Mato looked up at her and shrugged.

~*~

Sunlight pinked the eastern sky as Daphne came awake. Whatever had been rustling the bushes nearby had grown weary of her unwillingness to give up and become a meal. The air horn helped. She'd blasted it many times during the night. So often, in fact, that she feared it would soon run out of compressed air.

When she heard voices, she assumed Simon or her editor had finally gotten around to dispatching the cavalry for her rescue. It came as a complete shock to discover Indians had arrived instead. Roughly two dozen of them, all very small and none looking happy to be there.

Fortunately, Reyna stood in the vanguard. She even smiled, which gave Daphne a much-needed shot of hope.

"Food," the little Indian said, holding up an animal skin containing Lord-only-knew what. Then she waved at the others in her band, and they all moved forward at once.

Daphne tried to be stealthy as she reached for her camera bag and retrieved her trusty Nikon. The little tribe either didn't notice or didn't care. She raised the camera and looked through the viewfinder. She'd be able to get a ton of great shots!

Josh Langston

And then Reyna smiled at her again.

Daphne lowered the camera without taking a single photograph. Instead, she put the camera away and prepared to greet the rescue party.

~*~

"I don't understand it," the doctor confessed to Tori as an orderly wheeled Nate to a private room on an upper floor. "There's no way he should still be alive, much less improving. It's--I don't know--unheard of!"

She grinned at him. "Never underestimate the power of prayer."

"Oh, I don't," he said. "I've just never seen it work like this before."

Tori didn't add that her prayers had been for Mato to show up in time. She was still smiling as the doctor wandered away and Randy called.

"I just got the good news," the redhead said.

"Isn't it wonderful?"

"They wouldn't tell me how long he's going to have to stay, just that he's undergone a miraculous improvement. It's like nothing they've ever seen."

Tori chuckled. "Been there; done that. It doesn't mean there's no pain. That doesn't go away. But the healing part is amazing. Nate is the fifth giant to benefit from it, if my addition skills haven't totally failed me."

"Fifth *giant?*" Randy asked.

"As far as Mato's concerned, if you're not one of his people, you're a giant."

"Us and them, huh?"

"That's the way it's always been for them," Tori said. "But things are changing. Before, nobody knew his people even existed. Now-- Well, now, it seems like *everyone* knows. If not all of it, they know a little something--enough to be suspicious. I don't have any idea how we're going to get him back home without the whole world seeing him."

"No problem," Randy said. "I'll take care of that. For now, you need to concentrate on wedding plans."

Tori coughed.

"That's why you came out here, isn't it"

"Yeah," she said. "I guess so."

"Well, then. As Nate would say, 'Get a move on.' And don't forget to include invitations for me, Joe, and Ivan. We wouldn't want to miss it."

"How is Ivan?" Tori asked. "Mato wanted to know if he needed to help him the way he helped Nate."

"He'll be fine," she said. "It's not easy to take out someone that big."

"Glad to hear it. Mato thinks he's a good guy, even if he talks funny. Mato also wanted to know if they ever found the guy who shot him."

"We don't know who he is. All we have is who he claimed to be," Randy said. "His accomplice, a guy named Odom, provided a description of him, and the feds tracked him to a hotel in Honolulu. He used a false ID in the name of Rufus King. Does

Josh Langston

that name mean anything to you?"

"Nope," Tori said. "Should it?"

"Probably not, unless you're a presidential history buff. "

"You've lost me."

"I'm told one of the best forgers in the criminal world turned up dead a few months ago. The stuff he produced--passports, credit cards, whatever--was top quality, but odd in one particular respect. The forger liked to use the names of failed presidential candidates. It was sort of a signature for him."

"Okay. So?"

"Rufus King lost to James Monroe in 1816. The FBI and Homeland Security are looking for other similar instances. They aren't optimistic."

~*~

It took another full day for a rescue team other than Reyna's to reach Daphne. During that time the little Indians kept her warm and well fed. A tiny Indian woman about Reyna's size, but obviously much older, had confirmed that Daphne had broken a bone in her foot. Walking on it was out of the question.

The little woman, whose name was utterly unpronounceable by Daphne, seemed frustrated by her inability to be of more help. Daphne's size prevented them from moving her to a more comfortable spot. Instead, they worked to make the spot she already occupied more tolerable.

Few among them cared to venture close,

although Reyna and the old woman spent a great deal of time trying to communicate.

When the sounds of big people finally reached them, the Indians gathered their things and disappeared into the surrounding woods. Daphne was sad to see them go, but she understood their reluctance to expose themselves to her world.

She had attempted to explain that she no longer planned to call attention to them. Considering the risk they'd taken on her behalf, she had completely abandoned any thoughts she had of including them in a story. A Pulitzer Prize wasn't worth her self-respect.

One issue continued to bother her, however. Had Reyna stabbed the prospector, or was it one of her companions? And, if Daphne didn't report what she knew to the police, would that make her an accomplice?

She chewed on that while they loaded her into a helicopter for the ride out of the Cloud Peak.

"How did you guys know where to find me?" she asked.

An EMT sitting beside her in the chopper raised his voice to be heard over the clatter of the rotors. "Some guy from one of the colleges called it in. He claimed no one paid any attention the first time he reported you missing."

So Simon came through. Good for him! She'd have to deliver a thank you as soon as she could walk again. Playing footsie while wearing a cast might prove difficult, but she figured she was up to the challenge.

Her stomach lurched as the helicopter left the ground, and Daphne was momentarily glad she hadn't eaten much lately. Throwing up on the EMT would have been really bad form.

~*~

The wedding was small but fabulous, by any standards. Held on the private beach at Puck's Paradise, the ceremony included a luau and was officiated by a genuine *kahuna* in authentic native attire. Randy Rhoades made sure the event would be memorable with a band, fireworks, gourmet food, and an open bar with more options than a liquor emporium. She even had Tori's mother flown in from Atlanta and arranged for Tori's editor, Cassy Woodall, to be flown in from New York.

Tori appeared resplendent in a gown that mixed island comfort with mainland tradition. She and Nate went barefoot, as did the entire wedding party, and when the tide rolled in, Mato was the only one who noticed. Nate swept him out of the surf and passed him to Caleb for safe keeping.

Tori and Nate exchanged vows as the sun set over the water bathing the sky in a wash of pink, orange and purple. They became husband and wife in the presence of their closest friends and some of their newest acquaintances, and everyone celebrated late into the night. Nate, while not still fully recovered, held up remarkably well considering how recently he'd been seen as a source for recycled organs.

As the dancing, singing, laughing and drinking slowed and guests made their way toward their resort bungalows, Maggie found Mato sitting alone near a fire on the beach. It had burned all evening, and only coals remained.

"Did you have fun?" she asked.

Mato gave his head a minimal nod.

"What's wrong?"

"Mato failed Li," he said. "Man who took her dead now. Nate say."

"I don't understand. Who's Li?"

"A woman. One of the Island People."

Maggie frowned. "But not Reyna?"

"Reyna far away." He sighed. "Too far."

Maggie's phone rang. "Hold on," she told Mato, then she answered it. She never noticed Mato wandering away.

"Maggie? This is Daphne Cutter. From the newspaper?"

Crap. Her again? "Yes, I remember. What's up?"

"Not much. I just thought I'd call and let you know I won't need the names of those arrowhead collectors after all."

"Really? What's changed?" Maggie asked.

"It turns out the preliminary autopsy report was wrong. That prospector didn't die from

443

something on the spearhead. Someone at the hospital misread the guy's chart and gave him the wrong meds. That's what killed him. Whoever got him with the spear or the arrow or whatever it was, is off the hook. Officially."

Maggie felt elated. She couldn't wait to pass the word along to everyone else. "I'm so glad to hear it," she said. "That's wonderful news."

"It is?"

"Well, yeah. I mean, after all the confusion about a child's fingerprints-- I just didn't want to see some little kid get in trouble."

"Of course," Daphne said. "And I agree." She paused. "The little ones need to be protected."

~*~

As Mato walked slowly back toward the building he shared with Maggie and Cal, something struck him in the head. He dropped to the sand instinctively and gazed into the surrounding gloom. Whatever hit him wasn't a weapon; it was too light. He spotted a seashell at his feet.

"Mato!"

He looked up and saw someone standing in the dim light of a flickering torch. A double row of them lead away from the beach.

"Makani?"

"I've been looking for you," the youngster said.

"Why?" Mato asked. "I thought you didn't trust me."

"It's Li," he said. "I no longer trust her."

"She's *alive*?" Mato felt a surge of joy.

"She returned the night of the raid and now claims to be a great warrior."

"Li is very brave," Mato said. "But not very smart."

Makani laughed.

"What's so funny," Mato asked.

"She said you were very smart, but not very brave."

Mato chuckled, too. "Keep your eye on that one."

"It's hard not to. Anyway, I thought if you came back with me you could tell everyone what really happened that night."

"No," he said. "If she wants to be a warrior, let her. But see that she drinks the naukau with everyone else."

"So she sleeps, like all the others?"

Mato nodded. "As long as their battles are in their dreams, they will all live long and die happy."

"What will you do?" Makani asked.

"I have a mate, and a child. I have been away from them too long."

~ The End ~

About the author:

Josh Langston lives and works in Marietta, Georgia, with his amazing wife and two uninhibited dogs. His prize-winning short fiction has been published in numerous magazines and anthologies. He and Canadian author Barbara Galler-Smith have written a series of bestselling historical fantasy novels. All three books--**Druids, Captives**, and *Warriors*--are available in print as well as in E-book format.

Other Josh Langston titles you might enjoy:

A Little (More) Primitive --The sequel to the book you just finished reading! (Don't miss the sample chapter beginning on the next page.)

A Primitive in Paradise--Book three in the Little Primitive series has just been released!

Resurrection Blues--A novel of discovery and liberation set in a town that doesn't exist.

Mysfits**--A 6-pack of urban (and suburban) fantasies.

Six from Greeley**@--Timeless tales from a town that never grew up.

Dancing Among the Stars**--A 6-pack of science and speculative fiction.

Christmas Beyond the Box@--Seven holiday tales of mystery and magic.

Who Put Scoundrels in Charge?--A well-deserved break from the politics and politically-related nonsense we've suffered of late.

The Best Damned Squirrel Dog (Ever)**--A Civil War ghost story.

Co-authored with Barbara Galler-Smith:

Under Saint Owain's Rock --A contemporary romantic comedy set (mostly) in northern Wales.

Druids--An historical adventure that rumbles through the 1st century BC.

Captives --The Druids saga continues.

Warriors--The final book in the Druids trilogy.

**Available in e-book format only.
@Audio book from Audible.com
(List last updated December, 2014.)

Online: http://www.joshlangston.com

Josh Langston

And now, turn the page for a sneak preview of Josh Langston's stunning alternative history of the American Revolution: ***Treason, Treason!***

1

Treason, Treason!

Chapter One

"Remember that all through history, there have been tyrants and murderers, and for a time, they seem invincible. But in the end, they always fall. Always." --Mahatma Gandhi

At age 52, Raines Kerr had almost everything he wanted: a well-paying position, a secure future, and a loving daughter. But the loss of his wife had put a hole in his heart that would never heal. After ten years the ache remained.

He'd hoped to feel a moment of peace knowing that at long last he would either make her greatest dream come true, or die trying. Instead, turmoil churned his insides like a blender. Unlike Raines, Beth Kerr hadn't feared death. She hadn't feared anything. For her, death would be the start of "just another adventure."

A physicist and rational thinker, Raines admired his wife's attitude despite harboring doubts about her vision of the hereafter. Nevertheless, he was committed to the project, to his wife's dream, and to the possibility that the course on which he was about to embark would change the world.

Dramatically.

And forever.

He had already set the machinery in motion, quite literally. In a few moments, the cloth-bound package sitting on the ground in front of him would--if all went according to plan--disappear. Precisely ten minutes later, he would, too.

His daughter, Leah, stood a few meters away, wide-eyed and apprehensive. He tried to exude confidence, but his involuntary bodily functions betrayed the truth. Sweat glands and sphincters made damned good lie detectors.

He had great faith in his lab, his equipment, and the accuracy of his calculations. Still, he would have preferred to do more testing. Unfortunately, the power required to generate an Event made it impossible to run as many tests as he would have liked without bringing undue attention to his experiments. Even though he chaired the physics department, and enjoyed the considerable benefits of the accomplishments of his early career, he had no desire for scrutiny. He preferred secrecy. The project demanded it. If the Crown had any inkling of his intentions, he'd be thrown into a cell from which he'd never escape.

In that event, death would be a much preferable outcome.

So it was he found himself standing on the

threshold of the greatest scientific discovery of all time, and he could share it with no one except his twenty-five year old daughter, Leah. And not only was she sworn to secrecy, she would soon be joining him, and the equipment which made it all possible would be reduced to a smoldering puddle of slag.

A faint whirring sound got his attention as well disguised receptors gathered the high-voltage charge that would power the Event. Raines looked at the pitiful sack containing what would soon become all his worldly goods.

Bon voyage, he thought in the moment before his lumpy baggage winked out of existence.

The pop which accompanied the disappearance sounded ominously loud. So loud, in fact, that Leah jumped backwards in surprise even though she'd been expecting it.

Ten minutes remained. Either he would join the recently departed bag of stuff, or he'd be dead. He *had* to show confidence. He owed it to Leah. He owed it to Beth. Hell, he owed it to himself.

He squinted at the watch he'd placed on the ground just outside the targeting circle he'd scribed for himself in the rock. The circle he'd cut for his supplies stood empty.

It would soon be time to crouch down and grab his ankles.

And close his eyes.

And pray.

Nine minutes to go.

~*~

Joel's leg hurt. Again. He grunted as he massaged the deep scar in his thigh through thick wool trousers. The damned thing rarely *stopped* hurting. Whiskey helped, and he had an array of sympathetic pub-mates willing to self-medicate alongside him. Some of them also bore scars from the never-ending war.

"Bloody damned colonials," observed a red-cheeked Oliver Leahy as he lowered his bulk onto a barstool at the Small Arms, Joel's favorite watering hole. Rather than prove his ability to read Joel's mind, Oliver's comment merely restarted a long-standing conversation. He gave Joel's shoulder a comradely nudge. "Leg still acting up?"

"A bit." Joel raised his glass and looked at Oliver through the liquid lens, then tossed the amber fluid to the back of his throat and swallowed. The sudden surge of alcoholic heat made his eyes water and caused him to shift his thoughts away from his damaged leg, and the lie. He wondered if he should indulge in another.

"At least ya got the bugger what shot ya," Oliver said. "They grow snipers out there like we grow weeds. German guns, Spanish ammunition, and French--"

"Diseases," Joel said, though they'd shared the joke so many times neither man laughed at it

5

any longer.

Oliver continued with hardly a breath. "They call themselves Americans. As if they're the only ones living on this continent! Death mongering bastards."

"To be fair now, we shoot at them, too." *If only you knew.*

"Aye, but they *deserve* it! We're merely protectin' what's ours." Oliver took a sip of beer. "Most o' the time, anyway. Besides, they started it."

"That was a long, long time ago."

"Well it won't go on much longer from what I hear."

"And what's that?" Joel asked. "Suddenly you've got an ear at the Ministry of Defense? I thought you ran a bookshop."

"There's no end of uniforms popping in and out of that shop. I hear them talking. Come to think of it, maybe you should drop in and buy a book from time to time. You might learn something, too."

"Fiction bores me."

"Ruddy philistine! It's not all fiction. Buy something about philosophy, or cooking, or--I dunno--art!"

"I've always fancied history."

"Then, come by! I've got a huge selection."

"Maybe I should. God knows there's nothing worth listening to on the radio. It's all about the fighting; what the colonials are up to, or what we're going to do in reprisal. Nobody talks about how it all got started. Nobody cares anymore."

"Ha! Don't get me goin' about the colonials declaring their bloody independence. They started the damned war; that's all I need to know. And let's not forget they cost us the homeland."

"They've got no sense of history," Joel said. "All they want to do is fight."

Oliver bumped his beer glass on the bar. "Ain't that the truth! Even those what call 'emselves Torries don't share an ounce of loyalty to the crown. They just stopped shootin' is all. The rest have been at it for two centuries."

"Almost two and a half."

"They're worse than the bloody French. Why won't they give it up? They'll never win."

"They think they can wear us down," Joel said. "They want it all--the midlands *and* the coast. I swear--"

"Phone for ya, Joel," said a slender young woman behind the bar. She held out a handset for him, its cord draped across the bar and out of sight.

"Dawkins here," he said, covering his open ear with his palm. He listened to a brief message then responded with, "Right. Be there in ten," and handed the phone back to the barmaid.

"So much for lunch," he sighed, then waved his empty glass at the Union Jack behind the bar and shoved himself to an upright position. "Love

7

to stay and chat, but I've gotta get back to work." *Besides which, we've already had this conversation a thousand times.*

Joel dropped a two-pound note on the dark wood bar and winked at Mollie Evans, the Small Arm's proprietor. Everyone loved Mollie, and those who didn't lacked the stones to try and take advantage of her. She'd fought her way to New England in the last wave and, according to rumor, left a pile of dead Germans behind to prove her mettle. She put the cash in her apron and wiped the bar clean in a single, well-practiced motion. "Thank you, Inspector," she said.

The thickset bookseller raised his beer in a parting salute. "Yer a noble public servant, Joel Dawkins. Slow as a slug, and ugly to boot, but noble just the same."

"I love you, too," Joel said and limped to the door. He took a cautionary look around before pushing it open. One could never be sure if a Yank was lurking nearby. Being a cop in Boston was hard enough. He had no intention of posing as a target for some knuckle-dragging colonial terrorist.

~*~

Leah Kerr stood in the shade of a monstrously large oak tree and watched her father try to look nonchalant, as if he weren't in the least bit concerned that he was attempting something never done before. No big deal. Another day at the office. Another walk in the park.

Bullshit.

Even though she knew it was coming, the ear-splitting *Pop!* that signaled the departure of his supplies came as a shock. He never said it would be so damned loud. She rubbed her ears and watched as he tried to maintain a confident and good-humored expression. He had to be scared shitless. She felt that way for him, and when it was her turn, she had no doubt she'd feel that way for herself. It wouldn't matter that her turn would only come if the system worked--and worked flawlessly, an assurance he certainly didn't have.

"Five minutes," he said. "Everything's going to be fine. I'm sure of it."

Five minutes. Not nearly enough time to tell him all the things she needed to say. How much she loved him. How much she needed him in her life. How much she admired his intellect and his devotion to her mother's dream. How much she feared she would never see him again. How the hell could she pack all that into five minutes?

"I love you, Daddy."

He gave her that slow, wide smile that had always been a source of strength, confidence, and love--a smile that erased pain, restored faith, and promised hope.

"I love you, too," he said.

He kept looking at the watch laying on the

ground just outside the target circle. Her mother had given it to him, and Leah couldn't remember a time when he hadn't worn it. Now, of course, that was out of the question. She wondered if he really needed to see the seconds ticking away, or if he was trying to draw comfort from the memory of her mother's gift.

"Don't forget what I told you about adjusting the settings," he said. "Don't take any chances."

"I won't."

"Promise?"

"Promise."

"And be sure to flip the Doomsday switch to On."

She smiled at the reference. It would only be Doomsday for the equipment he'd built. Once she was gone, the power surge signaled by the pop would be directed back to the lab rather than into the power grid which serviced most of Massachusetts. As intended, the massive voltage spike would melt down the Event generator and pretty much everything connected to it. With any luck, the building would escape serious damage. After all, neither of them wanted to see anyone hurt.

"Will do," she said. "That's the big orange one on the wall next to the picture window, right?"

He looked up in sudden alarm, then saw her mischievous grin. There were no windows in the lab, nor any large orange switches for that matter.

Sitting on his haunches inside the scribed

circle, he twisted his lips to one side and raised an admonishing finger. She was waiting for him to shake it when the whirring sound she'd heard previously started up once again.

Raines Kerr wrapped his arms around his shins and lowered his head.

"Daddy," Leah cried, "I love--"

Pop!

"--you."

Standing alone in the now deserted clearing, Leah took a deep, shuddering breath. Phase One, as her father had called it, was complete. It would soon be time to determine whether or not it had been completed *successfully.*

~*~

Buried deep within the walls of the Ministry of Defense headquarters in Annapolis, Maryland, two aging senior officers sat at a table on which rested a high-definition map of the so-called midlands, an area defined by the Appalachian mountains in the east, the Mississippi river in the west, Canada on the north, and the Gulf of Mexico in the south. Most of the residents therein called it "America." The generals, like most citizens of New England, had other names for it, few of them pleasant, but all of them descriptive.

"I'd like to see this mess resolved once and for all," said General Sir David Fitzwilliam, Chief of the Defense Staff. He leaned back in his chair and squinted at his highest ranking subordinate,

11

General Sir Malcolm Nash, Chief of the General Staff.

"I certainly share that goal," Nash said.

"What I'm saying, Malcolm, is that I want to see it done. Finished! Completed during my lifetime. And, to be utterly candid, I don't have a great deal of time left."

Nash appeared instantly, and deeply, concerned for the welfare of his superior. "My condolences, General. I had no idea you were ill."

"I'm *not* ill. I'm old. Should have retired ages ago."

"Ah. Well. That's a very personal decision we must all--"

Fitzwilliam held up his hand. "Spare me your insight, please. Now, while I still have some time left, let me tell you what I want."

"Of course, sir."

"Simply stated, I want a plan. And I want it spread out on this table within a week. It must spell out, in detail, what we need to do to put an end to this war."

Nash pursed his lips and exhaled through his nose. "With all due respect General, if it were that easy, don't you think we would have done it before now?"

"I'm quite sure you could have," said Fitzwilliam. "Many times! I imagine there have been countless plans, mapped out in exquisite detail."

"But--"

"Yes, that's the problem, isn't it? There's always a 'but.'"

"I'm afraid I don't understand."

Fitzwilliam shook his head. "I'm talking about the politicians. They don't have the balls to see a real war through to the end. And that's what it's going to take to put an end to this absurd rebellion."

Nash cast about for something to say but came up empty. Fitzwilliam knew he would. Just as he knew the wobbly bastard would run to the prime minister the moment their meeting ended.

"Here's what you're going to do." Fitzwilliam tossed a thin file on the table. The cover bore the General's seal along with the usual hash marks denoting information of the most highly classified nature.

"Look that over, Malcolm. It spells out what I want done and who I want put in charge of every major element in the plan."

Nash left the document on the table. "It sounds to me like you've already got your plan, General. What is there for me to do?"

"I've merely outlined it in the broadest terms. You'll have to flesh out the details." Fitzwilliam carefully cut the end off a Cuban cigar, licked the seam, and struck a match. He puffed until nearly obscured by clouds of tobacco smoke. Nash waited in silence. "Pick up the damned file, Malcolm."

13

Josh Langston

"Of course, sir!" Nash stood, put the folder under his arm, and turned toward the door.

"Where the hell do you think you're going?"

"To start work on the plan, sir."

"You'll read that file in here," Fitzwilliam said. "Nothing leaves this room."

"But--"

"Or would you prefer to retire?"

"Retire?"

"Yes. Right now. This bloody moment. I've no doubt I can find a dozen people to take your place." *And do a better job than you've ever done.*

"I'd prefer to examine your plan first, sir. I need adequate time to--"

"You haven't been listening, Malcolm. I can't spare any more time. Either you get to work, now, on my terms, or you get out. Either way, that plan stays in this room. Furthermore, only the men and women I've listed in the file are to have any knowledge of this operation. Should anyone in parliament, or God forbid, any of the Royals get wind of it, I'll have you shot. Protocols be damned. Is that understood?"

"I-- Uh, yes sir."

"So, what's it going to be--'into the breach' or off to the beach?"

"You make it sound so easy."

"It is."

Nash returned the folder to the table, unopened. "I believe it's time for me to step down."

14

Fitzwilliam smiled. "Excellent decision." He pressed a button on the underside of the table. In response, an armed guard entered the room. "Sergeant, kindly escort General Nash to his office and help him gather his things. I'll be taking over the duties of the Chief of the General Staff. Please see to it that General Nash limits himself to personal items. Nothing else is to be removed."

The sergeant saluted, put a guiding hand on Nash's elbow, and led him away.

Fitzwilliam took several puffs on his cigar then rose slowly to his feet and smiled down at the folder. He knew Nash wouldn't have the nerve to accept his challenge. Still, it had been prudent to populate the file with bum fodder, and half of those pages blank. No sense in letting anything out of the bag on the off chance that Nash would actually peruse the file. He would almost certainly alert parliament that something was afoot in Defense. They could, and undoubtedly would, argue endlessly over details about which they knew nothing. *Bloody pols never learned.*

Meanwhile, he would put his team together. After that, the war's final chapter could be written at last.

~*~

"Welcome back, Dawkins," said Sergeant Billings, a ramrod-spined veteran of three decades with the constabulary. Though responsibility for the unit remained with the

15

Superintendent, Billings oversaw day-to-day operations of the precinct offices from which Joel worked. At nearly seven feet tall, the Sergeant towered over everyone and used his great height to intimidate troublemakers--in uniform or out. He nodded toward an interview room. "She's in there, waiting for you."

"Anything I should know about her?"

Billings shrugged. "Claims she's lost a loved one. My guess? 'E got tired of 'er and ran for it. But, in her mind, he's a missing person. That's still your bailiwick, isn't it?"

"It pays the bills." In point of fact, Joel *was* the missing persons department. Any and all such cases landed on his desk. He had a modest success rate despite the handicap of working alone. A half-dozen Joels could have made real progress. But except for the rare cases involving notables, the upper echelon paid little attention to him or his inquiries. The job paid reasonably well, and his skills had improved dramatically over the years. Special Branch would be hard pressed to find anyone able to match his productivity.

Joel popped a breath freshener in his mouth, chewed, and then opened the door to the interview room.

Based on the Sergeant's remarks, he expected to find someone shrewish and unpleasant, but the woman who sat waiting for him seemed quite normal in spite of her efforts to control her emotions. Plain, and soft-featured, she could have been a school teacher. Early grades, he thought.

Smiling, he introduced himself and took a seat opposite her at the wooden table in the center of the otherwise empty room. Extracting a pre-printed form from a drawer in the table, he filled in the date and the time. "All right then, let's start with your name."

"Sharon Doyle," she said, her voice shaky and too soft for a classroom.

He coaxed the usual personal information from her and entered it all on the form. With the preliminaries done, he sat back in his chair and gave her what he thought was a reassuring smile. "Now, who's gone missing?"

"My fiancé," she said. "William Smithers." She handed him a wrinkled and slightly faded snapshot then put herself back to work twisting a damp handkerchief into cordage. "I call him Billy, but to everyone else, he's William."

Joel glanced at the photo of a paunchy, slightly balding man in his early thirties sporting a wispy Van Dyke. The expression on his face could have been either a smile or a smirk. Joel doubted he'd like the bloke if he ever met him. "How long has he been missing?"

She glanced at her watch. "Almost two hours."

Joel fought the urge to close his eyes and shake his head. *What had Billings been thinking?*

17

Josh Langston

The 48-hour rule had been in effect since before Joel made it to Special Branch, and that meant a person wasn't technically "missing" until they'd been gone for at least two full days.

"Miss Doyle," he said, "I don't understand why you weren't informed when you first came in, but we have a policy--"

"My Billy disappeared into thin air," she wailed.

Of course. Didn't they all? "I don't mean to seem rude, Miss Doyle, but we--"

"He was right in front of me," she said, suddenly blushing. "Well, above me, actually. And then he was just... gone!"

"Above you? Like on another floor in your building?"

"No. I mean directly above me."

"Where you could see him?"

"Well, yes. Of course. Although I didn't have my eyes open the whole time." The distraught woman's complexion shifted from rose to radish. She lowered her voice to a barely audible whisper. "I believe it's called the missionary position."

Joel had spent nearly ten years investigating missing persons and assumed he'd heard just about everything, but this claim left him speechless.

"Please," she said, "swear to me that detail won't be included in the official report. If my mother ever saw it, I'd die."

18

Joel cleared his throat. "We often find it prudent to hide certain facts we uncover during an investigation. This one certainly fits that category. We needn't mention anything about it to anyone not directly connected to the case."

"Thank you." Miss Doyle's face gradually shed much of its color.

He shrugged. "Now then, let's go through this again, shall we? In, uhm, detail."

The blush returned with a vengeance, and Joel instantly regretted his word choice. "Forgive me! That's not-- I didn't mean--"

"I understand you have to do your job, Inspector." She gamely cleared her throat. "I'm-- I'm prepared to provide any details you think will help. But please, you must find Billy. I can't possibly go on without him."

"A little clarification, then, if you don't mind," Joel said, striving to be tactful. "Is it possible Mr. uh--" he checked the form "--Smithers merely left the room afterwards, say while you were--uhm-- recovering from... you know."

"No. It's like I told you, he disappeared *during* our... activities."

"During?"

"Yes."

"In the uh--I'm trying to be delicate here-- middle?"

"I think the proper term is *in flagrante delicto*."

Josh Langston

Joel coughed. "You were actually, sort of, that is to say, intertwined?"

"Inter-*connected*," she whispered.

He sat back and looked at her with a mixture of shock and admiration. It took a moment to collect his wits before he could continue. "I don't suppose Mr. Smithers is a magician by trade, is he?"

"Certainly not! He's a chemist, not some tawdry stage charlatan. And, I might add, a third cousin by marriage to Lord Middlebury."

"Middlebury, yes, I see. But he actually *works*, you say. In a laboratory?"

"A pharmacy."

"Of course. Has he ever done this before? Disappear, I mean."

She shook her head. "He's a very cautious, conservative, methodical man. He never does anything unusual. He doesn't like surprises. He positively thrives on routine."

"And yet, you're saying he disappeared." Joel snapped his fingers. "Just like that?"

"Well, no," she said. "It wasn't that sudden. He sort of just... faded away. He had a funny look on his face, but I suppose that could've been from--" Another furious blush. "--uh... Well, I think you can imagine."

"Right," Joel said. "He just faded away."

"That's about the size of it."

"Into nothing."

"Yes."

20

He squinted at her. "How on Earth could that be possible?"

She blinked at him. "Isn't it your job to figure that out?"

~*~

Treason, Treason! is available now in e-book and paperback formats at your favorite on-line retailer.

Made in the USA
Charleston, SC
30 July 2015